DIGGER'S IZY

By
NANCY WESTON

ACKNOWLEDGEMENTS

Mary Isabel Howse because she inspired this story.

Paulette Alden, author, because she is encouraging and smart.

Marilyn Rubinstein because she made it possible to tell the story.

Rosie Jones because she is the best friend ever and always.

Ethel Scholey for saving the day.

Linda Ames and the HAPPY BOOKERS for their time and input.

Comer's Printing for their "friend"ship and patience.

Claudia Harcourt/ODDDog Design for artistry and integrity.

IntentionMedia for expedience and excellence.

And perhaps most of all, Janet Basilone for brilliance and tenacity!

Dedicated to the Diggers of this world

PROLOGUE

It was 1927 but time did not exist, except in the measured movements of his busy hands. In his world, only the quest for knowledge of how a thing functioned was a meaningful reality—the reason there was a valve here or vacuum tube there. Curiosity was his constant and only companion. He was driven by one more conquest, one more mystery unraveled. His materials were scavenged, stolen or, if necessary, purchased. He monitored the feeble current from the photovoltaic cell as it passed through three amplification stations, then through a wire to the transmitter. There, light waves were converted into electrical impulses, leaving his control and entering the magical realm of the ether. All was within parameters. He bounded catlike to the next room. A makeshift shortwave receiver plucked the impulses out of the air, passed them through a series of amplifiers, and carried them to a lamp that was sealed and filled with neon gas. He watched, mesmerized. The neon gas glowed and flickered with varying intensity in response to the modulated impulses being transmitted from the other room. "It does work! Light transported like sound, captured and recreated. The possibilities!"

Abruptly, he was jerked from joyous triumph by a disruptive knocking, pounding, rattling of the hinges. "I know you're in there, you hooligan! Open up! Come on now, get out here! I have a warrant for you to be rounded up for the sixth-grade class again, and by force if necessary!"

Ducking low through the house, the boy crept to a safe corner and melted into the shadows. He held his breath, trying to detect how great the threat of force might be today. It was not unexpected. He played this game as many days as he dared. Huddling in the dark, his lanky body scrunched up, he waited for the offensive little man to pass through the familiar stages: autocratic threat, frustration, wearisome aggravation and, finally, departure. He wondered why the man never made good on his threats to break in by busting down the door or smashing a window. Sometimes the boy imagined him doing so. He fantasized various outcomes of such an encounter. He plotted escape routes and developed strategies for a brawl. He had all the advantages: surprise, agility, and wit. How tiresome and petty the little man's job seemed. Impotent. A waste of the man's efforts.

It didn't occur to the boy to reason which was more fascinating, his experiments or the game. It only mattered that he had both. One to feed his lithe, adroit mind, the other a distraction from his twisting, personal prison.

GRANDY

Isabella Reinhardt was born in the land of sunshine, the City of Angels before the concrete torrent at the end of the Great World War and just at the dawn of madness. She was on the precipice of staggering change. Nevertheless, she knew two things for certain: Grandy, her beloved Grandy, was going to leave her, and her father was turning into a monster.

It wasn't always so certain, and it wasn't always so scary. In fact, deep in the corners of her memory were pictures of herself as a baby, safe and loved. A photograph of the three of them: the proud man with his pretty wife and the baby, Isabella, on her father's lap, smiling. In her head, she knew they had once been a joyous threesome. In her heart, she could not begin to comprehend that she had been adored and cherished by him.

In the face of growing evidence to the contrary, a few precious, very early memories would flicker in her consciousness, sometimes in the twilight of her thoughts, before sleep. Music: something light and waggish, playing through her mind. She could hear it and, in time, had come to know it. Al Cooper and his Savoy Sultans playing loudly on the hi-fi: "Friendship, friendship, just the perfect blendship. When other friendships have been forgot, ours will still be hot! Da dadada da da da!" The first time she heard it, she was just a baby in her crib. She had turned toward the sound, expectantly, waiting to see a rose-colored lampshade with braided fringe pop into the room atop his shoulders, covering his head as he danced all around. His feet were bare, his pant legs rolled up. The fringe swayed, jigging and jogging to the music as he went round, moving backward, arms straight at his sides. The baby girl watched the aberration with glee. The music ended. He disappeared as he had come: like magic. As the last picture faded, Isabella would slide into slumber, clinging to a fragile notion that once upon a time, long ago, when she was too young to make sense of betrayal, he had loved her.

Isabella was always eager to learn. It began with those early flickering images. Pictures and sounds that existed on the periphery of awareness like the sound of her mother's voice, "No, no! Isabella! Get down!"

"What?" he said, entering the small bathroom.

"She's trying to get into the medicine cabinet! We can't have that! Isabella, naughty girl! No, no."

"Come here, Isabella." Gunter reached out and embraced his daughter, then lifted the toddler to the cabinet.

"What are you doing?"

"She's curious. Curiosity is a good thing. I want her to be curious."

Gunter Reinhardt emptied the cabinet onto the counter. One by one, he showed the child each item. The child watched the man take apart the razor, show her the blade, cut a label off a bar of soap. "Sharp, cut, Isabella." He pricked his finger with the corner of the blade. "Blood. Cut. Hurt. Smell the soap. Clean. Smells clean. Touch the soap." Next, a thermometer, a tube of something gooey, an aspirin bottle, which opened, spilling its contents. "One, two, three— count with me—four, five, six, seven, eight, nine, ten." The baby mouthed the names of each item until all were neatly back in their place.

The images were a great contradiction. They served to confuse her if she thought about them at all. She tried not to. Instead, she let them dance in the distance where they touched her emotions more than her thoughts. In their obscurity, they were cherished and sustaining against more vivid realities. She saved them in imaginary boxes and let them loose in quiet moments.

She remembered the sound of the needle skipping in the final groove of the 78, and again, her mother's voice: "What's going on? Why is the phonograph on the floor? What's going on? No, no, she can't be doing that!"

"Leave her. She is doing just as I have instructed her."

"She's far too young for that!"

"Nonsense! You'll see. Isabella, just as I showed you!"

"She doesn't even understand."

"She understands perfectly. Carefully, gently, that's it, easy."

The music started over from the beginning, his Savoy Sultans and "Friendship, friendship, just the perfect blendship." Isabella could hear her own squeal of delight. She could almost feel her hands patting together. And she perceived her eyes turn up to him for approval.

As the years passed, it was more difficult to bring these images into focus and recall what approval looked like when it had been available to her. The lessons continued, but over time, less endearingly.

"Don't start a sentence with 'well,' It makes you sound like an idiot."

"Yes, Daddy. Five billion years…"

"Approximately. Say it, a-prox-a-mat-ly."

"A-prox-a-mat-ly five billion years ago, Earth formed from dense gas. It swirled faster and faster, like an ice skater bringing in her arms." The girl spun around.

"Don't be frivolous. This is important. Continue."

Concentrating, looking into his face, she went on, "The more it got dense..."

"Condensed. It didn't get dense. When you say things that way, you sound dense.

"The gas condensed. Condensed. It was able to attract other similar bodies, colliding and reforming in accretion... Daddy, what is accretion again?"

"Accretion is the process of growth by addition of increments."

"What does that mean?"

He went into the kitchen, the child at his heel. Out came a bowl, flour, water, and butter. He mixed them together and turned. "This is a wad of dough. If I take this little wad and mash it into the larger one—that is the process of accretion."

She filed away wads of dough. "...reforming in accretion until it formed the basic structure of a planet."

"Adequate, but I want you to think of the whole concept, Isabella. See it happening in your mind, don't just recite the words," he instructed as they returned to the dining room. "Continue!"

The girl's thoughts got loose for a moment as he spoke. She had to quickly pull them back into order. "Elements eventually decayed."

"Only the active elements. So, certain elements."

"Sorry. Certain elements decayed, releasing heat and..."

"No! You must first explain how the surface was comprised of rock and formed a container."

"The rock surface formed a container, held in the heat of the decaying heat... No, wait, I know, that's wrong. The rock surface formed a container that held the... I'm sorry, Daddy. I don't remember what it held."

The man took her arm and led her back into the kitchen. He got out the cast iron skillet and a box of corn kernels. He put several dozen kernels into the pan and turned the flame on high, holding the lid in his hand. "Watch, Isabella. The heat is going to alter the kernels and they will pop, releasing energy, or heat." The first kernel moved, then another. One popped and jumped up and out. The man put the lid on the pan. "The crust is like this lid. It holds in the radiating

4

energy. Put your hand up here." He lifted the lid. A popped kernel launched into the air, onto the kitchen floor. The girl laughed. "Feel the heat?" he asked. "The lid held in the heat and allowed it to build up inside the pan. Do you understand?"

"The crust made a container like a lid and kept in the heat so it kept going up."

"Continue."

"The temperature reached a thousand degrees, which made the elements begin to break down..."

"The heat broke down the rock and separated the elements. And it's a thousand degrees centigrade."

"Right, sorry. Centigrade. ...Broke down the rock and separated the elements. Heavy elements moved toward the core while lighter elements moved to the surface."

"Well? That's it?"

"Ok, let me think. Oh, yes, the motion and separation of elements caused..." she paused, searching her memory.

"Convection currents! You know this, why do you hesitate?"

"Sorry, I just had to think, ...convection currents also moved heat to the surface?"

"Yes. But I want you to see the whole process in your mind. Any child might recite words. You must think! Now, if more heat moves to the surface, what will happen to the crust?"

"It will get hot?"

"You must learn to think. Not of obvious, simple things. Is the surface of the crust hot? Think, Isabella. Think as if your life depends on it!"

"The heat moves to the surface and cools?"

"Yes. But even more important, what is happening to the crust as the cooling process takes place? Think before you answer. Think!"

Isabella did think. She was also tired. It was hard to remember all the big words and their right order and meaning. "If it is cooler closer to the surface," she hesitated, looking at his face for some sign that she might be on the right track, "...the rock, the rock is less molten?" His face held expectation. "The rock is less molten, so it must be... I know: The rock is hardening, adding to the crust

5

by the process of accretion, which makes it thicker, holds in more heat, makes the molten layer even hotter."

"Very well. Now you have had a deductive thought." The small girl hoped that was a good thing. "Now you have a stronger container holding in the heat. What do we already know about heat?"

"It rises, Daddy," grateful for an easy question.

"Always. It is getting hotter and the heat is trying to rise, but the container is holding it in. What is going to happen?"

"It is going to explode."

"It is. That is the end? That is the formation of the crust?"

"Well…"

"I told you not to start a sentence with 'well.' You sound like an idiot. You don't want me to think you are an idiot, do you?"

"No, never. I'm sorry, Daddy. That was it, until the pressure under the crust, compressing, compressing something."

"There are three forms of matter."

"Solids, liquids, and gases."

"Yes. Think!"

"Gases. The gases formed by separation of elements. Compressing gases. Gases to the point that they were forced through small cracks."

"Say, fissures."

"Yes, Daddy. Forced through fissures. They pushed upward, forced out until they erupted into the premature atmosphere."

"The atmosphere was not premature. It was immature."

"Sorry."

"And? What happened to the gases?"

More thinking, remembering. "The gases formed an atmosphere. The atmosphere also formed layers of pressure to form and reform molecules, which became weather. Weather formed the crust by erosion."

"Just erosion? What about molecular accretion and oxidation?"

"I don't remember. I'm tired. Please, Daddy."

"Don't be lazy. Tell me the effects of accretion and oxidation."

"Oxidation is when the molecules break down and oxygen is released."

"You sound like an idiot. Stop, think, and then explain the process of oxidation properly."

"Daddy, I'm so tired. Can I explain it to you tomorrow? Please?"

"Explain it now."

"Oxygen atoms on the outside of the molecular chain… I don't remember, Daddy. I'm sorry. Please don't be angry."

"Missy, will you come in here? This child of yours is unable to remember what we went over and over just last night!" His words felt like a spanking. If only she were smarter.

"Look at her face. She's tired. It's late. She has to get some sleep before school. Let her go to bed now and she'll do better tomorrow night."

"School! What drivel they teach her in that kindergarten. She already reads, writes, and does her numbers. They are teaching her nothing of value. Fairy stories! They read my daughter fairy stories! Pixie dust! I don't think she should be wasting her time in kindergarten."

"She also interacts with other children and participates in the process of socialization. That's important at her age. Isabella, off to bed. I'll come in to help you in a minute."

"Process of socialization. What's that? Some hint that I am not socialized?"

"Of course not, dear. I'm saying that children need to learn to interact with their peers."

"I suppose I don't interact with mine?"

"I didn't make any reference to you, Gunter. I'm talking about Isabella."

"Right. But I know what you really mean." The child stood nearby in the dark, listening.

There were three things that kept Isabella steady in uncertainty. Play and its escape; her mother's unwavering affection; and her maternal grandmother, Grandy. Grandy was like a great oak tree, anchoring the land around it with roots, protecting with shade and shelter.

"Tell me the story of the Limerick."

"You know it well, Isabella. You should tell me."

"Please Grandy, please tell me the story, one more time, please."

"Very well, lass," the old woman poured tea to go with the oatmeal and berries, settled into her chair next to Isabella, and began.

"A great wicked storm came up from the south. The passengers were herded inside the great ship, for the sea and wind were far too dangerous to allow them on the decks. Inside the ship were cabins—small for first class, even smaller for second class—and huge open bays for steerage. Close quarters for all. With the wooden vessel heaving and pitching on waves rising into the sky, it seemed the ship would turn over on itself, sometimes crashing till it felt the staves and planks would burst apart and let the sea rush in. And the wind raging outside such as the devil himself might breathe his fury."

The old woman turned her head and glanced over the corner of her spectacles to see wide, brown eyes riveted upon her, begging for more. She bent in a little closer, holding the moment. "The captain was determined not to give up his lass to the storm. He rode the furor far to the north to survive. They lashed down what they could, lost what they couldn't, and hung on by the will of a stubborn man with his face in the way of disaster.

"There were rich, poor, man, woman, child, and terror aboard that ship when it came to a clear sky. They hadn't planned to go so far north. The captain told them the truth of their plight. A hardship loomed ahead. The crew would be sailing the stripped and weary vessel against the wind just to regain course. Supplies were not sufficient, causing everything to be rationed, including food and water. The seas were rough, the stench of sickness permeated the angst and fear. Ill tempers and deprivation became companions in every cabin. The disease began to prowl."

"Oh, Grandy. That's so scary," Isabella said with wide eyes. She scrunched them tight, her troubled face upturned, arms crossed over her heart.

Grandy smiled at her granddaughter. "It was that, child. And your great-grandmother, Mary Broun Prebble—heart full of hope, head filled with dreams, and womb full of life—was trapped in the belly of that ship."

"Did Grandma Mary get sick?"

"Nay child, you know as well as I, that she dinnary take sick."

"But others did. Didn't they, Grandy?"

"Aye, child, others took sick, died, and were left buried in the angry sea. Grandma Mary had letters and kept up their spirits reading them aloud. Letters of great vitality, possibility, bravery, and risk, fortune, and land. Men who were brazen, foolish, smart, and willful—building, expanding and always moving, mostly west. Change, always change. And Grandma Mary had a vision as well. Her poor life changed in this new land to one of great expectation. She envisioned Sean, her husband, your grandfather, would get into mining, work hard, and grow wealthy. They'd have sons who would do likewise. What a glory dawning for them she imagined!

"The ship so long come to land, Grandma Mary's labor came early. The pains started a day ahead. She tried to ignore them, praying not to have the time come in such a place. But early the next morning, she could no longer pretend there would be mercy. Her child was destined to be born aboard the Limerick, that storm-weary vessel on the sea outside of New York Harbor."

"And that was you, huh, Grandy? You were the child on the Limerick!"

"Yes, child, born at sea I was."

"It must have been a great ship, the Limerick. Don't you think, Grandy? And don't you think Grandma Mary was brave?"

"It was great enough to bring us in safe, most of us. I'll tell you, wee one, I think it was that Captain as well. Sometimes, a person has to set his mind to a thing, come what may. I think he was the bravest of them all, and as strong as his ship in my mind."

"What about Grandma Mary?"

"Grandma Mary was driven by her desire, her dreams. Her determination came from a fire called dissatisfaction, and it can burn bright, but it can also consume and destroy. Sure enough, it gave Grandma Mary strength to push on. Push on we did. Our destination was not New York, but the state of Ohio."

"Ohio? Why Ohio? O-Hi-Oh? What a funny name, don't you think, Grandy?"

"I suppose it is, in a way. It's an Indian name like most of the states, child. And they went there because Ohio was where Grandma Mary's uncle mined for soft coal, in Monroe County. They got through customs, arranged transportation, and pushed on to Ohio. The stress, exertion of the journey, and the birth were all so taxing. Grandma Mary arrived bedridden and unable to provide counsel, pleasures, or comfort to her husband. She could not even care for me without help.

"Your great-grandfather, Sean Prebble, immediately began to find fault with everything in the new country. He was stunned to learn his rich uncle expected him to find his own way by working in the mines, earning his due share of the fortune by proving his worth.

"Grandfather Sean looked around and saw tall chimneys like dragons belching fumes and black smoke; rail cars screeching 'stop,' then groaning 'go,' loaded up and headed out of town; and dark-stained men with eyes that saw nary a blue sky coughing up black.

"Coal mining's plain hard work. The coal is found deep in the earth, down manmade shafts, hand-built elevators. Great gaping mouths swallowed up men and machine, and down they went. Once underground, the manner of digging the coal is coarse and raw. They used crude tools, sometimes made of a single piece of iron with one tool on one end, another on the opposite. The men used sledgehammers, wedges, and grit mostly. It was hard labor in dangerous conditions. Every breath is dust, and that dust was fuel. A wee spark could set the air afire, and explosions were common.

"Grandfather Sean, my father, did not fancy hard work or get along with miners. He looked for other work—cleaner, easier—but found none to his liking. He did not like his uncle by marriage. They made a bad start. No, my darling girl, Sean Prebble drew no friends or progress. Very soon he determined to return home to Scotland and his more familiar life and lot there.

"Grandma Mary was too weak to make such a trip, let alone care for the child on another journey. So Grandfather Sean took his things and stole away, got passage back to Scotland."

"He just left Grandma Mary?"

"Aye, he did. He left us."

"That's an awful thing, isn't it Grandy?"

The old woman paused and allowed herself to ponder abandonment. "A furious awful thing! But justice comes round on you. Don't you forget it! Diphtheria an awful thing as well: choking gag of pus building in your throat till you cannay breathe or swallow. It's not a pretty death, I can tell you."

"Did you ever know anyone with diphtheria, Grandy?"

Aye, child, too many. When I was young, it came, a plague, spreading like cold in the night. One year, not another, then again, stealing in and taking what it wanted, lusting for the young, but not too proud to take the grown." The old woman's eyes were on fire, dancing and holding the child's. "On the journey home to Scotland, Sean Prebble took sick with it." She spat the words, with a decided nod of her head. "Far from land, he had little chance and died without ever sighting Edinburgh!"

Isabella lived in a house with her mother and father. Behind their house was a smaller house, set back deep on the property, where Grandy lived. It was situated near the back fence and the big wooden gate that opened onto the Southern Pacific Railroad tracks running directly behind the property.

The proximity to the trains had made the land cheap when her Uncle Clay, a building contractor, purchased it. He built six modern suburban homes (seven counting Grandy's little house). Two other contractors built another six, for a total of twelve. The postwar boom in California was placing demands on everything: highways, schools, utilities and, most of all, housing. Another six lots located on the west end of the block would not remain vacant for long. Uncle Clay sold the lot with two houses to his sister Missy's husband, Isabella's father.

Isabella and the other children had always loved the train yard and the trains. The great chugging engines and their clattering tail of cars punctuated the drama of their play. The powerful freight trains blew whistles at the major highway crossing—Vermont to the west and Figueroa to the East. They ambled past their houses, then would pick up speed and race away through the less residential areas. Sometimes, when the trains slowed just enough, children lying in wait would run to catch the steps of the caboose and ride the train—hanging on precariously, thrilled by the mischief, oblivious of danger. The railroad yard served as the official boundary between two worlds, the war zone for the only part of play that wasn't imaginary.

After school, Isabella burst out of the schoolyard and headed for home. Once there, shoes off, she bounded out the back door, skipping entirely the steps from threshold to pavement, eager to engage in whatever activity took her fancy. She awaited summers with hyper anticipation and pure glee.

"On three," Isabella spoke in a loud whisper so her troops would hear to her left and then her right. "One, two, three!"

They were up and out of the trench and over the top. It was a great surprise. They had had no warning. Her troops were on them, blasting them with a bombardment of dirt bombs and rocks. The usual counterattack was foiled by the surprise. She thought she might have heard a few zings from the newly-rumored armament, but it made no strikes. In fact, they ran like kangaroo rats through the tall grass, up and over their fences, and were gone. And just like that, the children were victorious.

The sacrifice was minimal: one casualty, little Barry's ear—and his own doing, at that. She had ordered him to stay down once he had sounded the alarm, but he disobeyed. He said he'd gotten caught up in the excitement of the charge. Being so close to the encounter, he was an easy target and got nailed in the ear with what was probably a piece of granite. Quite effectively, it cut a gash in the fleshy edge.

She called the troops to regroup. They headed back across the train tracks, cautiously watching their backs and staying low. It would be disastrous to let overconfidence turn victory into defeat.

Once back at the fort—actually blankets thrown over a stretched rope—she sought to protect Barry's wound from dirt. After cleaning it, she dressed the injury with salve. Barry squealed like a wounded cat. Then they all went about the day, planning tomorrow's attack and replenishing weapons.

She deployed troops to make fresh dirt bombs and to dig the holes in which to store them until they dried and became fully lethal. They also needed more rocks from the railroad track bed. So she set guards to watch out for an attack, as the rock-rich track bed was halfway between their territory and home.

Later, the band of children camped by the creek—a winding channel with water pumping through it that her father had dug through the yard. Her yard was like a miniature world in itself. In between the two houses, nut and fruit trees were abundant. Shrubbery and flowers grew so that passage was by way of a path. Calla lilies, her mother's favorite, grew by the creek bed. The yard was anything the children wanted it to be.

They played out great dramas filled with pirates, knights, monsters, and heroes. More than any other fantasy, there was the Wild West—cowboys and Indians. She loved to play-act tales of the west. And when they did, she was always an Indian because Grandy had told her she had Indian blood. Her brown eyes were proof.

This day, the yard was their camp after the battle, and they regaled themselves with individual impressions of the triumph. But this drama was more than fantasy. The Mexicans were very real.

"I heard a BB gun!"

"How do you know it was a BB gun?"

"Just do. It was a BB, all right."

"Darn! We're doomed! How can we fight against a BB gun?"

"If they had one, why'd they run?"

"Yeah! If they had a BB gun, they'd have just stood there and fired."

"I heard it too," Isabella stated calmly. "And that's the point! They ran even with superior weapons. I think that says a lot about tactics versus weaponry. But we need to get our hands on a BB gun ourselves. Ronny, your brother has one."

"Yes, but father gave that to Matthew for hunting. Besides, Matthew would never let me touch it, let alone use it."

"Then maybe we should just borrow it."   There was a definite preference to not anger Matthew.

"Anyone got a better idea?"

"We can't fight a BB gun with rocks."

"Maybe we should surrender."

"That would mean we'd have to give up the train yard and, worst of all, we'd look like weenies to the Mexicans!"

"Yeah, and my dad says they're gonna ruin the whole neighborhood."

"Then we gotta get a BB gun, too."

"Oh man, Matthew!" Veronica, who was called Ronny, uttered in dismay.

"I'll take care of Matthew if it comes to that," Isabella assured them, making eye contact with Ronny as she spoke. "We've gotta figure this thing out."

"You mean you gotta figure it out, Izy."

"Sure, I just gotta think." Izy was what the children called Isabella.

Izy listened while the conversation reverted to bragging and laughing. She began plotting. She'd figure out something. She always did.

Her best friend in the whole world was Ronny. No matter what, Ronny came to visit and play with Isabella. When they met they instantly fell into a bond of friendship based on some unnamed knowing, some intrinsic sense of trust and commonality. Nothing could shake them, no matter what. It was a different kind of bond from the one between Isabella and Grandy. Both were intricate, vital threads in the fabric of Isabella's world and her survival.

Outside, in the children's world, it was always a magical time. Outside, Isabella felt she had control. She used that control to purge herself of things in her heart, things she did not contemplate but endured. She likened herself to the beetle she was now watching plod like a juggernaut over the boulders of hardened clay, rocks, and twigs that made up its world—unstoppable, irrepressible. It was driven by a force it did not think about, only obeyed.

Later that night, before impending curfew, Isabella went to check the repository. The cool evening breeze from the Pacific softly cooled the desert land. She clomped over the uneven terrain of the railroad yard, through the waist-high grass down the block to the empty lot. The sun was near the horizon giving Izy little more than twilight to see as she scouted the path through the construction debris toward the old shack.

Uncle Clay had left the shack when he finished building the houses. The construction crews had left the shack padlocked. It took little effort for the children to dispense with the old lock and replace it with one of their own. Izy looked around carefully. It wouldn't do to be caught inside alone. If the Mexican gang attempted an assault on the shed, doubtless she'd get the worst of such a chance encounter. It wouldn't be the first time she'd gotten beat, but she prided herself on being cleverer than that.

With an open view to the train tracks, the coast appeared clear. She went inside and inspected the accumulated props and paraphernalia of childhood fantasies: a bedspread and old blankets, rope, sticks, clothespins, drawstring bags, boards, hunks of abandoned concrete, remnants of furniture, broken and discarded tools, kitchen utensils, an old cloth hammock, and some adult clothing.

She picked up a small box, sturdy and undistinguished, and opened it. Inside was an old rag. She picked it up and tilted the box to allow the small metal balls she had recovered to roll around and make a sound. Was this the future? All-out war? Where was this going? Someone was likely to be seriously hurt. Thoughtless escalations could even get someone killed. This was crazy. Why had the Mexicans gone and upped the ante? Why couldn't they be content to facilitate skirmishes with rocks and dried mud?

It was in their blood, this battle. Something they inherited from the adults, like children handing round the measles. You didn't have to do anything to get it. It came upon you because you showed up, listened, and watched. They heard derogatory remarks and saw the subtle and not so subtle slights handed out in jest, but with meanness and rancor. In the end, it came upon children to play out this puzzlement across the train yard.

"Tell me about the Mexicans, Grandy."

"Ah, they were poor like us, but not at all dreary. Their skin was brown and their eyes black. At first, we seemed to be very different. But in time, we tried each other out a bit and found we had more in common than we had differences. And even the differences, well, they were more like distinctions."

"Distinctions?"

"Everyone's distinct in their fashion, every single person is, child. That's what makes us each special."

"Is that like you have blue eyes and I have…" she trailed off, hesitant to say it.

"And you, wee lass, have brown. Yes. That's a distinction. The Mexican children were distinct in their ways, their clothes, and their language. But inside, they were just like me."

"Daddy says they are members of the dark races."

"Well, now, I dinnay think that has good sound, do you?"

"But they are dark. Even you said that they were brown-skinned. Ronny's dad says they're no better than niggers."

"Isabella! That's the talk of fear, now. Maybe you should be a brave lass and get to know them. All that name-calling and denigration, that's talk of fear. Don't be listening to the grown-ups so filled up with it they can't see the truth."

Even as she watched the BBs roll around in that small box, she knew that they had to get Matthew's rifle. She was afraid of the potential of those little metal balls. She had dug these two shots out of the posts that made up the back gate. She saw that they set into the wood. They would set deeper in flesh.

Fear would destroy her troops unless they could match terror for terror. She didn't want to see this new day dawn. It sure wasn't going to be she who'd turn tail and run. If they could demonstrate equal power, maybe there could be some understanding. She had to make sure that no one got hurt, but how to do that was the question. She finished her inspection, locked up the shed, and headed back home.

The sun was down and dark was descending by the time she got close enough to hear the voices on her porch.

"Well, just look at his ear! All swollen and red!"

"Oh, Mom."

Isabella ducked into the bushes and watched from a safe distance.

15

"I assure you Isabella wouldn't do anything to intentionally hurt Barry."

"Well, he didn't have this before he came over here today, and look here at the shirt! I didn't send him out all bloodstained!"

"I'm so sorry about your ear, Barry. Can you tell me how it happened?" Missy said, bending down to his height.

"He's not talkin', but I don't need it spelled out for me! What did she do to my son?"

"Barry, how did you cut your ear?"

"Don't think you're going to interrogate my son! Where's your daughter?"

"She's not home... ."

"There, you see? Not home. After dark! I'm telling you, Missy Reinhardt, that tomboy of yours is the scourge of the neighborhood! If you can't control her, then I have no choice but to forbid Barry to play over here anymore!"

"Aw, mom, no," Barry whined as his mother dragged him off the sidewalk by the shoulder, still carrying on. Isabella suspected Barry would be forbidden from the frontiers for a while anyway. No great loss. Barry was one of the youngest of her troops. He was good for espionage and any sort of skulking, but not an asset in a fight.

It occurred to Isabella that this was not an opportune moment to appear. So she headed to the fort in the back near the train tracks to allow her mother's disapproval to subside. Missy would worry just a bit if she were late, and that would lower her threshold for punishment.

The ear issue was troublesome. What had gone wrong? She checked the first aid kit upon entering the fort and realized she had made a big mistake. She thought she had put Vaseline on Barry's cut. Instead, she'd put Vicks. "Oh, drat! No wonder the little weenie had made such a fuss. Man, oh, man!" she berated herself. A bunch of stuff washed over her any time she was not astoundingly brilliant. She was relieved her father didn't know she'd goofed up.

In a situation like this time was on her side. Better stay away for a while. So she climbed high up the walnut tree to where the branches swayed in the evening breeze. "Ahoy mates!" she called, imagining herself aboard the Limerick aloft in tall seas. From there it was easy to look up at the clear desert sky and see the stars spilling across the darkening heaven. That night, amid the images in her mind, Isabella Reinhardt both loved and hated her life.

In the distance, she heard the music. It was so different. Their music. She could even see lights flickering. Lighted only by the rising moon, Isabella descended the tree, slipped through the tall grasses, trekked up and over the train tracks, then veered cautiously toward the fences that separated their world from hers. Light shone from behind the boards, and she found her way to a gap she could look through. There were colorful paper covers on lights and a table outside set with food that smelled like Olivera Street. One man played guitar, another a drum, and someone shook objects that rattled.

In the center of it all, a large man with a great belly held court and lavished smiles upon people who must have been his family. His hair was black like that of all of his children. One child, a beautiful girl with huge eyes, watched everything. "Iyana." The little girl's head turned. "E-yon must be her name," Izy thought, mispronouncing it. How exotic it sounded. A woman, the mother perhaps, brought out a platter of something steaming. The music stopped and they came to the table and began eating. She heard laughter and happy chatter, but she could not understand their language. They were different. Very different from everything she knew.

Back in her world, she paused at Grandy's house, but the lights were all out. Grandy went to bed early. Izy longed to share her secret trip to the other side of the tracks with the only person who might understand. Grandy was her most special relationship of all. She could share things with Grandy that she could not share with anyone else. Grandy shared things with her that broadened her view of life. She never regarded Isabella's youth as an impediment to her ability to know and understand the world.

Isabella went into the house and took her licks over Barry's ear, claiming she'd only tried to be helpful, which was the truth. She agreed to apologize to his mother and him in the morning. Then they waited for her father to come home to dinner. She prayed to be forgiven for her mistake with the Vicks. She prayed to be ignored, that the night would pass without incident.

FAMILY

At the end of summer, following Isabella's first year of school, new people entered onto her stage and into her awareness. One was a tall man with a mustache who walked with confidence and talked with a rich, booming voice: Uncle Micheil. He had a pretty wife, two sons, and a daughter called Kathy. He didn't stay long. He had brothers to visit and took his boys with him. But his wife and Kathy stayed with Grandy and spent the days with Isabella and her mother.

Izy looked at Kathy—her dark hair and blue eyes. If Izy had known the word, she would have said Kathy had a coquettish face. She was dressed in ruffles of organdy. She had on ankle stockings and patent-leather pumps. On her head was she wore a bonnet.

At first, Izy was ill at ease until Kathy flashed a disarming smile that ended in big dimples.

"That's a pretty dress," Isabella said.

"Thank you. I like your pedal pushers," Kathy leaned way forward and whispered, "I'm not allowed to wear them, ever."

"I would think it hard to climb a tree or get over a fence in a dress."

"I'm not allowed to do that either."

"What do you do?"

"I play with dolls and I have tea parties."

"I have tea parties, too. At Grandy's."

It was an occasion since Izy didn't know her cousin Kathy, who had never been to the West Coast. The two mothers chatted, eager to be better acquainted. The girls were close in age. It made for a comfortable foursome.

"Mother, Isabella has no bonnet!" Kathy announced to her mother, Isabella's Aunt Renée. So it was decided they should all go shopping to buy her one. They found a blue bonnet that matched one of Isabella's dresses. Afterward they went for a ride on Angel's Flight, a trolley that rises steeply up the incline between the shopping district in downtown Los Angeles and the grand houses on the hillside. They walked along the avenue and marveled at the rich folks' homes. They visited Olivera Street where they became intoxicated by the brightly-colored trinkets, rich smells of exotic food, and music from the mariachi bands. Back home, the mothers fussed over their daughters like children with new dolls. Izy did her best to be ladylike, admiring Kathy to whom it came naturally. The visit lasted almost a week and, when the time came, Isabella was sad to see Kathy leave.

Before they left, there was a great feast at Uncle Willy's house.

To Isabella, her family seemed very big and made up of mostly men—the women a background to the men at center stage. There was an exception, a contradiction: Aunt Emily. She stood out, unique in the forest of tall people. She was short and somehow also very large—background to no one at all. There was a lot said and done about food. There was a sense of comfort in it. Everything was given with pride to nourish and sustain those loved. For the young, there was touch football on the front lawn, stories, teasing, and laughter. Isabella and Kathy giggled the day away. This was family. It was the first time Isabella could remember seeing so many of them all together. It evoked new feelings in Isabella. She took her curiosity about them to the person she thought could best explain.

"Grandy, did you feel something funny at the dinner?"

"Funny? How so, child?"

"Well, there were so many of us. It's hard to explain. Somehow it made me feel kind of good. And Kathy, it was good to have Kathy here. And all those other cousins, too. Do you know what I mean, Grandy? Didn't you feel it too?"

The old woman paused and looked at her granddaughter. "I think I know what you're feeling. It's like belonging to something, being a part of something that is bigger than just your wee self. You know what that's called, child? You were feeling akin."

"Akin, yes, that must be it. I was feeling akin. It's a good feeling, huh, Grandy?"

"It is, lass. Your kin is cut from the same cloth as you. In them, you will find bits and pieces of yourself, and they in you, the same. Together you carry forward the treasure of strengths and weaknesses of all who have come before you, and you will pass them to the future."

Isabella knew the words were important. And while she could not have known that her grandmother's joyful feelings were mixed with sadness, her intuitive nature helped her to recognize that she had also been moved by the family gathering.

A few days later, Isabella was with Grandy when she suddenly set down her Bible, went to the table where she kept photographs, and picked up one of herself sitting in the midst of all her children. She looked at it for a long time while Isabella quietly, deliberately, tried not to intrude on whatever it was Grandy was contemplating. Then Grandy walked into the bedroom and over to the dresser. She paused and looked into the mirror. She took off her spectacles and peered at the reflection before her. Her hand went to her cheek and then her neck. Isabella watched silently.

Isabella had another family on her father's side. Grandma Hauser had remarried after Isabella's grandfather died. Her new husband was a bald, round man who was quiet. He smelled like cigars and usually held one, lit or not, between his chubby fingers.

Grandma Hauser was not at all quiet. Her given name was Alberta. Isabella called her Grandma Birdy, partly because she often wore feather boas, coats with fur collars, and hats with big brims and lots of feathers, and partly because others called her Bertie.

She frequently asked that her only grandchild come to visit. Isabella would enter the house to the familiar smell of onions, garlic, and tobacco all mixed together and hanging on everything. Grandma Birdy's house was full of large and small furniture crowded together like a maze. Adornments included shiny satin pillows with fringe, bright-colored embroidery, a statue of a Spanish lady in a lace dress, a black velvet bull with Tijuana written on the bottom, and other mementos—souvenirs of Grandma Birdy's life.

Grandma Birdy smoked cigarettes, but never in front of Isabella. She drank liquor, but never in front of Isabella, although sometimes she talked funny and Isabella learned that this was due to her being 'tipsy.' Grandpa Hauser sat in his big chair, smoked his cigar, and read the paper. Sometimes he gave Izy a silver dollar to keep.

Mostly Isabella sat on the big sofa with Grandma Birdy watching wrestling matches on a blaring television set and listening to her grandmother tell her about each contender, her favorite being Gorgeous George. Grandma Birdy also adored Liberace; if Isabella was there when Liberace came on everything stopped so they could look at what he was wearing. Sometimes Grandma Birdy taught her to play poker and made Isabella promise not to tell her mother.

"Look here how she learns, Arnold, do you see? And so young. She is smart like her father, the genius." To her grandchild, "You and your father are all I have. You will make me proud. I know you will, Kinda!" Arnold, in his big chair, peered over his spectacles with a smile.

Grandma Birdy had another son. But Uncle Hartmut had died in the war.

"Who is this with Uncle Hartmut?"

"That is no doubt one of his many women. Bring it here, let me see. Ah, yes. That is Hazel. She was crazy for your Uncle Hartmut. He was a rake, he was. Not like your father. He was not so bright, but the women! Oh, how they loved him. When we had his funeral, they came in droves, and they cried. You know, sad as I was, and I was that, I had to laugh at them all there weeping for him altogether as if each were his own true love. It was grand. He was a rake, that one, he was."

Then laughing, she broke into a deep, rugged cough. She often wheezed and sometimes spit up phlegm into a hanky she carried tucked in the cleavage of her generous bosom.

Back then, most days came and went in relative peace. Isabella might be at school or at play in her fantasy world with other children, or alone in the walnut tree that was to her a great sailing ship. She might be with Grandy listening to stories about her great-grandmother's endeavors to survive in the New World, along with her daughter, Katherine Margret, Grandy's real name. When Grandy entertained Isabella with stories, she never missed the opportunity to point out facts she believed to be important.

"There were exceptions, child, but it was not common for a woman to venture out into the world. Education for women was not even compulsory in all states. And even when it was, it was not necessary for them to follow through with all the educational requirements. Grandma Mary came from a world where women were only thought of as assets in the home." The old woman paused. "Grandma Mary was not a forward thinker. She thought little of her daughter, Katherine Margaret."

"That's you. Katherine Margaret."

"Aye. That's me. I could not be apprenticed or work in the mines. I needed to be cared for and to Grandma Mary, all alone—that seemed a great burden. It was a time of great growth and expansion in this New World all right, carried out by men and their sons."

"Couldn't Grandma Mary get a job?"

"Not likely. A woman was lucky if she could even read and write. There was a woman who advocated the education of women and promoted reforms that eventually got them into schools. Her name was Catherine Beecher. But she did it saying that a woman was better prepared to serve in the home if she had a basic education. Mostly, a woman's training was for housework, and expectations for more were limited. Prospects were glum indeed. But your great-grandmother was cunning, and she set about to do the one thing a woman could do in such a circumstance. She found a man willing to marry. And that

21

wasn't easy, her having a daughter with another man and all. I don't imagine she had her pick."

The old woman told her granddaughter tales of her own mother venturing out west with her new husband, Mr. Nigel Way. The west was still very different from the industrial east. Out west there was adventure, skullduggery, and dust, Grandy told Isabella. If you went far enough, where there was little law or security, the land was cheap and enticing.

"Women out west were two groups. There were those who set themselves to carve out a life from the land—partners working alongside their husbands. They toiled every day with little regard for anything more than necessities. Theirs was a very different life from that of the women in the cities of the east. Then there was another sort of woman. Nigel Way was the sort of man who used up whatever was given to him and exploited whatever could be used as barter. As such, Nigel Way gave no good life to his new wife. Other than six more children, Grandma Mary got very little. And all the while Nigel Way regularly took mistresses, squandered his money—save enough to purchase a small farm—and took out his frustrations on his stepdaughter, whom he expected to work for her keep!"

For the Reinhardt family, an extraordinary episode rattled the foundation of peace and shattered accepted normalcy, changing all the rules and elevating tension. When it was over, life became more complex, maniacal.

On that particular night, Gunter was late. It was dark. He arrived angrily. Eyes huge, face flushed, and his hair mussed and standing in clumps at attention.

"Red is butchers. They kill pigs, cows, and a red river of blood flows on the floor at their feet! Yellow is for cowards. Yellow, lily-livered, slithering, chicken-hearted, traitorous cowards!" He spoke in machine-gun bursts and spit with each consonant.

Isabella heard the words but struggled to find context and comprehend their true meaning. What she did understand was that her father was disturbed—raging against some force or code that pursued and tormented him. What she sensed terrified her. It pushed her over the edge of calculated behavior and into the realm of fearful reaction. She couldn't grasp the situation. She only knew to stay one step ahead of the overwhelming chaos suddenly infiltrating her world. Survival instincts began to form and strengthen. Her father raged, unstoppable, irrepressible, driven by a force he did not comprehend but clearly obeyed.

Izy's mother grabbed her up and pulled her away from the frenzy, sheltering her as she strained to watch what she didn't want to see in the other room. Isabella looked into her mother's eyes to see the same terror looking back. Missy quickly forced her face into a smile, as if she realized what Isabella had seen. "It's all right, Isabella. Dear Lord, help us. Thank you, Lord!" With that, Missy appeared to recapture herself and she took Isabella's face in her hands. "You must be brave, Isabella, and try not to be afraid. God will protect us."

"Why is Daddy so angry?"

"I'm not sure, honey, but I don't think this is really your father. I think that something overtakes him sometimes and he is not himself. I don't understand it, but I know your father would never do anything to hurt us, or even to frighten us if he could help it. Whatever this is, he cannot help it!"

Gunter Reinhardt went through the cupboards, shelves, drawers, and closets. Red and yellow things had to be ferreted out and destroyed. Cups and plates were smashed, books torn, and dresses cut up. All of it, out. Out of the house right now!

From that day forward, there was no more red or yellow. In fact, the idea of any bright color became unnerving. Muted shades or, better yet, neutrals, were the safer choice for just about everything.

When events or emotions threatened to career out of control, Isabella bound them up in imaginary boxes and filed them away. When it was time to play and she could be outside, she never thought about the dramas that unfolded in the interior of her house. Outside she exerted maximum control over her world and usually got her way. She was skilled at managing the children in the neighborhood and, when necessary, their parents.

The children were evenly divided between girls and boys. Izy could lick every one of those boys, except for Veronica's brother, Matthew. Matthew had played in little leagues almost from the time he could walk. His father was a big man with domineering ways. His son was going to play ball! Ronny's mom was timid and made fun of herself. She could be quite funny at times, and Izy liked her. Izy did not like Ronny and Matthew's father.

Matthew was big and strong like his father, and there was no getting around him. But he had no interest in leadership, so Izy ruled the neighborhood.

Being the leader was clearly not all about muscle, it was also about the ability to understand what would appeal to each child or adult. Izy had an agile imagination and could think up entertaining things to do. She was skilled at games and when it came to war, she was the strategist and the commander, without question. Well, almost. There was this one kid next door: Shelly.

Shelly was a genuine genius, a whiz! He was also clumsy, gangly, self-conscious, and had a quick temper. It made him mad that Izy could beat him and even outthink him in ways that didn't require objective calculation. Even in science, Izy could keep up with him, thanks to her father's relentless schooling. But not so much in mathematics and engineering, subjects in which Shelly excelled.

One day, after little Barry's mother relented and allowed him to play with Izy once again, she found him and his big sister arguing in their front yard.

"But it's mine, not yours!" little Barry wailed at his older sister, while Phyllis tried to take whatever it was he had wadded himself into a ball to protect.

"Hey, Phyllis, what's he got?"

"Our dad brought us home a kit to build a kite last night but didn't have time to put it together. I'm just trying to help him out."

"He didn't bring it to *us*, he brought it to *me!*"

"Now, why would he do that, you little cry-baby?"

"Wait a minute. Let me get this, now. You have a kite kit that your dad brought home to you, right?"

"Yes."

"Do you know how to put it together?"

"It has instructions inside."

"You can't read, Barry. You're going to need help!" With that, the three set about assembling the paper, balsa wood, and string.

"Ok. You carry the kite, but keep it up over your head. If you don't the thin paper will snag and tear, and you'll have no kite at all. Let's go out on the train tracks where there are fewer power lines to worry about."

"If you let him carry the kite, he'll wreck it."

"Will you wreck it, Barry?"

"No, I won't wreck it."

24

"Yeah, well, hold it up high. Let's go."

Off went the happy band of three, headed for the sky in the only vehicle they had that could carry their imaginations on the afternoon ocean breeze. They went west on the train track where the wind from the ocean would blow the kite back toward their houses if it became overpowered. They were soon joined by a fourth. "Where are you going?" Veronica asked.

"To the train yard to fly Barry's new kite."

"It's really our new kite. But he has to think it's his," Phyllis announced with an accomplished tone of the superior, older sibling.

"It's my kite and I'm going to fly it!"

"Okay, you can fly it. Come on."

Once in the perfect location, far from any obstructions, they began to tie together rag tails to get a steadying effect. When they thought they had it right, Phyllis ran down the track until the first good gust pulled the bright red, aerodynamic shape out of her hand and sent it aloft. Ronny and Izy kept their hands on the string, letting it run through their fingers. Squeals and laughter followed it up, and sighs and moans followed it back to the ground. "Too much tail, I think."

"No, you morons, not enough," Shelly yelled, running toward the group. No one had seen him enter the train yard. "What do you know about flying a kite anyway?"

"Just as much as you, Clarabelle!" But that was a lie. Shelly knew what he knew, and flying a kite definitely fell into his zone of expertise. But it was difficult for Izy to admit. Shelly grabbed up the brightly-colored shape and began adjusting the tail, adding rags until he was satisfied. And what a satisfying and magnificent thing it was. Because this time, when Phyllis ran down the tracks, the kite flew up, steady and high. "All right, Shelly!" Ronny and Izy kept their hands around the string and lifted and pulled to ensure flight. And Barry was content. He had the ball of string.

"Told you so! It's Bernoulli's principle applied to the lift of the kite and the drag of the tail. Too little tail and the kite is merely a leaf in the wind. Too much tail and the fragile paper cannot bend enough wind around it to lift all the weight."

"Yeah, yeah, bend enough wind." Izy knew that he was right. She was grateful her father hadn't witnessed the episode.

"That's why things fly, you know." Shelly went on didactically. "The wind doesn't push them up; they fold in the air around themselves, sort of making a pocket in the air through which they fly. That's why the kite is bent taut in a curve. That curve creates the pocket. And it needs a tail to give it stability to stay in its pocket."

"Wow," said Phyllis.

Izy thought to herself, "Show off."

The children watched the red paper arch in the air climb higher and higher, its funny tail swaying back and forth like the well-designed rudder it was.

Izy wondered what the kite could see from up there. How wonderful to be a thing flying so very high. She could feel the wind pull it and lift it. "Who is controlling whom?" she thought, "Barry is so determined to have the kite be his, but the kite holds our thoughts, commanding attention with its dance in the sky. Does it belong to us or do we belong to it?"

All thoughts came back to earth with a *crack-zing-kerplink*. Izy knew in that instant she had made a terrible mistake. Although it was not a day scheduled for war, she'd let her fancies get the better of her reason. She had posted no lookouts. They were had, and it was her fault! Sick feelings washed through her, and she felt awful. And to make matters worse, they were looking at the instrument of their fears. The Mexicans did have a BB rifle, and there it was!

"Give the string to me!" *their* leader commanded.

"The hell we will!" Izy said, desperately calculating the situation. There were eight of them and the rifle. Two had jumped down and were moving toward the small band while the rifle was pointed at little Barry. Izy's group didn't even have a rock. The nearest stash of weapons was at least a football field away.

"If you do not give me your string, I will shoot you, *Niño*."

"No. You can't have my kite. Izy, don't let them have it!"

"You would shoot a boy for his kite?"

"You want to take a chance with me, huh?" She heard some of *their* language but could not understand, as the rifle moved and was now pointing at her.

She tried to think. She didn't believe he would kill Barry or anyone. Not

26

really, not kill, not on purpose. But she didn't want to feel the pain of that little metal ball. What if he just hurt one of them? Izy was afraid. She tried to be rational, but she also wanted to run away. One thing was for certain: She knew this was a defining moment. What happened here would not be forgotten.

The one who spoke did not have the rifle. He was on the fence and she was pretty sure they called him Miguel. He was older, bigger—her counterpart on *their* side. She had to be careful. For one thing, the Mexican boys didn't take anything from girls. She hadn't licked any of them one on one. They had no call to be afraid of her, no reason to respect her. She was pretty sure they were in deep trouble. She assessed her resources: Ronny, girlie Phyllis, little Barry, and bright Shelly who could trip on his shoelaces at any moment.

"Where was Matthew when you needed him?" she thought to herself. "Practicing his pitching, no doubt."

With no one paying attention to the kite, it floundered, even with its amazingly-designed tail. It landed in a tree on the other side of the train track in *their* territory. Izy grabbed the ball of string and threw it at the boy on the fence. "Take it, you creeps. It's probably ruined, thanks to you." She secretly hoped it was. Then she turned and signaled retreat. They ran all the way back to her yard, through the gate, and dropped behind the bushes where they could assess the possibility of having been followed. The train yard was empty, but they could hear voices speaking *their* language heading toward the treed kite. Barry cried, and inside Izy cried a little with him. What a wonderful thing it had been. It was her fault. She had taken them out in the train yard without proper precautions. She had let them down, lost Barry's kite. "Man am I going to get it for this," she thought.

No one explained the Mexicans to the parents, not ever. It was a thing only the kids knew, a part of their outdoor world. And you didn't rat out other kids even if it was *those* kids. When children cannot tell the truth, they tell what they think is expected of them. So it went down that Izy had taken Barry's kite away from him, treed it, and lost it. What a problem she was. The mothers of the neighborhood kids decided that playing with Isabella should be restricted for the rest of the summer, or until she learned to respect other people's property.

As such, Izy spent even more time than usual with Grandy. She helped her with the washing. The Reinhardts had a big, round washing machine with legs that locked down so it didn't "walk" away with the wash. It also had an arm that swung out of the way when it wasn't needed. When the washing was done, the arm swung into place so the wash could pass through its thick, motorized rollers that squeezed out the water. When they washed sheets or towels, Grandy would wring the items yet again and get even more water out. "How'd you get so strong, Grandy?"

"I'm not as strong as I once was, lass. There was a time when life was filled with hard work. When I was a girl, my stepfather had no sons. Well, he did have, but they all died, mostly of diphtheria. So when he finally bought a farm, it fell to me to do the work. There's always a good that can come of the grimmest of plights, my little lass. What came of that was I grew very strong. And I was tall, so I became formidable."

"What is formidable?"

"Formidable is, well, it's... best I give you an example. When I grew up, in the house of a man, not my father, there came a time when I realized his interest in me was not as right as it should have been."

"How should it have been?"

"Well, now, how shall I say this? First, shake out this sheet with me, crisp and hard! That's it, again! Now we pin it up so the sun gets blown into it. That's the way." Finished with the sheet, the child paused, looking up into Grandy's face, waiting. "Plain out's best, I think. Into some men's minds come thoughts that a daughter, not his own blood, well, she can be a second wife to him. Do you understand that, child?"

"I think so. Is it like a mistress, Grandy?"

"It is, child. That's it exactly. But it's not right. Nonetheless, as I matured and became more of a woman, the more insistent was my stepfather. When I was 17 years old, on an afternoon in summer, I was in the barn mending tack. The barn door flew open.

"'Well girl,'" he said, "'you're a fine sight, all shiny with sweat. Let me wipe it off so's you look akin to a lady. You know you are no lady, don't you girl? You're nigh onto orphaned and lucky to have me givin' you shelter. No law says I have to. Come hither, now!'" He turned and swung the barn door closed and brought down the bar across it with a thud, punctuating his resolve.

I stayed still and felt the sticky sweat on my clothes. I'd loosened the collar of my dress and turned my skirt up into my waistband to make the work easier and now regretted it.

He came toward me, slow and steady, cutting me off in the corner where I stood. "'Come now, girl, don't be difficult. You're not blood to me. It's no sin for you to be nice since I give you shelter.'"

"What's that mean?" Isabella asked.

"It means, well, it's not proper to have carnal relations with our own family."

"What is carnal relations?"

"That's a bit sticky, lass. When a man and woman want to make a baby, they have carnal relations. It's a fine enough thing when it's all proper done. But sometimes, a person wants it when it's not proper. And this was the thing. My stepfather thought because we weren't actually blood-kin, it would be a proper thing. But I did not. And if both don't agree, then it is always wrong. Plain as that!" The girl nodded her understanding, unaware of the deeper meanings and implications.

"He came on very close so I could smell his breath full of liquor and anticipation. My eyes were locked onto his, and I could see he looked forward to me struggling and crying for him to stop. I had played this scene with dreadful certainty in my nightmares for years.

"I was afraid, but I was determined. I puffed up my courage as big as that barn. He paused as if making final calculations in his plan for assault. Maybe he expected me to make a plea before he, at last, forced his will upon me—all the more exciting. But he didn't figure on me, the strong, able lass he had made me!

"I, too, had been plotting and knew the barn well. In the pause, I lurched for the halter and flung it at his head. As he ducked, I grabbed the buggy whip and licked him, again and again—cutting the fabric of his shirt and leaving welts and slices—until he was no more than a whimpering heap." Isabella gasped.

"Outside the barn, I felt the air hit my damp skin. I knew my life had veered sharply, unalterably. I headed for the house, through the kitchen door and up the stairs past where my mother, your Grandma Mary, was drying dishes. She watched me pass and stood, motionless, but I think she turned to look at the barn."

Izy stood with her mouth slightly opened, her eyes glued to her grandmother telling her tale. "I grabbed a few things, needed and dear, and left on foot toward town. With each step, I expected Nigel Way to come with the wagon to fetch me or beat me. He did not. I had left him behind me."

Isabella exhaled as if it was finally safe to breathe. "What then, Grandy?"

"Well, first we must put in the next load, donyee think?"

"Okay. But keep on with the story!"

The old woman went on to tell her granddaughter how she had gone to the town and sought work when work didn't come easily to a woman. How she had found the determination to overcome adversity. She told Isabella, no matter how meager her plight, she had believed in herself and in a dream for a better life. She told Isabella about faith and friendship, friendship in particular with the two brothers Hume.

That same summer when Izy was six, Grandpa Hauser died. Missy sat Isabella down and explained that the old man had bad lungs, and eventually, he just wasn't able to breathe.

"Was it the cigar?"

"I think maybe it was."

"Where is he now?"

"He's with God, I think. He was a good man, kind man. I think he is with God. But his body is still here just as you remember him."

"What will happen to his body?"

"We will go to a funeral, and then they'll bury his body in the ground."

"A funeral. I've never been to a funeral."

"No, sweetheart, this will be your first."

"What's going to happen at the funeral?"

"Good things, mostly. There'll be a big box, and Grandpa Hauser's body will be inside. We will be there to pay respect to the man he was, and listen to words and prayers."

"Will I see him?"

Isabella sat in the front row with her mother, father, and two grandmothers. She could just see her grandfather's nose sticking up above the box he was in.

"I didn't know there would be so many flowers. It smells better in here than Grandpa ever did," she whispered to her mother. Missy smiled at her daughter and touched her face with her hand.

Grandma Birdy cried a lot. Gunter helped carry the casket of his stepfather and stood by his mother at the grave. In the cemetery, at the end of the prayers, Grandma Birdy stood over the casket and crumpled rose petals over it, letting them cascade where they would. "My men have all died and left me alone in the world. Except for you, Gunter. You and Isabella are all I have."

Miguel read the words carefully. Izy watched him study the simple message as if searching for a hidden meaning:

Meet me at the pile of old tires near Figueroa, high noon, tomorrow. Come alone and unarmed, or else. The Claw

Izy had written it in her very best penmanship, intent on evoking fear and awe with her confidence and brevity. The question was whether he'd come or not. He didn't know who had left the note. He didn't know it was a girl. She hadn't figured out how to deal with that part yet.

She watched as he turned to look across the tracks toward the houses. He knew that much. That it was one of the children from across the tracks. She watched him turn back to those around him, other Mexican kids like himself. He tore up the paper into small pieces and threw them to the ground as he said something short and forcefully.

They stormed away into one of the houses, speaking all at once. She watched them go through a chain-link fence. He was the last through the door. He turned and looked across the tracks once more, then disappeared. That was when she knew that he would come and come alone.

She handed the binoculars back to Ronny. "He'll be there."

"Oh great. You're nuts. Now what are you going to do?"

"Well, someone will have to meet him."

"And that means you. It certainly isn't me. And what will you say to that great big Mexican boy who has a BB gun?"

"I won't say anything. It's up to The Claw now!"

"Claw? What claw? What are you talking about?"

"Listen, here's what I'll need. I'll write it down, and you've got to help me get it as soon as possible."

"I've got to help you get it? Get what? Oh, gads, this already feels like

31

trouble. My stomach hurts. That's always a bad sign."

The Mexican boy, Miguel, arrived at the tires 15 minutes past noon, causing Izy's anxiety to surge. He came discreetly, clearly not wanting to be seen by anyone on either side of the tracks. As soon as he made it to the pile of tires, he ducked behind them so he could only be seen from Figueroa Street, and waited.

The Claw didn't keep him waiting, but stood up from a small, concealed gully surrounded by tall grass. Miguel stood up tall, dressed in all black. He was impressive, but hadn't realized The Claw had been waiting there all along. He was obviously equally impressed by the image of his adversary. Miguel surveyed The Claw from head to toe. Izy watched him search the grasses around them, and then his gaze settled on the figure before him, just as The Claw began to speak. "You are Miguel, right? I am The Claw, but you can call me John."

"John? I don't remember seeing you before, and what's that getup?"

"It is not a getup! It is a means of disguising my true identity. And you are correct: I do not usually play with children."

"Come on little man, you are just a *niño* yourself." Miguel relaxed his stance as if to demonstrate his command of the situation. He turned his head over his shoulder. For a second, she thought he'd leave. "I don't know what you think you are doing with your disguise and that note. But I have better things to do than talk to little *gringos... ."

"Do you want to die, *amigo*?"

"Are you threatening me, *niño*?"

"Of course not. But you are already threatened by your actions."

"Oh yeah? How's that, *niño*?"

"You think you have the only BB gun in town? We have one, too."

"So what if you do, *niño*?"

"Why do you insult me with this *niño* business? And now you show up and wave around your BB rifle. You use our gates as target practice. I gotta ask you, where do you want all of this to go, Miguel?

"Wherever it goes, little gringo. I don't care, but I can tell you one thing: You will never win this thing. So why don't you all pack it up and go home to your *momasitas*."

"We will not pack it up. We were here first before any of you even moved here. And I think you know this is heading for real trouble. I would like to have an agreement not to use the BB rifles on either side."

"Bold words for one who has no rifle."

"But I do."

"You don't have a BB rifle. You're bluffing."

"Matthew!"

Kerplink-zing, kerplink-zing. Matthew stood up from the gully and fired impressively at the tracks, then pointed the rifle at Miguel.

"Now, will you agree?"

"You said we should come alone."

"I said you should come alone and unarmed. How better to prove that I mean you no harm than to set you up for a thrashing and let you walk away? It's a show of good faith. I saw it on T.V. Now you're supposed to say you agree because you can see I am trying to do a good thing here."

Miguel stared hard at Matthew and the rifle, certainly the more serious threat. Izy observed Miguel's facial expression as one of calculating his situation. The expression shifted to fear and, quickly, became anger. Izy began to worry that her plan was not working. Then Miguel's confident manner returned. The Claw spoke again, "Look, if we wanted to hurt you, we could, and we didn't, and we won't, so that's got to be worth something."

Just then, Miguel let out a howl like a coyote, and three bodies leaped up on the nearest fence on their side of the tracks. He was not alone after all. The Claw hadn't seen that coming, but never flinched or looked away, recognizing the threat peripherally.

"You have made a mistake, little gringo."

"And you have broken trust."

"You tricked me."

The Claw thought about that for a moment. "Okay. I did that. I tricked you. But I did it for a good reason, and I didn't hurt you when I could have because I thought you might be alone. Now, here we are, all of us and the rifles. Don't you get it? Someone's going to get hurt. I don't want it to be Matthew or Ronny."

On cue, Veronica stood up next to her brother. "Or Shelly, Phyllis, or Barry." And one by one, they stood up armed with rocks and dirt bombs. "Or any of my friends. Do you want it to be one of yours? Do you want it to be you?"

Miguel stood there for a minute. Then his posture broke and he tossed his head back with a grin. "I will remember you, Juanito, and you better just leave well enough alone. You are dangerous for a little *conejo*!"

"Say, what's this *conahoe*?"

He never answered, but took a step backward, and then another, never shifting his eyes. Then he casually turned and walked toward the fence where his compadres guarded his retreat. He looked back at The Claw one last time, then heaved himself up and over the high fence. Then they were all gone.

The Claw watched him go. She thought him to be a truly powerful person, liked him even, wished things could be different. Then she turned and motioned everyone back, low, to the first opportunity to cut into a yard. Once safe in the yard, Izy removed her mask and cape, took a rag from her pocket, and removed the mustache drawn on her upper lip.

She grabbed Ronny and hugged her, "It was great! He thought I was a *niño*, a boy. Ha, ha, ha!"

"Ha, ha, all right, but do you think he bought it?"

"I'm not sure. He sure wasn't going to concede anything right out there in front of everyone. I was kinda hoping we could keep it between him and me."

"Right. Private between you, him and all of us," Matthew chimed in.

"But he wouldn't have known that. And then it could have been a private honor between two warriors."

"It can't be a private honor between two warriors when it is really between a crowd!"

"Look, Matthew, really, thank you for the backup and the rifle. You were the key to making it work. Without you, we wouldn't have had even a chance."

"Okay, well, against *them*, any day. But I'm not sure it wouldn't have been better to just ambush Miguel and thrash him good. Send him home with the message and see if they want to continue to escalate!"

"Oh, absolutely, Matthew! That's a great way to get someone to back down. Humble and hurt them! I know you'd back right down in a minute, huh?"

"No, but I wouldn't have been stupid enough to meet you alone."

"Well neither was he. You got to trust me. He's got to think we were trying to make some point. Given time, I think Miguel will come around. I like him. I didn't expect to, but I do. And if not, The Claw will ride again!"

"The Claw? Huh! You just look goofy."

"I do not! I am The Claw! Anyway, I couldn't just meet him as myself. He wouldn't listen to a girl. My Grandy says that Mexican boys live by their own code, and you have to get to know them and do things their way. I had to approach him as a boy. Even a younger boy is better than a girl. And sometimes, you just have to put out who you want people to see. Sometimes, you have to be something you're not just to be heard. Besides, it worked. It fooled Miguel. Bet it woulda fooled you, too."

"Miguel thought you were a boy. That doesn't stop him from thinking you're a goofy boy."

"It worked. That's all that counts."

"We'll see," Matthew mumbled, as he took the rifle and headed back home.

"I don't think he thought I was goofy."

GUNTER

With Grandpa Hauser in his grave, Grandma Birdy wanted Isabella to visit all the more. Missy told her daughter that it was a lonely time for Grandma Birdy, and Isabella felt good about being needed.

"Grandma, when did you come to California?"

"I was born in California, Kinda." Grandma Birdy had two wooden matches held between her teeth, one on each side, sulfur side out. She stood squarely in front of her aged, wooden chopping board and cut the end from an onion, pushing the end to the edge of the board.

Isabella held her matches in her hand because they interfered with her speaking. "But you are German. My Grandy is a Scot and she came from Scotland, born on the ship. Didn't you come from Germany?"

Grandma Birdy cut slits in the onion while she spoke, "My father, he came from Germany, as did your grandfather, my husband, your father's father."

"Why did they come here?" Isabella could feel the sting of the fumes and put her matchsticks between her teeth as Grandma Birdy had shown her.

"Why everyone came here: possibilities. And in the case of your grandfather's family, a chance to start over." The woman chopped the onion into chunks with practiced leverage from her wrist. "You see, sometimes a person can get in such a circumstance that they just need to escape and make a fresh start. Such was the case with that family. They were, all of them, either very smart or, well, very different. Oh, and I can tell you, when they were of a different kind, well, they were unruly, inexplicable characters. There was trouble with that group in the old country. They came to California to start over." She paused to sniff deeply, "Ah, these are good onions. The fumes are strong so they will make a good flavor!"

"So you met grandfather here?"

"That is so, Kinda."

"And was he of a different kind?"

The grandmother stopped chopping and looked at Isabella. Isabella turned her gaze, wondering what the expressions shifting across the woman's face might mean. And then Grandma Birdy began speaking again. It was rare for Grandma Birdy to speak of serious matters. "Your grandfather was exacting in his beliefs, strict, unflinching in his ways. His parents would not speak English, even after they had settled in this country. Only German would they speak. My German is not so good, but I had to manage best I could, especially with your great-grandfather. His son, your grandfather, I think he would have preferred to return to Germany, but he could not. That fact came to embitter him over time, make him hard, but not at first. Early on he was quite the charmer, daring and dashing with his blonde hair and blue eyes. Especially here in California where there were so many darks."

"Darks, Grandma?"

"Indians, Mexicans, all with black hair and eyes." Izy thought about that statement but let it pass without comment. "Your grandfather stood apart from them in all ways, Kinda. In all ways! I met him here in the new state, the Golden State, California! But it was not so much like it is now. It was great, rolling land, and so few people. Now it changes, every day it is changing!" Grandma Birdy paused from her chopping to blow her nose, Isabella's, and then coughed a good deal. So much so, that she went to the kitchen table and sat in a chair, fanning away onion fumes. "Everything changes, Kinda, change is what life is; don't you know it!"

Isabella knew already that what Grandma Birdy said was true. Even though she was young, Isabella knew all about change. In fact, it seemed to her she was on an invisible means of conveyance—like the escalator in the department store—slowly, almost imperceptibly, moving even when she was standing perfectly still.

It happened most subtly with common events repeated often and regularly. It happened most relentlessly at home with her mother and father. Meals, once a time of togetherness that were anticipated, shifted to being necessary, morphed into obligatory, then endured.

"Shut your mouth when you eat! And don't clank your silverware on the dish! Why can't she eat like a civil person? Your daughter has no manners at all!" Gunter barked at Missy.

Isabella pressed the fork slowly into her food, pulling up just short of touching the plate underneath.

"Don't slurp!"

Isabella hadn't even got the glass to her lips. Her eyes looked up to Gunter's, his glare cut through to the back of her skull. She took a tiny sip, carefully.

"She eats like a pig. She is a pig. A brown-eyed pig! Wipe your mouth!"

There was no way to eat appropriately. That was the point. Every mistake was an opportunity for Gunter to admonish Missy for the failings of Isabella. "Disgusting! Do you see? She eats like a pig. I think it comes naturally to her. She is a brown-eyed pig!"

"May I please be excused?"

"Honey, you haven't finished your food." The mother spoke and touched her daughter's knee under the table. The child looked pleadingly into her face. "Well all right, honey."

Isabella went to her room and curled up on her bed. Tears were in her eyes, but she would not let them fall. She opened her eyes wider and wider to contain the fluid and forced herself to think of dirt bombs, pirates, sailing ships, and other things until her eyes fell closed in sleep.

Missy took Isabella's shoes off and tucked her daughter under the covers. "I love your beautiful brown eyes, my darling, my little angel. Sleep tight, and don't let the bed bugs bite." Isabella rolled over, off safe in a dream somewhere.

When Isabella began regularly depositing her food in the toilet after dinner, Missy decided it was enough. She bought a folding device called a TV tray, and from then on, Isabella ate alone in the living room with her new dinner companion: the television. It didn't occur to her to question why she was the one banished. She was simply grateful.

Izy watched Cisco Kid, The Lone Ranger, Jim Bowie, Kit Carson, Rin Tin Tin, and Roy Rogers. There was also My Friend Flicka, Sky King, Superman, I Married Joan, and The Andy Devine Show. The television reminded her of the hours with Grandma Hauser. Later, it would be difficult for Izy to remember why she had been such an ardent fan of television. But the imprint of adventure, daring, and heroics was deeply etched.

When Missy watched with Isabella, she sat next to her daughter, usually with her protective arm around her. Missy preferred family programs: The Andersons especially, and also Lawrence Welk. Izy didn't care about family shows depicting sane, jolly groups of people. It wasn't until much later she learned all families are a little crazy.

Television was more than a dinner companion. It was instructive, compelling, and consoling. Television taught Izy to ride a horse so naturally, as if she were born with all the knowledge required. Izy learned easily, intuitively.

For Isabella's eighth Christmas, Gunter bought H.O. Train kits, three of them at first. They were wrapped in holiday paper, and the tags said they were for Isabella. She opened the packages enthusiastically, and when she saw the pictures on the boxes and realized they were trains, she was thrilled.

Gunter and Isabella set out immediately to assemble each kit. First, they put together the boxcar, which they painted brown, then the caboose, which was much more detailed and had tiny lights on the side. The steam engine, intricate and fully functional with soft pellets that made smoke rise from the stack, came last. Gunter was exacting and rational so long as Isabella was articulate and responded intelligently. She endeavored for the sake of them all.

He brought home sections of track and a power transformer. They assembled them this way and that, inclines and descents, ovals and circles. More kits appeared: gondolas, flatcars, coal tenders and tanks—all assembled with care, precision, and deliberation. She prized the time enough to endure the tension and anxiety that naturally accompanied sessions with her father. When it was time to work, she became filled with angst, fearful of any mistake or misspoken word. Underneath, driving her, was still a need for his approval—a faint flicker of hope that she might once again win his acceptance.

One not enough, a second engine was assembled, and a transformer, more cars, and additional track. Soon the trains ran all through the house: around the sofa, over trestles, and under tables and foot. The winter passed into summer that way.

"Someday I will travel to many places, like Paris. I'll bring you something. What do you want?" Isabella stood on the piano bench and handled all the mementos on top of the piano.

Grandma Birdy, coughing and reaching for her hanky, thought for a minute. "Well, I should think an Eiffel Tower, if you're going to Paris," she coughed. "Or one of those high-kicking dancers with the ruffled bloomers. But why Paris?" She coughed deeply again.

Isabella paused and looked over her shoulder at Grandma Birdy coughing. Then she said, "I don't know." Returning to her examination of the mementos, "It's far away and it sounds so different, fancy." Her grandma coughed still and gasped for her breath.

"I'll make you some tea. That'll fix up your cough." Isabella jumped down from the bench and headed for the kitchen. "I don't know if I have tea, Kinda," Bertie called after her. "Look up there. If not, maybe some coffee." She struggled to talk, and as she did, the coughing neared gagging.

Isabella raced back to her side. "Grandma, you're scaring me. Please stop. I'll make the coffee." She hurried back to get the percolator and the coffee. But Grandma Birdy was not stopping. Isabella ceased her efforts to make coffee, grabbed a glass, filled it with water, went to the woman and patted her back. She had pulled out her hanky and was spitting into it. Just in a flash, Isabella saw awful globs of bloody phlegm. "Grandma!" Isabella set down the glass, feeling panic. Though Isabella patted her and fretted, the woman couldn't speak. She struggled to breathe at all.

Isabella went to the phone and dialed her own phone number. "Momma, momma! Grandma's sick. Momma, she's really sick! Spitting up blood. Momma help me!"

Missy and Grandy arrived and put Grandma Birdy in her bed. They prayed for her and in a while, she seemed to feel a little better. They stayed huddled over the sick woman. But when Gunter arrived, they decided Grandma Birdy should go to the hospital.

Grandma Birdy had cancer in both lungs. The doctors said there was nothing to do except make her comfortable. He gave her strict orders not to smoke anymore. He put her on a diet of bland foods that Grandma Birdy hated. So he relented. Once a week she could have whatever she liked. She came to live at Grandy's house where Missy and Grandy took care of her. For her special meal, she always chose sausage and sauerkraut.

"We can only make her comfortable. There is very little time," Missy told Grandy as they made up a tray with a plate of her favorites.

Isabella listened to the discouraging words with a heavy heart. As Grandma Birdy ate her sausage, her granddaughter kept watch and prayed quietly for a miracle.

One day, Izy came home from school to see her father was home. Sadness hung in the air. Grandma Birdy was gone. She had died and been taken away. Izy looked up in the sky to where she thought God might be and asked, "Why?"

There was another funeral. Isabella felt this one much more deeply. She saw Grandma Birdy in her coffin surrounded by satin, a satin pillow under her head. Isabella knew Grandma Birdy would have liked that. Missy cried. Grandy cried. Isabella cried. Gunter carried the casket and stood by the grave, yet shed not a tear.

Gunter Reinhardt got up every morning of the week and dressed for work. He had a natty preference for muted colors and subtle patterns and styles. He was particular about the crease of his pant and the starch in his shirt. If a thing were not to his liking, he would point it out to his wife and suggest she do better. He wore a fedora cocked ever so slightly, and small, gold-rimmed glasses. His only other adornment was a plain band of platinum on his left hand. His hands were square and balanced with fine, long fingers—hands of an artist.

When he was ready, he walked up to Figueroa Avenue to catch the Little Red Car, the colloquial reference to the Pacific Electric Rail System that ran in and around the greater Los Angeles basin. The system was extensive, running from the San Fernando Valley and Ventura to the north, and Newport and Balboa Beaches to the south. At that time, during the early postwar boom, it covered four counties with 900 cars and carried over 100 million passengers. The Red Car lines were charming, efficient, and beloved. But they were also doomed. Meanwhile, Gunter rode them daily to work.

Grandma Birdy had told Isabella that as a boy, Gunter was endlessly curious. He took apart just about everything, reassembled what he pleased, and avoided school as much as possible. He was advanced beyond the studies there and preferred, instead, to learn on his own through experimentation and inquisitiveness. She had nothing but praise for her son. She did not mention that Gunter was highly narcissistic, that she had never disciplined him and was tolerant of almost anything he did. But she did remark that Gunter's father was distant, callous, and disdainful.

Missy had told her daughter that Gunter, who did not graduate from high school, obtained his diploma independently after returning from the war, and then took the civil service exam. He had a natural acumen for the way things worked and enough knowledge of science and engineering to become a fine draftsman, a profession that drew on both his intellectual and artistic talents.

He got a job at Los Angeles Water and Power in the project development division. Before long, he was recognized as the very best in his department—revealing a hidden talent for just about every aspect of the department's work. In time, even the engineers would seek out his thoughts on problems. Gunter had found a place open to allowing him to apply his vast mental abilities. But they weren't about to formally acknowledge him for his talents. He didn't have a college education. He was a valuable asset to be used but not deemed promotable for his contributions. In the beginning, the arrangement worked for everyone.

Gunter worked directly for the department head, a man named Louis Goodman. Mr. Goodman found the young German interesting, intelligent, and even fascinating. Although Gunter was moody and occasionally overreacted or behaved a bit irrationally, Mr. Goodman overlooked it—in a sense, protecting the man from himself.

Mr. Goodman sometimes visited at the house. He always asked to see Gunter's paintings. Gunter would oblige, and Mr. Goodman spoke encouragingly. Then he would turn to Missy and say that she was fortunate to have such a brilliant and talented man for a husband.

One time when Gunter left the room, Mr. Goodman looked at the trains winding through the house and rolled his eyes saying, "Brilliance is fraught with eccentricity. You have to be glad he doesn't cut off an ear, yes?"

After Mr. Goodman left, Gunter said, "That Jew comes here to keep an eye on me, you know. They got to keep an eye on me. We live in a Jew state and Aryans are nothing more than fodder to serve their purposes."

"He is genuinely interested in you, dear. I think you should be grateful. It is an honor that he would take the time to come here."

"It is no honor. It is humiliation. He is a Jew spy and I don't trust him. He's determined to ferret out secrets, important secrets about me. But I'm onto him. I'm one step ahead of him and all the Jew masters!" Isabella listened to all being said that night from another room.

The next day, as soon as she was able, Isabella bounded into the little house out back, "Grandy, what is a Jew?"

Grandy was fetching the pie crust dough from the freezer. "Jew? Well, a Jew is a descendant of one of the twelve tribes of Israel. The tribe called Judah after one of the sons of Jacob. Why do you ask, child?"

"Are Jews spies?"

"Jews are no different than anyone else. There are spies, so I suppose some spies must be Jews. But spies are also every other sort of person." The old woman looked at her granddaughter for a moment as if puzzled. "There are always people in this world who will single out a group with some differences upon which to lay blame. It doesn't matter so much what the differences might be, so long as they serve to isolate that group from everyone else."

"So Jews are a group who are different?"

"In some ways they are distinct. Some of them hold to a faith in God that harks back to Abraham and Isaac. You know those stories."

"Yes, Grandy. But don't we hark back to God, too?"

Her grandmother paused, pondering the subject before continuing. Isabella watched her closely, sensing the important nature of the discussion. She held tightly to each facial expression and word. Grandy took in a breath and saw an opportunity to change the subject. "Here, let me show you again. Hold the knife-edge flat to the apple like this and keep just under the skin as you go. But go quick and smooth in big stretches. There, you see? Off it comes, clean and nice." She handed the dangling skin to Isabella, who chomped it with her teeth, grinning. Soon she turned her gaze back to Grandy, awaiting the answer. "Yes. We believe in God, the very same God. But we worship God in a different way. We have different beliefs. That is the glory of this nation that we live in, child. We are all free to believe how we choose."

"How do we believe differently?"

"Oh, dear lass. Now you've hit on one of my own personal and sacred beliefs. How shall I explain? Oh, Lord, help me here! You see, child, that's the tricky part exactly. I believe what I believe. You are still forming your beliefs. I cannot tell you how you believe. What I can tell you is that I believe that God himself visited us here on Earth as a man. A man called Jesus."

"Yes, Jesus. I know about Jesus."

"I believe that when God visited Earth, he came to change the way humans approach God. He came to change the Law that had been given to Moses, the very Law that Israel upheld and that the Jews still believe to be the Law."

"So they believe in different laws? Is that it?"

"Well, in a manner of speaking. Laws about God and how to relate to God."

"But they are wrong."

"It is not wrong to believe. It is wrong to judge. Judging is for God. He has the plan for our lives in his hand. It is not for any of us to judge one another, and certainly not for how we believe. You either believe or you dannay believe. How can one judge another for believing or nay?"

"The judge in a court is a person, and he judges people."

"Yes. That is true, lass." The old woman paused, possibly searching for wisdom. "But he judges behavior against a set of laws. The judge does not have the right to judge people for who they are or for what they believe. That is a sacred trust. It is between God and the person he created alone. The judge in the court can only have say over the laws created by man, not the relationship of a human to God. Can you understand that?"

Isabella took from her grandmother's words all that she could and put them away for the future. She knew their weight even if she did not know their implication. She recalled her father's words spoken the previous evening. What possible calculation could she make of it all: Jews, spying, vexing him in the night? She could not solve the equation. She bound it all up and put it away in an imaginary box. Then she nodded, looking into the face of the old woman, silently affirming the moment. They made a green apple pie. While Grandy worked, she told Isabella that the world could be a hard and difficult place. That joy was something to be sought after, and sought after diligently. "Seek out the little joys, lass. They are precious few, like little treasures, easy to pass over and miss. Then life is drudgery and sorrow. It is up to each of us to choose the one or the other."

Isabella played outside a little less than before. She felt an obligation to stay on top of things, things that she could not exactly define, but things that mattered a great deal. It was necessary to control as much as she could: what she said and what she did while her father was at home until he had left again. A level of anxiety began to build, and her sense of responsibility increased with it. If she could anticipate and prepare, there might be peace in the house. The thing inside him that said and did inexplicable, scary things might sleep if only she were careful enough, smart enough, brave enough.

When it was time for lessons with her father, she forced herself to stay alert, to be correct—aware of pitfalls and precise in her navigation around them.

She learned that she could not control the situation when others were around. Always, when someone intruded, no matter how innocuous the intrusion, there was trouble.

"It's not enough, all day long at work! Tell me the truth! Do they come while I'm at work?"

"No, Gunter. No one comes."

"You lie and lie, always, you lie for them."

"Gunter, please, there isn't anyone. No one comes when you're not here."

"They come when I am here? How? How do you deceive me?"

"No one deceives you."

"Everyone deceives me or tries to. Now, let me think. Saturday, the doorbell, that was an agent!"

"What doorbell? There was no agent."

"I heard a doorbell when I was in the yard."

"Girl Scout cookies. The only doorbell was a child selling Girl Scout cookies."

"Even the children are coerced against me!"

"Gunter, it was a child selling cookies. The child was just selling cookies."

"No one is to come here, do you understand? I don't want anyone to come into my house! You are my wife. You're supposed to be on my side. No one, I tell you, no one! What have they done now? What did this child smuggle into my house? I'm going to find it!"

He went out to the garage, and Isabella went to the kitchen. Missy grabbed Isabella and held her tight. He was back in a flash with a sledgehammer. When Missy saw it, she began to scream, "No, Gunter, no!"

Isabella knew this would be bad. He turned to the wall between the living room and the hallway as Missy continued to wail in protest.

Missy lurched toward him and he turned, threateningly, to face her. Isabella pulled back on her mother's skirt. Missy grabbed Isabella and, half stumbling, led her daughter into the dining room. There she sobbed and held Isabella tightly while her husband vented his suspicions of listening devices hidden in the walls. When, at last, the entire wall lay upon the floor, Missy, in shock, took Isabella into the bedroom and closed the door.

Missy and Izy slept together in the bed that had once been Isabella's alone. Deep within Isabella, something shook. At least tonight there were no grueling lessons—that was something for which Isabella could be grateful! It was a means of escape: seeking out the little joys and being grateful. Find something to be grateful for and somehow the terror would come down a notch. Thank you, God, for a place to sleep. Thank you, God, for food to eat. Thank you, God, that he did not hit my mother.

Over time and without conscious decision, Izy avoided the house if her father was at home. Inside she waged a quiet battle between her need to control circumstances in order to keep herself and her mother safe, and the inevitable failure of those efforts and the guilt and terror that ensued. Another emotion was taking form. In these first days and weeks, it was weak and small. It didn't have a loud voice, only a sense of heat.

In the beginning, until compelled by darkness or a promise to her mother to be home at a specific time, she would stay out long after dark, simply to avoid the house. But more and more, the reason she stayed away was to be by herself, high up in the walnut tree or alone by the creek.

It was nothing to miss meals. She would usually grab something that could be stuffed in a pocket and pulled out later for quick consumption. There were avocado trees, orange trees, nuts and berries in abundance, even sour grass that could be eaten if necessary. Sometimes she made it a game of wits and stealth. She would sneak into the kitchen and grab something handy. Often she found a sandwich on the counter, neatly wrapped in waxed paper and meant just for her.

When she did return to the house and he was there, she did so with caution and trepidation. Usually, she succeeded at a completely surreptitious entry and stealthy passage to whichever area of the house was compelling, then exited through a window for the most expedient and covert escape possible. Sometimes, on the brink of discovery, she would duck into the bathroom and hide in the dirty-clothes hamper.

On one particular Saturday afternoon, hungry and without provisions, she was determined to check the kitchen for a possible sandwich. As she approached she heard the elevated anxiety in her mother's voice. "They gave it to you because you are a hero, Gunter. Why else would they give it to you?"

"To shame me, that's why! You shouldn't get a medal for murder, unless it is to hang around your neck as a reminder, mocking and marking you as what you are. Don't you see? It's all so clear."

Izy thought to flee from the apprehension welling up inside her but was held captive by something she could not name, only obey. She leaned in closer to listen.

"I read the citation myself. You got it for bravely staying in that forest alone and spotting for the bombers. You could have been blown up, shot, or captured. Most people would never have braved going out there in the first place, let alone stay there." Missy's voice turned rich with compassion and tenderness. "You were very brave, Gunter." Izy tilted her head back, lifting up so she could peek through the window in the door.

"You don't know what happened! You don't know anything!" He pushed away from Missy and turned his face to look out the window as if through it he could see the past. His voice was low but clear. "We hid in that village all day and into the night. The lieutenant pulled the company out of the village. All but one platoon. I stayed because I was in charge of communications. We got pounded all night by the artillery hidden in the forest. The platoon leader sent spies into the forest under cover of darkness. But they were never heard from again. By morning, I couldn't raise anyone on the walkie-talkie. I figured they were all dead. All but me and this young private."

Missy stood perfectly still, transfixed, as was Izy, still peering, unnoticed, through the window.

Gunter continued, "The private was scared. He was just a boy. I could see it in his face. But I wasn't. For some reason, I felt wonderful, as if the air itself was charged with energy. I volunteered us to go out into the forest to spy on the enemy. We crept, the private and I, on our bellies from gully to haystack, fence post, and rock, until we reached the creek bed. Then up, out, and on the ground, to cover of trees we went.

"We were certainly nearing our objective, hearing the sounds of the quarry in the distance. I heard a gasp, turned, and saw the private hit the ground, his throat cut. A tall, blue-eyed young man in a German uniform set upon me with his bayonet. I managed to use the quickened impulses within me to gain the advantage, overcoming the element of surprise. I knew the man wanted to kill me, wanted to do it close up and in my face. I could feel a rabid glee in him, and I knew he liked what he was doing. I began to gain the upper hand. I had to keep him from sounding the alarm. Wrenching the soldier's own blade from him, I plunged it into his throat. I watched those blue eyes, so like my own, intent, then horrified, then frantic at the lack of air, then bulging, bloodshot, then fixed upon mine, looking into my soul as if to take it away with him, until still, vacant, and yet he stared at me."

Izy watched her mother reach out to touch her father. He grabbed her hand and twisted her arm until Missy's shoulder hunched up. Then, close into her face he said, "A sound from the nearby entrenchment tore my gaze away from the dead German. I looked around to be certain I was unseen, then ducked behind a tree to collect my wits. The tree was low-slung, with branches I could easily mount with stealth. I did so, moving higher and higher, careful not to rustle the leaves until I could, in fact, see the tanks in their places and the troops who manned them."

"Gunter," Missy said softly, "you're hurting me."

He paid no mind to her plea. "I contacted my company commander and whispered to him what I could see. The planes were ordered into the air. Soon, while I remained, wedged in that tree, the bombs were falling all around me. It was strange. I thought I might be killed. I didn't care. In another way altogether different, I was invigorated, impervious, and omnipotent. They were trying to get me, but they couldn't. And do you know why they were trying to get me?"

His eyes were burning holes in the woman. He was grinning on one side of his face and spitting out his words.

"Gunter, dear heart… ."

"They were trying to kill me because I had killed, murdered one of my own. The whole thing was a test, don't you see? I was tested. And I failed."

"I don't understand."

"My father told me not to go. He said that no German should take up arms against the Fatherland. I defied him. I went. So they tested me to see if I was a good little soldier. And I was a good little soldier. And a murderer. I killed my own kind! An Aryan, like myself, like my father. And do you know what happened next?" He didn't wait for a response. "They sent me to a hospital. They said I was fatigued. While I was in that hospital, they gave me a telegram telling me my father was dead. Don't you get it? And that same day, they pinned this cross on me. I hate this god-cursed, damn… ," he was ripping open the little velvet box, "piece of burning, cursed… ." Out came the shiny, gold cross and eagle on a deep-blue ribbon. Then he was out the back door just as Izy leaped sideways off the top step and out of his way. She quickly ran inside to her mother. Missy clutched her child as the door banged open, and he was back with a ball-peen hammer raised in his hand. The golden cross hit the tile counter just before the first blow struck it, deforming its surface, breaking the tiles beneath. He pounded the metal until it was unrecognizable in the dust of the tile on the counter.

MISSY

"Tell the story of the Indians!"

"You mean the Hume boys," Grandy answered.

"But they were Indians."

"Aye, they were. Their mother was full-blooded Huron Indian and mean!"

"Why was she mean?"

"Well, that's a hard thing for us to say, here and now, not knowing all her life and sorrows. But it is fair safe to say that she was bitter of white folk in general, and with good reason."

"Why? And if so, why did she marry a white man?"

"Oh my! So many questions. I don't know for sure that. I know after defeating the Huron, Europeans split up the tribe into two groups. They marched one group south down to the United States from Canada. Your great-grandmother Empee's family was in that group. I can imagine that she received no good treatment from the Europeans in this country as she grew up. The Indians suffered far more than defeat at the hands of whites, and in their own homeland. It is a shameful thing. A shameful thing Americans shall carry with them until they make it right."

"And how will they do that?"

"I dinnay know, lass. Maybe there is no way to put such a wrong to the right. But it's probably all that and much more, we cannay know, made your Grandma Empee who she was—mean and spiteful."

"Tell me the story!"

"She married your great-grandfather, a Scot, just as my father; they came west, just as my family. And he died young, just as my father had. Only instead of diphtheria, old man Hume had diabetes. When he died, he left Grandmother Empee alone with two wee sons to fend for herself. Her solution was to beat them, work them hard. She took her anger and disappointment out on those around her, including her brother. He came to her, sick with the disease in his lungs. He should have had rest and care. Instead, she sent him to earn his keep at the sawmill, where his lungs worsened and, in no time at all, he died. Much blame fell upon her for that. So much so, her sons turned against her, took off on their own—though they were still quite young and with no training for anything but hard work."

49

"And that's the town you lived in after you left Mr. Way's farm. You fell in love with George Clayton Hume."

"Aye, over time, I did. The Hume brothers and I had a good deal in common. First we were friends, kindred spirits. Your Grandpa George was a gentle, kind man. He loved animals and the land. He was quite different from his brother, Micheil, in most ways. Micheil was clever, good with his hands, handsome, and bold. George was shy and cautious. But he was just as good looking. Yes, we were all three friends at first, but over time, it was George who took my fancy and my heart."

"So, you married him."

"Yes. We married and pooled our wee pocketbooks to buy a farm way up north of the City of Angels, in the north-central valley. Land was cheap and crops could thrive. But there was little else, it was a life of toil. Everything had to be made and done by hand. But the weather was kind, and soon, we began our family.

"First came George Clayton Junior, named for his father of course, but also my uncle who paid for our passage to the New World. George Clayton Junior was a large, blue-eyed child who walked early, weaned himself, and quickly took to following his father in his work, rather than hanging with his mother, as most children do.

"The second child was a daughter. We named her Mary Elizabeth after my mother, but we've always called her Mary Beth. She had hazel eyes. Then came David Norman, named for Grandma Mary's father, with brown eyes, and Micheil James, named for his father's brother, with blue eyes. George Senior was pleased to have sons to help with the farm as it grew and the work increased.

"Soon there was Emily Jayne with blue eyes and William Sean, whom we called Willy. He had brown eyes. More children to care for and love, but your Uncle Clay thought his brothers and sisters were only more work. Every time a child would come along, George Junior would make his feelings clear. He thought only about the escalating chores and most of them mine, his mother's. It was impossible for him to understand that the children were a reflection of his parents' love for each other.

"Last came a wee little daughter. To her we gave all the names that were left, I guess. Margaret, Isabella, Sarah, Sian—so many names! So we called her Missy for her initials, and that was your own dear mother.

"I was so content. I loved your grandfather. Oh, I knew he was perhaps too gentle to ever be a good farmer. He was attached to his animals and slow to slaughter them, and he gave his grains and corn for too good a price. We managed, nonetheless, and I tried to make my eldest son understand that. The more I tried, the more he saw things his own way. Soon it became clear that George Junior thought his father a fool. George Junior began to dream of college and longed to get out on his own to make something of himself. I think he planned to make his fortune and then take the burden from my shoulders himself, probably to spite his father, never understanding it was no burden on me."

"Why do women have children, anyway?"

"Let me think. I guess it's because they want to pass on part of themselves. No, it's more than that. It's not just passing part of you. It's passing on everything that came before you and passes through you to the future. Can you understand that?"

"Like the stories?"

"Yes, but much more than that. You see, from the beginning of time, each generation is given something from the generations who came before. They use what they are given, best they can. Like George was given a gift of raising up fine animals, bringing forth abundance from the land, and rearing children. He got that from his father, certainly not from his mother. But from her, he got courage and strength, I think. Anyway, he takes what he's given and in his children, he passes it along."

"But his mother was mean and George wasn't mean."

"True enough. I think there's far more to it than I know, child. True it is that some take the good and others take the bad. I don't know the reasoning for it either way. Just that we must make as many choices as we can for the good because plenty enough comes to us in our born nature where we have no choices!"

One day, Gunter construed an idea, went underneath the house, and began digging. He excavated a hole such that he could get under easily and study the structure of the house and its foundation. He dug more and more until he had room to work. He measured, calculated, planned, and measured again. Isabella observed his steadiness as he worked, as though he were in some world of his own making, where the only things that mattered were his thoughts. In his world, the laws of physics and engineering were supreme and the trivial machinations of the outside world no longer held sway. In this special realm,

51

only the quest for solutions and the reach for possibilities were a meaningful reality.

Concrete was the answer he came up with—concrete to hold up the house! Materials were listed, Missy was sent to the hardware store, and the digging resumed. First through the clay, eight to ten feet and then to the pure, lovely sand underneath. Straight down with a post hole digger, deep and narrow he dug. He constructed a pulley and winch over the hole. Isabella's tiny feet were fitted tightly into a bucket, and her slender body was lowered down the long, narrow hole. With the hand shovel she was given, she was instructed by her father to dig out the remaining sand.

When the bucket was filled, Isabella called up and pushed back into the walls of the hole. Gunter would raise the bucket and empty it onto the pile, then send the bucket back down the hole.

The excavation provided a cool place to spend the summer: down in the hole, out of the heat. Isabella's role was essential. A feeling of importance drew her to her father once again.

"Daddy?" No answer forthcoming, again, "Daddy?" Silence. He would come. He always did. When he didn't, she tried to climb up the rope. But dirt fell and she thought of the walls caving in. "Daddy!" She listened to silence. "Please, Daddy, come!"

She closed her eyes and smelled the earth that surrounded her. Soon she began to feel cold. Outside, far away in the distance, barely penetrating the walls of clay that imprisoned her, a Southern Pacific engine blew its horn. She heard the screeching stop and groaning go. She imagined chimneys like dragons belching fumes of black and great, gaping mouths swallowing up men and machines. "I'm grateful for breakfast, and Grandy, and tea." She let her imagination take over. She was pouring boiling water into small china cups sitting in their saucers—one covered with rosebuds, the other with lilacs. She could hear Grandy's voice, "A good cup of tea steeps three full minutes, lass. Check the clock and take note. Too soon and it's weak. Too long and it's bitter. Just right and it warms the cockles of the heart.

"Now, a lady holds her saucer and balances the cup steady so as not to spill a drop. Grandma Mary always held hers so. I think in her heart she saw herself that way, a lady, all her dreams and such. Did I tell you about the English ladies?"

"No, I don't think so."

"Once, on the farm, three English ladies came from town for a visit. I was curious, so I hid where I could hear what was said. When Grandma Mary got up to fetch the tea, the one said to the others, 'You'll get a fine cup of tea at this house, though in clay, not porcelain!'"

"Isabella, sweet child. Gunter!" Missy hollered until he appeared. "Get this child out of this hole! Right now! Gunter!"

Not a word did Isabella say when she came up and out. Missy took her daughter's hand and turned to leave. "Poor thing! Come with me, Isabella!"

"No harm came to her. She has more work to do! I'm not done with her!"

"Oh yes you are, for today!"

Isabella didn't look to see his face. She'd deal with that tomorrow. "Thank you," she whispered, once upstairs. She paused, looking into Missy's face, wanting her to know the deeply felt nature of those words. Then Isabella was off, outside, and away.

With support for the weight of the house completed and the structural integrity secured, the hole grew until Gunter could begin work on his vision. He gave Missy more detailed lists for the hardware store and lumberyard: chicken wire, hardware, plywood, and two-by-fours. He built forms, into which he poured concrete, which he mixed in a wheelbarrow. More holes, more sand, and bags of cement were purchased. The men at the store came to know Missy and sometimes inquired what "the little lady" wanted with all the cement. Missy smiled shyly at them but gave no reply.

Before long, mountains and valleys were formed. Plumbing was added so water could be delivered, flowing in concrete banks, cascading over a precipice. A trestle bridge linked the cliff banks of a river that careened through the emerging landscape. He painted the entire thing so that there were dark green pine trees, grassy meadows, and golden fieldstone. One direction was the sunrise and the other, the sunset. Lighting determined morning or evening.

Out of the project he created, there appeared a rich, dramatic landscape for the H.O. Trains. He embedded the tracks in cement, covered their beds with sand, and wired the transformers so that, as fantastical as it seemed, the trains were ensconced. Isabella watched her toys become a part of a giant sculpture, a reliquary for her father's demented genius. She observed this in a cloud of emotions. Her awe was knotted with dismay, and her excitement was glued inextricably to her helplessness. It left her insides as cold as the pit in which her trains were now enshrined.

Gunter showed off his creation to Isabella's uncles, and Isabella didn't know whether to feel proud or ashamed or to succumb to the anxiety she endured whenever people intruded on their delicate equilibrium.

Uncle Willy walked around the sculpture and mumbled sounds, "Uh-huh, uh-huh." His arms were folded over his chest. When he had seen everything, he said, "Now, Isabella comes down here, in this hole, to play with her trains, I guess. In this... cellar?" There was a tone to his words that Isabella recognized as dangerously close to admonition or ridicule.

"Of course. What do you think I built this for?" Gunter's head snapped away and he gestured toward his creation, "This is worthy of the trains. No more trite tracks set up in the house where they are jostled. These are not factory trains. Each one is a minor work of art, handbuilt, crafted with great care. They are not mere toys. They deserve to be showcased, to be given a place in the imagination, a place in history! This is here forever. What do you think of that?"

Isabella looked from her father's face to Uncle Willy's. He was staring at Gunter, perhaps in some state of wonder, or disbelief, or maybe it was confusion. But he pulled himself back and said, "Well, so long as Isabella likes it." Then he looked down at the small face turned up toward him.

Isabella looked back at her father and lied, "Yes. It's much better now." She looked again at her uncle. Couldn't he see that she was a prisoner, just like the tracks in the concrete? Was he blind? Was he afraid of her father? She saw it as a failing on his part. Worse, she feared the inevitable repercussions.

The girl stood looking up at the two men. Uncle Clay took extreme care to check the foundations and the support Gunter had installed to hold up the house.

"I must say, you have accomplished something remarkable, Gunter. I would not have thought it likely to excavate, such as you've done, with any safety at all. What is under the concrete?"

"Pounded clay, compressed eight to one. The weight compressed it even more if anything, but the density should be sufficient to prevent seepage or liquefaction."

"Impressive. How'd you raise it?"

"A joint at a time, with a five-ton jack. Same as I used to form the bricks in the mold."

"Astounding! You are an industrious son-of-a-gun! I'll say that. Isabella, your father is, well, inventive and clever. More than that, he is quite able!"

Isabella looked up at Uncle Clay and took in what he said about her father.

She knew that it was true. She knew that her father was not like other fathers at all. She knew in her heart that Gunter was capable of the extraordinary. She hoped that because Uncle Clay spoke so favorably, perhaps everything would be alright.

After extensive evaluation, Uncle Clay said, "It seems sound as far as I can tell." Isabella was relieved to know the house would not fall down. She noted that her uncle seemed as stunned as he was impressed. "How did you convince the city?" Before her father could even reply, Isabella instinctively shuddered deep inside her small self.

"I don't care about the city!" Gunter fired back at his brother-in-law.

"You did get a permit, Gunter?"

"I don't need a permit. This is mine. I paid you for it. It's not your business or the city's!" Isabella was filling with horror.

"It's yours, sure enough, Gunter, but you must have a permit to do this. I can help you get one retroactively." Isabella began backing away, and then she went forward, stepping between them as if she could somehow halt the unavoidable.

"I don't want your help or your permit. You think I'm stupid?" And then there was the moment of breakage. "I know why you want the city in here. You are a spy, nothing but a lackey for your Jew masters! Get out! Get out of my house!"

Isabella's hands were on her ears, trying to block out the sound, the embarrassment of her father's words, the truth that they represented, a truth she could not name, but that felt like shame. Uncle Clay left shaking his head. Isabella watched him hug his sister as he passed her. Missy looked at her husband's face and then closed her eyes tightly. Uncle Clay looked back one time and his eyes fell upon Isabella. They stayed affixed for a long moment, and then he was gone.

From then forward, Gunter accused Clay of being an agent of the dark-race conspiracy, and he insisted the house had been infiltrated with listening devices. He announced that there would have to be further modifications to the house that Uncle Clay had built.

When her father was at work and she was home after school, Isabella observed her mother. Missy had a private life she kept inside herself. It was most evident when she unpacked her crystal and cleaned each piece, rewrapping it carefully and replacing it in the wooden crate in which it was stored. Inside the crate, Missy also kept her wedding photographs. Whenever she opened it, Missy would take out the photos and look at each one for a few minutes before setting it aside to take the next. Isabella watched Missy perform this ritual, trying not to stare, wanting to understand the expressions that spread across her mother's face. Isabella didn't want to intrude upon these moments that lit Missy's features, especially her eyes, like no other moment ever did.

As Isabella grew older, Missy let Isabella help unwrap, clean, and replace the pieces. It became a secret ritual shared between them. At first, inclusion was sufficient reward for Isabella. But in time, she longed to know the meaning behind the ritual. So one day, after Missy had laid aside a photograph, Isabella picked it up and looked it over, allowing her mind to absorb what there was to be learned from the faces, the poses, and the clothing, "You were a pretty bride, Momma," she said.

"They say all brides are beautiful, but I didn't feel all that pretty. I was what you call plain. Nonetheless, darling, on that day, I did feel very special. On that day, I thought all my dreams had come true."

"What dreams, Momma?"

"When I was just a girl, not much older than you, I went to work in the home of a rich lady in Boyle Heights."

"That seems young to be working."

"Yes, I guess it was, but we all had to chip in to help out. My mother had a hard time with all of us children after my father died—feeding, clothing, doctoring. I was proud to contribute. So I got the only work I could, being so young."

"What did you do for the rich lady?"

"At first, I'd go after school to do laundry. The lady was pregnant and the doctor told her she had to stay in bed if she wanted her baby. She hired me to wash, hang, and iron their clothes, linens, and such. I had to stand on a chair to reach the ironing board." She smiled looking at her daughter. "Then I began to go earlier, before school, to help get breakfast, clean, and then race off to class. After school, I'd go back and dust and sweep. Well, pretty soon, I'd spend the afternoon keeping her house, way after dark sometimes, helping with dinner."

"That doesn't seem fair—working and going to school. When did you play?"

Missy gave a little laugh. "I didn't have your imagination for play, Isabella.

It was a lot of work, but I also loved it. The lady had a beautiful home and beautiful things: dishes, stemware, silver, crystal. And the sheets, well, I've never seen such sheets, so fine you couldn't tell the weave at all. She had heavy linen tablecloths with matching napkins. Every time I set the table, I'd dream of having fine things myself someday. I also wished I could give my own mother, your Grandy, things such as I saw there. Your grandmother worked hard all her life and never had much, except those teacups!" The two giggled at the thought of the precious, little cups and saucers.

"That's in case English ladies come for tea someday!" And they giggled at that, too.

Looking back at the photograph, a sad look fell across Missy's face. "When your father and I got married, the church people got together and, instead of giving individual gifts, they gave us this crystal. I could not believe my eyes as I opened each piece, just as we are today—bowls, goblets, and all. Well, I just thought I'd died and gone straight on to heaven!" Her words sounded misty and joyful, but her eyes were bright with unsurrendered tears. "All I wanted in the world was to be the very best wife ever, to be a helpmate to your father. I'm afraid I'm a failure. Sometimes, I don't know how to help him, Isabella. Sometimes, I just don't know what to do." Then she recovered herself, seeming to realize what she was saying and to whom. "I know that it is all in God's plan for us. Everything is God's will, and we must endure and endeavor. I promised before God to love, honor, and cherish your father as long as we both shall live on this Earth. And I will do. And you must do, as well. He is your father, and we must stand by him no matter what!"

Isabella looked up into her mother's face, attempting to comprehend what was being said and the meanings of words not spoken, but so powerfully conveyed. And then Isabella nodded.

Gunter's instructional sessions carried on throughout Isabella's grammar school years. The subjects shifted, and the intensity increased. Geology thoroughly covered, they moved on to biology, physiology, chemistry, physics, and electronics. But physical science was not all that Isabella was expected to learn.

"Your daughter is either entirely deaf or incredibly stupid! She can't take simple direction, even when it is repeated over and over and over. Is she brain-dead? If so, she gets it from you. Do something with her to get her to pay attention!"

"She is not stupid. You can't expect a child to paint like an adult, Gunter! Not like you. You are an accomplished artist."

"I don't expect her to do anything but follow directions, but she is incapable of doing that!"

"I would find it difficult to follow your directions. You can't instruct a child to have skills that take time to develop. Who knows, maybe she isn't an artist like you. Maybe she will never have the ability with a brush and color that you do. And even if she does, it will develop over time, not right now. She is just a little girl."

Gunter ignored Missy's reasoning altogether. "Take the brush in your hand and do it again! Right this time, unless you're without the ability to think at all!" He barked his words, ladled with disgust.

Isabella took up the brush determined her hand would not shake. She carefully dipped the edge into the blue paint and touched it ever so gently into the gray-blue, so that when the brush touched the canvas, the colors could mix and blend just how Daddy wanted. She watched her hand move toward the canvas. She concentrated on its not shaking. The brush touched as she made sure only the edge made contact as the paint was being deposited. Then with great care, she pulled the brush down and out to blend the colors in a smooth sweeping motion... .

"No! I told you not to glob so much paint at the top!" His hands moved efficiently to wipe the paint off the canvas with the paint-stained cloth that smelled of linseed oil and bore record of her shameful failures. "Now do it again, and stop wasting my time with your insolence. It is a simple stroke. A moron could do it."

"I don't think I could do it any better myself, Gunter... ."

"Well, there you have it. You'd have to wise up to be a moron, Missy. You are not the yardstick by which I want my daughter measured." Isabella noted unconsciously that when she erred, she was her mother's daughter. But all the expectations were for her father's daughter. The challenge was to meet those expectations, to spare her mother humiliation, and also to obtain that which it seemed she could no longer elicit from her father: acceptance.

"Gunter, it is so late. Isabella has to go to school tomorrow. She should have been in bed three hours ago. Can't she do this tomorrow night?"

"No! She must at least get this one stroke correct tonight! She has to do one thing right or what is the point?"

"What *is* the point, Gunter? I mean, why don't you let her paint the way she wants to. It is her paint set. If she is to be an artist, shouldn't she be able to paint how she wants?"

"You see? You are in cahoots with that school of hers. You are all in this together. It is a conspiracy of mediocrity. Do you think I buy these things for her pleasure, for her idle play? No! I do all this for her proper education so that she can achieve excellence. I want a kaleidoscopic child. Can you ever grasp the possibilities? I doubt it. You want this child to be coddled into a prosaic future. She will never amount to anything if she doesn't learn to push herself. She will end up commonplace, ordinary, just like her mother! If she is going to do a thing, she should do it right."

"Mom is not ordinary. I can do it. I can!" Isabella didn't know whether to flush to the expectation or pale to the denigration. She filed away the confusion in an imaginary box and picked up the brush. Holding her nerves as tightly as she could, she brought the brush down on the canvas, taking care not to blob the paint, then smoothly… .

"Again you do not listen! Too much of the gray. Now the color is muddy! An artist must protect the light at all cost!" He wiped off the child's error and Isabella set out to try again, and then again. Always it was incorrect.

"Please, Gunter!" Missy was weeping and begging. Isabella was unnerved. Of course, she wanted to be correct, to be the child he wanted. He was so bright, so talented. How could she not long to please him? But she also agonized for her mother, and she secretly longed to have her mother prevail and save her. She was tired, and it seemed overwhelming, all of it: what he expected, her mother's obvious pain, her failure. She could not understand how her father could ignore her mother's pleas. Isabella began to cry, just a little, tears spilling over beyond her control. She hoped her tears, once they had escaped, might have some effect on Gunter. But it was in those moments that Isabella learned something painful, yet very valuable: Tears and self-pity brought nothing but contempt. The only way out, the only way to save her mother and herself, was to buckle in and paint as he expected. Somehow, from the depths of her soul, she found the strength to control her mind and her body and was able to focus. And then, only then, did the lesson stop for the night.

"Uncle Clay is a smart man. He is, isn't he, Grandy?"

"Yes, he is that. He could have been a great architect, I imagine. Instead, he is a contractor. That means he carries out the dreams of architects, and I think that is a great sadness to him. You know your Grandfather George died when Uncle Clay was only 18, and me with all the children, Uncle Clay stayed by me instead of going off to college like he dreamed."

"How'd Grandpa die?"

"He pulled something in his belly and it never healed. Doctoring was not the same so long ago. He tried to manage, but only grew worse and more of the farm work fell to Uncle Clay. Finally, he sold the farm and we headed up north to the Central Valley and bought one closer to the city, thinking it would be easier. But it was in the desert, and the promise of water never came. He died knowing he'd made a mistake. We lost him and the farm the next year. Made it all the harder."

"If you lost the farm, where'd you live?"

"Came to the City of Angels, lass. Rented a big old house and took in boarders. Course, that meant lots of work, and I'm afraid the children got little enough discipline after that. Uncle Clay tried to help out, but Uncle David and Micheil, well, they were pretty wild. David got work at the local garage and learned to love cars—the faster the better. Micheil worked at the dairy. When he wasn't working he drank and got into brawls, often dragging David into trouble, as well. Mary Beth was beautiful and attracted a good deal of attention, more than she could handle, especially from one boy who was 'trouble looking for a chance.' Your Aunt Emily, well, she was always self-possessed and able to take care of herself, always purposeful and filled with an inner power. The boys either hated her or worshipped her; she paid them no mind either way."

"What about Uncle Willy and my mom?"

"Willy was a clever lad. He had a way of charming and getting away with more than I should have allowed, I suppose.

Your mother, on the other hand, well, she had it most difficult. She was the last, the youngest, and the rest seemed to take out their frustration and regrets on her. All but Uncle Clay, he was like a father to her, shielding her when he could."

From time to time, there were such explosive episodes of erratic behavior in Gunter that everyone endured the repercussions and no amount of denial or rationalization would suffice.

The Scattergood Steam Plant was planned to take pressure off existing facilities straining to cover the demand for energy in the Los Angeles Basin after the postwar boom. Gunter had been assigned to the team as chief draftsman. He proceeded to devise novel solutions that would greatly benefit the project. But there was no formal recognition of his talents.

One Friday afternoon, certain of conspiracy and angered by perceived persecution, he destroyed all the drawings he had completed for the project. This was, of course, a disaster for the organization. With energy demands increasing exponentially, the project would incur unforeseen costs and suffer damaging delays.

Mr. Goodman was furious and could no longer overlook Gunter's antics; he suspended him and reassigned the work to someone else.

Gunter came home that Friday night, rambling and ranting about the ongoing conspiracies around him and his rationale for why he was held back in the world. There was nothing novel about his ravings, and although his level of agitation was acute, Missy and Isabella thought little of it.

It was clear from the moment of his arrival that it would be wise to avoid him as best they could. When they did encounter him, they endured endless tirades from this person who looked like Isabella's Daddy but was not really him at all. In fact, as the weekend evolved, the person's eyes would bug out and when he spoke through a crooked, gaping mouth, spittle flew. Sometimes a grin twisted up one side of his face, and that was the scariest of all.

Gunter didn't sleep, bathe, or eat all weekend. As the hours passed, his disposition became increasingly intense. On Sunday, after church, Izy and her mother spent most of the day at Grandy's house. Grandy and Missy prayed and read from the Bible. When they weren't praying, Missy paced and watched out the window. Grandy tried to keep her granddaughter entertained by telling her a story, but for the first time, Isabella didn't listen.

When it was nearly dark outside, mother and daughter crept back to their own house where Missy quietly got them into their small bed. But he discovered them and burst into the room. By this time, he was no longer her father, but some terrifying monster who made no sense at all. Isabella feared what horrible things this monster might be capable of. She tried to be brave. She wanted to be strong for her mother's sake, but failed. She trembled and sobbed as the monster ranted on, occasionally smashing things to punctuate his rage.

By Monday morning, no one had slept. Gunter had stopped yelling, but he didn't cease making noise. There was pounding and crashes and the music was turned up loud. They all prepared for the day as if nothing had happened, even though another wall had been destroyed. The lathe and plaster laid in chunks all over the floors. Missy signaled Isabella should hold herself together and get on as best she could. Isabella left for school worried about her mother, wondering if there would be anything to come home to.

When Gunter arrived at the office of Water and Power, Mr. Goodman reminded him that he was suspended and told him to go home. Gunter began a tirade that made no sense at all and started breaking things. Mr. Goodman called the police. When they arrived, Gunter wouldn't go peaceably, so they beat him into submission and hauled him off to the psychiatric ward at Los Angeles General Hospital. Mr. Goodman then called Missy, who had no idea that Gunter had been suspended. At a little past ten that morning, Isabella was summoned from her class to the office. When she saw her mother, she knew that something so incredibly awful she could not even imagine had, indeed, happened.

At the hospital, they took an elevator to the correct floor. When they stepped out of the elevator, Isabella felt her mother's hand tighten around hers, and she felt frightened. Each section of the floor was locked. When they explained who they were, they were let into the next section. After passing through several sections, they came into a room where they were asked to wait. Two men brought Gunter into the room. He was wearing a colorless one-piece pajama and his head was shaved. Isabella could see where his head had been split open and stitched closed. His face was bruised and his hands and feet, which were bare, were shackled. Missy and Isabella stared in shock at the sight of him. Missy gasped and began to softly weep. Crazy or not, this was her prince, her Gunter, for better, for worse, in sickness, as well as in health.

He was subdued now. His eyes were slightly bleary from drugs, and the monster was gone. He was pretty much Isabella's Daddy once again. This was all the more wrenching. The three spoke in whispers. He told them the truth about the suspension, how he'd gone in even though he wasn't supposed to be there. He said he got angry because they were stealing his ideas. He thought the police were going to attack him, so he fought back.

Isabella listened and pieced his words together with her own experience. She could sort it out. All too recently, she had seen the scary monster that the police had encountered. They didn't have time to distinguish Gunter was someone's daddy or husband. They saw a large man, belligerent and threatening, a madman out of control. They did their job, a brutal job. She understood, but it did not ease her anguish for him, her shame, her fears, and confusion.

They took him away. A man directed Missy down the hall to the doctor's office.

"Perhaps we should talk without the child."

Missy turned to Isabella, smiled and motioned her into a chair, then entered the room with the doctor. Isabella sat by herself. She felt ice-cold and tried not to tremble. She felt everyone in the vicinity were looking at her and saying, "That's the daughter of the crazy man!" And, of course, they were. She kept her chin upward and looked down her face at them from way underneath her eyelids. She wanted her mother. She wanted her father. She sat there, more tired than she could ever remember, looking at dingy-colored walls, the floors, heavy bars, and locked doors. She listened to the sound the bars and doors made when they were opened and then closed with an echo of finality. She wondered if she was crazy, too.

Gunter was placed on medication and after seventy-two hours, released from the hospital under psychiatric care and back to work with a severe reprimand. His demeanor was restrained, but underneath was a current of emotion that Isabella could only attempt to decipher. It was akin to anger, and it smacked of belligerence even though, outwardly, he seemed calm, even tranquil.

Now Isabella looked at her father with increased scrutiny. She watched his great hands at work and then looked back at her own hands. When he wasn't paying attention, she would study his face and then look in a mirror and study her own. She reached out with her mind, attempting to connect with his in hopes of unraveling the mysteries knotted there, but she had only modest results. She felt his anger about something she could not fathom. She was certain that he was the smartest person she had ever known and admired his ability to unscramble the most complex puzzles in ways her teachers seemed to lack. She also recognized that her father was living in a world wholly different from the one in which she lived.

When he worked out a problem, he would burrow into it until he almost could not be found. His body remained while his brain was far away. His brow would furrow in a particular manner, indicating that no one should disturb him.

She longed to know him, this stranger who was her father. She wanted to talk to him in the way she could with Grandy. She imagined conversations with him during which he would actually speak normally to her and answer questions without disdain.

As the days passed, the distance between Isabella and her father seemed to expand and those answers seemed forever confined in a half-life or half-space. They could come half the distance, but the rest of the way was always yet to be traveled. Eventually, she stopped visiting her memories of his lost affection. Instead of a desire to please or even to appease, she preferred to dismiss her pain by forming a new layer over her heart, a layer distinctly more impervious than the last.

Standing at the curb, Grandy pulled the contents from the mailbox, kept some, and handed the rest to Isabella, who stood like her shadow, jabbering about the haze in the sky. She was speaking with authority about its components: How it was the combination of morning fog and smoke produced by combustion and was called *smog*. But at a point, Grandy ceased listening and read from a letter she had torn open. Isabella said, "Who is the letter from?"

"Aunt Emily."

"What does she say?"

"She's telling me about your Aunt Mary Beth, lass."

"What about Aunt Mary Beth?"

"I need to read this now. Take these to your mother for me, please."

Isabella did as asked. "What could be going on with Aunt Mary Beth, Mom?"

"Why do you ask?"

"Because Grandy's got a letter from Aunt Emily about Aunt Mary Beth and I think she's concerned. What could it be about?"

"Oh, dear. I'm afraid it is likely not good news." She looked down at her daughter and knew that was not going to be enough, so she continued. "I'm afraid Aunt Mary Beth has herself in quite a situation. Years ago, she married a man who treats her badly. For many years, my brothers have tried to convince her to leave him and come home, but she will not. I believe this letter bears only more bad news."

Isabella looked at her mother and heard the words. She wondered if Missy heard them herself.

The next few days were filled with phone calls and visits from Grandy's sons. The letter was like an alarm. A family intervention was needed to get Aunt Mary Beth out of St. Louis. Isabella listened as adults conversed about consequences of prolonged ill health, the poor children and what effects they may be suffering, and someone named Buster being out of control, abusive, and shirking his responsibilities. This was big, and Isabella found it difficult to get all the information she yearned for, despite asking questions at every opportunity. Often, she was shushed or ignored. The conclusion was really big: Grandy was going to fly away on an airplane so she could get to St. Louis pronto!

"Aunt Mary Beth, what's she like?"

"Here she is in this picture," Grandy said, handing the framed photograph to her granddaughter.

Isabella looked it over carefully. "Yes, but what's she like? Is she like Mom?"

"No, not at all like your mother. No, no, they are different."

"Are you sure, Grandy? They are sisters, from the same fabric and all."

"Well, in some ways, maybe. But they are very different."

"Tell me about her."

Grandy stopped her packing just for a moment, looked out into her memories, and then began. "In order to understand anything about Mary Beth, you have to look back on what the children went through after George died. As for me, for a while, I thought I had no reason to go on. It was all these children gave me purpose. Before he died, George made me promise I'd keep the family together and raise them up the best way possible. In that big, old boarding house they had to double up—three girls in one bed, three boys in another. George Junior decided he wanted to be called Clay. He rented a room on his own but stayed close, helping me and keeping an eye on things. He got work in construction and gave me money to ensure the children had good shoes and oranges at Christmas.

"I went about life in straight fashion: set up my house on propriety and plain, simple rules. I charged fair prices, cooked good food and plenty of it, and stood by the principles of Christ. There was no drinking or smoking in the house, no gambling, fighting, or foul language. And no women. On Sundays, I'd put on a clean dress, ready the children, and encourage my boarders to walk with us to the Presbyterian Church.

"Every one of the children had to help out. And those mostly grown had to look out for themselves a good deal, find their way without a father's guidance and discipline. It was difficult at first, but it got easier. Trials make you brave or they beat you down, one or the other. You have to decide which it will be. I'd made up my mind way long ago I would not be beaten down. "Mary Beth was good with her hands and did the family sewing and mending, keeping us in clothes. She could make a shirt or a dress, pants, even a coat. All she needed was a picture and the materials. I marveled at her ability. She'd lay out her fabric and cut away, basting and sewing with apparent ease. She made it look effortless, but it was not. It was a talent. I did my best to place value on her, but she hungered for something I could not give her.

"Mary Beth had a beautiful smile and wore her chestnut hair long and flowing. I'd tell her it was unseemly, so she would tie it up till she was out of the house. Then she'd let it down and as she walked it would sashay behind her, sparkling in the sunlight. It wasn't long before she attracted this character named Buster, Buster Petty.

"Now, Buster Petty was a slick dresser and could talk his way into or out of just about anything. He had brass. He liked to gamble and drink, and his audacious behavior made him popular with the faster crowd. She was smitten. I didn't like Buster. But the more I tried to talk to her, the more determined Mary Beth became. I saw threads of my mother in her—desperate for a man—and hints of her father's trusting nature. Buster lured Mary Beth into a web of glamour, excitement, and eventually, sorrow."

The old woman looked as if she might cry, holding back tears and looking away. "I must decide what to wear, lass. Should I fly in this gray suit or my navy dress?"

"The dress, Grandy, it's your very best."

"Then so be it, lass." She continued, "Buster didn't take to the family, and as soon as he could, he took Mary Beth away with him. After some wandering around, they settled in St. Louis, Missouri, where he made friends and began cavorting around. It was not what Mary Beth had imagined, I don't think. But she kept her peace. Little was heard from her until just after the war. Home safe from the war, her brother Micheil visited his brothers in California. On the way back home to Chicago, he stopped off to see Mary Beth. He found her in ill health and unable to care for the children. There was barely food in the house and bad trouble between her and Buster. He talked to her about coming home, to no avail.

Next, Clay went back there and did his best to convince her to return to

California. I think your Aunt Mary Beth inherited a stubborn streak from Grandma Empee. Mary Beth has made a sorry life for herself and her children. Now, well, we shall have to see what can be done."

On the day of her flight, everyone got dressed up. Isabella wore a Sunday dress. Her mother did too. Grandy put on the navy blue dress with white polka dots, a hat, and gloves. Uncle Clay picked them up and took them to the Los Angeles airport. It was a place that woke up the senses. The sound of propellers and messages on the public address system filled their ears; all around were people in lines, shiny airplanes, and fancy uniforms. Hustle and bustle and anticipation filled the air.

Grandy was consumed with the business of flying. Isabella thought her Grandy was very brave, but felt a twinge of loneliness as she watched her pass through the gate in the fence and walk toward the big plane. Isabella had not known a single day when Grandy hadn't been in her little house, always available to be a friend. It didn't feel good. A thought occurred to Isabella: What if Grandy didn't come back?

"How long will she be in St. Louis?"

"We don't know for sure, Isabella."

"What if she doesn't come back?"

In Grandy's absence, Isabella was drawn closer to her mother through their shared loneliness. "I miss her too, darling. But she will be home as soon as she can be, and when she comes, she'll have family with her, family you've never met. Won't that be a nice thing?

"You have been fortunate to have her. Think of all your cousins, her grandchildren, just as you are, and they don't have Grandy to tell them stories and fix them tea. Most hardly know her, not like you do."

"I guess I've never thought about that."

"You and I have been lucky. I was the youngest, so I have always had Mom with me. First, as a child and now as an adult. I still have her. I don't know what I'd do without her!" And for an instant, Isabella witnessed a stunned look on Missy's face. There was a prolonged silence during which both mother and daughter pondered unspeakable apprehension.

It was the first time Isabella had given thought to her mother's strong relationship with Grandy. They were together a lot, but she always thought of herself as the connection between them, not the two of them as connected first and then herself as an effect, rather than a cause. "When you were a little girl, did you have your Grandy around?"

"No. I barely knew Grandma Mary, and to tell you the truth, I didn't really like her that much. Isn't that an awful thing to say?"

"Not if you mean it. If you didn't like her, it's no good to pretend that you did."

"How'd you get so smart, young lady? Grandy will come back to us, honey. Right now, others need her even more than we need her. Do you understand?"

Suddenly Isabella felt an emotion she had never experienced before that she was not proud of. "If all those people come back with her, will they live with Grandy?"

"I don't know, precious child. I don't know."

While Grandy was gone, Isabella went to her little house every day. She walked around and looked at the tea kettle, her doilies, and the photograph of Grandy surrounded by all her children. She looked at Aunt Mary Beth and decided she looked a lot like Grandy. In the photograph she was smiling and happy. She seemed okay enough. Isabella went into Grandy's bedroom to touch the quilt covering her bed, then opened the linen closet and inhaled the sun-scented sheets. She opened the clothes closet and stood among the dresses hanging there and imagined having a tea party.

Izy still played with neighborhood children, but she had less zeal for the dramas. Tiring of them, she found she preferred to be by herself or with Ronny. The old shack was gone and six new houses and families had replaced the vacant lots. The new children were younger and held no interest for Isabella, who was growing up fast. After the summer of The Claw, the war with the Mexicans had cooled to an informal truce. They did not become friends but shared the train yard in an uneasy armistice.

Aunt Emily came home on the train with Mary Beth, her children, and their grandmother. But wild Buster Petty was not along. Isabella heard the adults talking about how Mary Beth had been completely exhausted and slept all the way home. They said she was ill with malnutrition, dehydrated, and had weak reflex responses. There was a general concern for the state of her health. As such, her brothers had taken her directly to the hospital. Mary Beth's children were divided between her brothers, Willy and David. Esther, the youngest, was to go home with Grandy. It was not ideal since the children had been so abruptly uprooted and whisked away, but it would have to do until their mother was in better health.

When Grandy arrived with Esther they were riding in Uncle Clay's car. Isabella followed them to Grandy's house and watched as Grandy made tea, which she poured for the three of them. Isabella felt uneasy. Something was amiss. Something was all wrong. Grandy made conversation while they sipped, telling Esther about Isabella and vice versa. The two girls eyed each other carefully while they sipped their tea.

When the precious amber liquid had been consumed, Grandy had the girls spill out their leaves onto their saucers. "Ah, just as I thought."

"What, Grandy? What do you see?"

"I see a tall friend come over the hill, Isabella. She has her feelings in a bag tied to a stick propped over her shoulder. She's afraid you won't like her, and she'll be sad. But I say you're one to surprise her with generosity and kindness.

"Now, what have we here, Esther dear. Ah, yes, there it is. There's a wee little friend who thinks you've come to take her place. But I see right here, you've a good heart and can share." Esther and Isabella giggled. They knew the secrets of the fortune telling.

"I've unpacking to be done now. Isabella, take Esther outside in the sunshine and play. Go on now, the two of you. Out!"

Esther was gleeful in the warmth of Grandy's care while Clay looked for an apartment for his sister. He visited Mary Beth in the hospital every day and then came by to report to Grandy, carrying away her messages of encouragement back to Mary Beth. When she was released from the hospital, Clay brought Aunt Mary Beth to Grandy's house, where they'd have to make do till the apartment was ready. New energy swarmed around the little house out back, and Gunter took particular care to avoid it. He became invisible amid the flurry of attention placed on the new arrivals.

Aunt Mary Beth was not at all like her photograph. She was thin and didn't smile. She ate mostly raw vegetables and fruit, remarking on their quality and abundance in California. Grandy told Isabella that cooked vegetables turned to sugar and that was not good for a diabetic. Isabella saw the small bottles of insulin Aunt Mary Beth kept in Grandy's refrigerator. Her aunt used them to give herself injections, which caused Isabella to decide Mary Beth was brave. Almost blind, she wore thick glasses that helped only marginally. Her mannerisms were stern. She addressed Esther in harsh tones, often critically. She was unhappy and suspicious of gladness. Isabella tried to imagine what may have happened in St. Louis to make her so bitter.

Aunt Mary Beth chastised Missy for allowing Isabella to wear pants and play with "worldly" children. Worse, she said there were "heathens in the neighborhood who might contaminate the child."

When it was time, Mary Beth collected her children and moved into her own apartment. Grandy told Isabella that the state of California would be helping Mary Beth. Upon their departure, Isabella felt a sense of relief that she hoped no one had noticed, just as no one had noticed that the prescription bottle in Gunter's medicine cabinet was empty and had not been refilled.

Visits to the apartment became a part of life's routine. Aunt Mary Beth walked with a red and white cane and learned the Braille language. Missy and Grandy bought her a Braille Bible. Aunt Mary Beth's health wavered between fragile and poor. Eventually, Buster Petty found Mary Beth and beat her, which put her in the hospital once again. There was a big to-do followed by a court order disallowing wild Buster to go near his wife or even call her on the phone. Buster went back to St. Louis.

Mary Beth's children grew up fast and married young, anxious to escape their mother's tortured existence. Only Esther, still in school, was at home to care for her mother.

Isabella took note of each turn of events associated with Mary Beth with intense curiosity, patiently waiting for things to add up, to make sense. A mean man. An order from the court. If Missy had witnessed the tragic events in Mary Beth's life, why, then, couldn't she recognize the similarities in her own circumstances? Why could no one else see it?

The visits to Aunt Mary Beth's apartment aside, life had returned to normal. Isabella went to school, which she found boring and condescending. But she did enjoy the playground. Every day when she returned home, she rushed to the little house out back, so glad to have Grandy back home.

After pondering the recent events at length, Isabella finally asked Grandy, "Why did the judge order Buster to stay away from his family?"

"Because Buster drinks and becomes abusive. We brought Mary Beth out here to rid her of Buster. Buster had no business coming here where he wasn't wanted, and he certainly had no right to cause anyone bodily harm!"

"Is that it? The bodily harm? Or is it that Aunt Mary Beth left him to get away? I don't think I understand exactly what caused the judge to order him away."

Grandy paused and looked square over her spectacles at Isabella. She seemed to be giving an inordinate amount of thought to her answer before speaking. When she did respond, it was with a question of her own. "You're asking about your father, aren't you, lass?"

Isabella did not speak, but in her eyes the answer was there, clear enough.

"Truthfully, it is plain difficult to give you an answer. There is a difference. Maybe it is subtle, but it's there. Buster was always careless and thoughtless in his ways. He made choices that brought him to his circumstances. Your father is different. He is himself caught in the grasp of something no one understands. Can you take that meaning?"

"I think so. But sometimes, well, it just seems like someone should do something."

"People don't know what to do. He's so intelligent, talented, and so trapped. I don't think anyone knows how to help him. So they, well, they don't do anything at all. They feel sad for him, helpless."

"Why doesn't God fix him?"

"I can't answer that, lass. God holds the plan, not I. You must have faith that there is a purpose. And no matter how difficult a thing is, it will work out in God's time."

"Is it wrong to wish it were different? Sometimes, I do. Sometimes I have a dream that he loves me and that he cares about me. Then I wake up. I hate those dreams because they make it harder, not easier. Why does it have to be so hard?"

"That's really a difficult question. But I think in your heart you know the answer. If there were only easy times, then you wouldn't know what easy was. If every day were a good day, how would you know that it was good at all? Life is plain difficult. Then when it is easy or good, we feel blessed. That's the truth of it, lass. Life isn't meant to be easy. That's the thing of it. It's a struggle to find the moments when it is all so wonderful."

Isabella completed the thought, "And we have a duty to look for the moments, even when they are almost invisible, almost not there at all, we must find them.

"Aye! Then, even more so, lass, that's it indeed."

It wasn't long before Mary Beth's health began a steep decline. Then one day Esther phoned and told Missy that her mother had been taken to the hospital again. This time it was for kidney failure; within a week she was dead. Mary Beth's children came home to say goodbye to their mother. Isabella watched as they sorted out their emotions, shedding tears of shame, their faces scrunched up in anger.

Aunt Emily came home, as well, and tried her best to comfort her nieces and nephews. But they resisted, choosing, instead, to hang on to their bitterness. Everything about these cousins was uncomfortable for Isabella, who was old enough to surmise the damage caused by prolonged anguish. Isabella recalled Grandy's words and was determined that life would not beat her down!

"Aunt Emily is not like Aunt Mary Beth, is she?"

"Aunt Emily is not like anyone I've ever known, really."

"I can tell."

"You hardly know your Aunt Emily, lass."

"But I can still tell. I remember her from the time that Kathy was here and everyone was at Uncle Willy's.

"Aunt Emily met with the church council to request that she be assigned to a church of her own."

"What does that mean?"

"Emily was an evangelist. She traveled from congregation to congregation, preaching and allowing God to work miracles through her. I admired her very much for her work and her courage. It was not something done by women, although Sister was herself a woman, of course."

"Sister?"

"The Church referred to Sister Aimee Semple Macpherson as 'Sister.'"

"They call everyone Brother this or Sister that, don't they?"

"Yes, they do, indeed, but only one is called 'Sister.' Sister was quite the celebrity for a while. Then she fell into scandal and that seemed to turn a lot of folks away from her ministry, including your Uncle Clay. But not the boys and not Emily. Emily wanted to be just like Sister. Emily was always unique, always somehow set apart from all things ordinary or expected."

"She even looks different from Aunt Mary Beth and my mom."

Isabella's grandmother paused and picked up the photograph of her family. "You're right. And she has a lot of Grandmother Empee in her; she has her spirituality."

"Spirituality?"

"Yes. Emily is not so much a religious force as she is a spiritual force, as if she were sent straight from God on a mission. Once she found her calling, well, lass, she was quite something. In fact, there have been moments when I thought my greatest contribution was my children, and that of them all, Emily was anointed by God."

When the sun rotates back toward the equator, the desert begins to collect heat, radiating warm air toward the cooler air of the ocean. The cool and the warm air mix together to form a layer of low clouds. They lie thick and heavy along the shore and ooze up the creek beds into the valleys. The clouds come in the spring and provide a brief respite from the heat of summer to come.

On just such a day, Gunter took advantage of the coolness to make new screens for the windows of the house. He cut the wood to length and mitered the ends. He painted the frames, then cut mesh and fitted it into the frames. Isabella was captured by the creativity of his task, considering the level of destruction that was wrought periodically inside the house. When her father invited her to help, she was proud to assist him in his efforts—once again seduced by a sense of feeling needed by him.

So pleased to be a part of his day, Isabella allowed herself to indulge fully in the enjoyment of the moment. She pushed away her usual hypersensitive awareness as they teamed up to make the work go more quickly. The minutes passed seamlessly into hours, and she was flush with a sense of tranquility. They worked efficiently together. She began to feel as if she were an asset instead of the usual, more familiar image as a failure or inadequate. She dropped her guard and found herself humming a tune she'd heard on the television.

Catchy, little tunes burrow into the unconscious mind and wiggle out at the oddest moments—without invitation or reason—floating along on happiness before they spill over lips, meeting haphazard words that attach themselves to humming until a person is singing while they work.

"A robber and killer of trains is his art
He rides, and he ropes with a mighty black heart
No mercy is known, or leniency shown
He rides, and he ropes and they call him Black Bart."

Gunter stopped working. "Shut up!"

Jerked back into the moment, Isabella looked up at her father to see his eyes, squinty and cruel.

"Shut up and go in the house!"

Isabella's heart seized, but she obeyed. She entered the house, stunned. Her mother saw her and asked, "What's wrong, Isabella?"

"Not sure. We were working on the new screens. Suddenly, he told me to shut up and come in here."

"What did you do, what did you say?"

"I... ," she thought for a second, "I wasn't saying anything." Her mind rewound. "I was singing." Her heart suddenly filled with concern. For the first time, she was aware of what she had sung. "I was singing a song. From the TV. About Black Bart, who had a black heart... ."

Missy went to her daughter and folded her in her arms. A shiver went through them both, and Isabella continued, "Oh, my God! What was I thinking? How could I be so stupid? What have I done?"

They had little time to wonder. The door burst open. Gunter stood with the claw hammer he'd been using raised in his hand, his eyes glaring and bugged out and exposing white all around the iris. His face was a menacing red; veins protruded at his temples and neck.

"The song you sing, who taught it to you?" he demanded of Isabella.

"No one, Daddy, I heard it on the TV. I'm sorry. I know better. I wasn't thinking. I am so sorry."

"Liar! You are lying. Did your mother teach it to you?"

"No, Daddy, honest, it was the TV. Please, I am so sorry."

"Do you know why they want you to sing that song to me? It's because your father is a villain and has a black heart, and they will never let me forget it."

"Daddy, I don't think you're a villain. You don't have a black heart. I just wasn't thinking. Please! Oh, God! Oh, God!"

"Poisoned my own daughter against me. Clay! Your uncle is behind this! There is no end to his meddling or your treachery!" His face near purple, he backed up Isabella from the kitchen into the dining room, step by step. "Don't look at me with those eyes!"

"Sorry, Daddy!" Isabella, now in the living room, continued to step back from her father.

"Gunter! What are you doing?" Missy approached and grabbed the arm with the raised hammer. He tossed her to the ground and continued stalking Isabella who, afraid to show her brown eyes, kept her head low, furtively sneaking glances when she could.

He swung the hammer, and Isabella quickly moved to her left. There, behind her, he spied the television. "Oh, Daddy!" The hammer went through the glass with explosive force, the blows that followed shattered all that remained.

For some completely dark reason, Gunter turned and stomped through the debris and into the kitchen, where he placed his hand on the counter and smashed every finger of his left hand with the hammer. He winced with each strike but never faltered. Isabella screamed for him to stop and fell to her knees sobbing. When he had exhausted himself, he turned, rigid with many kinds of pain. Holding up his hideously damaged hand, he asked no one in particular, "You want me punished? I must be punished! Is this enough? Do you want more? What must I do? How shall I sate your cursed demons?" In those moments, mother and daughter were helpless, transfixed with silent, breathless horror.

In February 1959, when Isabella was almost twelve, Grandy got sick. Grandy had never been sick. Missy took her mother to the doctor while Isabella was in school. The doctor checked Grandy into the hospital overnight for tests. When Grandy returned, things had changed.

Grandy would get out of bed in the morning, put on her robe and sit in her rocker, a knitted shawl around her shoulders and a blanket on her lap. Now Missy brought over food. Grandy rarely cooked. Isabella made her grandmother soft-boiled eggs in the morning before school and took responsibility for tea in the afternoon.

The foundation of Isabella's world was quaking. Though she woke up every morning and found the sun still there, she was not reassured. She went about her routine; still, the regularity of it did little to relieve her anxiety.

One day in early spring, Isabella was with her grandmother when the rocking slowed and finally stopped. She looked at her Grandy. Her eyes were shut and her breathing soft and even. Her face had deep wrinkles, and it occurred to Isabella that Grandy was very old. Grandy's skin was pale. Maybe it was the light. Isabella's gaze fell to the floor and she listened to time slipping by. When she looked up again, her eyes found Grandy's hands, folded one over the other in her lap. And at that moment, a sweet little memory came to Isabella beginning with Grandy's voice.

"In with the tip and then cover the yarn and catch and loop back, yes, that's it! There, you've got it."

"You do it again so I can watch."

"All right. Here we go. Sit here and I'll put my arms around you so you see it right in front of you."

Isabella had watched the fingers, so practiced, the motion smooth. "It looks so simple when you do it. I like to watch you knit."

"I'm not so good anymore. Rheumatism and time make everything a little harder. But we manage still and as long as I can, I will."

Isabella thought Grandy looked quite thin. The door opened softly and Missy crept into the room. "Mom, is Grandy going to be okay?" Isabella whispered. Her mother motioned her to the other room.

"Isabella, Grandy is very ill. When she was in the hospital, they discovered she has cancer of the liver."

"That's very bad. When Grandma Birdy had cancer of the lungs, she died." Isabella paused and pondered a moment before asking, "Is Grandy going to die?"

"I am asking God to work a miracle and heal her, honey, because I just can't imagine living without her. But I think we need to prepare for the fact that she may die, yes."

A cold new reality settled in upon Isabella: life without Grandy. She was stunned by the thought. She had known the possibility existed, but not to the point of accepting the notion as real. She struggled with this new truth.

Isabella was eleven years old, and now there were only two certainties in her life: Grandy was going to leave her, and her father was a dangerous man. Isabella no longer pretended she wanted anything to do with Gunter. That day under the hammer, she had seen something in his eyes that went beyond terror or rage. It was ignorant madness. He had been unaware of her and yet intent upon her at the same time. She could not allow herself to bring the image into

76

focus. Instead, she locked it away in one of her imaginary boxes, very far toward the back of her mind. She barely acknowledged his presence now. She avoided him at every opportunity. Grandy's illness provided an excuse to stay by her side, and for this she was grateful.

As soon as she arrived home from school every day, Isabella hurried to Grandy's, bursting in on her grandmother like a fresh breeze. She was Grandy's elixir. Isabella was young and strong, and despite her inner torment, she was boundless in her energies.

Grandy no longer did laundry or ironing. Her step had become cautious and her movements deliberate. Isabella took over the chores at Grandy's house. When she was there, her grandmother would smile and perk up. Isabella would jabber on about school, her friends, lessons, her thoughts and perplexities while Grandy listened. One day, Grandy took Isabella's face in her hands and looked into her granddaughter's eyes. Then it was Grandy's turn to talk.

"I have some things I want to tell you, and I want you to listen, so be still for just a little while. My mother's family came to this country from Scotland to make a better life for themselves. Some of them did that. Others just made trouble for themselves. My life was about putting down roots, making a start in America so my children could have a better life. Isabella, you are very smart and you are one who can make a difference in the world. Now go and make us a good cup of tea, because I have more to say."

Isabella put the fire under the big kettle and took down the precious tin of tea. She placed the tea in china cups and when the kettle was boiling hot, she poured the water over the leaves and looked at the clock on the wall. A good cup of tea steeps for three minutes, not a second less or more. She carried the first cup in to Grandy, set it beside her, and went back for her own.

Grandy continued, "We came to the New World with high hopes, and some of us got our wishes. Some of my mother's brothers did very well. My mother was deeply disappointed, however, and for all her willfulness she could not seem to get it right. She died without her dreams coming true."

"Did your dreams come true, Grandy?"

"In a way, no, and in a way, yes. My dream was to become a chef in a grand hotel in the great City of Angels."

"You never told me that."

"Because it is spilt milk. That dream didn't come true. But I gave up that dream of my own free will. I chose your grandfather over that dream. I loved him a great deal. It is lovely to live in a state of blissful love and trust with another person. There is nothing that could be better than that, wee darling. My mother never had anything like that. In that way, I got better than I had ever imagined. And I got to see my children grow up. I'm glad for that, but there is some sorrow in that as well."

"Sorrow? I don't understand."

"When your grandfather died, he asked me to promise that I would keep the family together. I gave that promise and I kept the family together. But God rest his soul, I'm not sure that was the best thing to do. Sometimes, I think it was at the expense of our children, rather than to their advantage as George had intended. It was hard for us all. So much was denied, so much taken away, for the sake of that promise. But I kept it, sure enough.

"And you, young lass, what path awaits you? You have strong wits and a big, brave heart. But I also think you'll have a struggle until you overcome it to find yourself. You must take care, my lassie!"

"I can take care of myself, Grandy, don't you worry."

Grandy looked for a moment into Isabella's face, then she nodded. "Spill out the leaves and let's have a look at your future." Isabella did so.

"Ah, yes. You'll need all that you have in you today and more. You can have great, big dreams, Isabella. And you should have. You are very capable, and in a strange way, God has given you a marvelous gift that must first be a thorn. When the gift is fully known, it will give you all you need to achieve great things. But they won't come easily to you like your schoolwork and your play stories. You're going to have to battle if you want them. I want you to promise me you will never give up the battle."

"I do promise. I will battle always. I want to achieve great things."

"It's not fair to place this last burden on a wee lass, but I must. You'll have to look out for your mother, as well."

Isabella had already felt that weight drop on her shoulders. She didn't need tea leaves to know what it meant. Isabella did not answer. She just looked for a long time into Grandy's blue eyes.

Grandy's condition remained stable until late spring, then rapidly deteriorated in the summer. She would get up a little in the morning and a little in the evening, but mostly she lay in bed. She drank broth and could eat a few crackers, things that did not require her wearing her dentures, which no longer fit. Some days she would barely open her eyes and there'd be a small tremble about her in between shallow, quick breaths taken in and held as if something hurt very badly.

Missy prayed over her mother every day; at church the congregation prayed for her as well. But Isabella knew Grandy was going to heaven and that their talk had been Grandy's way of preparing her for what would happen when she was gone from her life. People came by all the time, bypassing the front house, heading to the house in the back. They'd stay a while, maybe pray or read something from the Bible. Isabella prayed for her grandmother's suffering to end. But still, with all that was happening, she could not imagine how the sun would come up without Grandy.

Without Isabella's really noticing the changes, Grandy became unable to get out of bed and could only sip water.

The family started showing up. Emily came first, which helped Missy a lot. Clay came every day, as did David and Willy. Micheil came home as soon as he could.

Emily moved right into Grandy's house. After all the weeks of Isabella's mother taking care of Grandy, suddenly Emily was in charge. Missy stepped back and allowed it. Isabella was glad for Aunt Emily's power and strength, but to Isabella, it seemed Emily was coming late and doing little, yet ready to take the credit from Missy.

Uncle Micheil stayed with Uncle David's family, but they all spent as much time as possible in the little house in the backyard. Isabella sat like a mouse in Grandy's room, watching each of Grandy's children receive their final message of love and encouragement. Grandy never sent Isabella away. Then Grandy went to sleep, and Aunt Emily told Isabella that her grandmother was in a coma.

A couple days later, deep in the night, Aunt Emily knocked quietly on the bedroom window where Isabella and Missy slept. "Call the boys, and then I think you better get over here."

Grandy was wide-awake when Isabella got to her side. She seemed incandescent—lit from inside as if a warm, glowing spotlight shone through her from an invisible source. She saw Isabella come in and motioned with her hand for her to come close. "I am going to be with your grandfather now, lass. And there he's come to get me." Grandy pointed to the shadows at the foot of her bed. Isabella turned her head but saw nothing. Grandy continued, "I see my mother and she's beckoning me. And now I know that she loved me after all. It's so lovely over there. I see my grandfather and a thousand people behind him. Your Grandma Birdy waves her hanky. They've all come to welcome me home at long last. And there's Mary Beth all strong and well in the arms of her father, whom she loves so dearly. It's a grand thing to see!" Missy came in and Emily said, "Mother's seeing right into heaven, Missy. She sees the family gone ahead." Isabella looked around the room and still saw nothing.

"Yes, and I see angels too, Emily. One sits there on the end of the bed, and one stands here beside me. It's so fine and so glorious." The boys came in together and their hustle was stilled at once by the rapture on their mother's face. They stood in awe around the bed.

"Clay, your father is so proud of you. He says to tell you there's still a dollar owed you." Clay gasped a tiny bit of air, knelt down, took his mother's hand, and began to sob. The other boys were shaken at the sight of their big brother weeping.

"Margaret Isabel Sarah Sian, come here close to me." For a moment, Isabella had no idea whom she was talking to. Missy came close and knelt, touching her mother's hand. "Here I am, Momma."

"You must be very brave and strong, and trust in Isabella. She is a strong child. You will need each other."

"I know, and I will, Momma."

"I know I should have done better by all of you, but I did my best. I hope you can forgive any mistakes I made and always love each other."

Grandy's children wept wordlessly and nodded. Grandy was in a halfway place. She looked around at her six children and prayed a blessing on each one in turn. Then she fell back into a coma with a smile on her face.

Night falling, Isabella sat in Grandy's room with Aunt Emily who rocked in her mother's chair. Bored with silence, Isabella went to fluff Grandy's pillow. Her body was completely still, her skin very pale, her face peaceful. One tear ran from her left eye down her cheek. Isabella said, "Aunt Emily, why is Grandy crying?"

Aunt Emily stood up immediately and came to the bedside. She took Grandy's wrist for a minute, touched her neck, told the girl to fetch her mother and to tell her mother to call the boys. "When she comes, you stay in your house. Do you hear?" Isabella didn't want to leave, but she obeyed.

When Missy was about to go, Isabella remained motionless and said with a choke in her voice, "Aunt Emily told me to stay here." If she hadn't known before, Missy knew then. She flew out the door to the little house in the back where her mother's body lay emptied of its great spirit. The uncles came and so did the black hearse. Isabella watched through the window and saw her Grandy carried out on a thin, velvet bed and driven away.

There was a simple, yet magnificent funeral. There wasn't enough room for all the people who came. There were as many outside as inside. Isabella knew very few of them. They were folks her grandmother had touched with her life and her prayers. Isabella's uncles arranged for a pipe band. Isabella watched people parade by the coffin, crying and sobbing. Some left little things: a flower, a letter, a book, a cross on a chain, a poem written in longhand. Four sons and two grandsons carried Katherine Margaret Prebble Hume from the church to her grave, and bagpipes mourned the brave, bonny lass gone to glory.

ISABELLA

That year, Missy sent Isabella to summer camp in the mountains with other Christian youths her age. For the first time ever, Isabella questioned Missy. "Why do we go to church anyway, and why do I have to go to church for a whole month?"

"We go to church to celebrate our faith in God."

"What exactly does faith in God mean, Mom?"

"Faith in God is, well, it is a belief in a higher power, something greater than anything we can fathom as human beings. Something that is creation itself and, most important, something that is all-powerful, especially in moments when we feel powerless. And we believe that God visited this Earth in the form of a human being, Jesus Christ. That makes us Christians."

"I guess I understand that, sort of, but if God is all-powerful and created the entire universe, why would he be interested in the affairs of this one little planet?"

"He created this little planet along with everything else. Why wouldn't he be interested?"

"Okay, but if he is interested, why doesn't God answer our prayers?"

"God answers prayers, just not always as we envision it when we pray."

"That sounds like an excuse."

"I think God will always follow the plan set out for our lives. Sometimes we get an idea in our heads about how life should be and we ask God to make life as we want it instead of as it is planned."

"Then what's the point? If God is going to do things however is planned, why pray to begin with?"

Missy looked at her daughter, "Isabella, I don't know." Isabella kept looking at Missy, expecting more. "I think humans have a need to pray, to cry out to a higher power at times, and I think God hears our cry, answers our prayers, but maybe the answer is more in the form of comfort than delivery of our wishes." Isabella did not move, awaiting something more. Missy continued, "Once upon a time, when I was young, the kids played a baseball game, sandlot softball, between two churches.

And I went along to watch my brother, your Uncle Willy, play."

"Uncle Willy played ball?"

"Oh, yes, he did. And he was very good. He might have been a professional but for the war. Anyway, I remember before the game, the man who was the coach for our church team said a prayer. In that prayer, he asked God to help them win the game. Now, I don't think there was anything wrong with that, but I remember asking myself why God would help out one team at the expense of the other team. I watched our team, bolstered by faith that God was on their side, go out and defeat the other church team on the field. But I don't believe God took sides that day or any other for that matter. I think that the prayer maybe provided a comfort that allowed our team to do their best, and maybe that's why they won. In that way, their faith carried a lot of weight. But playing better than their opponents is what won the game."

Isabella pondered her mother's words carefully at a time when she had arrived at an intersection in her life. Soon she would have to choose a path of her own. She left for camp aware that it was her mother's way of helping her get over the loss of Grandy. As she boarded the bus, it did not seem as if anything could fill the huge hole in her heart. She did not know how to pray for help, nor was she sure there was any prayer that could help.

Upon arriving at camp, the bus was greeted with enthusiasm, which was, at least, a distraction. Campers were sent to cabins for orientation and Isabella allowed herself to become absorbed in the new information. The girls were given rules about boys and told to beware of the effects of altitude. It could cause shortness of breath, fatigue, or even start menstrual cycles.

As the days passed, Isabella bound up her feelings of loss and placed them in precious little compartments in her soul. The more she refused to dwell, the more time passed easily. Games, sports, and crafts by day... bible lessons, songs, and campfires at night.

Because she was the only one from her church at the camp, Isabella was assigned to a cabin with girls from another church. When she introduced herself, she made an important decision without thinking much of it. She said her name was Isabella, but that people called her Izy. It was a minor distinction, but it was also a veer in the path.

The other girls in the cabin had matching outfits and Izy didn't, so she stuck out as an oddball. Undeterred, she sought other oddballs and managed to have a good time. However, underneath the merriment lurked an undercurrent of ache, a loneliness she couldn't completely shove away.

Even before Grandy had gotten sick, Missy had explained the facts of life to

Isabella. Isabella took it in as a matter of fact, although she absolutely could not believe the part about the penis. When Isabella found blood on her underwear, she went to a counselor, as instructed. She was given the belt, pads, and a pamphlet with pictures of reproductive organs that explained what was happening to her body. Isabella followed the instructions in the pamphlet and assembled the protective apparatus as she wondered if the person who had come up with it had ever had to wear one.

She thought of Grandy's story of finding blood and not knowing what it was, washing her underwear in the creek, embarrassed to tell, and learning she was now cursed. Was Grandy in heaven? Could she see? Isabella wandered off by herself and sat down under a tree. "Grandy, got my period." She waited, listening for a response as the loneliness stabbed at her throat. Then she snapped her head to attention, stood up, and walked on.

There wasn't much blood. Sure enough, as soon as she left the altitude, it ended. It didn't come the next month, or the next. She forgot all about it. Soon enough it would come for real with pain, emotional extremes, and even more transformations.

When Isabella returned home from camp, she found Grandy's house had changed. Missy had gone through and sorted her mother's belongings: every apron, stocking, dish and spoon, doily, linen, and dress. She noted great care in the way everything was placed reverently into boxes, folded in tissue, or tied with ribbon and labeled for who should get what or what to keep for herself. A box was set aside for each son with things just for them. A box for Emily was filled with items she had requested: her mother's Bible, some hankies, her shawl, an old pitcher and bowl. For herself, Missy set aside old photographs, a wooden rolling pin, china teacups and saucers, and the kettle—keepsakes for always.

Isabella came upon Missy kneeling on the hardwood, her body weight pressing her knees into the floor. Isabella thought it must be uncomfortable— the way she was posed, as if she needed the sensation of pain to help her grasp this new reality. The sight brought a stab to Isabella's throat. Then she saw her mother was softly weeping. With that came another realization: They had all left. Missy's brothers and sister had returned to their own lives. Missy hadn't been able to process anything while her siblings were there, talking, so certain of themselves, so in charge. Missy had ridden their presence out like driftwood to shore. She even sent Isabella away so she could have these last, precious moments with Grandy's things. A sorrowful, intimate task. The final task. Isabella turned and left Missy alone.

Not long after that day, Uncle Clay took them both by surprise with another loss. "Just about sold everything, won't be long now."

"But Clay, dear, you can't, oh, I wish you wouldn't. It won't be the same without you."

"It's best. Lil's diabetes is my main concern now. I want to devote myself to her. Don't want her to end up like Mary Beth. Oregon is beautiful, peaceful. I have two acres on the Ompagua. Going to build a home there, fish for trout and salmon, grow our own fruit and vegetables. Mom's gone now. I always felt I needed to stand by her, but now, well, it's time to move on."

"If that's what you want. What about George Junior?"

"Willful child. He don't listen to me, goes his own way, don't need me. Wish he did. I could be a help to him. You know how it can be with fathers and sons."

Isabella watched the big man with bear-like hands and rugged face. She saw him as the protector whose first thought was for the safety of their house, to be sure it wouldn't collapse after Gunter had dug out the cellar. Clay had taken over the farm for his father when he fell ill and was faithful to his mother. Isabella saw the things passed down to him—the threads in his fabric. Like his mother, he was a great oak tree, but also like Indian grandmother—bitter and intractable. There was something else. When Uncle Clay liked you, he liked you deeply, favored you. Isabella knew in her heart that Uncle Clay liked her, and she was glad. Isabella had a thought: No matter how many things come to you, something is always leaving.

Later Missy told Isabella, "I'm not sure he really knows why he's leaving. He says it's Aunt Lil, and it is, at least partly. But not completely, as he states. He's lost his heart. That's why he's leaving. If a man is to get ahead in business it is more than just the work. There's the socializing, the dinners, functions. All that Lil would not do! She couldn't stand for Clay's attention to be elsewhere, and she didn't like people paying attention to him. Your Uncle Clay has gone as far as he is ever going to go when, in fact, he could have gone so much further. This is his way of escaping the disappointment."

"Where did he meet Aunt Lil?"

"She is the eldest granddaughter of an English banker who came to this country, to California, at the end of the Gold Rush. He was quite established and Clay went to him to borrow the money to start his construction business. She was there visiting her father that very day. That's how it started. I think Clay thought it was a means to getting what he wanted in this life. She wrapped herself around him and, at first, I think all the attention was enticing, such that he did not see the pitfalls. When your Uncle loves, he loves deeply. That's the thing when you are young. You can only see as far ahead as your inexperience allows. We all make mistakes and we spend the rest of life straightening them out with God's help."

Isabella wondered if her mother was speaking about Uncle Clay in words that Missy could not bring herself to take personally. Did Missy think of her life as a mistake that had to be straightened out? Then, Isabella thought of Emily and her innate power. Why didn't Missy have any of it?

"Grandy said Aunt Emily used to travel around working miracles."

"During her evangelist years, yes. She traveled all over the country, back and forth, up and down. I think Mom worried about her at first. She had another lady who traveled with her. Sister insisted on it, it not being at all proper for a single lady to be on the road alone. But still, just two ladies, all by themselves, it was extraordinary! But I never worried for her. In fact, I felt sorry for anyone who tried to tangle with Emily!

"She wasn't just an evangelist. She was also a troubleshooter. If the Foursquare Gospel Ministry opened a church and all did not go well, Emily was sent in to straighten out the problems.

"Once there was such a case. A church opened in the Midwest somewhere. Shortly afterward, they just lost contact, were never heard from. So out went your Aunt Emily. Turned out the would-be minister was a scoundrel who had taken the money to bankroll a gambling syndicate. Imagine what the community thought! Emily had to get rid of him, chase out his minions, then try to salvage what was left and rebuild the trust of the community. And she did it! Turned it around in less than six months. But then they sent in another man to take over the church. It was a long time before Emily finally got a church of her own."

"That's odd. The church was started by a woman."

"Yes. Sister MacPherson started the church. But then she died."

"How'd she die?"

"I'm afraid it was amid controversy, Isabella. She died, and by her bed was a vial of sleeping pills. Gossip was she'd overdosed, committed suicide. But her son Ralph fervently denied it, and I'm not sure it was ever clear how she died. She died as she had lived: flamboyantly and at the center of a furor!"

"What does that mean?"

"Aimee Semple MacPherson was a gifted speaker, and I think she was really in touch with God. God seemed to bless everything she did. But Aimee the person, well, she was something else. You must remember we are all just people; we all have strengths and weaknesses. Sister was no different. She was flawed. But she was a very public person. She enjoyed the visibility and there is a price to pay for courting fame. Her flaws became very public and even scandalous!"

"She was in the newspaper?"

"She disappeared while swimming at a beach. Didn't show up for days. They thought she'd drowned or been murdered, eaten by sharks. Then she just showed up miles away in the desert. She claimed she'd been kidnapped, but the police didn't believe her. Gossip went wild with all manner of possible explanations. Nothing was ever proved or disproved. To this day, it is a mystery."

"What do you think happened?"

"I think it doesn't matter, really. I think she was a human being and whatever happened, it is between her and God. Everyone has lapses, even Emily. After her husband died, she had a dark spell."

"She was married?"

"Yes, briefly, but it was as if they were soul mates."

"What's a soul mate?"

"It is when two people find each other and become as one. So it was with Emily and Tom Evans. When she received the telegram that he had been killed during the invasion of Normandy, I'm told she fell into a chair and cried out, 'Oh, my Lord God, why hast thou forsaken me!' And then, she just went away, vanished for a while. We didn't hear from her for months. But when we did, she was bolder and brighter than ever before. So, maybe our trials and our lapses make us stronger."

Over time their childhood vanished, but Veronica and Isabella remained friends. Sometimes, while off in some private hideaway together, a great silence would fall between them. Discomfort would fill the space as if there were nothing left to say but the truth. For that, there was no vocabulary. Izy wanted Ronny to know her secrets. Ronny was the only one Izy trusted enough to tell, but she just couldn't. So they would part. Their meetings grew less frequent and did not last long. The funny thing was that Izy felt Ronny had a secret, too.

That fall, Isabella went to junior high school, reluctantly leaving her mother alone. Izy was assigned to Henry Clay Junior High. It was brand new. Isabella's class would be the first to go through the grades. She didn't go to one classroom. Instead, she was assigned a homeroom class, then went in different directions all day, changing classrooms, subjects, and teachers. Right away, it required more attention just to figure out where to be and when. Izy found it more interesting as she had never really cared much for school before. She was assigned a locker for stowing her books, gym clothes, and personal items since she had to move around all day. School became a world unto its own, and although she did not think about it, she was both drawn to this new world and pushing away from the old. The new world was not completely affable. In fact, some experiences were downright uncoupling.

The girls' bathroom had a new sense of energy. Makeup was being applied and garters for nylon stockings were adjusted. These were things only grown-up women wore, so far as Isabella knew.

Young people were coming together from various grammar schools and there was much to sort out. To Isabella, it seemed a puzzle fraught with stings and hisses. But it was fascinating.

"Do you know that boy, the one with the blue jacket? He is just *the* cutest!"

"Oh, that's Cindy's brother, older brother, and he's dreamy!"

"I've just got to meet him!"

"Ask Cindy."

"I couldn't do that! She's such a drip! How could *he* be *her* brother? She still wears her hair in braids! Can you imagine?" Everyone was judged on criteria Isabella didn't know existed. She seemed to be enrolled in some cosmic contest in which the prize was popularity. And how one looked and dressed actually mattered. Isabella's clothes were functional. They warmed and covered her. Her shoes were sturdy and worn with socks. She had never given thought to her appearance, at least not in this new and particular way. The fad was big hair! Isabella didn't have a clue about how to get it and wasn't sure she wanted it. "What do they say about my hair?" she wondered.

She looked in the mirror to size up her appearance. She saw freckled skin, reddish-brown hair, and, of course, brown eyes. Her features were well-placed, but not alluring. She wore no makeup and had no inclination to do so.

The world was divided into boys and girls; there was no unisex, genderless play. Boys hung with boys. No "tag-along" girl allowed, even if she did know the Dodgers won the World Series—beating the Chicago White Sox 4-2—and scored

705 runs and won 82 games for the season. While trying to make friends, Isabella attempted to express her love of baseball to three girls; they made faces, turned, and left her, laughing as they went.

At the end of the first day, Izy was confused. The end of the first week brought suspicion she might be "uncool." By the end of autumn, Isabella was unequivocally an outcast.

Undeterred, Izy sought out others outside "the circle." First, she tried the "brains." Shelly fell right into that group. His science, math, and naturally-inventive nature made him a shoo-in. But Shelly's socialization skills were lacking; he soon became isolated, even within a group of his apparent peers. Izy was disappointed to learn that these "smart" kids used their grades as weapons, then whined when they were persecuted. She found no fellowship with them.

She abandoned the brains for the morally-solvent young Christians club, where she reasoned she would find some commonality. There she found a similar flaw: self-proclaimed moral superiority. This was righteousness, not the humility of Christ. When she pointed this out, she was shunned; she moved on.

Next, Izy fell in with the budding lesbians, a rough group of girls who, among other things, were good athletes and took their sports seriously. Izy was skinny but strong; she found a bond. These girls did not obsess over boys. This was more comfortable for Izy, who had no sense of the blossoming hormones that seemed to affect most of her peers. She met Gina.

"Setup! Setup! Setup! I'm not having anyone on my team who can't setup! Volleyball is a team sport and I intend to win, get it?" Isabella watched the forceful girl wield her will on her newly-selected team, for which Izy was proud to have been chosen. Gina had deliberately chosen girls who, like herself, were tall, agile, or strong. Some acted a little like boys, but not Gina. Gina was shapely and developed; her shorts hugged her backside, unlike Izy's, which hung from her waist to bag around her strong, but woefully-skinny legs. For some inexplicable reason Izy, accustomed to being captain herself, was simply glad to be on the team.

Gina took in Isabella as a friend. It was good to find a friend, and Gina, brave and strong, was a good one to have. When she wasn't in gym clothes, Gina wore a thick, black, leather jacket with silver rivets and skirts made of the same material as Levi jeans. She had pierced ears. She took abuse from no one, at least not to her face. Isabella felt a measure of safety with Gina and gave herself over to her new best pal.

At home, Gunter was busy. He cleared out enough of the walls so that you could see the whole interior of the house from the front door, except the bathroom and little bedroom where Isabella and her mother slept. He slept in the rafters, where he had made a space for himself. Underground, he went tunneling. He wanted to be able to go from the front house to Grandy's house without being seen. Whenever he was not at work, he was digging and pounding the clay into walls. The walls of the tunnel ended roughly chest high for Gunter and were topped with a shelf. He built wooden forms on the shelf that went up and over from one side of the tunnel to the other, which he filled with concrete to form a rounded ceiling. Like an eggshell, the tunnel was actually strengthened by the weight of the earth above pushing down on the rounded concrete. He installed electrical outlets for lights as he progressed, like a mole, toward the little house out back.

Missy appeared to have just given up. She stopped arguing with him about the house modifications. She went about her normal duties and endless chores as the housekeeper in the destruction zone, quietly seeking to keep the peace and avoid conflict or confrontations with her husband.

Gunter and Isabella occasionally had "lessons," but the remodeling projects were consuming more of his time. The lessons quickly deteriorated into ranting sessions, full of inane accusations, plots, and tyranny. In those moments, Isabella was trapped with the monster. There was no reasoning with him, no acceptable response. Missy would swoop in to rescue her if she could. Then they would hurry into the bathroom, lock the door, and wait for him to head off to his projects. When he was rational, Izy would search for her daddy, pray for mercy, and do whatever it took to appease him, keep him focused. If she made an error or dared to ask a foolish question, he would still use her failure to punish Missy. Missy didn't cry anymore, she just looked at the floor and waited.

Isabella spent less time with the neighbor kids, including Ronny. Instead, she chose to hang out on the volleyball courts at school with Gina. Pubescence wrapped around her and made everything seem crazy, not just her father. Without Grandy, Isabella was on her own to make sense of her leap into adolescence.

"Mom, did you still work at the rich lady's house when you were a teenager?"

"I worked there until I was about sixteen. She had three children by then. In some ways, they were like siblings to me. I was around them from their birth and as they grew."

"But you had so many brothers and sisters."

"Yes, but they were older, grown before I could relate to them. They had no time for me. I was a nuisance to them. Willy with his baseball, Emily lit with her own flame, following her own path. But the rich lady's children, I was important to them. They were my charges and that meant a lot to me. I was sad when I left."

"Why did you?"

"Well, things changed. Our family got caught up in the Foursquare Gospel and we started going to church, not just on Sundays, mind you. Wednesday for prayer meeting, Thursday for choir, Friday for young people's service, Saturday for outings. It was all-consuming. The Foursquare Gospel was salvation for my siblings!"

"Salvation? Why, Mom?"

"You see them as pious ministers now, but there was a time when your uncles David and Micheil were wild and heading for real trouble. David stole a car and took it for a joy ride. He was obsessed with automobiles. They put him in the pokey! Micheil was in one fight after another; he drank and had a vile temper. Grandy worried for them and prayed that God would forgive them.

"Then they went to this tent meeting where this amazing woman evangelist, Sister, spoke the word of the Lord. Well, she was quite something! She was dressed in a white, flowing robe with a dark blue shield and a red cross over her breasts. Her hair was twisted up in braids like a crown or halo. It was no time before they had all converted. They started to attend church regularly and gave up stealing, drinking, smoking, and fighting!"

"Did Aunt Emily smoke and drink?"

"Oh, no, honey. Emily always followed her own ideal, waiting for something to come along and harmonize with her own inner song. It was the Foursquare Gospel. Soon Emily was Sister's protégée. Emily followed Sister everywhere, braided her hair before meetings, and stood in the wings, breathless at every word. The boys joined the seminary to become preachers. As soon as she could, so did Emily, which was rare then. But your Aunt Emily, she was something rare herself!"

Isabella nodded, knowing that was the truth. She did not know her well, but Aunt Emily was a force to be reckoned with, for sure. Something about Emily resonated with Isabella.

Gina didn't care for schoolwork, so neither did Izy. Isabella could easily get decent grades without homework or study, and she did. Gina couldn't, and her grades were poor the first year. The following year she flunked and was left behind. Izy would have helped her, but Gina said she didn't give a damn and seemed to be proud of failing. There were a group of students emerging at the school who shared her attitude. They hung out, smoked cigarettes, and wrote on the clean, new walls. They were angry about something Izy could not understand, but she was sure it had to do with being on the fringe of everything. Gina drifted toward them and Izy went along out of loyalty, hoping to hold on to Gina by gravitational force, even as she felt Gina slipping away.

In the spring of 1961, President Kennedy made a speech to Congress. "I believe that this nation should commit itself to achieving the goal, before this decade is out, of landing a man on the moon and returning him safely to the Earth." It was intended to inspire, and the world turned its head to see what the United States would do with the challenge.

The press was alive with talk of space. It was uplifting toward some unknown possibility. Izy's heart and mind lifted with it to a brand new sense of the world around her. In school, they studied Sputnik, the Soviet Union, and the latest U.S. rocket to explode during liftoff. Shelly became an expert rocketeer. He designed and built his own, with periodic launches that were far more successful than those of the National Aeronautics and Space Administration. At least at first. His designs included sophisticated launching systems with electronic ignitions and automated countdowns.

Tunneling beneath the earth, Gunter reached Grandy's house and was burrowing up through the floor.

Once he had private access to the little house, he boarded up the windows and padlocked the doors. He took the remainder of Grandy's things—bentwood rocker, treadmill sewing machine, wrought iron bed—and sold them to the "Jews downtown," whoever they were. Isabella watched it all disappear and hoped the "Jews downtown" knew that the things were precious. She wondered what they would do with them. She saw the ripping away of each item as an act of brutality; her feelings were inexpressible. In time, Gunter turned the place that had defined safety and love for Isabella into an arcane fortress from which she and her mother were verboten.

Gunter expressed a liking for Diane Lennon of the Lennon Sisters on Lawrence Welk, and also for Marilyn Monroe. Isabella didn't like it when he talked about them and would often detect a reaction in her mother when he did. Although she kept quiet, Missy would lower her head. He announced his intention to do portraits of the celebrities, in oils, out in the little house. He always went by way of the tunnel. It became the place he stayed almost always and there was relief in that. Missy mourned her losses silently. Izy took her first sips of bile and felt the fermentation inside her innermost self, thick and frothy. She watched as Missy put on her apron and smile each day after Gunter had left for work, hiding her pain, seeking out little joys, making the best of the day until it was time for him to return. The only time she saw Missy truly happy was in the facets of the crystal on those rare occasions when she would unwrap her beloved collection. What Izy felt when she watched Missy was not pity, not empathy, or even sadness. It was dull and empty and might have been on the fringes of disdain. It was a draining of respect. But not a lessening of love. Love is a very strange thing.

There was another feeling. That curious, nameless feeling—the one that had first surfaced years earlier—began to take hold. Plodding like a juggernaut over the boulders of longing, rocks of disappointment, twigs of betrayal—it tore away the last bonds of allegiance.

SEDITION

In the fall of the final year of junior high, Gina came to school with a tattoo on her arm. It was awesomely bold: a red heart with a dagger through it and a single drop of blood dripping off the dagger. Izy was impressed. One day after school, Gina took Izy under the bleachers and pulled out a pack of Marlboro cigarettes and offered Izy one. That was the first time for Izy. Afraid and thrilled, she cautiously took one and lit it. She watched Gina inhale and blow it out her nose, wowed. She had to learn to do that. Izy inhaled gagging and choking.

"I love you, Bella," which is what she called Izy, who was now clearly Izy to everyone else except her mother. "You're a sweet kid and I will never let anything bad happen to you." Izy smiled and tried another inhalation and choked, nodding her head, a little dizzy. She liked that Gina called her Bella. She liked that Gina said it like a big sister, something Izy had never known. But with all the camaraderie, they never went home together. Izy never went to Gina's house and Gina never came to Izy's. No one ever came to Izy's house anymore. In some ways, it was a relief. It was safer being isolated from outsiders. It was also a means to propagate the surreptitious nature of their existence, the threesome, in their cloistered nightmare house.

In October of that year, 1962, news broke of Soviet missiles in Cuba. With enough nuclear power on that island to blow up America, tensions mounted with fear of war, or worse. It occurred to Izy that madness was a global issue.

Sunday, October 21st, rumors were rampant, even in church. "And in this special week of prayer, we will meet daily in the hope that God will intervene to vanquish the Godless tide of communism and give our President the wisdom and the courage to stand up to the Soviet Chairman!" Izy listened and felt rising terror all around her. She pondered words like godless tide and wondered what could delude whole sections of the planet into communism. What was communism?

On Monday, October 22nd, President Kennedy announced an embargo on Cuba.

Tuesday, October 23rd, during homeroom a voice over the speaker broke in to announce, "Once a day from now on, until further notice, there will be an air raid drill to prepare us for the threat of nuclear attack. The following procedures are to be followed without exception. You will cease whatever you are doing and identify the nearest object that may provide protection. A desk or table, a door jamb are examples. You will move to get under protection. If you are outside, move immediately to the nearest walled structure, huddle as close as possible, and cover your head. Regardless, be certain to close your eyes and do not open them under any circumstances. You will remain as such until the 'all clear' is sounded." They showed film of nuclear blasts on television and Izy wondered what good it would do to get under anything or huddle next to anything since it would be blown away completely. She wondered if it might be better to take one last look around and find something unspeakably wonderful to look at, to take with you inside your mind as you were blown into... into, whatever it was, heaven, or maybe, smithereens!

In social studies class on Thursday, the teacher seemed to be reciting, "Communism is an evil doctrine of collectivism whereby ingenuity and self-determination are suppressed. Individuality is discouraged and the society is trapped in its own mediocrity.

"Under the rule of communism, faith in God is considered the 'opiate of the masses,' lulling the poor into subservience to the rich. Capitalism, on the other hand, is how America has become the richest country in the world, where the standard of living is the highest and where there are fewer poor and hungry than in any other place on Earth.

"The godless leaders of the communist world are bent on world domination. It is a part of their doctrine that until the entire world is united as workers in a workers' state, there will always be a chasm between classes. This edict is why Communism must be our enemy and stopped at all cost!"

Tremors of concern rippled through the nation and the world. The young people of America were now aware that the world as they knew it was in danger of coming to an end—or that they were going to be Godless commies within days.

On October 28th, while the churches were busy praying, the commies backed down. Missy was certain God had been merciful. The press said that President John Kennedy was a great hero for standing up to them. But that week when he made his regular call on the phone, Uncle Clay said, "He's a damned Irish idiot who nearly got us all blown to bits!"

Clay didn't trust anyone that rich or that Catholic. Although he had moved north, Clay would call to talk with Missy and always had a conversation with Izy, something she began to anticipate and value. Uncle Clay, as usual, was riled up about politics: "The only thing good about Kennedy is his stand on corruption in the unions. But he better not turn his back on that Hoffa guy. He's a crook with long arms!"

The next fall, Izy went to George Washington High School. It wasn't new like Henry Clay. It was old and built in a great square like a fortress with a huge open area inside called the Quad. The Quad was mostly grass, but there was a sidewalk that ran around the outside under an archway and a central sidewalk through the middle where the flagpole hoisted the Stars and Stripes and the Great Bear of California. On one end of the Quad was a stone bleacher section where meetings could be held out in the open.

Behind the school to the east were the athletic fields and courts. West, in front of the school, there was a large lawn and then the road where the cars and buses dropped off kids and where the parking lot was to the south. For the first time, Izy was in a school of mixed races. Again, everyone had to check out everyone else. Like pack wolves coming together, every pup had to figure out where it stood in the hierarchy of coolness, style, and power. This time it didn't come as any shock: Gina flunked badly at Henry Clay, so she didn't graduate and Izy went on alone. Nonetheless, looking out for her sweet kid, she hooked up Izy with friends who were already there. That raised Izy one notch in the pecking order.

The first day, Izy went to the girls' bathroom as instructed by Gina. It was an out-of-the-way facility. When she entered, she saw a band of dark girls.

"Who are you, bitch?"

"Bella. My friend Gina told me to come here, ask for Delia."

Gina didn't say you were a gringa."

"Well, I am."

The girl who spoke circled around Izy. Izy followed her, turning, realizing too late that she was surrounded. She felt eyes peeling her, sizing her up. "I'm Delia."

"Well, then I guess you're the one in charge, huh?" Izy tried to put out her best mind lock.

Delia stepped up and pushed Izy against a wall, menacingly. Izy tried to be tough back without being provocative. "Uh-huh, we'll see, you little gringa bitch." Izy felt the control slip away. She knew she was in trouble, but unsure what; she tried to act as if she could handle it. Before she knew it, Izy was on the bathroom floor, looking at the base of a toilet, with Delia straddling her and two others holding her arms and legs. One girl lit a cigarette, dragging on it deep and hard. Izy's eyes grew wide, her breath coming fast, shallow; she did her best to be brave and thought: Gina said these were going to be my friends, try to relax. What could they do? Really, what? But Izy was terrified.

Delia spoke in Spanish to the others and reached up. The grip on Izy tightened and the cigarette was put between Delia's fingers. Panic set in. Izy wanted out, she'd begun to struggle way too late. The girls laughed, mumbled. Delia shushed them, dragged off the cigarette, brought it down on Izy's arm, burning her flesh. Izy cried out. Delia slapped her hand over Izy's mouth, grinding the back of her head into the tile floor, told her to shut her mouth. She left it burning till Izy was nearly passed out from the sensation and hyperventilation. She lifted it, took a drag, and got in Izy's face.

"We'll see if you are one of us, you little bitch. You take your brand, you keep your mouth shut, and maybe you can ride with us!" Izy was freed and helped up. There were slaps on her back and a fist briskly dusted under her chin. Her initiation had begun.

The hotshots from junior high were nothing in this world. They had to start all over again. On the other hand, Izy was welcomed into a group known as "The Lil' Road Dancers." They were very cool in a criminal sort of way. If you were a Dancer, no one was mean to you. They might look at you, but only when they thought it was safe; they might talk behind your back, but people got out of the way when the pack walked together. The Dancers were dark and mysterious. Izy was afraid of them and intrigued just the same.

She got the lay of the land and figured where to hang out in the Quad. The sororities hung out on the stone bleachers and, therefore, so did the fraternities. They were demonized by the Dancers, but not nearly so much as the Preppies and "Sosh" Clubs who hung out in the cafeteria.

The Dancers hung out in the shadows under the bleachers where no one ventured. The first time Izy was taken there, "You're going to meet El Uno, you may pay him respect if you know what's good for you." She blinked and looked close. There was no mistake. "Miguel Costas, he is El Hombre, Numero Uno, he's it. What he says goes." Izy knew him well, of all people in the world, Miguel from Figueroa. Suddenly she remembered it all so clearly, The Claw and the strong, confident young boy who had been her admirable adversary.

He looked at her without recognition. After all, she was grown up and a girl. He had grown up handsome and very, very cool. Izy felt the first twinge of something completely foreign to her, but lost it in the deluge of new experiences.

The Dancers wore black as much as possible and metal, lots of metal. All the Dancers smoked, which Izy could do well by then. They drank beer after school if they could get it. The girls ratted up their hair and wore black eyeliner. Izy still wore her hair straight and plain. In fact, she was going the other way. The bigger the hair craze, the shorter she wore hers, slicked back and no makeup. Izy was different and only marginally accepted by many. Dancers walked in packs around the campus. They ditched school just to be cool. When they did, they went to nearby stores, shoplifted stuff they didn't need, and took pleasure in unsettling everyone and everything, willing to be provoked. It was all part of the ritual and Izy's initiation into their world. Izy was living a double life.

On Sunday mornings Isabella went to church in gathered skirts and little cardigans. She pretty much refused all the other church-related activities now. She had tried to fit in with young people at the church—then in the all-white suburb of Inglewood—where her Uncle David was the pastor. They had nothing in common. At first, Isabella tried to understand how that could be. Then she didn't care. In the end, they didn't even share faith because Isabella's was faltering.

Isabella had prayed to God that her father would be nicer to her mother. She prayed to God to heal her grandmothers, and her father from mental illness. She had even prayed the Dodgers would win the '58 World Series. They wound up losing more games than they won. Isabella was beginning to think God didn't like her or that Gunter was right, there was no God.

During that school year, the news cackled with President Kennedy and the fragile nature of Southeast Asia. A new word was filtering into everyday topics: Vietnam. President Kennedy invoked idealistic phrases. According to the President, the United States had to do whatever was necessary to defend Vietnam against Communism because the spread of Communism, one country at a time, was dangerous. Kennedy would talk about "the situation in Vietnam; complicated and unique circumstances; particular historical significance; legal obligations; and relationships with NATO partners." In school, Izy asked what these might mean. She learned about the relationship France had once had with the country now called Vietnam. People were talking about Kennedy, space, and communism.

Shelly didn't care about politics. But that year he designed circuitry that was patented and sold to the Jet Propulsion Laboratory in Pasadena. He and Izy no longer maintained a relationship. Word traveled from his parents to Missy. He got enough from the sale to ensure a college education at Caltech when he graduated high school. It seemed completely fitting to Izy.

In the fall of 1962, Gunter had an episode, a major psychotic break at work. He started destroying things and the cops were called again. He was beaten again and sent back to the psychiatric ward for evaluation. This time the Los Angeles Water and Power, over Mr. Louis Goodman's objection, was determined to press charges. At Gunter's hearing he was declared incompetent to stand trial. He was committed to the state mental hospital at Camarillo for a period of no less than ninety days, after which he would be reevaluated to determine the appropriateness of further incarceration. In the meantime, he was suspended from work without pay.

This was bleak news for Missy, who had no savings, little cash, and no other means of support. Missy had to find work and fast. Uncle Willy came to her rescue and put her in touch with a woman at his church. The lady worked for a credit bureau in the city and she got Missy a job answering phones and giving credit ratings. Izy had to come straight home after school and do chores to help out. There was less time to run with the Dancers.

The holidays passed by them that year, barely noticed. On weekends they filled the tank and drove to Camarillo to see Gunter. Isabella became familiar with the formidable horrors of a mental hospital. Missy said, "We have to support him now more than ever."

"What does that mean, Mom?"

"It means that we are his family and we're going to stand by him come what may."

"I don't understand that. I mean, he doesn't get any better. He gets worse. Where is this going? Where are we going? At some point, isn't it enough? Can't it be enough?"

"Marriage is for better and worse. Your father, whom we both love so very much, is trapped inside the very strange and twisted person who lives with us. Now, I know that's an awful thing, but we have to honor the man inside."

"I know all that, but I think we may be going too far with our allegiance."

"Isabella, do you remember when you and he were best friends?"

"No. I don't remember him even liking me!"

"Listen to me, my sweet darling, he did love you. He does love you. Inside, the man who is your father loves you. When you were a baby, you were the center of his world. He believed in you absolutely, he adored you. When I tried to deal with you as a child, he would intervene and treat you as if you were a treasure to be encouraged. He always had time for you and together you were inseparably intertwined. I remember the day the doctor told me I was pregnant. Your father was so happy. He told the doctor that you would be a girl—a blonde, blue-eyed little girl."

Then she realized what she had said, "I didn't mean to say that." She knew that the spell had been shattered.

"But it's true. I don't have blue eyes. I'm a brown-eyed pig, and I hate him for that!"

"Don't hate him, honey. That's not your father talking. That's the sickness." But by then they were both crying and there were no words to change anything.

They'd finished their bowls of chili, cheap and filling. They got back in the car and drove on. Isabella tried to connect what Missy was talking about. "Her father, whom they both loved." What did that mean? She was pretty sure she didn't love him. But if she didn't, how could he hurt her so deeply? She wasn't sure of anything anymore.

She loved her mother, but Missy seemed powerless and gullible. Gunter was crazy but he was very powerful. President Kennedy seemed to have it all together. He was powerful. Then there were the Dancers. They seemed powerful. Isabella began to see Missy as embarrassingly weak. But she was her mother. She remembered something that she had been only barely aware of at the time. Gunter had seemed uncomfortable around his own mother. It dawned upon her that she had no memories of Gunter with his mother. She realized that Grandma Birdy's flamboyant, sometimes vulgar, nature offended Gunter's sensibilities. Yet, she was his mother. Why didn't he cry at the funeral? Who was this man?

"I better find a gas station or we'll run out."

"Oh, I don't know. After that chili, we could make it home on the gas in my stomach!"

"Isabella!" They both laughed. They needed to laugh. Once they started, they could not stop. They laughed out of control until Missy could hardly drive, tears cascading down her cheeks.

Money was tight but they managed. Outside of school, Miguel and Izy formed a bond. Miguel's mother showed Izy that rice and beans made a whole protein and a nourishing meal. Izy got pretty good at making simple, plain meals interesting.

Mom didn't like spicy, so she added corn and tomatoes so it would be flavorful.

Izy spent more and more time with Miguel's family and became friends with his sister, Iŷana, whose name Izy finally could pronounce. They were a comfort, and there was that causal friendliness Izy imagined Grandy would have loved. She liked Miguel in a way she could not yet comprehend. Eventually, they started to meet and talk, but not at school—in the train yard. One day, Izy asked if he remembered The Claw and he said he did. She looked at him, searching to see if he would get it, and smiled, "Don't you know that was me?"

"No, really? Yes, well maybe. Ayeee! You? Bella? Why did you do such a thing?"

"Well, I was afraid you wouldn't talk with a girl. And if I talked to you as a girl, you'd think I was just soft and wouldn't think seriously about the B.B. gun. I just wanted you to listen. You were so impressive, so big, and so bad. I was trying to do what I could to be respected."

"So the little niño was a niña." Izy felt a twinge of embarrassment.

"You know, the reason I listened was that I thought the same. It was all getting out of hand. We were told that the gringos didn't want us and so we came out expecting to find trouble. The fact that it was there, well, one thing leads to another."

"I heard all kinds of things about Mexicans. That most of them were not very nice. But my grandmother, she had a different point of view. She would tell me to be brave and get to know you. I wasn't so brave. But if Grandy could respect Mexicans, then I didn't really want to hurt anyone."

"Grandmothers, they can be wise. Mine is in Mexico, but she sends letters to my father. Well, actually my uncle writes them for her. She has no schooling at all. She is the one who encouraged my father to come to California. She said that he should have children in California or not have them at all. So he came here and picked grapes in the fields until he could get a job. He worked hard to buy our house and have his children go to school. It hurts a lot to think that anyone would not respect him for that."

"Grandy told me that her mother came here dreaming of a better life and didn't find it. But she made it possible for her children to have dreams. So in that way, we are a lot alike, Miguel. We are the children of dreamers. I don't know why people are mean, but they are. It hurts me to think of your father and the people who don't respect him. But what hurts me more is I think some people are just mean for no reason and they're going to hurt someone. Maybe they got hurt and they want to pass it on. Everyone passes on something and some people pass on hurt."

There was a silence that meant it was something they both wanted to think about. Then, "You were quite a character with your pencil mustachio and," he paused looking at her, "I don't know what I would have thought of a girl."

"My friends told me I was goofy." They both laughed. Izy dropped her head, remembering how absurd she had been with her costume. But Miguel said, "I think you were goofy. But also, inside you, Bella, there is a brave heart."

At school or after school with the Dancers, Miguel was more distant. Izy ran with them but she was also an outsider. She had the feeling Miguel thought that was the way it should stay. At school, he hardly acknowledged her at all and, although she wished the other Dancers knew of her special relationship with Miguel, she respected his preference.

She was always home when Missy got there—dinner cooked and her chores done. Then they'd spend the evening together. It was the best time that Isabella could remember, except maybe the time with Grandy. In the house without fear, they talked and laughed and slept through the night in quiet. One night, they sang washing and drying dishes. Overcome with the privilege, they grabbed each other and danced there in the kitchen. For just a second they were looking in each other's eyes, then away. Isabella wished it could stay like that. She hoped her father would never come home. She was ashamed of herself, but couldn't help it. Isabella didn't want to stand by him anymore, but she didn't want Missy to see that in her eyes.

Isabella wanted to take back the house from him but wasn't sure how to do that. One day after school, she ventured down into his underground world and out into the tunnel leading to the little house. At the end of the tunnel was a pull-down ladder she used to see inside the little house. She jumped up, missed, jumped again, caught the end with her weight and brought it down. Then Isabella carefully climbed up into the monster's world.

He had covered the walls with oil paintings of Marilyn Monroe and Diane Lennon, naked in various poses. Diane sat naked sewing what looked to be her wedding gown. Marilyn, wearing only a tiny organdy apron, lifted the lid of a steaming pot at a stove, and so on. The place had a handprint on it. Isabella felt creepy, like he would jump out at her any moment. In a corner was a pile of bedding, towels, and a pillow. She figured that was where he slept. A wire stretched from one post to another like a clothesline; on it hung women's clothing, mostly satiny nightgowns and matching robes, like that. The furniture that remained was covered in satiny covers. There was a perfume in the air that made her sick to her stomach and she could hardly breathe. She struggled to comprehend what she was seeing without words to articulate, yet she knew there were clear indications. It wasn't what she had expected, but it was why he had to have his secret place.

She went down the stairs, pushing them back up, through the tunnel, back to the front house. She tried to regroup her thoughts. "Did mom know? Oh my God! What if someone saw it? What should I do?" Her system was in shock. She couldn't take it. She puked into the toilet in the bathroom and then collapsed in a puddle on the floor till Missy came home. Suddenly shaken from her muddle, Isabella wasn't ready to face her. She lied, told her mother she had come from school not feeling well… upset stomach. "Sorry about dinner, Mom, I'll get something quick."

"Don't bother honey, you look pale as can be. Go to bed and I'll take care of myself." Isabella did so, relieved that she could be alone for the evening.

Isabella went to bed wholly certain that in the hands of professionals, it would be evident Gunter was a completely twisted, sick individual. She was sure that Gunter had finally crossed a line like Buster Petty had years earlier. At long last, some judge would order Gunter to leave them alone. They would keep him locked up forever!

Izy had no idea how the system worked. She had no way to know the system was helpless to deal with mental illness. In fact, Izy had more in-depth experience than most professionals, and a far more comprehensive understanding of its ravages. In order to keep Gunter in the hospital, a legal commitment order was required. A commitment resulted when the court determined that confinement in a mental hospital was appropriate punishment for crime. Or, a responsible family member could request that Gunter be evaluated; if he were found incompetent, his rights to determine his freedom would be taken away. The family member could then commit him. Otherwise, only Gunter could commit himself. He did his ninety-day evaluation period medicated and made a good show to the "professionals." After all, he was crazy, not stupid.

At the end of the ninety days, the professionals recommended to the court that Gunter Reinhardt be released on the condition he take medication indefinitely and undergo regular psychotherapy. The Water and Power Company dropped all charges. Unless his wife wanted to commit him by taking legal action to do so, he was free to go. When the moment came, Missy declined to do so. Izy was stunned. Her mother could not possibly let him come back! But she did.

Mad Gunter certified back into society and back to work and back into Izy's life—this indicted all social order and authority in Izy's mind. They were all nuts!

When Gunter came home, he took his medication for exactly two weeks. Then he threw the pills in Missy's face, bouncing off her cheeks onto the kitchen floor.

"You are incredibly stupid. Stupid, stupid, stupid! I thought you had me! Now I'm out. And you will never have another chance. Get ready to rue the day you made this mistake. Stupid!"

Isabella was numb at first. She heard the words, but it took a while for them to filter through her psyche. There were conventions and expectations to get past. A lifetime of effrontery and indignity compressed into seconds as Isabella watched her mother crumble in surrender and terror—something flared. That curious emotion, long fermented, ignited now and blazoned blue-white rage!

Isabella no longer feared him. She knew his little secret and somehow that gave her power over him. She could take no more. She found the soul behind her brown eyes, Indian Great Grandmother had arisen.

She flew across the kitchen, unstoppable, irrepressible, driven by needs she did not think about, only obeyed, grabbing the iron skillet as she went. She shoved him into the cabinets with her arm out, bent and held like a steel ram. With her fingers in his chest, "I have had it with you, you prick! I hate you. You think you are so bad? You think you are so tough? Well, I've learned from the best and now it's my turn." Gunter was actually afraid, if only temporarily and only because of the shock. "You touch her," Isabella raged on, "you dare throw anything at her and I'll make the cops look like pansies. I don't even care if you live or die. I wish you would die." Missy fell to the floor, mumbling for God to help them. "You are evil. Now you get your evil ass out of here!"

He was stunned, but recovered, pushed away from her. His lips quivered and snarled, and she thought he might attack. She leaned in and stiffened her grip on the iron skillet. Missy tried to speak. "Shut up, mother!" He turned into his hole and went through the tunnel; he didn't come back to the house that night. Izy was taking back her life.

Missy kept her job and Izy respected that decision. It was smart. Gunter ordered her to quit. She refused. It was a time of sedition on all fronts. He continued to be crazy and Izy allowed him to rattle around being as crazy as he liked. If he went too far over the top or was mean to Missy, Izy went right in his face. She didn't care anymore. It was better to die than to exist in his grasp.

Missy wasn't so sure. She read scripture to Izy about honoring her mother and father. Izy told her to shut up. Izy had to push away from Missy as well if she was going to survive. Missy prayed fervently for Isabella. She was tired, overwhelmed. The psychiatrists had all told her mental illness ran in families. Could Isabella be losing her mind as well? Was she possessed of the devil?

That summer, Izy began to see the Dancers differently as well. Their banter seemed affected, designed to impress when underneath, there was fear. She could smell it before she could name it. They were definitely serious and dangerous, but Izy began to see it was all the same game as the one played on the tracks years before. Like The Claw, they were in their costumes, being bolder than reason. The posturing and bravado became more and more targeted. They began to have trouble with colored kids. Izy watched Miguel confidently. He would know what to do.

In southwest Los Angeles, white families were moving to new suburbs that set outside the city. The population boom during the 50s and into the 60s included every race on earth. California was the new melting pot of the United States. There were jobs, housing, and the most liberal and lucrative welfare program in the nation. Soldiers were coming home to start their families. Those overwhelmed with futility and repression left other parts of the country to start over in the Golden State. White people in Los Angeles thought of themselves as progressive because they didn't have segregation laws.

Izy heard about Reverend Martin Luther King, Jr., a minister in Alabama who was protesting segregation. She heard white people say just about everything imaginable on the subject. One thing was curious to her. As colored people moved into neighborhoods, white people moved out. There was talk of blockbusting and there was fear of it. Izy understood it took a concerted effort to get a colored family onto a previously all-white block, then the whites would sell out fast and cheap. She knew white people had slanted ideas about Mexicans and she suspected they had the same ideas about the coloreds. Ronny's father always called them niggers and coons. He spoke about defending his home with his guns, if necessary. Izy listened to him and watched him. She thought of him as scary, crazy. Her father wasn't the only nut!

In a southern jail, Reverend King wrote a letter to other local ministers, black and white. He wrote of his cause as just and nonviolent. He explained he didn't want any violence and asked for their support. The letter was read in school.

At church on a Sunday, Izy asked Uncle David if he was supporting Reverend King or actively seeking to integrate his all-white church. Uncle David said, "Isabella, honey, it is not right to hate black people or to cause them any harm or hindrance. But I believe in the segregation of the races. They should have theirs and we should have ours. That's the best way. King is stirring the pot. That's not right."

Izy listened, thought, and replied, "Uncle David, if colored people can't eat at a diner or sit in any ordinary seat on a bus, isn't that hindrance? And I saw on the television where the police were squirting the colored people with fire hoses. Isn't that harm?"

"It may well be, but I think we should leave it alone and let the citizens of Alabama sort it out. That is certainly what's best."

"I just don't think Grandy would agree with that point of view. If Grandy were alive, she'd support Reverend King."

"You don't know that and even so, she wouldn't get involved in the affairs of people she didn't even know."

"Grandy was a Christian and lived her life the way she thought Christ would live his. If Christ were alive, you think he'd not get involved?"

"Isabella, I'm not going to argue with you. We are not supporting lawbreakers and that is that!"

"Then Uncle David, you know what? You can take your church and your piety and your religion and stick them all!" Uncle David spoke to Missy about her daughter's behavior and they both agreed that she was becoming radical. Izy refused to go to church to hear what she termed, "Phony, bullshit, religious dogma that would make Christ puke his guts!"

In school she began to notice that white students thought of themselves as the center of the world. It was their country and their school: History was theirs, science was theirs. They studied European history that led to Columbus and the thirteen colonies. They did not study the civilizations of the Americas who had survived for centuries without Europeans, where they came from or how they lived. They barely covered the brave and desperate revolution just south of the U.S. border or the nature of those brought here as slaves. It seemed enough that they had played an important role in white history.

Izy expected the growing tension at school to be aimed at white students. But it wasn't. They existed in a world completely separate from the world of the Dancers: Some parallel strata where they could appear to walk the same halls, sit in the same classrooms, yet be in two different universes. Izy watched the conflicts mount. She tried to comprehend what was happening. There was no doubt that the prejudice and bigotry of the campus cliques made it clear who was on the top of the heap and who wasn't. Why were the colored and the Dancers, who were largely Latino, in conflict with each other? Pressure was on to hate. It was heading nowhere good. Izy had an out and she took it. No one in the Dancers greatly valued her presence. Except for her brown eyes, there was nothing about her that belonged with them. Everyone knew she had trouble at home. More and more, she used her obligations to bow out. Her time with the Dancers was coming to an end.

She hoped that with Miguel at the helm, they would surely steer clear of real trouble. When the time came, he'd be The Claw.

In 1964 the United States Congress passed the Civil Rights Act. That year the California ballot contained proposition 14, an initiative driven by outrage. There were billboard signs and notices on telephone poles for and against it. On one side, it protected property owners and the value of property. That made sense. People work hard and invest a lot of money into their homes. They should have the right to protect their investment. On the other side, it was a direct and flagrant attempt to preempt the Civil Rights Act. Angry debate ensued and everyone had an opinion.

Izy wished she could go back to the sweet days of play and sunshine. The days of the old shack, vacant lots, barefoot fantasies, and innocence had long disappeared. Maybe insanity was contagious: The whole world had gone mad. Looking for a taste of the past, Izy began seeking out Ronny again and hanging with her.

She wasn't sure why they had drifted apart. Different schools, probably. The fact that Gunter had forbidden visitors. When the plumbing went south in their only bathroom and they couldn't flush the toilet anymore, he wouldn't let Missy call a plumber. Instead, from then on, they had to fill a bucket with water in the bathtub and pour it down the toilet. The water created the same effect as the flush action and that was that. Taking a dump required manual labor. And it certainly wasn't conducive to having company.

Neither Missy nor her daughter ever shared these secrets with anyone. Missy and Izy lived a nightmare but went on outside as if they were the Nelsons or Andersons. Izy's shame, embarrassment, and lack of vocabulary to explain what was going on in her home were probably why she avoided Ronny. Now Izy longed for the friendship and trust they had once shared.

Ronny was beautiful now. Her long blonde hair draped her shoulders and her blue eyes had grown large. Her figure had blossomed. Izy was sure there wasn't anyone who could fill out a pair of jeans like Ronny. Izy loved her all over again and hoped Ronny could forgive her for betraying the friendship. Ronny seemed glad to see Izy and to be together again. And though she surely recognized Izy's family was a little strange, Ronny never questioned anything or intruded on Izy's privacy. Izy took it as a measure of heart, knew Ronny loved her truly.

Ronny's father was a tyrant over her in a completely different way. He watched her like a hawk. No neck too low or skirt too high, no tight or revealing clothes, and no boys in the house. He was obsessed with where she was and what she might be doing. He gave Izy the creeps.

A letter arrived for Missy in the early summer. It was from Illinois. That meant news of Kathy, and Izy was anxious to know what was mentioned of her. Missy read the letter out loud. As it turned out, it was about Isabella. While Izy wasn't paying any attention at all, her cousins had grown up. It was the first time Izy fully comprehended that life went on all over, even when she wasn't involved at all.

The eldest son, Micheil Junior, or Micheil J as he was called, had flipped out or something. He was drinking, getting in trouble, and had run off. They didn't know where he was. They asked Missy to pray for him. But that wasn't all.

The second son, Patrick, was ordained and leaving to be a missionary in the Congo, a very dangerous place for white missionaries. Between the two sons, Aunt Renée was very upset. To help her out, could Isabella come to visit over the summer? It might help Aunt Renée get her mind off her boys, and Kathy would love to spend time with her cousin.

"Oh man, could I, Mom? Please, I'll do anything!"

There were phone calls: Mom to Uncles David and Clay, who happened to be down from his home on the Umpqua River and in Los Angeles visiting his son.

"David says it would be good for her to visit. But she is too young to travel all alone."

"She's a smart one," Clay assured his sister. "She'll be fine. I trust her far more than I do my own son. She listens and takes heed of good advice given! And it is always good for a child to have new experiences. I think you should send her, Missy. I'll be here with George Junior for a while. If you want, I'll arrange everything."

There were long distance calls to Illinois and to Iowa. It was finally decided Isabella should go to Illinois as a family ambassador.

And so Izy got to go on an airplane. Not like her Grandy's, but a jet engine plane. Izy had never even imagined doing so, and it was more exciting than anything she'd ever known. Missy and Uncle Clay took her to the airport. Missy prayed that God would take the girl safely and give her traveling mercies. Uncle Clay hugged her and said not to talk to anyone. If someone tried to talk to her, she should say, "Buzz off!"

"Oh Clay, that's not nice. Don't teach her to talk like that."

"Missy, she has to know how the world really is. You do as I tell you, young lady!"

"I will, Uncle Clay." He was so to the point. Izy liked him.

Izy sat in a window seat and spent most of the flight looking out. She remembered what Grandy had told her about her flight to St. Louis.

"I was looking out the little window and there was all this smoke, everywhere. I couldn't imagine what could have happened. So I asked the stewardess. Well, was I embarrassed! That wasn't smoke. It was clouds. I never, you just don't think of a thing like that. Well, I hadn't. What an amazement!"

Izy saw the clouds and the United States of America passing beneath her. What a marvelous concept that was. Bernoulli's principle at work, the great metal machine folding air all around its wings, creating a pocket through which they were flying. At last, Izy was the kite up in the air. She thought about Shelly and his great brain. Wondered for a moment what scientific breakthrough he might be up to and how he might someday change the world.

On earth below, people were walking, talking, and driving in cars; farmers and businessmen going about their work, kids playing—no one giving thought to the plane flying above them. Down there, up in the plane—there was something staggering about it. Something about the persistence of life and, at the same time, an oblivion that lets people concentrate on their lives and ignore the vastness of life itself.

In that airplane, Izy began to comprehend planet, humankind, and universe in a way that all her science classes had been unable to convey to her before. It wasn't just about her, the details of her life, facts, or events. It was a miracle that it could all even happen. What happened might not be quite as important as that it *was* happening and everyone alive could experience it. Well, that is until death, like Grandy.

Then what, she wondered? Do we go to heaven? Did Grandy really see into heaven? Where was this heaven that she could see into while on Earth? How could Grandy see it so clearly, and yet she couldn't see anything at all? There were still wonders to be contemplated.

The plane landed in Indianapolis because Uncle Micheil's church was now in a town called Danville, Illinois, which turned out to be closer to Indianapolis than to Chicago. Uncle Micheil, with his crisp mustache and confident stride, and Kathy met the plane. They drove Izy through farm and mining communities, west toward Danville across the Vermillion River.

They lived in the parsonage just two houses down from Uncle Micheil's church. Their house was on a busy street and they didn't have laws like in California where if you hit a pedestrian, you're in big trouble. In Illinois, pedestrians were on their own, fair game, expected to watch out or else! Izy's uncle was very clear on the consequences of making a mistake.

The house was small, simple, and nice. Izy arrived on a Thursday. On Friday, Uncle Micheil took her to his farm. It was really only land. He had a crop of corn and six white-face cows. Aunt Renée and Kathy rode along. Izy could tell this was her uncle's special place. He walked her out to meet his cows. She was surprised that they seemed to know him and pay attention that he was there.

The greatest wonder of all was that he had a horse. It was the most wonderful horse Izy had ever seen. "Please, Uncle Micheil, can I ride the horse, please?"

"Well, I don't know. Have you ever ridden?"

"Yes, yes, I have. Please?" What a wondrous stroke of good fortune!

"Very well, okay. Come here."

He motioned her to follow, went to a little shed, and opened the door. They went inside where it was stifling hot and smelled of leather. The tack hung on the wall. He took down the bridle and hung it on his arm. "My saddle is far too big for you. You'll have to ride bare. Done that before?" "No, never. Is it hard?"

"You must use your knees and the insides of your legs, especially your calves. Think you can do that?" He opened a sack and took a handful of oats and put them in her open hands. "Yes, I can do it," she stated.

Out of the corral again and he opened the gate. The horse turned, trotted a small circle, and made straight for them standing just inside. Kathy swung up and onto the corral fence, her mother beside her. Uncle Micheil intercepted the horse and cupped its face with his hands, talking nice and low, "Good girl, easy now. Good girl."

Izy peeked out from behind him, watching with anticipation. "Look here, girl, there's a treat, come with Isabella now. Come around child, let her have the treat. You must pay if you want a ride." The horse knew exactly what she had in her hands. She nuzzled big, soft lips into Izy's hands and licked up the grain.

"It tickles," Izy laughed with delight!

When the horse had licked the last oat, Uncle Micheil, talking low and sweet, eased the bridle onto the mare, petting and patting her all the while. Izy did the same. He put out his hands locked together and hoisted her onto the back of the mare. Step, step to steady her weight, Izy settled in for a ride, feeling the muscles of the back as the mare walked out. Just a touch on her sides and she'd pick up the pace, not like the stable horses at the dairy. Izy rode around the corral, out and down the road and back. Then Kathy rode. Uncle Micheil rode as well. He was a fine rider; the mare pranced, sidestepped, and reared up. He clung with strong legs and praised her obedience.

He walked Izy out into the corn. The rows high over her uncle's head, he explained to her the art of raising it up, how important rain was to the crop. It was impossible to see where they were. Completely disoriented, Izy was glad to be with her uncle, who loomed tall and straight just like his corn as they walked down one row and up another. Izy thought of Grandy. "When you were young, you worked at a dairy."

"Yes. How'd you know that?"

"Grandy told me. She said you were good with animals and farming. She said that's why you stayed in the Midwest, 'cause it was farm country."

"I suppose that's true. I like it here. Like the people. Wholesome, honest folk who work hard and love the Lord."

"She also said that you used to like to drink and fight and sometimes you got into trouble."

"Yo ho! That's in the past, now, all behind us. I don't even think about that. It was before I found God and accepted the blood of Christ as my savior. Now we're as pure as a lamb, praise be to God!"

On the ride back Uncle Micheil pulled into a roadside creamery for ice cream. There was a black couple in the creamery. They got cones and left. In the car, Uncle Micheil commented, "You see that, Renée. I'm telling you, the darkies are getting very arrogant. Something should be done about it before the apple cart's upset." Izy rethought every moment in the creamery, and yet she couldn't think of anything that had seemed arrogant.

In the morning, Aunt Renée made cornmeal cakes for breakfast along with eggs and bacon. They had roasted corn for lunch, or dinner as they called it, and cut corn for supper with lots of butter and beef. There was lots of beef: roasted beef, grilled beef, stewed beef, and beef burgers. Izy had never seen so much beef. All meals but breakfast were served outside on a table with a gingham tablecloth.

"I bet you eat out here 'cause Grandy used to serve her meals outside."

"Well, so she did, so she did. I like it because you can smell the Earth a growing. But you're right. Mother used to serve great meals outside. Everyone liked to come to our house for meals. Those were the days! Yes, indeed. You might be right. Never thought about it. Might be that's where I got the liking for eating outside, when the weather permits!"

Kathy and Izy settled into a routine that allowed plenty of time to catch up on their two lives playing out in different settings. Kathy's life was full of Midwestern children—white and poor to middle class, mostly farm kids. Her teachers had grown up in and around Danville, largely educated at the University of Illinois. They knew all the families of the children in their classrooms and socialized with their parents.

Izy's life was urban and her schoolmates diverse. Many of the kids and most of her teachers weren't even born in the state. The number of kids Izy knew personally was limited and the teachers were strangers who struggled to learn all the names; some they couldn't pronounce.

Kathy lived in a house where there was family prayer and bible study. Isabella and Missy prayed in hiding. Kathy's house was bright and orderly, Izy's in a constant state of demolition and disrepair.

Izy never mentioned her father or the state of her house or the house where Grandy had lived. In the completely reasonable environment of Illinois that summer, it was nice to forget, easy to pretend there was nothing to tell. For a while, she had left her father with her mother, who faithfully loved him, while Izy was in another world, one that seemed much more like the "Andersons." She exhaled.

Uncle Micheil spent time in his office studying the word of God, preparing his sermons, and praying. Sometimes Izy could hear him pray. He was not quiet, like Missy. He spoke to God as if God were deaf. His voice would boom as he prayed for his flock, his wayward son, Micheil J., and for Patrick in the Congo. He prayed for the nation and that the Lord would bring a great revival. He called upon God to put to rest all the tensions in America. He told God to rid the hearts of the darkies of the influence of the devil.

Every day but Sunday, he went to his farm. Izy went if he'd have her. Sometimes he'd say, "Not today, dear, I have to work."

"I'll help you."

"Farm work's not women's work. You stay, help your aunt. She has work appropriate for a young lady."

"When Grandy and Grandpa George started the farm, they worked side by side. She did farm work."

"Well, she shouldn't have. Women needed to be cared for and protected from manual labor. They have their own time of labor, and that's enough. You're staying here today and that's final." Off he went alone.

Uncle Micheil took Izy around Danville, showing it off with pride.

"Now that is the Barnum Building. That's where Mr. Abraham Lincoln had offices in 1850."

"Wow. That's even before the Limerick sailed for America."

"The Limerick. Where'd you hear about that?"

"Grandy. I know all about it and the storm, the angry sea and her being born before they could reach New York."

"I forget, you grew up with her and her tales." Uncle Micheil pointed to the courthouse up the street. "Mr. Lincoln walked this very street many times when he was a lawyer, before he became a politician."

"Uncle Clay doesn't think much of politicians."

"No, he don't." Micheil laughed. "You're just a little storehouse, aren't you?" She smiled. "Come over here. Now, here's the memorial. It was right here Mr. Lincoln gave his farewell address to the people of Danville on his way to Washington D.C. Yes, he spoke eloquently, wishing a bountiful blessing on the Vermillion River area."

Aunt Renée took Kathy and Izy to a quilt show; Uncle Micheil took all of them to a baseball game between Danville and Springfield.

"This girl knows her baseball, dear. Smart as a whip, she is! I dare say, she knows more facts than I do. Not only that, she can call those plays better than even Micheil J." Aunt Renée smiled, nodded, and lowered her eyes to hide the sadness. "Sorry, dear, didn't mean to make reference to him. It'll be all right. He'll come home or I'll find him for you. I promise. If only he wasn't so willful!"

There was a community picnic and a fireworks show and church potluck dinner. Summertime in Danville was pleasant enough.

Sundays, Kathy and Izy sat on the front row at church with Aunt Renée. They were kin to the pastor and had to set a good example. Also, Uncle Micheil could keep an eye on them from the pulpit, and he did. Uncle Micheil kept a close eye on everything. He was the man in his house. It felt secure to know that someone was in charge and that things were orderly and sane. In exchange for this, there was a small price. At home Izy got away with things not permitted here, not even imagined. Certainly, smoking was one thing not permitted.

Izy was never alone, never let out of the house alone, not even to a store. Danville was not like Los Angeles. Everyone in Danville seemed to know her uncle whether or not they went to his church. And everyone went to one church or another. The people of Illinois were not what Izy was used to. One thing, they were white! Izy didn't see any black people except in the ice creamery. She didn't see any Mexicans at all. She'd have to manage without smokes; for the first time, Izy felt cravings for the addiction she could not feed.

On their last Saturday night together, Kathy and Izy were trading clothes, trying things on, and playing with each other's hair. "You have such beautiful dark hair, all curly and bouncy. I hate my hair; can't do anything with it," Izy lamented.

"I could do something with it. What you need is styling gel. I could fix your hair real cute, if you want."

"Yeah? How?"

"Well, I'd put curlers in it with this pink gel. That's the trick. The gel will curl your hair right up. I'd goop it on real thick. Then we'd dry it so the curls would stay. I'm sure it would work. Then brush it out, maybe even put it up. I'm sure it will look beautiful. It will look great!"

"Really? You think so?" Izy was imagining herself with stylish, curly hair.

"Really. Let me do it tomorrow morning for church. We'll get up early and wash your hair, I'll set it. It's your last Sunday. You'll be a smash!"

Izy wanted to believe it could be so.

The girls stayed up talking. They fell asleep without remembering to set the alarm extra early. Aunt Renée woke them up in a panic.

"Now you can't do it. Oh no. I'm so disappointed."

"Yes, we can. I have a dryer. We'll put the dryer bonnet on you. Come on, hurry!"

They scrambled, putting off Aunt Renée's calls for breakfast until they brought down orders from Uncle Micheil, "Get out here to the table. Food's ready. Come on now. Hurry!"

Izy's hair was in curlers, all sticky wet, but up and as high as her hopes for a grand, new look.

After breakfast, the girls hurried to Kathy's room and the bonnet for Izy's hair. The two worked in concert to get dressed, saving Izy's hair comb out for last. Difficult gyrations performed by teen girls for a feat of beautification.

The hair wasn't drying. They stalled as long as possible, until Aunt Renée was waiting on the porch. "This won't do. I can't go like this!"

"I don't know what to do. I thought it would dry. Maybe I put too much goop, but there's so much hair. I don't know. Why is it taking so long?"

"I don't know. I never set it. You go on to church and I'll stay under the dryer. Once it's dry, I'll just brush it out. You can fix it up later."

"Father insists we be there on time."

"I'll be right along. Go."

"I don't think that's a good idea, Isabella. You'd better come along."

"Like this, no way! Go on! I'll come as soon as I can."

Aunt Renée wanted to know where Izy was. Kathy told her what had happened and Renée shook her head. "I hope she gets to the church before the service starts!"

When Uncle Micheil came out onto the platform, smiling to greet his flock, he saw that Isabella was not sitting with Kathy and Aunt Renée. His smile faded. His eyes searched the congregation and Kathy tried not to make eye contact.

While the assistant pastor led the congregation in song, Uncle Micheil came down from the platform and over to Renée. "Where is Isabella?" he whispered to her. She whispered back that there'd been a little delay and that Isabella would be along any minute."

"A little delay?"

"It's nothing, Micheil, don't make a scene, please."

"We'll see about this!"

Uncle Micheil left the church down the center aisle and headed straight

115

down the block to the parsonage, while the congregation sang or muttered. "What could be up with Pastor Hume?"

He strode into the house, banging the front door as he entered. Izy could hear it even with the bonnet blowing hot air past her ears.

"What exactly are you doing, young lady?"

"I'm drying my hair, Uncle Micheil, we got started late and... "

"I don't give a hoot for your hair! You get to church right now! What will people think?" He started ripping off the bonnet and curlers out of her hair— and took hair along with some of them. "God comes before everything, especially vanity. Hasn't your mother taught you that? I'm ashamed of you!"

With her damp, sticky hair in curlers sticking up in every direction, Uncle Micheil took her by the arm and all but dragged her down the block, into the church, down the center aisle, plopping her down next to Aunt Renée. "Keep an eye on her. She's a lesson coming when we get home!"

Izy watched his every move but with her head down, looking through her eyebrows. Her embarrassment flushed her face.

She whispered to Aunt Renée, "Do you have a brush?"

"Shush girl!"

Izy sat there with all the eyes witnessing her shame and wondered, "What lesson?"

When Uncle Micheil got up to preach, his topic was the sanctity of the Christian Church in trying times. His great booming voice rang out with conviction and power. The congregation affirmed their agreement, punctuating his words with shouts of "Amen!" "Preach it, brother!" and "Alleluia."

"We are at the end time, folks. Jesus is returning to Earth! Before he comes, there will be a great tribulation! Yes! The anti-Christ will first come and wreak havoc upon the world. Yes! I tell you here today, the evidence is clear. The anti-Christ is already here on Earth! Yes! He is already wreaking havoc! It is he who is behind the darkies' uprising! Now folks, God himself has ordained that darkies be subservient to the white man. To have it otherwise is against God's will and the order of things. But that is the mission of the anti-Christ, to disrupt the order of God's will!"

Izy twisted in her seat. Her shame was no longer just for her hair. She was stunned to hear such things come from her Uncle Micheil. He was a forceful preacher. Every sermon had been of hellfire and damnation. That was one thing.

116

But he had never assaulted the dark races. Not any time Izy was in the congregation. Izy had a lot of questions, but she was in enough trouble, so she tried not to think about what was being said.

After church, there was handshaking, a certain amount of jawing at the door. Then Izy was marched to the parsonage where her punishment was announced. "You will spend the entire day in Kathy's room by yourself, without lunch or dinner until the evening service. During that time, you will think about the sin of vanity and repent of your iniquity. And I can tell you, if you were my daughter, I'd take the hairbrush to your backside. Yes, sir! A good blistering would teach you a thing or two! If it were Kathy, she'd get licked till she wasn't mad, but only glad it was over! That's the way to raise up a child in this sinful world!"

Izy thought, "Poor Kathy!" Though stunned, Izy accepted her punishment quietly. Alone, Izy had time to think about the sermon and Uncle Micheil. And after a while, she thought about Micheil J. and about Patrick. She began to comprehend why they had run away. Patrick went to be a missionary, all the way to the Congo where it was very dangerous, but where his father approved of what he was doing. It was still running away. The humid summer air seemed thicker than ever. She felt like a prisoner, and she was.

Kathy came to the window of the room.

"I'm sorry. It's as much my fault as yours. I talked you into the goop."

"It's okay. I stayed behind. Besides, if it were you, he'd beat you with the hairbrush or something."

Kathy looked down and a wash of discomfort fell over her face. Looking up, "Well, I just wanted you to know, I feel real bad."

"This is no big deal, believe me."

That night at evening church service, Izy's stomach gurgled and growled but at least her hair was brushed. Izy was careful to be barely seen and certainly not heard. When they got home, Izy went straight to Kathy's room. She had no interest in encountering Uncle Micheil. Aunt Renée quietly brought her a small stack of wheat toast with honey and a cup of tea. She ate it all up and was grateful for the kindness.

Uncle Micheil and Izy did not get on after that. Izy didn't want to go to the farm anymore. He would ask, but Izy said, "No. Thank you, just the same."

"It's a good thing, Renée! She is in need of responsible authority. A little discipline! Her unfortunate family situation is leaving its mark. And it's a shame."

Izy overheard them in the next room.

"She's a teenager, Micheil. It was just a teenage thing, experimentation. I'm sure it won't happen again. You made your point. Let it go."

"I can't let go the fact that she's miffed, pouting. It's because she's not accustomed to discipline and order in her life. David says that her father is no help to Missy raising this child. That child should be taught a thing or two before it's too late. Lord knows Missy has no backbone in her to do the job!"

"She's a sweet girl, Micheil. Missy's doing a fine job, and she's smart as a whip."

"Too smart, if you ask me. That's her father in her. Too smart for his own good! That's what's wrong with him. Too smart! A child has to learn discipline, not to question authority, and to respect the rules! That's all that's wrong with her! If I'd given her a sound thrashing she wouldn't be going around with her nose out of joint."

"She's at an age when things like her hair matter a great deal, Micheil. You embarrassed her. She'll get over it. Just give her a little time."

"I embarrassed her? She'll get over it? Nonsense! That is not the point! This is just a ridiculous incident. It's her life I'm worried about. What's going to become of her? She's all but grown up. I should have given her a licking. If I had, she'd get beyond vanity and this would all be over. That is the value of a good licking."

Uncle Micheil was a good size and strong. Izy thought about it. "If I see him with a hairbrush in his hand, I'm not going down without a fight!" She lay in bed that night, sleep elusive; she thought of how satisfying it would be to give Uncle Micheil a whack with a hairbrush.

During the last week, the tension mounted between the man and the girl. Finally, something utterly unremarkable touched it off. Something small, a word or deed that later no one could even remember because it was a wee flick of a match amid amassed kindling repressed for days. Izy had the time to get over the shock and humiliation of that first dreadful encounter. She had been bested, but not beaten. It was no longer in her nature to cower or to easily digest abuse. In the days after the hair episode, she had festered and decided it was not over at all for her. When the opportunity presented itself, Izy grabbed it. The banter began in the living room of the small parsonage. At first it was about rules and Uncle Micheil's expectation of unquestioned obedience, but it quickly shifted direction. Izy was up for it this time, her wits clear, her resentment out in front of her fear. She wanted him off his high horse.

"You think you are so smart. Standing in your pulpit talking about the darks and the whites. Who the hell do you think you are? You're just an Indian, a member of the dark races! You know, the ones who are to be subservient to the pure whites—which you are not, by the way!" He was stunned, his mouth was slightly open but nothing was coming out. "But oh, no! You got to act like a racist pig hypocrite! You take me 'round where Mr. Lincoln walked like he would approve of you. You bigot! Your own mother would be ashamed of you!" He slapped her face. She took it without a flinch, staring him square in his blue eyes with her brown Indian eyes!

Everyone was glad when it was time for the girl to fly home.

Back up in the air looking down on Earth, Izy wondered if there was anywhere that made any sense in the world. Then, it dawned on her. She was so busy being angry with Uncle Micheil, she had failed to help out Aunt Renée. In fact, she had probably made things more difficult for her. Izy felt awful.

In the fall Veronica started Washington High School. They went together and even though Veronica, a freshman, was completely uncool, not at all hip, Izy hung with her gladly. Izy was done fitting in. She was who she was. Ronny was the best friend she ever had. Izy showed Ronny the ropes—where to and where not to hang. Matthew, who was already there, had a car and drove them to and from school. When they could, they met for lunch, ate on the front lawn away from the cliques and gangs.

Izy had a class called Government—officially, the way humans chose to rule and be ruled. They examined history, not for events, but for the evolution of human civil relationships beginning with tribal communities and their leaders; forceful warlords; divine rule, imperialism, and the revolution of peoples' right to self-government. Unofficially, it was the first forum for Izy's generation to examine the reasons for Vietnam.

"I think the whole thing's flawed!"

"Why do you say that, Josey?"

"You know, lady, my name's José!"

"You are in America now and you should have an English name: Joe, Josey or Joseph."

"Oh yeah, well I'm in California, and Mexicans were here long before the

English!"

"That is irrelevant! You are in America and we do not speak Spanish in this country! But you were saying, young man?"

"Yeah, I think the whole Vietnam thing is a bunch of crap!"

"If you can't speak without vulgarity, then you can be quiet," the teacher turned away. "Isabella?"

Izy wondered what business it was of hers if José's name was turtle! She thought the teacher should be fired, taken to the woodshed, her mouth washed out, something—none of which was likely to happen. So she just said with disdain, "I also think it's flawed." That stunned the woman for a moment. Izy continued. "On the one hand, there's President Kennedy saying the commies are threatening and we should duke it out in this little country. Stop them here! Stop them now! On the other hand, there's our alliance with France, which seems to put us in league with some twisted colonial thing between them and Vietnam. You know, frankly, this reminds me of *our* colonial struggle. George Washington, throwing out the British. We seem to be backing the redcoats in Vietnam. Explain that!"

The teacher, back in control of herself, replied, "The colonists in America were not communists threatening to take over Great Britain. That's the difference."

"Well, that's troublesome too, this whole commie thing. The way I see it, it's either the most reasonable thing I've ever heard: Overthrow the rich who repress the workers. Or it's doomed to fail for all the reasons the capitalists fault it. What was the big deal anyway? Either way, it seems to me we should sit back and leave it alone. I mean, if America is the great experiment in democracy, then communism is the great experiment in utopian ideals. Maybe we should give it two hundred years to prove itself or die trying."

"Winston Churchill said if you're not a communist when you are young, you have no heart. If you're not a capitalist by the time you're thirty, you have no brains. Keep that in mind, Isabella!"

Another young man spoke up, "Well, all I know is there's a lot of high talk, but it's my ass going to Vietnam in less than two years. So somebody better come up with a better story than I've heard so far. You know, I think it's all a bunch of propaganda to get me killed! You understand that? Get me dead in some stinking, little country. I want to know why I gotta die!"

Izy was on the yearbook committee. "We need a theme!"

"Right. So what's your bright idea?"

"Well, I think we should do research and find a student, you know, someone who went to high school here and then went to war and died. Some guy who was like us and just didn't get to grow up."

"Yeah? What's your point?'

"Simple. We remind the world that soldiers who fight wars were once high school kids, hoping, dreaming of growing up. If they are to be deprived of that, then it should be to save the world, not to further economic or political agendas."

"Yeah, like anyone cares what we do with the yearbook, really."

"Someday, it will matter. Someday when there's a reason, someone will look back at our class and ask why. This will help answer."

Government class was on the third floor of the south wing of the great fortress. The students heard shouting from below the Quad, in the halls. The teacher stepped into the hall as one of the boys opened a window to the Quad. The words coming from all directions were "...dead, shot in Dallas, Kennedy has been assassinated." The students were stunned before they could be upset. They closed the school and sent everyone home.

The following days for Izy were surreal. Kennedy, whether or not you liked him, was vital, charismatic. "What are we if someone can just kill the president? How can this be?" Isabella wondered. A waft of self-doubt pierced her thinking, struck deep, and stung badly. "You know, Mom, everyone talks like we are somehow endowed by God to right wrongs and call the shots on Planet Earth. Then suddenly God stands aside and lets the president get his head blown off. What was the message in that? What does that say about everything?"

"It just says that there are people in the world with evil in their hearts and they do things that are not ordained by God, awful things. That's what it says, dear."

"It's bigger than that, Mom. I'm not sure what it is exactly, but it's bigger than that."

Lyndon B. Johnson took the Presidential Oath of Office and tried to bring order back to the country. Scandal persisted, the war in Vietnam and its controversy heated up. The Lil' Road Dancers found trouble with a specific rival gang of colored kids called The Avenues from Fremont High. Just like the children across train tracks years before, the game itself sucks them into war. Once ignited, the fire grows. Little things feed it, things far less significant than hatred, injustice, and cruelty. In the spring, before school let out, there was a Righteous Brothers concert at a local park. It was a big deal: They were world famous and they were from the local area. People from all strata of life turned out to see them: preppies, clubbies, the frats, sororities, the gangs—not a likely formula for a quiet evening. Izy didn't go. If she'd had, she'd have been there with the Dancers.

There was a fight. The sheriff's department called off the concert right near the end, during Ebb Tide, which just pissed off everyone.

The next day at school everyone blamed everyone else. Talk of the concert was everywhere. Threats were flung here and there, escalating bravado. There was tension until summer break.

The summer was hot and it simmered more fights than usual. There was trouble at the public pool, in the parks, on the streets. Come fall, the tension was palpable, molten, like the center of the Earth, from deep underneath, up through the fissures—accreted, crusted yesterdays demanding to be heard.

Early in the morning, on campus, behind the stone bleachers, two outsiders called out a Dancer. First there was name-calling and shoving, then fists flew. The fight swirled to the lawn. There were shouts, screams, fury, and chaos. The pack frenzied to the flagpole, more piled on. Whistles blew, men came running, and students fled, all but one. He was cut, low in his back.

There was blood, gasps, and horror.

The faculty cleared the Quad and sent the students to their homerooms. The wounded boy was taken out to an ambulance, driven away.

"As you are all aware, there was a truly unfortunate incident this morning. I think it's something we must all learn from. There are appropriate ways to settle differences and there are inappropriate ways. Violence is inappropriate. Now I can tell you, the young man who was injured is going to be all right. Now, everyone, please settle down and we will resume our regular schedule right after lunch." The principal let go of the button on the public address microphone, pleased with his comments.

At lunch, the administration and faculty were intentionally visible. Behind the stone bleachers, a student named Delia got into it with a girl dating a member of the gang at Fremont. Miss McKinsey, the girls' vice principal and a former Marine, subdued the fight. Both girls were expelled.

The next day, Miss McKinsey, fearless and undaunted, set out on patrol behind the stone bleachers. When she passed, a small pack of girls attacked her in revenge for her interference. McKinsey was game, but there were too many and she went down, out in an ambulance. More girls were expelled.

The sheriffs were called to the campus and posted at strategic locations to keep the school in line. That lasted for two weeks. Then they left.

The following Monday Izy was in biology when the class heard noise on the front lawn; they ran to the windows in front of the school. Across the lawn—two boys with two boys after them. The two in pursuit stopped cold on some cue, held objects outstretched, fired, wounding one boy, killing the other.

The sheriffs returned. A meeting was called in the Quad. The principal spoke once again, "I know you are all upset. You have a right to be. I am upset. We all are. Now I want everyone to just take a minute and calm down. I think if there is any good in this awful situation, it is a clear demonstration that violence only reaps more violence. Violence solves nothing. Furthermore, it won't be tolerated! We are trying to get to the bottom of this, but we need your help. Anyone having any information about the perpetrators of the shootings this morning should come forward immediately. If you do not feel comfortable talking to an officer, then talk to me or to Sydney Brickman, the boys' vice principal. You may think you are protecting a friend, but as you can see, until we put a stop to whatever is going on, it is possible that your friend will be injured, or worse."

The sheriffs stayed longer, but when they left, the school was vulnerable again. Although there was a period of seeming peace, underneath the gangs were seething. Izy wondered if the adults even realized what was happening. The white students talked about it as if it were some great mystery that had nothing to do with them.

"That's what they get for putting all these coloreds and Mexicans in our school. My father says that when he went to this high school, it was a model of civility. The fights only took place in the boys' gym."

"Well, they better do something or my parents are putting me in private school next year."

Izy listened as she moved through the days. She knew an explosion was unavoidable.

To minimize the chance for trouble, night athletic events were suspended. Games were played in the afternoon or not at all. And when Fremont played Washington, sheriffs were on hand. As expected, trouble broke out. The troublemakers were expelled from the game. They went elsewhere.

A meeting in the park late that night went badly. Thuds, cracks, oaths, groans, and sirens, and then, two lay dead.

"Killed, who, tell me, who?"

"I heard Miguel Costas got stabbed, killed."

"Miguel!"

The Dancers arrived on campus with their colors on, their jackets, strictly forbidden. Miguel's death had become a conflux of emotion for the Dancers. There was a big scene in the Quad when the sheriffs, once again, arrived and saw the jackets. They told the Dancers, "Take 'em off or we'll escort you off campus!" Some did and some left.

After school Izy and Ronny waited for Matthew to pick them up in front. Both were anxious to get away from the campus. Everyone was, it seemed. Everyone except for those who wanted more, still. A light drizzle fell softly on the uneasy afternoon. Ronny held books and an umbrella, which she didn't bother to open.

Cars lined the street extra heavy, the traffic unusual. It was boisterous with kids yelling back and forth. People sat silently in their vehicles with their windows up, just wanting to be done with the tension. All in all, it was a traffic jam. A man, one of the shop teachers, moved through the traffic. "Let's move along. That's right. Just load and move along. Good, next!" Mr. Cody was a large man of about fifty. The two girls stood at the curb and watched him work. He had on a slicker spattered with rain, but no hat. His thinning hair was wet and dripping as he motioned this and that to the cars and the kids.

He came upon a convertible, four good-sized colored boys in it. He gave direction to them like all the others. "Fuck yo self, honkey son bitch!" Mr. Cody moved to the front of the vehicle, began writing down the license number. One of the boys in the back stood up on the seat and yelled, "What you think you doin'? Hey, asshole, I asked what you doin'?" First one boy from the back came up and out, followed by the others. They attacked Mr. Cody with surprise, overwhelming force. He was on the ground instantly.

First stunned, Ronny dropped her books and lurched forward with the umbrella, Izy with her book bag. One boy turned to face them and shoved Ronny to the soggy ground. Izy stopped, swung, and missed, fell over Ronny. The big man tried to get away, they were on him kicking and stomping. There were sickening sounds. The force of their kicks lifted and wrenched the big man's body. Izy felt the backswing of a boot in her side and groaned. In his struggle, the man almost made it to the curb, his hand outstretched. Then a boot forced his skull into concrete, then again. His outstretched hand began jerking. His eyes rolled back in his head and his hand fell limp; no longer struggling, he was unconscious.

Mr. Brickman was out the front of the building, over hedges and into it, other teachers behind him. The boys left their vehicle, logjammed in the traffic, and beat it on foot, police sirens coming closer.

Matthew had left his car and arrived, "Oh no, not Mr. Cody. He's the best!" Izy wished that Matthew had arrived sooner. Matthew was big and strong. A far better defender than Izy and Ronny had proven to be.

The blood from his head and face ran down the gutter. Mr. Brickman knelt, took his pulse. "He's alive."

The ambulance arrived. They were all shooed away so the attendants could work, then take him away.

The police took statements. "Yes, I saw the one clear and close. He shoved Ronny, I saw him good!"

"Good. I doubt we'll need it. We have their vehicle. But good, just in case." They were sent home. Ronny was bruised, soaked, and angry.

This time, the sheriffs stayed through the end of the year. There were no more incidents. Mr. Cody visited graduation rehearsal. They brought him in a wheelchair. He waved to the students. But he had brain damage and did not return to teach.

Izy went to the Costas home to see Miguel's parents. His mother was devastated and his father could not speak to her. In his silence, there were tears that did not fall and anger he could not hide. There was nothing to say. It was enough to come for a while and share the burden of their pain.

Iŷana walked Izy out. They sat on the porch. "You know, they are sending me away. We have family in New Mexico and my father is afraid if I stay, there will be more trouble. I don't want to go, but it doesn't do any good for me to protest. I think he will sell this house and move."

"What about the other families?"

"I don't know. You know how it is. It is not likely to change. In fact, now it is far worse. I don't think the parents realized how much tension was building at school with my brother and the other gangs. The Dancers turned their fear into hatred and even now, they churn each other up to revenge on revenge. I hate to leave, but I think maybe my father is right. This thing is probably not over.

"You know, Miguel did not want this for me. In the beginning, the Dancers were a way for Mexican kids to feel we had a place in the world. Then it was good. Now, it has become something altogether different. If my father had known what was happening out there, he would have beat Miguel within an inch of life before letting him remain in the Dancers, let alone be the leader. I have anger toward the boys who murdered my brother. But I know that it is the same anger that killed my brother. Those boys who stabbed him were just the weapons of hatred. The parents over here are worried. Worried because they know about the gangs, and they also know it is too late to stop them."

Izy wondered if Miguel had gone to the park to negotiate peace, like The Claw. "He must have. Why had it gone so wrong?" she wondered.

"You are a wise girl, Iŷana. I don't want to see you go either, but I know that things are going to get much worse. I wish there were someone or something that could stop all this. Let me know if you go and where. We could write." But they didn't. The last time Izy saw Iŷana was at her brother's funeral, a Catholic mass. Izy had never been to one before and spent most of the time trying to figure out what to do and when. Church had never been about ritualized participation and she felt conspicuous. Twisted thoughts plagued her—thoughts about the day at Figueroa, the dangers they had avoided as children, and that came again to take Miguel's life. It was so insane, it was all so insane.

The class graduated. The kids who could afford it went to college; Iŷana went to her uncle's in New Mexico. The poor boys went to war. The gangs continued to form alliances and grow powerful.

Izy's class was on the crest of their generation—741 students in all. Of 367 boys, 78 died or went missing in action in a jungle across the Ocean of Peace.

Izy didn't go to college. She wasted any chance of a scholarship. There was no money. Instead, Izy got a job.

126

SEDUCTION

During Izy's last year of school, her art class took a field trip to Long Beach Harbor. Their assignment was to draw the boats in the marina. The most visually interesting vessel was a Barkentine Schooner called the Killing Shark. It was made of wood that was painted black, had scrubbed wooden decks, and a Jolly Roger flying from the mast. As the class settled in to fulfill their assignment, a swarthy man emerged from the cabin of the Killing Shark to watch them work.

He was short, but all muscle, and might have been forty, but his thick leathery skin made him look older. His hair, black with some gray and dull from saltwater, was combed back and caught at the nape of his neck with a thin black tie that matched the tee shirt clinging to his chest. To Izy, he was more interesting to look at than the boats, so she drew him. She had her father's talent, and the sketch turned out well. The man saw the girl looking up and down from her pad to the place where he stood aboard the Killing Shark. After a while, he sauntered up to where the students were spread out.

He spoke to the teacher, "What will you do with these sketches?"

"They are part of their workbooks and will be graded along with everything else."

He took a few short steps to where Izy was seated, "Well grade this one now, and I'll buy it from the girl."

"I can't do that, sir. We have to be going."

"Oh yes, you can. You can say whether it's good or not. And if I'm buying it, how can it not be an A+?"

"The artwork is not for sale; it is for school. Come on everyone, on the bus." Izy understood that the teacher did not like the man. Before Izy got on the bus, she looked at the stranger. He stared back with a grin and winked.

The week of graduation, Izy got her workbook back. She tore out the sketch of the dark man and boarded a bus bound for the harbor. Once there, she found the marina they had visited earlier and scanned the slips for the Killing Shark. The Shark was out, the slip empty. Izy waited on the far end of the dock, watching pelicans and gulls sky dance and dive. Hours passed, and uncertain why, Izy remained. Finally, she spotted the black hull, the tall mast flying the skull and crossbones. The sails were tucked away; a small motor propelled the Shark to its place of rest. Izy trotted down to greet them. "Grab this line, honey." The swarthy man threw her a rope. He pointed, "Tie it off on that cleat." She did as asked.

He threw off rubber bumpers between the Shark and the dock, jumped off, and secured the other lines.

Then, inspecting her work, "You tie like a landlubber, honey. Look here, I'll show you." His broad hands untied her clumsy knot and skillfully threw a hitch on the cleat. "Did you see that? Can you do it? Go ahead." Izy undid the knot carefully to see how it twisted and then recreated it herself. "There! Now you've learned something. That's the most valuable knot in the world. You'll use that. What you want down here?"

"I brought the sketch."

"Sketch?" He looked closely as if he had just recognized her. "Ah, yes, the sketch. Come aboard, we'll have another look." Yes! Izy wanted to go on the Shark. She was glad.

She had her work rolled up in a tube on a strap over her shoulder. She took it off, opened the tube, and carefully pulled out the rendering. He took it from her and spread it on the plank table in the main cabin below deck. "It's good. I'll take it."

"You'll buy it?"

He looked at her for a moment, "Aye, I did say that didn't I? Very well, I'll give you five dollars."

"You'll give me twenty."

"No, that I won't. But I'll go ten."

"Eighteen or not at all."

He grinned at the game and said, "Fifteen."

"Seventeen and it's done."

"Sixteen and it's done."

"Seventeen, if you want it."

"You're a hard, wicked girl, but I want it, so here it is." His eyes twinkled as he went to a drawer in a sideboard. It was locked with a combination but he quickly twirled and, opening the drawer, extracted a ten dollar bill. "It's all I have, you'll have to trust me for the other seven."

"Then I'll have to hold on to this until you get it."

"Ohhh, what a wicked girl you are. Here it is, then."

128

"You lied."

"So what if I did?"

"Lying is a sin."

"And who are you to tell me about sin? Do you think I care what a girl like you has to say?"

"You should. If you lie, you can't be trusted."

"I can be trusted to do what's in my best interest and that's all that matters in this life. Take care of yourself, no one else will."

That rang a small bell inside of her; Izy began to like this rascal.

"Is that your business, then?"

"Guess so. I better go. I'm looking for a job."

"How old are you?"

"Eighteen. And I've graduated."

"That so? Well, you can work for me if you like."

"Work how?"

"I charter the Shark in the Channel Islands. For groups. You know, like your class and such. I always need a hand. You can crew for me."

"But I don't know the first thing about a boat or sailing."

"You know how to deal, that'll come to good use and I'll teach you the rest as we go."

Izy was at the Shark bright and early the next morning. She beat on the hatch and woke up Captain Jaime Almador, who crawled out in his underwear to let her know not to ever do that again. He had the stature of a little bull, robust and very strong. He was brown and his hair was loose, not tied up at his neck like the day before. "You can call me Captain, sir." He spoke with a Portuguese accent, so slight that Izy barely noticed. "And you'll do as you're told, not complain. If you act like a sissy, you're through."

"Agreed!" Izy said, and they shook hands. He set about teaching and Izy, to learning. First, there was cleaning; the Shark had to be maintained. There were decks to scrub, brass to polish, wood to scrape, and teak to varnish. Then came mending and fixing. Izy was eager to learn the proverbial ropes. And then there were the actual ropes: knots particular to every purpose.

"The wrong knot can lose a ship more easily than a storm can sink her," said Captain. He had her take a long plank, sand it smooth, and paint the letters that spelled out the names of the most important knots: a half dozen versions of a hitch, figure eights, square, double fisherman, and mooring. The board was then varnished and fitted with small posts, cleats, or eyes, so that Izy could tie and untie to his satisfaction, again and again, until they were familiar.

From time to time, one of his cronies from the marina would stop by to jaw with him over a beer. Izy kept her distance from them; she felt their eyes, knew they were watching her. They smelled and talked cheaply. She didn't like them.

"Keep your feet hard to the outside of the rigging and your weight as balanced as you can or you'll twist!" Izy tried but it was far more difficult to climb rigging than it looked. When she made progress, he'd jiggle the rope to confound her efforts. "You'll be doing it under sail, and it won't be easy then."

"It's not easy now!"

"Easy enough. Get down. I'll show you again!"

Mainsails, foresails, staysails, squares, and jibs. All had to be learned. Which was which, how they were rigged and raised, and how to tie them fast when they came down. Sheets were not sails, but lines. Facing forward, port was left and red, like the wine; starboard was right and green. The helm was aft, or near the stern.

He taught her to use an air tank, a diving mask, and a regulator. Then, in they went to go over the workings of the keel, rudder, and the prop of the small engine.

"There's a Boy Scout troop that's paid a charter to Catalina this weekend. You can crew, and I'll pay you $120. You'll work, not play, mind you."

Izy did work. From stowing gear to assigning bunks, then checking the rigging and casting off. The early morning went by quickly. Once out of the harbor, they turned southwest with barely a breeze; the going was slow. Captain kept the small motor puttering and called for adjustment of the canvas to catch what little wind there was. Izy didn't care. It was grand! She had never felt anything like it. The walnut tree was nothing compared to this.

When land was only a thin line behind them, Captain set troll lines aft. He assigned boys to watch the lines and alert him if they saw fish jumping out of the water. Sure enough, Captain soon pulled in a large bonito and then more. He called the Scout leader aft, instructed him to watch the compass, and allowed him to take the helm. Izy was jealous. In between checks on the helm, he taught her to gut and clean the bonito and store them in the cold locker below.

The boys were curious and surprised to see a girl for a mate. They eyed her sideways when Izy was busy and envied her for knowing the commands barked by the Captain. She worked carefully, pretending she'd been at sea all her life, relishing every minute.

The Captain headed just north of the visible narrowing in the center of the island. When they could see it, he called to Izy, "That's the Isthmus, or Twin Harbors, as it's named. It is important to know it by sight. On the other side's a small fishing village and a store." The wind had picked up and Captain brought the Shark to anchor at Emerald Bay under sail, laying anchor smoothly. The boys were quick to begin playing, jumping into the water, squealing with delight. Captain and Izy set the bowline to the rocky shore, then headed out in the dinghy to set lobster traps.

They left the boys to the Scout leader and rounded the jut of rock to the south of the bay. On the other side was another smaller bay with jagged rocks jutting out from the shore. "There's bugs here, for sure," the Captain said.

"Bugs?"

"Yes. The crawly things of the sea: crabs, lobsters, clams, and such. Bugs."

"I've never had lobster."

"Aye, well you will before this weekend is done."

He rowed the dinghy to where he wanted each contraption: near the rock, where the bugs dwelt, under the golden seaweed that crusted the surface of the water. Izy lowered the trap down till it rested as square as possible and left a tethered milk bottle at the surface to mark its location.

Back at the Shark, Izy was set to peeling and cutting potatoes, rinsing them in lemon juice so they wouldn't turn brown. Next, she cut up carrots and onions. Captain fished again, pulling in whatever was close to shore. The waters were rich with marlin, tuna, barracuda and swordfish, halibut, moray, snapper, sole, and shark, not to mention the delicious golden perch that flickered through the seaweed. The bigger game fish were just off the edge of the long sloping shelf, but often wandered into the bays to feed on its riches. With luck, a big one would make for a good dinner! But not today. Plenty of fish, nonetheless.

When the sun set, Captain filled the dinghy with a huge kettle, all the fish, the vegetables, plus Izy and the last of the boys not already on the shore, and rowed toward the beach. He built a fire, made a thin chowder with the bonito, and cooked up big steaks of fresh fish in tin foil. He said nothing to the others but gave Izy a cup of sangria. She drank it down and helped herself to more. After a while, everything blended together for Izy. Tired, but content, she sat back, waiting to be entertained. She could not recall a happier day in her life!

Captain told stories of the patrols that came sometimes to chase everyone off the shore because camping wasn't allowed. He described the wild animals that roamed free on the island: deer, buffalo, cattle, goats, and hogs. He said the hogs were vicious, that it was dangerous to sleep on the land. He said a rich man named Wrigley owned the island, that he lived in Chicago and made gum. It was he who forbade people from accessing the island shores and hired the patrols to guard it. The island had come to him with a long list of previous owners who, rumor had it, included slave traders and pirates. The Captain mesmerized his audience with a plethora of steep island lore or captivating malarkey. No one seemed to care which.

The first recorded owner, a man named Robbins, received a grant from Governor Pico in the final days of Mexican rule in California. From him, it passed to men who had dreams of raising cattle, mining the land, or building great sports fishing resorts. In the end, only a few came to the tiny paradise, settling only in the areas they were allowed to inhabit: Avalon and Twin Harbors, mostly. No automobiles were allowed. Life in the towns was slow. The only businesses were those evolving to meet the needs of the tourists who rode the Great White Steamship from Long Beach on weekends.

He told of secret tunnels, miles long, where pirates' treasure was buried. He gave a bone-chilling recitation of ghost tales, victims murdered and left. He described an abandoned, lofty mansion, haunted and windblown, at the peak of the island. He was crafty with his stories; they were punctuated with 'oohs,' shutters, gasps, and laughter from his audience. Izy was sure they couldn't all be true, but in the dark, by the firelight, they came alive.

He took up his guitar and played and sang songs everyone knew; all sang along.

After a few tunes, Captain saw something move, doused the fire with a can of water, and ordered everyone into the water.

"Be quiet about it, and swim for your hides."

Back aboard, the scout leader and the Captain counted noses as a small patrol boat quietly rounded the rocks.

"Well, if it isn't the Shark and her keeper. Amador, you best stay off the beach. You think we don't see the smoke from that fire?"

"Aye, you see the smoke, but you don't see me ashore, do you now?"

"We'll catch you one day, and then we'll impound the Shark."

"You'll take the Shark when you've sent me to hell, you landlubbers!"

As the patrol boat moved out of sight, only their searchlight could be seen as it made its way around the island checking one bay at a time.

Izy watched the Scout leader, sensing his discomfort. Rules had been broken, right in front of the boys. There was a moment when she thought the Scout leader might protest. But then his expression lightened, and Izy figured it had been so much fun that somehow it outweighed any evil.

After another day of swimming and diving, the Scout leader was on shore that night for the same high jinks. Only this time they extinguished the fire early and were off the island long before the patrol came. They did their singing aboard the Shark and fell asleep to the lapping of the water against the hull.

When, the following day, they set sail for home, there was a brisk wind in the sails and a chop to the sea, making the trip hectic and difficult. The Captain, with his strong, experienced arms, was needed at the helm, which meant the task of managing the sails fell to Izy; it was more than she could handle. She let slack a sheet to the foresail, which then became tangled in the rigging. She freed it but, in the process, the ladder twisted on her and she was caught. She flopped helplessly and was told she was useless. As the Captain chided her for her carelessness, she felt stung by his words but didn't have the luxury of reacting. There wasn't time. The boys enjoyed her humiliation, which only made Izy feel worse. The Captain told her she'd have to get herself down, "It'll teach you not to be so stupid." Izy was hurting, almost willing to throw herself overboard to be free of the mortifying predicament, but that wasn't an option. She was stuck.

Izy felt a familiar sense of dread in her gut. She had to pull her wits together and just do it! Carefully she untwisted herself, navigating the pitches and rolls of the waves, concentrating, making her body work. As soon as she had a chance, she slammed her sneakers to the outer corners of the rope squares, which helped tremendously.

Once she was down, Captain took pride in her, giving her dignity back; he relieved the boys from her tasks. "You may have salt after all, Bella," the name Captain called her reminded her of bygone days and Gina. "Not bad. You know, I thought you'd ride to harbor up there. I'd have let you, too, you do know that?" Izy didn't reply but she believed him. More than that, she felt curiously good inside. She'd earned a bit of respect. It felt so wonderful and chased away the hurt. She felt tears well up in her eyes, but they were flicked away by the wind before they could fall. No one knew.

For a while, the journey was swift and smooth. Izy settled in at the bow to watch the water as it was cut by the Shark. Her thoughts were tiny tendrils floating back to Grandy and the Limerick crossing the Atlantic. The sea, the adventure, even the painful situation in the rigging—as a whole, it was the grandest thing she'd ever experienced, and she was delirious with a new joy. Captain would have to be far crueler than that to break her.

Summer passed with charters every weekend and one or two week-long outings to visit Avalon Harbor or other islands, which were mostly owned by the government and used by the military. They were forbidden to go ashore on these islands. Instead, they anchored and went diving, exploring deep water and encountering big fish. In Avalon they ate tuna chowder, visited the grand casino, or walked along the boardwalk. Captain always complained of the prissy, white boats in the harbor. He called their owners "landlubbers" and "weekend sailors," and none too quietly, either. Izy never knew when he might cause sufficient trouble as to be chased out of town by the constable. No one on the charters seemed to mind. Whether or not they were aware of it, the Captain and his swagger, his bellicosity, were part of what they paid to enjoy. It was a chance to be a pirate, a renegade, adding spice to the journey.

Izy collected her earnings and saved whatever she could. Soon weary of the bus, she bought a shiny-red used Triumph III convertible sports car. It was hot! She was very proud of it and tore around with the wind in her short hair, downshifting instead of breaking; screaming around corners: It suited her well. She didn't bother to put the top up. It was summer, who needed it?

More often than not, the trips were to Emerald Bay. It was the Captain's favorite, and hers as well. Soon Izy was managing to lay traps on her own, fish, and dive. Once, while diving at a thirty-foot depth, Captain tapped her shoulder, pointing up. Near the surface was a huge school of jellyfish as far as the eye could see. They moved in formation, shifting their hue like a kaleidoscope.

Captain purchased jugs of Red Mountain wine, oranges, limes, potatoes, onions, and carrots in big burlap sacks from the fish market outside the marina. Beyond that, they ate what they caught, whatever that might be. It was part of the adventure. The sea was rich around the islands. Everything from octopus and sea snake to sea snails, fish and, once in a while, some great, proud swordfish.

On one particular trip, they caught nothing. Captain sent Izy in the dinghy to the Isthmus, up and over to the windward side and into the village. There, she bought fresh clams, milk, and eggs. The Captain made chowder and in the morning Izy scrambled eggs. It was okay but took a bite out of profits and put him in a foul mood. They began arguing and fussing over everything.

Once, Izy was fishing and accidentally left a line with a hook attached on the deck floor. Captain stepped on it, tearing open the sole of his foot. His temper broke loose and he came after her. Izy moved quickly to the top of the cabin and over the mainsail boom to get away. He was right behind her, cursing and bleeding. Down to the deck and around to the stern she went, but only inches from his grasp. Izy wasn't sure what he would do if he caught her, so she chose the sea and in she went.

She could hear his oaths before God all the way to the rocks as she stroked through the water. When she reached the rocks, he'd quieted and was mending his wound, with an occasional burst of blasphemy. Izy stayed on the rocks for more than an hour watching crabs scurry. The dark rocks absorbed energy from the sun and kept her warm. She found a huge boulder worn smooth by the tide. She folded herself over the rock, hugging it and feeling connected to planet mother.

"Bella girl, catch this line and we'll drag for perch in this seaweed." Izy looked up and there he was in the dinghy, all smiles and sweetness.

She didn't answer.

"Now Bella, you're not gonna sulk on me. Look here, I've brought you a soda. After all, you did splay me tootsie wide open. Give a man a break for the sake of the pain and loss of blood, not to mention fear and anguish... ."

"All right, all right, gimme the damn line."

"Oh, good girl, come around now. Yes, good, that's it, low to the water, now. We'll have tender fillets tonight!"

"You could watch your step."

"Aye. I could."

She learned to make sangria and enjoyed drinking it down, as well as eating the oranges and limes soaked in the brew. Depending on who was on board, they drank it all day long or sipped it discreetly at night.

Izy ached when she wasn't aboard the Shark. She started staying over a day before and after the trips to prepare, clean up—making any excuse just to be with the Captain and his ship.

Sometimes, there were other females aboard. The Captain had an eye for women and could sense any willingness on their part to join him in his cabin. If he liked one, he was not shy and would slap her butt playfully or be openly affectionate in front of Izy—something that never failed to make Izy feel uncomfortable. She was jealous of the women who got attention, and did not wonder why he never touched her in those ways. There were times he was so engaged in his wooing that Izy felt invisible. Once she caught him deliberately looking at her over another woman's shoulder while he played with her hair. Izy had looked away, burying her embarrassment by busying herself.

The voyages were splendid. Sun, wind, and all manner of sea life—a common treat swimming alongside the bow, flying up out of the water and splashing down again—would accompany them at various stages of their journey. Sometimes they saw humpback whales, always in groups, or pods, slowly gliding in soft arcs. Then, on some shared cue, they'd all dive deep and disappear for a long time—twenty minutes or more before bursting again through the surface, ejecting water vapor and air through their blowholes. "This is nothing, Bella! Wait for the winter, then you'll see them in hoards!" Sea lions and seals swam by or rested on buoys; there were great schools of tuna or bonito and all manner of other fish, which they'd catch and eat if they could.

Izy went home less and less until it was only occasionally, and Missy was clearly worried. Izy told her just enough about the Captain and her work for Missy to have cause for concern. Now Izy was the cruel one. But Missy had no more control. Izy was free.

Late into summer charters slowed, bringing a free weekend. The Santa Ana winds came early that year. Also called "devil winds," they sweep down from the deserts and out toward the coast, bringing hot, dry air. The early Spaniards shortened the name to "Santana," which sounds similar to the Spanish term "Sataná," meaning Satan. The air has a choking effect, making you feel you can't breathe. You don't sweat because the wind steals the moisture away and eliminates the body's ability to cool itself. You just bake. Crime, murder, and suicide rates climb, tempers flare and, if there's trouble brewing, it's bound to boil over amid the winds, for sure.

Captain decided they should use the time for maintenance. They worked hard all day Saturday and then went up to the Red Witch Inn in the marina for a shrimp feast and some margaritas.

The next morning he blew into the cabin where her bunk was, "Get up you lazy lubber, coffee's on with eggs and potatoes. We have plans to make!"

"Plans?" She stumbled to the main cabin and plopped down at the galley table.

"We'll go under today for an inspection."

"We did that in June."

"Well, it's a good hot day, we'll do it again. You know, Bella, when the season's ended, I'm pulling the Shark for the cradle. It'll take me two to three months to get her ready. That gets us through the hurricane season on the Mexican coasts. Then I'm going through the canal to the Caribbean. I want you to come along."

"The Panama Canal?" Izy was overwhelmed with excitement and took nothing else at all into consideration. She was going!

"Aye. Then we'll spend the winter hopping islands and taking charters. We'll have a good time, I promise you that."

"Have you been there before?"

"Aye, many times. I know all the great places and all the great people. As for now, I think we'll take a cruise, just you and I, to the islands this week. What do you say to that?"

"Great! I'm all for it." She pictured herself sailing the world—an adventurer.

On the morning of August 9th, they motored out of the harbor with a hot wind at their backs. They put up sail as soon as they were free of the buoys, tacking north toward Santa Barbara Island. They sailed all the way and, in between tack changes, Izy climbed out on the bowsprit, clinging to the forestay. There she'd breathe in the salt air, flexing her knees with each wave, and fly through the spray like a gull. Two great orcas came to play and crisscrossed the bow, rolling and diving. There was nothing like it. She wished Grandy could see her.

When they came into a cove it was Izy's job to tie up to the mooring with the knot Captain had taught her. They set the shoreline, then went in diving. Santa Barbara Island drops off suddenly into the deep ocean, unlike Catalina, which has a sloping shelf on the lee side. They were hoping for albacore but found nothing. After being out for forty minutes, Izy was thinking about air when she felt a tap on her shoulder. She turned to see Captain pointing into the shadows beyond them. Two, then four, large, gray shapes were circling. There was no albacore because they stay away from sharks.

They had encountered sharks only once before on one of their trips to the Islands. She and Captain were in the dinghy setting traps when, suddenly, the oars began banging on the surface. They had drifted into a school of leopard sharks feeding on the fish in the seaweed forest that filled the bay. Izy looked at

Captain. He motioned her to sit down, be still. Then he slowly maneuvered them out of the bay. But in that instance, they were in a boat.

Now, they were in the water with the sharks. Izy's eyes were the size of her mask. Captain took off his regulator and gave her a grin, then replaced it. That helped a little. He made signs with his hands for her to swim toward one of the sharks. He jerked his hand aggressively. Izy shook her head sideways. He nodded and jerked his hand again. A dark flash in his eye told her to do as he motioned. She trusted Captain.

Izy looked out toward the shadow to her right and made a decision. She began kicking and heading straight for the nearest of the gray sharks, her heart pounding. The shark broke its pattern and swam down. She caught a glimpse of Captain in the ring of sharks opposite her; he had done the same. They were so far apart she felt terror. Captain motioned for her to swim toward him. When she reached him, he gave a jerk of his head toward the ship. Her breathing was so rapid she was afraid she might run out of air. They made it to the ladder without further incident, but Izy could still feel the sharks in the water around them.

Scrambling up on deck, regulator out, she said: "They were following us, I know it."

"I'm counting on it, and so are you if you want an excellent dinner!"

He went into the cold locker and came out with some cleaned mackerel to use as chum. He chopped them up and threw them into the sea. The pieces floated near the surface, drawing interest from the gray scavengers. He threw Izy the large snag net. Then he grabbed the spear gun and climbed down the ladder. He stopped just above the water where he tried to hang out further while holding onto a rope. Izy couldn't tell how many sharks there were. From where she stood looking over, the water was dark. Occasionally she saw a dorsal come nearer and break the surface. Captain hung there like a tightly-wound spring. Finally, he fired into the water. Then there was thrashing.

The harpoon danced in the water, then dove under. But he was quick to secure the line. Now there was only the battle of pulling in his catch. Once he had the gray body against the hull, Izy could see that it was a small one, or maybe they had seemed bigger when she was out there with them. It was arching its head up and she could see its eyes and, lower, its broad mouth and sharp teeth. It was still terrifying. Captain killed the shark with the machete while it was still in the water, leaving parts for the friends if they wanted. Captain said, "No moonlight swims tonight."

They ate well that evening and drank sangria. Later, the Captain played his guitar and sang Caribbean songs into the blackness of night.

"Sharks kill what they can, you know. They look for the slow, small, and weak. It's far more dangerous if you are splashing at the surface than down below. As divers, we appear to be sleek beasts like themselves. They circle to size us up, see what we'll do. If we fear and do nothing, they get brave. One will come in for a bump to test the danger. The thing to do is to beat them to it and be aggressive. That gives them pause because now you're a threat. That's what a dolphin does. It's rare a shark takes on a dolphin or another shark. So be brave and smart, Bella, always be so, for the world is full of sharks!"

They downed shots of Cuervo and looked at the stars. Later, Captain, who was now quite drunk, opened up the main cabin hatch so that the entire cabin was open to the sky. Topside, Izy heard him banging and clanging down below. Then he reappeared.

"Come, see what I've done," he said with a loose jaw. It was all she could do to move, but she managed to ride the swells of the tide over to the cabin door. He'd turned the table into a double bed.

"I didn't know it made a bed."

"Well, it does. It's for special nights, for tonight. Too hot to sleep inside. You can lay here and see the stars. Come on down."

A tiny thought ran through her mind and back out, and then she swung her way down the steps and flopped onto the bed. "Not bad."

"Not bad? It's great! What more is there than to ride on the wind, eat what you kill, drink till you're blind, and fall asleep counting the stars? Well, there is one more thing... ," he said, slithering beside her on the bed.

Izy was suddenly sober. She heard little alarms going off and felt a hot sensation in her gut. She felt something cold explode inside her chest as her heart began to race. She moved away and he moved with her, rolling on top of her. Izy knew what was happening, but she wasn't ready. "Please, Captain, don't."

"Don't what, Bella baby? This will make it perfect."

"Please, no, I don't want to."

"Yes, you do. Do you like to play coy? Do you like to struggle?" He laughed, "All the better! I like to struggle."

"Don't like to play at all. Please!" He had ripped her tank top. Her breasts were exposed, and she was frantic. Izy struggled against him but had waited too long, or maybe there never had been a chance. In the struggle her top disappeared. He held her arms and licked her breasts. She tried to get her legs out from underneath his weight. She was uttering sounds of effort, revulsion, and fear. He put his open mouth against hers, his tongue licking her. When her lips parted, he was inside. She jerked her head up and to the side so he couldn't get to her mouth. He lifted up to grab her bathing suit bottom. It was her chance. She lurched out from under him and made a lunge for the edge of the bed, face down. He pulled her bathing suit bottom down around her knees before his body landed on top of her. Then he was struggling with his own briefs.

"Please don't do this, pleeeeze!" Izy felt tears in her throat. With her fists clenched, she flailed at him, to little avail. Suddenly, he raised her up and turned her over, flipping her like a pancake. The bottom was gone. Izy was naked and looking at an erect penis for the first time in her life.

He was thick and brown; only a small area of his torso was light skinned as if there were a spotlight on his penis. His legs straddled her. She jerked her legs up as a reflex, hitting him in the buttocks. For a second he thought she was trying to hurt him, so he slapped her hard in the face. She was stunned, terrified. His eyes were blazing and his face was stern. It finally occurred to Izy that she had nowhere to go. She began to sob softly in acquiescence.

He sucked on her nipples, fondled her breasts, and kissed her. She tried to kiss back but was completely inept. He was trying to make love to her. He separated her legs and pushed them out, placing his hands under and lifting them so that her knees were bent. She looked from leg to leg in wonder and fear. He cupped his penis with his hand, bent over her and came in, low, toward her face, kissing her gently on her lips. She felt something hard press against her and knew this was it.

He tried to put it in but it wouldn't go. He brought his hand to this mouth and wet his fingers, moistened her vulva, and tried again. Then again. It wouldn't go. Izy thought, "Maybe he can't do it and I'll be spared." He lay down with his full weight upon her and whispered into her ear, "Relax, Bella. It's going to be so good, so nice for us. I've wanted you from the first day I saw you sketching. I wanted you when I fucked other women. I would fuck them because you made my blood so hot, I had to, just to function. I want you, I want you now, my Bella." And she did relax a little. Then he just put it inside her with a single thrust.

She gasped at one, sharp pain, then it was gone. There was only the complete fullness of something in that place where nothing had ever been before. He was making small kisses all over her face, neck, and breasts. "Ummm, so tight, Bella, so like a virgin."

"I am," she said in a sob. "I mean, I was, until now."

"Oh, Bella, Bella, this is your first time?" His voice held a tinge of tenderness and surprise.

"I've never even had a date or a kiss."

He cocked his head just slightly as if trying to decide if he believed her or not. Then he smiled and a new look spilled over his features. "Gentle, we must be gentle from here on, my Bella." And he began to stroke in and out of her, slowly at first. "You will like it, sweet Bella. I will help you like it." He raised up on his arms, took her buttocks in his huge hands, and proceeded to give Izy her very first fucking.

When he was finished, he collapsed on her, all wet, smelling of sweat and odors new to her. With his weight on her, she realized her chest was heaving. She was glad for him to be done, yet she felt oddly special, like this powerful man was weak now, submissive. It was an emotion she felt but couldn't quite claim.

It didn't last long. He soon was kissing, sucking, and touching her between the legs, stroking inside and outside, moaning and muttering. She felt the spring of his penis against her leg. This time he held her head in his hands and kissed her tenderly, then passionately. Now it slipped in easier because she was wet and gooey down there. He lasted longer the second time. Partway through he pulled out and turned her over on her hands and knees and came back inside from behind her. At least he wasn't kissing her. Her breasts hung down and she thought of a cow. Then he ran his hand over her back and pushed her down so that her face was pressed into the bed. His one hand pressed over her buttocks as he kept the other holding her belly up to expose her whole backside in a way she could never have imagined. She felt flush with embarrassment, which was nothing compared to when he began stroking her anus with his thumb and then trying to poke in. "No, no, please, don't!" And she wrenched away from him, but he held her firm in his grasp, skewed.

"Bella, this is so beautiful, just relax and let me teach you about pleasure."

"It's not pleasure for me! Pleeeeze!"

He pulled out and grabbed her up on his hip like a bundle and took her into the tiny head where he set her down in front of him, facing toward the small mirror over the sink. He ripped the mirror out of the small, wooden casing and propped it up in the sink. Then he lifted her up so her legs straddled his knee, pulling her back against his chest, his huge hand smashing her breasts in his grasp. His knee was wedged into the sink, exposing her private parts. He wiggled out and got a grip on the edge of the mirror and brought it between her legs.

"Look at you Bella, you are beautiful, so pink and fair. Do you know this is the prettiest cunt I have ever seen?" His use of that word made her flush even more. "You are lovely, and I want to touch all of you and know all of you. It is what lovers do with each other. It's so special, just between us, here, in the moonlight."

She was thinking. She was feeling.

Then he was moving somewhere else, toward the open hatch, with her in tow by the wrist—up into the night and the sound of the sea. He took her to the rigging where she had been tangled that first voyage. He took her hands and lifted them into the rigging above her head. "Bella, grab onto the rope with all your might, throw your head back and smell the salt air, think of the wild things in the sea all around us and trust me that, here, tonight, I love you as I have never loved a woman. He lifted her up. "Wrap your legs around me, little girl, and I will make you a woman, under the stars."

She felt overwhelmed. She did as he asked; he pushed into her, thrusting hard. She was suspended by the cradle of his hands to her hands in the rigging. She felt the rough rope sawing the skin of her hands and wrists while convulsions in the pit of her stomach rose up and into her chest. She could feel herself getting wetter and wetter till she could hear the wetness. When she dared look, she saw her naked body bouncing in the warm air, her lover's features contorted, his lips curled back displaying his teeth, so intense, and she found pleasure in it.

In the early morning, while the Captain was snoring in the bed under the sky, she awoke. The wind was still blowing and the waves were lapping hard against the hull. She could feel rawness, a mild ache in her crotch that immediately told her it had not been a dream. "Oh, God! Grandy how you must be ashamed of me." She felt a small but distinct emptiness where something used to exist, as if she had lost something precious, something she could never have again. She rested a minute, trying to comprehend what it might mean to be a woman. Sex outside marriage was a sin, or so said her mother and the Bible. She thought about being a sinner.

She needed to be alone. She took great care not to wake Captain, got up, and made her way to the head. There was the little mirror in the sink. She urinated. It stung just a bit. She wiped herself gently, put down the lid, but didn't run the bilge pump for fear of waking him. An irresistible urge compelled her.

She picked up the mirror to look at her face. Maybe there was something different about her mouth or her eyes, maybe not. Then she put her foot on the lid and held the mirror so she could see herself. She'd never looked before last night.

Then she heard a bump to starboard. Bump again. Below the water. And again. She ran to the hatch, up and peered out. They were very near the rocky island. "Captain, Captain! Wake up, wake up!" She was on the bed shaking him. He jerked with alarm, then heard a bump.

"Come!" He commanded. Izy obeyed.

The mooring line had come loose and they'd drifted into the low-lying rocks. By the time they were on deck, the Shark was already beginning to list to port. Captain pulled out two huge oars, ten feet long, maybe more, and gave one to Izy.

"Go forward to port!" He went aft, starboard.

"Brace it down on the bottom and hold fast, whatever." Izy did as she was told.

He went up on the rail, made fast in the rigging, and began to push off with all his might. He gained a few inches. Izy held, but the waves were too great. "Be brave, Bella, don't give up!"

Naked and desperate, they worked but were held firmly against the rocks. Suddenly Captain ceased pushing off, "Push off on starboard, Bella!" She switched positions, then loaded the mighty oar in a lock. Her arms shook with exhaustion. She was too afraid to climb up on the rail. She slipped and slammed her foot into the casing of the open hatch, ripping open her big toe. The blood made the deck more slippery. The waves were coming softly over the hull. Izy knew their prospects were bleak.

"Load your oar in the port lock, Bella, then go forward and cut the shoreline free!"

Izy loaded the oar, then fought her way to the locker forward of the cabin, pulled out the machete, went to the bow as quickly as she could, and hacked through the line.

"Hurry, Bella, give me a warning when it's going to go!" He yelled from the stern, where he was wielding the oars to hold their position.

"Now, Captain, now!" When the line snapped free, there was a violent lurch. She thought they were done for as she crashed to the deck with the machete in her hand. Springing up, prepared to jump for her life, she saw Captain at the stern, feet wedged firmly, leg muscles bulging, his powerful arms and shoulders straining to row the Killing Shark against the wind and the waves out to sea. He was determined, like the captain of the Limerick. Izy began to sob at such a sight: Magnificent, heroic Captain raging against nature to free his ship to save them.

"Take the helm hard to port!" He barked. Izy, stumbling, moved as fast as she could to do so. Captain brought the Shark over the shelf as they jibed, "Start the engine, Bella, fast!"

Without a thought, she followed his order. "Take her out, Bella!" They were saved.

He took over the helm and they motored around the point till they found shelter from the devil winds. "Bella, girl, you saved us."

"No, Captain, it was you! It was me that put us in danger. Yesterday, I should have done a better job tying up to the mooring. I nearly dashed us."

She expected abuse. There was none. Exhausted and grateful, they collapsed on the deck until sunrise.

When they sailed, they stood at the helm together. He held her with his great arm. Izy looked around at the Shark under sail on the chop of the sea, a beautiful thing to behold. They spent the next two days at Catalina. Because it was the middle of the week, they were alone. They swam naked and ran through the shallows, falling on the rocky beach in an embrace. They had sex two or three times a day and in every position. She allowed him to touch her, lick her, whatever he wished. He wanted her to put his penis in her mouth. At first, she couldn't believe it. But with his constant urging, she succumbed and survived. It held no pleasure for her.

By Wednesday, the 11th of August, they were heading back. To her shock, she felt saddened. There was something about the intimacy—the rapt attention they bestowed on each other—that overshadowed the shame she had felt that first night and the fear of being alone with him on the sea. She realized the experience would enhance her life. She just didn't know quite how.

The Red Witch Inn was a welcome sight—a full bar and a menu offering something other than shark. While they were eating, some of the Captain's cronies came in and approached their table.

"Ahoy, can we join you?"

"Why not? And you can buy us a round," Captain said with an open grin and a wave of his hand. The server brought over a bottle of Cuervo.

"Where you been? Slip's been empty for days."

"Bella and I took cruised up to Santa Barbara," he winked. She felt sick. So now they all knew. Izy felt their eyes on her in a way she never had before.

"Bella, you shouldn't go with this old dog. Come sail with me," one of them said.

"No, she's mine, and I'll lick any one or all of you says another word to my woman," the Captain slurred.

She was his trophy. He was so proud. She felt like she had a big, brass Captain's penis hanging around her neck and, suddenly, she hated him. How could a heart so grand and heroic also be small and cheap? No one she loved would be vulgar and boastful. She knew how to be crafty. She was on land now.

She laughed and kept her anger deep inside. She made jokes and drank less, but she poured for the lot. She kissed her Captain hard on the mouth, touched his nose, and coyly told him to wait right there while she went to the head. He clopped her a smack on her backside, as he had to other women, as she left the table. Izy went straight through the kitchen, out past the garbage bins, and got into her car and drove away. She steered onto the Harbor Freeway toward the only place in the world she had left to go.

All she had was what she was wearing: shorts, a tank top over her bathing suit, and flip-flops. Everything else was on the Shark. Thank goodness she had her keys. She didn't know why she had put them in her shorts pocket. Maybe she'd intended to go to the car for something after they ate. All that was gone from her head. She only knew she was through with Captain, her Captain before she became his handoff. She could read it well. She could see it coming.

She got off the freeway at Imperial, as always. As Izy sat at the light, a car full of colored guys pulled alongside her. They were yelling and talking trash, would she like to do something obscene? Izy wondered if everyone knew she was no longer a virgin, now a loose woman. Am I wearing a sign? Then one boy got out of the back seat and tried to jump into her car. Izy went through the light with him half in and half out of the car, until he lost hold. His friends in the other car picked him up and stayed right behind her.

She saw a flicker of motion in the rearview mirror. Then heard a crash, a whoosh—the back of the Triumph was on fire. The flames were streaking behind her like the tail of a rocket. She could hear shrieking, laughter, and shouting and knew the coloreds had done something but she had no clue what. She had to decide whether to keep going or stop and get out before the gas tank blew. What to do, what to do?

She heard a siren, then another. There were cops everywhere motioning her to the curb. She pointed the car at the curb, braking until the tire hit, not even bothering to downshift, and jumped out. Still in gear, the Triumph lurched to a stop and was quiet.

One cop jumped out and pulled her behind his patrol car. Another car chased after the coloreds who had made a U-turn and had disappeared by then. "What the hell is going on? I'm a slut! Has the world turned into hell? Has everybody gone crazy?" Her thoughts raced.

The Triumph burned and she begged, "Call a fire truck, damn it!" The cop told her, "None available. No life endangered here."

"None available?"

The cops crouched behind their patrol cars, waiting. Sure enough, her car blew up, spraying window glass and shrapnel everywhere. There was a fireball. She could feel the heat, even from behind the cruiser. Dizzy with the cacophony and smell of toxic fumes, she struggled to grasp what was happening.

"You'll have to leave it, Miss. We're going to take you home right now. Where do you live?"

"Take me home? What about my car? Don't you guys carry extinguishers?"

"Believe me, Miss, if we had them, they were used up a long time ago." He was shoving her into the cruiser, "What's your address?" She gave it to him and they sped in the cruiser toward the nightmare house.

The radio blared the whole way as they drove. They let her off at the curb. "Get inside your house and do not come out till morning. Do you understand?"

Izy nodded and went into the house. Right away she knew something was dreadfully wrong. She turned on a light and a whole section of the floor was gone. You could see clear through to the trains down below. "Oh man, what's he done this time?" Missy came in and whispered, "Turn off the light, Isabella."

Izy obeyed. "Has everyone lost their minds? You would not believe what just happened. My car got set on fire and blew up!"

"Oh dear Lord! Your little car? Are you all right, honey?"

"Well, I have a busted up toe, but I'm fine."

"Thank you, Jesus! Well, it's no wonder. Where have you been? I've been frantic with worry. You don't know. Don't you know?"

"What? Know what? I mean obviously, something's up!"

"There was a riot today in Watts, and there's been killing, and fires, and vandalism. There's trouble everywhere, and… and I thought you might be dead or injured. I was so worried and I've been so frightened." Missy was weeping and shaking and, suddenly, Izy felt like a rat.

"Momma, Momma, Momma. I'm here, safe. Are you all right?" Missy nodded in her daughter's embrace, sobbing. "Well, then everything's going to be okay. Where's Daddy?"

"I don't know for sure. I think he's in the back house."

"He left you all alone?" Of course, so had she. Giant rat feelings cascaded over her. She'd forgotten about the Shark, Captain, and the sins committed. Izy had come home to a brand new America born while she was at sea fucking the Captain. As Izy held her mother, a thousand thoughts flew through her mind.

They lived in the area of the city adjacent to Watts. When martial law was declared, the National Guard was called in and a perimeter was established to contain the violence. The nightmare house was inside its boundaries. If you went out of the zone, you had to stay out; there was no coming back in. If you weren't already inside the zone, you weren't allowed to come in. You couldn't go out after dark. The National Guard patrolled the streets in little jeeps with big machine guns mounted on the back. Using bullhorns they broadcast warnings that they had orders to shoot curfew breakers on sight.

Izy snuck out of the house, ran across the yard, and crouched under the hedge by the fence, inching to the end so she could see both directions up and down the street. No jeeps. She flashed her light twice; Veronica came out and dropped by her porch. Still no jeep. Three lights flashed meant it was safe to cross. She came straight away. Then they crept through Izy's backyard and out onto the railroad tracks. There was plenty of cover. They huddled there for a hug.

"I'm so glad you're okay and you're back. Your mother was really upset!"

"I know. What, is it the gangs?"

"No. Some guy got pulled over by the cops. Some say they were roughing him up and a crowd gathered. Others say the crowd was just edgy, you know, with this Prop 14 business, and it's so hot and there's no relief. Anyway, one of the cops took his club to someone in the crowd, and they mobbed him and the other cop. They called for backup, and all hell broke loose."

"You're kidding. Wow! Are you all okay?"

"Yes. My father has all his weapons out, cleaned, and loaded, and he and Matthew take shifts guarding the house. He keeps saying, 'No f-ing niggers are going to burn his house!' I'm glad they set a curfew to make people stay inside. He was talking to Matthew about taking matters into his own hands. Matthew was just staring at him, and I was scared he'd take Matthew, go to Watts, and well, you know my Dad."

"Maybe you should come to my house. Well, maybe not. But I wouldn't want to be there with all those guns."

"I hate them too, but right now, well, honestly, I feel pretty safe, under the circumstances. They keep an eye out over here, too. Matthew told me to ask if you want a shotgun or something."

"This is crazy! No, I don't want a shotgun. But tell him thanks for the thought."

"Yeah. Crazy! Say, where were you?"

"I was out with the Captain. I'll explain later. Actually, it's a pretty good story, but nothing like this. It can wait. You better go back home. I have to get back to Mom."

They slipped quietly through the yard, low to the front. No jeep. Over she went, home safe.

That night, Izy sinned once more. After Missy, fully dressed including shoes, was settled on the bed, Izy took a butcher knife from the kitchen and grabbed her old baseball bat. Then she lay down beside her mother, wide awake. Not many in Los Angeles would sleep that night.

Smoke hung in the air for days, fed by the occasional new blaze. That night, the fires were fresh and not far away. She heard sirens, explosions, and weapons being fired in the distance. She listened, intently, for any sound near the house or the neighborhood.

Izy tried to understand why anyone would want to hurt them or come down their street. Then she realized the city was in total chaos. No one was really thinking, only raging, and desperate to be noticed instead of ignored. It was like Reverend King, in a way, protesting to bring attention to injustice. Only Izy didn't think Reverend King would do anything like this. He planned and acted rationally. His letter had said "...civil disobedience is a nonviolent confrontation with those who are unjust." This was a confrontation, but extremely violent, and it was a spontaneous thing. The news said that most of the rioters were likely to get away without even being arrested or tried, if they were arrested.

And then it occurred to her, "What if they did come down those tracks and come into our yard and see that little old house all boarded up out there. Maybe they'd just torch it for fun. It looks empty. Who would imagine there was a monster living there? What if I sneaked out there, clubbed him in the head so he couldn't get out, and set it on fire myself? Everyone would assume it was rioters, wouldn't they? We'd be free!"

Izy wanted to do it. She thought about how. "Cleaning solvent, the oil paints, turpentine, linseed oil. It would go up like a torch. All I have to do is get up and go down into the cellar, creep down that tunnel, and catch him in his sleep. But what if he's awake?" She got up, went to the window, and looked out at the little house through the trees. "I don't see any light at all. But that doesn't mean anything. He is so weird. Maybe he's doing something obscene out there in the dark, or using those little spotlights on all his wicked paintings. Gross! All the more reason to be done with his sick self. Gads!"

By dawn, Izy was convinced she was crazy for having such evil thoughts all night long. The light seemed to lift her terror. Izy was ashamed of her fantasies. He was her father. No, he was her Daddy who had once been her colleague, her teacher. Even if she didn't like him anymore, how could she club him and burn him to death? Last night, it was she who was the monster.

The riots lasted for six days. Thirty-four people were killed. A thousand or more were injured. Whole blocks of Los Angeles were demolished, burned to the ground in most cases. There were so many blazes, the fire department could not keep up. All told, there was 200 million dollars in damages—destroyed buildings, looting—and, of course, Izy's Triumph was hauled away. The news said an estimated 45,000 people had participated in the riots, but only four thousand were arrested. Everyone had an opinion about the riots. Ronny's father said, "...outside agitators from Martin Luther God Damned King were sent here to stir up trouble! The FBI oughta arrest him for questioning and prosecute him. That'd put an end to this outrage!"

Izy saw a guy on the television at Ronny's house who had been arrested. Someone asked what he thought Martin Luther King would think of his actions. He replied, "Martin who? We don't need a preacher. We need action!" Izy decided that if agitators had come, they hadn't been sent by Reverend King.

The governor set up a commission to investigate the riots. They came back citing overcrowding and an overwhelming strain on housing, utilities, and just about every other aspect of life in the area as chief causes of the tension that led to the riots. High unemployment in the inner city, shoddy housing, and bad schools contributed, which seemed to explain why colored people were trying so hard to get out and move into other neighborhoods, white or otherwise. The report also noted that the attacks were specifically targeted at white-owned businesses and that establishments owned or operated by blacks were left alone. And finally, it stated that the hatred was greatest toward the all-white Los Angeles Police Department whose officers routinely used brutality to subdue and suppress the black population of Watts. It was an explicit indictment of racist attitudes thinly disguised as tolerance and segregation by covert exclusion. Izy thought, "Finally! With this public exposure, punctuated by the rage of the riots, things are bound to change!" They did not.

The riots and those that followed in other cities around the nation fed the fires of racism. That's when Izy became convinced that King was correct in his approach. She read everything she could about Reverend King. One thing that caught her attention was that he got his ideas from a man in India named Mahatma Gandhi. So Izy read about Gandhi.

It was a new concept for her: Win by refusing to fight back. She read about the salt mine campaign of civil disobedience in India when the British ruled over the Indian people in their own country. Hundreds and hundreds of Indian citizens had willingly walked into beatings. As they fell to the side, they were pulled away so the next in line could step up to be clubbed to the ground. It continued over and over until the British were exhausted by their own brutality. What was this? Sacrifice and surrender to the brutality of another until the other comes face to face with the devil inside?

Izy remembered the feelings she had in the airplane on the way to Illinois. She began to see the grand design. Not a design in the way of a plan, but more like meaning or purpose. To give meaning to our existence by choosing to see beyond ourselves and serve a higher purpose. A little overwhelming, but it felt very fine. Still, Izy knew she would never have the courage to walk up to a soldier knowing he would club her to the ground. Izy was having enough trouble living with her mistake of being so naïve about the Captain.

Others were adjusting to the new America as well. While Reverend Martin Luther King was gaining momentum and respect, the gangs of Los Angeles were quietly forming underground repositories for rage and backlash. When the time was ripe, they would reemerge and be called the Black Panthers.

FRIENDSHIP

For days, Izy sorted and sifted through the events at Santa Barbara Island, analyzing how she had been incredibly, unforgivably stupid. "Why had it not occurred to me what was up with that situation? I should have known! Am I the greatest idiot who ever lived? Grandy would never have been so naïve! I will have to do better in the future."

Izy decided two things: She wouldn't tell anyone about Santa Barbara Island, not even Ronny, and she needed a real job. It wasn't that she was less adventuresome. Santa Barbara had been a wake-up call. She was not as prepared for life as she had assumed. She was neither invincible nor infallible. She went to see Uncle Willy.

"I think it's a sign of hope that you come to this conclusion, Isabella. Frankly, we've all been a bit worried about you."

"You've been worried about me? Who's we?"

"Uncle Micheil and I have talked." Isabella's face warmed. "And we both think you're off kilter."

"Kilter?"

"Yes, not that it's your fault. It's entirely due to the environment in which you were raised." Something was irritating Izy. "But this shows good sense. Of course, I'll help you out in any way I can. First let's talk about the car. No more silly, old convertibles. They are unreliable and cost a fortune, too. You can't lock them, and soft tops can be cut open. They're not safe. What if you'd flipped the thing over? Uncle David's the car expert. We'll get you something reliable, American built, not too expensive. It probably won't be new."

About halfway through her Uncle's "coaching," Izy stopped supplying her undivided attention. She didn't like the sound of any of this, but she felt it best to surrender to the advice, at least until she could get back on her feet, both financially and psychologically. "Sounds good," she concurred. "Sure, Uncle David, it doesn't have to be new. But can it have a little pizzazz? I don't want to drive a washing machine."

"We'll see. Now, about the job, I can get you an interview for a position as an operator."

"You mean like dial 'O' for operator?"

"Exactly. The Phone Company is a great place to start. Look at what it's done for me. I have a home, cars—everything anyone could reasonably want. All thanks to The Phone Company and years of dedication on my part, I must add. You can dedicate yourself to a job and who knows how far you could go." Izy swallowed deeply as she listened. "You could be a supervisor or even a manager. You'd have to buckle down and work hard."

"I'm not afraid of hard work," she said, trying not to think of herself as supervisor in some office. She didn't mention the nasal voice impersonations of long-distance operators echoing in her head.

She started work at The Phone Company. From the beginning, there was an order to things. Rules were straightforward and strictly enforced. She started out listening to an experienced operator working the job. She caught on with ease and was assigned to her own position at the huge switchboard, a supervisor seated behind her. She worked from prescribed scripts. Creativity was discouraged or forbidden.

The work was easy, boring. Izy daydreamed about being on a ship in the Caribbean, standing on the bowsprit, riding the waves. But the dream always ended up at the Red Witch Inn that last night with the Captain. She collected a paycheck, meager, but regular, and counted herself fortunate.

She and her uncles came to a compromise: A nine-year-old Chevy with a hard top for Uncle Willy, an engine that passed Uncle David's inspection, a blue and white interior, and modest payments for Izy. As Uncle Willy gave the car one last examination, David put his hand on Izy's shoulder. When she looked up at him, he winked at her and smiled. In that brief moment, she knew there was value to having these men in her life. Then she felt terribly sad and fought to keep the tears from rushing to her eyes.

The very next paycheck was enough for a month's rent, and Izy moved out. She took with her only what was needed or dear to her heart. Missy begged her not to go. Izy begged her mother to come with her. In the end, they parted. Izy wept as she drove off, but didn't look back.

She met new friends at work who were not at all like Captain, not wild, in their own groove. They hung out in bars, approved of each other, and lived for the next good time. Izy felt attracted to their assured attitude, the sense of being part of a pack, and the predictability of their lifestyle. She partied but stayed out of bedrooms and backseats. She discovered vodka: She mastered the art of building, then sustaining a buzz, and recognizing the signs just before she went blind, or fell over drunk. Soon she was good at achieving the delicate equilibrium. Contemplation of higher callings and the meaning of life no longer fit the shape of her mind.

Although she was glad to be free of the nightmare house, Izy still returned to visit her mother.

"Here's your mail, honey."

"Thanks." Izy noticed the large, ugly bruise as her mother handed her the mail. "You've hurt your arm."

"Yes, I'm so clumsy. Banged into something."

Izy wondered and worried. "You know, you should come with me. Pack up your things. I'll help you. Let's get you out of here. We could make a plan if you want. You don't have to come right now."

Missy replied, "If God wanted me to leave your father, He'd give me a sign. I took a vow for better or for worse. I can't break that vow without God telling me to do so."

"There's been a neon fucking sign over this house for years: "LEAVE NOW! RUN FOR YOUR LIFE!""

"Mind your language, Isabella!" Missy admonished, then continued in her usual gentle tone, "In Ephesians 5, Paul tells us that a wife is to submit herself unto her husband as unto the Lord."

"I can't believe that God wants you to be abused by this nut! I don't care what Paul said. I bet there's nowhere that God said stand by your man even if he's cruel! What about the duty of the husband to the wife?"

"Jesus loves me just as he loves you and your father. I believe Jesus is going to heal Gunter and, in the meantime, he'll take care of both of us, because I've asked him to do so."

Izy felt a familiar box close around her head and she changed the subject. The house deteriorated with each visit. The visits were all the same and grew shorter and shorter.

Izy read her mail: a class newsletter from a student who kept everyone up to date. It contained the usual bragging from the preppies now in colleges across the states. "Rah, rah for the suck butts," she thought. At the bottom of one of the inside pages was a small square filled with a block of text headed "Vietnam Update."

The item read: "War heats up and class of '65 hit hard with draft call-ups. Student Body President, Frank Duffy, in basic training at Fort Ord." The words gripped Izy. She didn't know him well. He was one of the preppies, clubbies, and a sosh, one of *them*. But he was one of *her* them. She knew his face, the sound of his voice, the way he walked. That little war was getting very close to home. It somehow mattered that Frank had been drafted and was probably going to war.

A year passed quickly. Izy visited Missy regularly, albeit briefly, each time looking for the next newsletter. She could have submitted an address change, but she didn't. The newsletter was a tether to her mother. It arrived every couple of months, not like clockwork. She ignored the latest exploits of the campus crowd and went straight for the little square. It grew over time. The first classmate to die was noted in the first quarter of 1966. After a while, it was common to see a list of dead or missing. Names like Cortez, Almaraz, and Fuentes. Later that year Veronica's brother, Matt, was drafted into the army. He was on his way to the jungle.

On the day shift at The Phone Company Izy felt management scrutiny; she transferred to graveyard. It was very different. The crew was on its own from midnight to 6:00 a.m. There were four to six operators, a lead, and a switchman in the back in case of equipment problems. They became a tight group.

The board was busy from midnight to 2:00 a.m. when the bars closed. Then things got crazy for an hour or so with everything from murder and mayhem to perverts and lonely, old drunks. It was certainly more interesting than days. And then, there were the quiet hours between 3:00 and 6:00 a.m.

The shift could relax, get loose. The switchmen played tricks on the operators and vice versa. They covered for each other and took extended breaks, exploring the building, leaving, bringing back food, celebrating birthdays with a cake—occasionally, a bottle of cheap champagne.

Izy resented management. She enjoyed the harmless impertinence of the graveyard shift. On the day shift, she had been noticed. Words like arrogant, difficult, argumentative, resistant were already being typed in her file alongside competency ratings of excellent and outstanding. She was flagrant in her dance along the boundary of rules, crossing it whenever she could, displaying an intemperate edge in her attitude.

She wore her hair longer now. Her dress took on a dark, sleek austerity that made her look poised and powerful but made others feel uncomfortable.

Church held no interest for her. She no longer attended Sunday service or gave thought to God. The only identification she had with God was that he lived in the house her mother refused to leave. That fact implicated God in some personal crime against humanity.

Ronny visited Izy's apartment, eager to spend time there. Izy embraced her and made it clear she was welcome and wanted. But Izy lived close to her work, which was inconvenient for Ronny, who was still in school. Ronny came on Friday nights and stayed over until Sunday afternoon, which soon slid into Sunday evening, and then Sunday late into the night. If Izy had to work the weekend Ronny came anyway, slept while Izy was at work, and hung out while Izy caught some sleep during the day. She met Izy's new friends; she approved of some, thought less of others.

Ronny had mixed feelings about Francine Gavin. Francy and Izy had become pals on the graveyard shift and ran together outside work most of the time. They shared things in common, and had things in common not spoken, but somehow understood. They were attracted to each other by their differences. The workers of the graveyard shift did not take the job to heart, preferring short-term gratification over long-term goals. But they were unique in their means of self-expression. The big redhead liked gossip and hair spray. Another, a shy brunette, had a hubby and kids. Francy had a weakness for sweets and men. Izy preferred alcohol and thrills.

Francy craved male companionship and usually found it. She was tall and curvaceous with long, dark hair that dusted the apex of her buttocks as she walked. When it came to men, she knew exactly what she wanted. She judged them based on looks and what she called animal magnetism. Izy called them sluts. They'd make love to Francine gladly, then disappear, leaving her to weep and wonder what had gone wrong.

On one visit to Francine's apartment, Izy let herself in, only to find the blues blaring from the stereo speakers and her friend nowhere in sight. "Francy? Where are you?" she yelled, heading for the bedroom.

Izy saw on the floor the heap of bedding, shaped suspiciously like Francy's backside. She pulled back the first layer and a foot appeared. Then, slowly, Francine emerged from a fetal position. She was in her underwear, her hair in tangles, makeup smeared down her cheeks.

Izy went down to the carpet beside her. "Come here, let's have a look at you. Ohhh, what a sorry thing you are."

Izy pulled Francy's limp body into her arms and gathered the comforter all around her. Now, now, tell me, what did the nasty Jerry do?" When there was no response, Izy just rocked and held her. Francy sobbed softly, and Izy wiped away the tears. Even in the depths of despair, in Izy's eyes, Francine looked beautiful.

"He wanted to break it off last night. But he comes in here and fucks me first, and then tells me!"

"Ah, the blob lives!"

"I hate you!"

"No, you don't. At least you're talking to me. You had me worried there for a minute."

"I'm through with men! I hate them all!"

"Might not be a bad idea, at least for a while, France, baby. I think you should just lay low and get your balance back." She was sitting up on her own now. "I swear I don't get it. Guys always talk about wanting a woman who's as interested in sex as they are. Then they find me, and they act like I'm a one-night stand."

"Madonna-whore. That's what they say. Jerry was not a one-night stand."

"One month. Big deal! You weren't here. It felt like a one-night stand this morning. I felt like a whore and he made me feel that way." She got up and threw the bedding vaguely in the direction of the bed.

"Well, maybe you should play harder to get. Be the Madonna for a change."

Francy stripped off her underwear and made her way to the bathroom, then turned on the shower and plopped down on the toilet. "Like you? Is that what you are? A Madonna? I don't understand you. What are you saving it for, anyway?"

"Let's just say the price isn't right. And no, I'm no Madonna." Izy got up and went to the open bathroom door.

"And you talk about me. What's that supposed to mean, Izy? The price isn't right? You sound like a whore. You talk so rough, but you act like a virgin." She paused, looking at Izy, her head cocked slightly, her chin jutting out defiantly.

Eyebrows raised, Izy said, "Well you can't have it both ways. Am I a whore or a virgin?"

"Sometimes I don't think you're even a woman," Francy said as she pulled open the door and stepped into the shower.

"What the hell is that supposed to mean?" Izy dropped the toilet seat cover? and sat down.

"I mean, you don't, well, you stiff-arm everyone. Plenty of guys are interested in you. And you're attractive. What's the deal? What are you saving it for? Always with the hard-ass, aloof act. You're neither." The water poured

156

over her as she scrubbed away the fingerprints of Jerry's crime.

"Who says I'm saving it? Besides, where do you, with the biweekly broken heart, get off telling me, with the sound, well-adjusted heart, how to run my sex life? You don't know who I am, not really. I didn't come here to be lectured and certainly, not by you." Francy was gorgeous and shiny with soap all over her body. Izy found it stimulating and annoying at the same time. "Got anything to drink?"

"I'm not lecturing. Yes, in the fridge. I just don't get you sometimes."

Izy stayed in the small living room, sipping a Coke and rifling old magazines until Francy came out with her hair up in a towel.

"Come here. Give me a hug and let's forget all this fussing," Francy said. "I'm sorry. I really am."

Reluctantly, Izy stepped up and pulled herself into Francy's body. She wrapped her arms around her friend, who was still damp and warm from the shower and smelling of lemons: Jean Naté. Nestling into her neck, Izy took a deep breath of the scent. "I didn't mean to be sharp. It's just that I don't like to see these guys walk all over you. And you let them. You invite them, actually. You're allowing them to hurt someone I love, and I want you to stop. Maybe I don't get any action, but I don't go through piles of blues albums." They let each other go.

Back in the bedroom Francy said, "I know. I got a problem. I admit it." She pulled out panties and a bra from her dresser drawer. "I see a guy that's got real magnetism and well, I'm just gone. That fast. I can't help it, I swear." She stepped into the panties, tiny and delicate. "I thought Jerry was, well, you know, the one. Maybe that sounds crazy, but there was a connection."

"I believe that France, but a connection can be just that: a sexual attraction, lust. It doesn't have anything to do with love. And it isn't 'The One' if it's all in your belly. It's got to be there, and there's got to be trust. Trust takes time. So love has to take time. You can't fall in love over margaritas!"

"Well, what's that all about anyway? Love! I'm not sure there is such a thing. I've never felt it. That's for sure."

"Sure there's love. There are all kinds of love. I love my mother. I loved my Grandy. Don't you love your mother?"

"I never knew her. She left for greener pastures when I was two. My father raised me."

"I didn't know. Sorry. Don't you love your father?"

"In a way, maybe. But I also hate him."

"Really? I hate mine, too! Why do you hate yours?"

"I hate him because he remarried!"

"That's not a reason to hate him. He's got a right to go on living."

"He married a woman who hates me. And because she hates me, she farmed me off on my father's brother and his wife whenever she could. And whenever she did that, my uncle would find a way to be alone with me and, well, you know." Her voice, which had been racing with a decided twinge of anger, trailed off. She glanced sideways to see Izy's reaction.

"He raped you?"

"He would have sex with me. I don't know if it was rape."

"Did you want to do it?"

"Not at first. But I figured it was just the way things were. So long as I had sex with him, things went okay while I had to stay there. So I went along, and I gotta say this: He taught me just about everything there is to know about it."

Izy watched Francy as she perused the inside of the refrigerator. She thought about Santa Barbara Island. Francy turned to look at her. "What?"

"Nothing. Just thinking." Izy wanted to be reciprocal, but she could not. She had the memory tucked away under lock and key and was afraid to set if free. "If you didn't want to do it, it wasn't just sex. I mean, if a girl doesn't want to have sex and for some reason she thinks she has to, well, it is rape. I think that's awful, France. Couldn't you tell your Dad?"

Francy held out a spoon to Izy, inviting her to share some Cherry Vanilla. Izy opted for an apple. "Are you kidding? My father thinks the world of his brother! I don't think he would have believed me. And I didn't think of it as rape. I thought of it as our secret. Is it rape if I consented? You think it was rape? I'm not sure." Izy opened a drawer, pulled out a knife, and began peeling her apple without even thinking about it.

"It was all so mixed up and complicated. But in the end, it all blew up in everyone's face. My aunt caught us fucking one day and had a fit. I, of course, was the villain, banned from ever going there again."

"Why, you, 'of course'?"

"Because that's how it was. Somebody had to take the rap. She called me a slut. She didn't think it was rape. There was a big brouhaha between the brothers. My uncle said I seduced him. My stepmother called me a whore and threw me out. I just, you know, hit the road."

"Just like that? Out?"

"Well, I was dating this guy in high school. So I went to his house, and we just sorta got married. But it didn't last."

"Just sorta got married? How can you 'just sorta' do a thing like that?"

"Well, we did. Doesn't matter. Didn't work out. Guess that's your point. Well, anyway, after the marriage broke up, I came down here from San Francisco. Then I got this glamorous job at The Phone Company. And that's my life story."

"Wow! I didn't know you were ever married. What did your father say to you?" Absorbed in Francy's story, Izy ate the apple skin as she dangled it in front of her, a comforting, familiar act she didn't even notice.

"He was angry—I'm not sure who he blamed the most: his brother, his brother's wife, or me for being the cause of all the trouble. And I'm not sure it was rape. See, after a while, I enjoyed..., well, it was like I had this power, you know? I could get him to do things for me. I'd promise him a blow job so he'd let me have the car or whatever. I seduced him, actually."

"Yes, but in the beginning, did you want to? Was he the first man you were with?"

"No and yes. I was a virgin the first time and, no, I didn't want to. It felt, well, dirty, and I tried to push him away." They were both remembering. "I was ashamed, you know? I'd never seen one and I'd never been seen, well, not since I'd got breasts and all. I hated it, okay? I hated it, and I hated him. But it happened, so that was that, and I just learned to use it to my advantage. So I guess in the end, I was as bad as he was."

"What did you think after the first time?"

"I thought it was disgusting. I locked myself in the bathroom and took a bath for an hour to get the feeling of filth off me. I remember that bath sometimes. I think of it a lot when something ugly happens, like this morning. It all feels like scum I can't get off me. You're right, men are scummy. Why do I fall for this shit?"

"Scummy, unreliable, and out to take advantage of a woman first chance they get. So keep your legs together, trust me. Did your father ever get over it?

I mean, did he ever see your side, say he was sorry?"

"We don't talk much. I call once in a while. I hang up if his witch of a wife answers. When we do talk, we talk about other things. I don't think I want to discuss it with him. You're the first person I've told since I left. So don't tell anyone else, okay?"

"Right. Who would I tell? I swear. Not a word."

"How did you lose it?"

Izy paused considering her options and made a decision. "I lost it to a brigand and a pirate."

"What?"

"Yep. At sea."

"Bullshit! No way!"

"Yes, it's true. I had an affair with the Portuguese captain of a schooner I crewed."

"I don't believe it! That doesn't sound like you at all. I've never even seen you flirt. In fact, I'd begun to suspect you might be, you know…, lesbian."

"I'm not a lesbian."

"Are you sure?"

"I would know! Besides, why does sex have to be defined by gender anyway? I mean it's just the manipulation of sexual organs for pleasure or procreation. What difference does it make what sex it is doing it? Well, I guess it does if you want kids. But if we're talking about morality, I would think that what you feel for the other person should carry the greater weight. Is there love between the two people? Are you being deceitful? Are you playing games? Or do you love the other person? Even if it is just for that moment."

"No way! Sex is sex. Love is love. One doesn't necessarily involve the other. I know that for a fact!"

"Well, then, that's nuts, plain nuts! But sometimes I think everyone in the whole world is nuts! I mean, have you ever thought about sex itself? It's pretty bizarre, really. Someone putting their tongue in your mouth, or vice-versa. Who thought that up anyway? Talk about a trust issue! Think of explaining it to a six-year-old. Then you begin to see how weird it really is."

"Well, everyone does it, and they have been doing it for a very long time. So it can't be that weird. It seems perfectly natural, and the only issues are with

160

society acting all snobby about what it is they do when no one else is looking."

"Society. Now there's an interesting concept. Social mores, the culture of the community of human beings. Civilization. There's a laugh!"

"What? You don't think we are civilized?!"

"I think we think we are. We don't carry around clubs or scratch our crotches in public; we pat ourselves on the back for being civil. And we'll never do better so long as we delude ourselves into thinking that we're okay. We don't see how primitive and completely insane we still are. What defines civilization is not its commitment to social behavior, but its commitment to social conscience. Indifference and complacency are the true measures of savagery. There are so many things that could be done to make life on Earth wonderful. But they are really big issues, really big. In fact, they are overwhelming, so we tend to just blow them off with easy phrases like 'What am I supposed to do about that?' or 'There's nothing I can do to make a difference.' Ultimately we allow ourselves to get away with doing nothing that matters."

Izy was starting to allow the things she'd put away to come to the surface. "Vietnam, for example, or oppression of minorities, or women's rights, or anything! Don't you ever want to do something that really matters? Something important that matters?" With these thoughts came other feelings, discomforts, and memories. "I guess I'm full of hot air. But sometimes these feelings come up inside, and I get so tense as if I'm going to explode. I feel like I have to do something, whether or not I know what it is. It makes me crazy sometimes. Haven't you ever felt like you would explode?"

Izy looked at her friend, trying to assess whether Francy was someone Izy could trust. Bubbling up was a compulsion to confess her darkest thoughts: the thing for which she carried a tainted scar. "Have you ever wanted to kill someone?"

"No! Well, maybe slap them, or hit them over the head like in the cartoons, but I never actually thought about killing someone."

Izy reached out, calculating if it was safe, wanting to know what another human would think of her if she knew. "Well, I have. I don't think I could do it. But once I was so angry, so crazy, that I actually thought of doing it. I thought of how and everything."

"Who?"

Izy was still calibrating her senses. She paused, skipping a beat, then two... , "My father."

"You wanted to kill your own father?"

"He's not really my father." Regret for having said anything at all was overwhelming her. "I mean he is, but he's different than most and, oh, you'd never understand. I shouldn't have said anything."

"No, no, tell me," Francy said tenderly, recognizing the signs of a wound needing salve.

Reason told Izy to fluff this off and shut up. But this one box wanted to be opened. Izy was compelled by things she did not understand, only obeyed. "Once, I was so filled up with stuff. Not just him, but all kinds of crazy, and it made me... crazy! I thought I should kill him—at least he couldn't be mean anymore, not to my Mom, not to anyone. It was sick. I felt awful for thinking it. But sometimes, when things get crazy and I hear about things that make me feel, I don't know, all jumbled, like they just don't make sense, I think that maybe, well, maybe if only I had the courage to do something that mattered, I could make things better. Maybe I should have killed him."

They sat together in silence for a long time as if there was nothing to say after that. Izy wasn't sure if she should have said what she did. Then Francy came to Izy. They melted together as one, taking comfort in one another, if only briefly. Love has been described as the fractures of two psyches fitting together, making whole what is otherwise broken. In that moment, Izy found someone, like her fractured self, who could hear her darkness and still hold her. It mattered.

They talked a lot after that in easy conversations which, with each secret shared, each confidence kept, wove them more strongly together. To Izy, Francine was a wounded soul with whom she shared a bond of affinity and understanding. Life was never simple, nor was it always fair. It brought new experiences, not all of which fit into familiar patterns. Sometimes life was downright cruel, throwing odd shapes into the mix, asymmetrical inequity. Like a three-sided object: Francine, Ronny, and Izy in the middle.

Izy planned a party at the apartment for Saturday and invited the gang from work. Friday night when Ronny arrived, Izy was filling an empty, cleaned milk carton with water to put in the freezer, making a brick of ice to cool the punch. Ronny was full of excitement, her graduation only weeks away. Would Izy come? Ronny's dad had gotten her a job at Southern California Edison, where he worked. Izy listened and sipped a martini until it was time to leave for work.

Ronny went to bed. In the morning, Izy grabbed some zzzs, then got up to prepare.

Ronny and Izy shopped in the afternoon, came back, and put out chips, dips, cheese, and crackers. Izy made a killer punch: frozen fruit concentrates diluted with vodka, wine, and a little soda.

"What are you going to wear?"

"A pale blue, taffeta dress, hemline to the floor with pearls and long, white gloves."

"Well, I can see where your brain is. I mean for the party tonight, not the senior prom! I'm wearing jeans and this tank. Too casual? Waddaya think?" Izy's body had grown tall and slender with broad shoulders, narrow hips, a flat butt and breasts that were adequate but small. Her hair, a sun-streaked reddish-brown, skin tanned, and brown eyes you could fall into forever, or that could cut through steel, depending on her mood.

"Casual, yes. But that suits you. Good color. You look best in earth tones. I wish you'd lay off the black. It's too harsh for you. I'm going to wear this!"

"Whoa, are you sure? Whoa. Tiny straps, cut, well, not like you usually wear, Ronny. Let me see it on."

"I'm going to shower now. Then I'll put it on. Wait till you see."

"Fine. But first, help me get stuff ready. Put the frozen milk carton in the punch bowl with these frozen concentrates." Izy was unpacking the bags of groceries they'd bought.

"Okay. I'm excited about tonight. But the prom, that's really exciting. I'm going with this guy from my history class. He's very nice and good looking."

"I'm surprised your dad ever agreed to let you go."

"He said no at first, but Mom begged him and I think he felt a lot of pressure. You know, it is prom after all. Why didn't you go to yours?"

"Wasn't asked. You know, it's strange, not even by an ugly boy or a dumb boy. No one even asked me if I was going."

"Are you sad?"

"Not really. I didn't have any taste for that sort of thing. I was a belated blossom. No, I was a reluctant rose, a no-show at the puberty prom… ."

"Okay. I get it. But now, aren't you a little sad?"

"I didn't want to go to the prom and if I had any sadness, which I do not, it would only be due to the fact that it's an event of a lifetime, you know, one of those things that comes once and only once."

"Yeah, in fact, I think that's why my dad caved and let me go. You know, he's just trying to look out for me." Ronny looked at Izy wanting affirmation. She got none.

"That's why he follows you on dates, spies on you, and picks out all your clothes, huh? Oh, never mind. I'm glad you're going to the prom."

"You have this thing about you, you know that?"

"What?"

"You have an air of inaccessibility. That's why no one asked you."

"What's that supposed to mean?"

"If you're tight with a person, then you're really tight. To everyone else, you're aloof, distant. You run the relationship by remote control, and then you're off somewhere else. Okay, for example, you never question anyone about who they are or where they've come from. Do you know why you don't do that? Because if you ask them, then they can ask you, and you don't want to be probed in any way. You want to be in control and, what, monitor your life from a safe distance?"

"Monitor my life? I'm in my life big time. More than you're in yours. Besides, who the hell cares? It's party time!" Izy turned up the stereo and danced back into the kitchen, beating the flat of her hands on the bar between the kitchen and the living room as the truth was drowned out by rock and roll.

When Ronny came out of the bedroom after her shower, she looked completely different. Her hair was swept up, revealing her neck, almost bare shoulders, and a touch of cleavage. Izy, pouring vodka over the concentrates and ice, was taken aback. "Ronn! What in the world are you doing?

"I just want to be different. I'm entitled to see what I look like all grown up."

"Well, you look all grown up, all right. I think you better be careful tonight, the way you're glowing and looking very sexy. Take it easy, girl! We don't want you breakin' any hearts tonight."

"I wouldn't mind if I broke one or two."

"Well, one or two." Izy couldn't stop looking at her. She was dazzling.

"Don't bend down like that. I can see your navel! Ronn, are you sure you should wear that dress?"

"I want to be alluring."

"Yeah, well, you'll lure all right. Just be careful." Izy wanted to take Ronnie in her arms and cover her up. To Izy she was sweet, innocent Ronny, now quite appealing.

"Ummm, good!" Izy declared the punch a success. "Watch this stuff, its dynamite." Izy cut up lemons, limes, and oranges and dumped them into the bowl, then added maraschino cherries. She smiled and raised her eyebrows up and down.

The doorbell rang. Izy opened the door, then Francy spotted Ronny seated across the room, "Oh, my God! Look what we have here! Up, up, turn around. Get a load of you, girl. I approve, honey!" And then Izy was even more uncomfortable.

From then on, the door was kept mostly open as an array of friends and acquaintances arrived. The music was loud but inviting. Some of the neighbors wandered in. Izy kept an eye on Ronny. Izy sipped punch, talked to her friends, and watched Ronny talking to some guy she'd not seen before. She sat on the couch chatting, "Say, know who that guy is over there?"

Someone wanted to dance. While dancing, Izy lost sight of Ronny and went looking for her. She found her in the bedroom making out with the new dude. Izy chased them out on the pretext of needing something out of the dresser. Izy felt guilty, uneasy, but continued to keep an eye on Ronny all night. She spent the better part of the evening feeling more nervous than made sense; after all, Veronica was a grown woman now.

Sometime around 3:00 a.m., the punch bowl empty, the music unattended, and everyone gone, Izy and Ronny went to bed. At the crack of dawn, Izy heard shrieking coming from the bathroom: "Oh, my God! Oh, no!"

Izy stumbled to the bathroom door, expecting to see blood or something. "Wha… . Oh hell, Ronny, it's just a love bite. Big deal. So you got a hickey." But Ronny was white as a ghost. Something else had to be the problem.

"Ohhhh, noooo," she moaned more than spoke. The sound was dark and foreboding. "It's not just that. You don't understand. He'll kill me!"

"Who?" Izy thought for a second, "Your Dad? You're worried what he'll do when he sees it?" Ronny nodded, tears welling up in her eyes. "Just wear turtlenecks for a few days, or we can put makeup on it."

"You don't understand. He will see it!"

"No, you don't understand. We won't let him. We'll cover it up."

"He will see it! You don't understand!"

Izy stopped talking and made Veronica look up, look her in the eye. Tears were cascading now, falling down Veronica's face. There was desperation in her eyes. Her face was contorted in a painful scrunch. Izy reached out and took her by the arms. "Ronn?"

"He'll see, he'll see… ," she trailed off, her unspoken words a plea for her friend to understand her secret. And then Izy did. She knew and released her hold on Ronny, who then slumped to the floor against the wall.

"Oh, my God! And you think it's somehow your fault? That bastard! Ronn, Ronn." Izy could do nothing for her right then. Ronny had to go where this was going to take her… , for now. Her hysteria had awakened Izy to something like a jigsaw puzzle that was now fitting together a thousand moments and expressions—a silence here, a glance away there—that over the years had gone mostly unnoticed. Finally, the ugly picture was all too clear.

Izy sat on the floor of the bathroom with her broken friend until she was quiet. Then Izy pulled the spent body up and into the bedroom, gently laying her down next to her on the bed. "It's okay, Ronny girl. He's not going to see. You're safe now. He'll never touch you again because you're not going back there. No. No. You're safe, Ronny girl. You're safe here with me."

For a while, Ronny accepted the comfort of Izy's arms and said nothing. Then it began. Her mind began to engage. "I have to go home. How can I not? How could I explain that? I should never have bought that dress."

"Forget the dress, Ronn. The dress was nothing. Or maybe everything. Maybe it was just your way of arranging an escape. It doesn't matter. You don't have anything to explain—not dresses, not hickeys, not anything. If there's explaining, let *him* do it."

"My mother! Oh, God! She can't know."

"It's time she did, Ronn. Way past time that she did."

"She won't be able to handle this."

"She's a grown-up. She'll handle it. She has no choice. You've handled her burden for too long."

"I can't let anyone know. I can't! I'm so ashamed!"

166

"Yes," Izy said, holding Ronny's face up so she could look into hers, "You feel ashamed because that's what he wants you to feel. But it's not your shame. It's his, and it's time he took it all back! Ronny, you haven't done this thing. He's done this thing! You are going to have to be very brave. I will help you. But it's you who must be brave." Izy got up.

"Where are you going?"

"I'm calling my mother. She'll know what to do."

"Do you have to?"

"I think it's best. Trust me."

Missy came immediately. Ronny told her story. "It started when I was eleven, during the time when we weren't so close, Izy, remember? When you were in junior high school." Izy felt a sharp stab of conviction. She did remember.

"He would come to me in the night when everyone was asleep. He would put his hand over my mouth and shush me very quietly. At first, I was startled. Then I became accustomed to the visits. He would want to touch me. At first, just rubbing my chest and little pinches, you know, on my nipples. Then it progressed. He touched me lower and then put his finger in me, then more fingers. Then he wanted me to touch him. On and on, almost every night, it became our secret, he and I. Pretty soon I felt trapped. He was my father. He was in charge. He said not to tell. And then because I didn't, I became part of it. I couldn't say anything then without admitting that I was, I don't know, naughty, something awful. I couldn't do anything. All this time... ," she trailed off, unable to find the next words.

"You'll have to tell your mother, Veronica," Missy said.

"I can't tell her."

"Yes, you can. She has to know. We'll be with you, right here. If you want, I'll call her and tell her she has to come here right now."

"Oh, God! What have I done?"

"Ronn, you've done nothing except been seduced by someone you trusted. This isn't your doing. You've got to believe that!"

Missy placed the call to Ronny's mother. She calmly told her that something had come up and that it was most urgent. She should come to Izy's apartment right away, and it would be best if she did so discreetly, at least for now.

Ronny's mother's face told a story as her daughter spoke. There was shock but not surprise. The knowledge that what her daughter said was the truth spilled out of her eyes, choked in her throat. Mother and daughter wept together, sharing the burden equally for the first time. Ronny's mother assessed the extent to which she had been aware and ignored the signs.

Missy was a rock. She stood strong and judged no one. She kept the priority clearly in focus for them all. She encouraged and comforted. She read softly from the Bible and prayed for them. She told the two women they had to be strong for each other. She told Ronny she was blameless, and she told the mother that she could make it up to her daughter if she took the responsibility of handling things at home.

Missy was sure Ronny should not go back there, that she had to leave the home for good, right away. Missy knew just what to say. Izy was proud of her and wondered why she couldn't do the same for herself.

Ronny's mom went home, packed up her daughter's clothes, and brought them back to Izy's apartment. The father flew into a rage and cursed Isabella when he heard what had transpired. He called Isabella's apartment. "Someone ought to teach you not to meddle in matters that don't concern you! You don't know anything about my family. Who do you think you are, breaking up my family and upsetting everyone and everything!"

"I know I'm a friend to your daughter and you're a pig!"

"You send her home immediately or I will come and get her!"

"No. But here's what I will do. If you call here again or dare go near Ronny, I'll report your incestuous behavior to the authorities. I'll call your work and tell them. I think you should be reported and locked up. For Ronny's sake, I have agreed to keep quiet for now. But please, come on. Be a big shot. Cause some trouble here. Give me just the tiniest excuse to rat you out to anyone who will listen!" He never called again.

He did attend graduation. Izy was looking for him. He came in and sat at the back of the auditorium. His eyes were riveted on the daughter he had violated. He wept when her name was called. Izy found it difficult to keep from walking up and slapping him. She tried to remember that he was a sick man, deserving of pity, not hatred. But she hated him all the same. He didn't approach his daughter. He left after he'd seen her accept her diploma. Amid all the rage, there was a hint of sorrow that stung and made Izy even angrier.

Nothing really changes from day to day. There is no waking one morning to find everything fixed and the past expunged. Actions and inactions linger, shackled to the heart as life shifts from yesterday to tomorrow. Izy was just learning this. She looked around at the people she knew. They all had secrets or crazy people in their lives who drove them insane. Everyone seemed to stumble along, passing the insanity back and forth.

Grandy had told her, "When a child had a temper on, best to send them wood chopping. Takes a lot of fuel to chop trees into kindling. Good use for anger. That's why God gives us vexations—so we can chop enough wood to cook and keep warm in the winter!"

BAD MOON RISING

Ronny, amid unsettling changes, found reassurance and refuge in Isabella. The jolt of a new life without benefit of a plan or conscious thought requires a period of adjustment. Ronny recovered quickly. She pulled together her reserves in remarkable time with a maturity, pragmatism, and optimism that impressed, and even surprised, Izy.

Isabella's apartment was far from the Southern California Edison offices where Ronny worked in the Land Rights Department, so rooming with Izy wasn't practical long term. After she acquired a set of sheets, blanket, dishes, utensils, two pots, and a frying pan, Ronny moved into her own apartment. Although the two friends spent time together occasionally, they were walking separate paths in new directions.

Ronny knew Isabella had done for her all she could, and that no one could heal the damage done to her soul. It brought a great sadness to Izy—she could read this in Ronny's face. And Ronny saw the sadness in Isabella's eyes. Without allowing herself to think of it on a conscious level, she made a decision: To survive, Ronny needed to put some distance between them so she could start putting this behind her.

Francine became Isabella's constant companion. She scarcely concealed her pleasure in Ronny's disappearance. Maneuvering to fill the void, Francy often stayed overnight at Izy's apartment. Isabella was grateful for her company, so she overlooked any ulterior motives she might have suspected.

At times, when Francy was preoccupied with some whirlwind romance, Isabella felt a hole inside. Despite the noise and activity around her, there was a sense of aloneness that made her yearn for Grandy. Already she had suffered great loss in her life. Rather than mourn, she put the sorrows and anguish away in tiny boxes in her mind and moved quickly to the next thing. Often, looking in the mirror, she'd say to the person looking back, "Ready. Bring it!"

When Francy was there everything was a little louder, and it filled the emptiness Izy felt. Francine was all records and radio, talk about men, romance, and love. And when she was blue, well, that was all-consuming in itself.

Missy didn't like Francy. "Francine is self-absorbed, a loose woman who's jealous of anyone or anything you find interesting, Isabella. I don't understand why you can't see that and the danger she represents!"

Isabella recalled that Grandy had said jealousy would ruin a person. "She's not jealous, just insecure. If anything, I feel sorry for her."

"It's jealousy, and it will only grow over time and come to no good end." Isabella determined from then on to do her best to keep her mother and Francy apart, which wasn't that difficult. An invisible wall had risen between Izy and Missy. Even so, Isabella continued to stop by, always intrigued by the little square in the high school newsletter that had grown to fill a whole column. It included editorials about the growing sentiment against President Johnson and his escalation of hostilities and bombing raids, as well as the Gulf of Tonkin Resolution that was cited as justification for the President's actions. Interested in the war from a personal perspective, Izy began traveling up to UC Berkeley— hopping planes when she could, driving when she couldn't—to participate in on-campus sit-ins and candlelight vigils.

She was not alone. Young people were making their voices heard. Kennedy had been murdered. Johnson was a liar. And as Johnson's popularity sunk, disillusions about the war surfaced, tainting America's image in the eyes of the world, but mostly to Americans.

Parents told their sons to be loyal Americans. Fathers shared stories from their wars and told their children that it was an honor to die for your country. The difficulties emerged when it was clear that parents assumed a cause was noble when it was unequivocally deemed so by the government. Young people's faith and trust were not that of their parents. Vietnam was murky. Sons did not understand why they were expected to die. The cause was polluted with contradictions. Families were splitting apart over it.

Missy and Isabella couldn't even bring it up without igniting anger, fear, and other ugly feelings. Trouble was brewing. The music was angry. Television had become a battlefield, and it wasn't all from Vietnam. Isabella saw it on the news as darkness and night encroached. At first there were sketchy fragments. Then all programming was interrupted by a tape of the great man standing on a balcony waving to people. He was shot dead. Assassinated, like Kennedy, like Gandhi. Martin Luther King had been murdered. It was like having the wind knocked out of you—an exhalation with no way of taking air back in.

"Why is everything so crazy in America?"

Uncle Clay answered, "It's the price of freedom. In order to be free, we have to endure the full spectrum of human desire and expression. There is desire to do good deeds, seek a higher meaning of life, to act nobly and outside ourselves. But there are also desires fueled by fear and destructive forces that foster cruelty and hatred."

"That's just what Grandy would have said," Izy thought to herself. When Isabella talked with Uncle Clay, he discussed issues and inquired about her thoughts. She enjoyed their conversations.

"There always seem to be wicked people. Maybe it's not so good to have so much freedom."

"Nonsense. Don't you want to be free to express yourself?"

"Yes. But I'm not wicked."

"There's the potential for wickedness in all of us. We each choose which parts of ourselves to express, virtue or wickedness." Izy recalled the night of hatred and her own wicked thoughts toward her father. Uncle Clay continued, "Now there's the crux of it. In order for you to enjoy freedom, you have to be willing to endure every single person's interpretation of their freedom as well, and that's not enough. You have to be willing to defend their rights to that freedom, even if you refute everything they say. Freedom demands participation. Liberty demands vigilance! That's the price we must pay. The day we stop caring, we take a step toward tyranny!"

"So what about the war, Uncle Clay. What do you think?"

"I think the commies are their own worst enemy. We only need to stoke our own fires. Southeast Asia is a political bog! That's all it is: politics!"

Peaceful protests on America's campuses were drawing more and more attention. School officials were stunned when rallies brought out thousands, not hundreds. In panic they called in law enforcement; they were afraid things would get out of hand. Students were organizing demonstrations across the country to express their outrage and anger.

The decade ended with increasing confrontations. Film coverage of both wars aired on the evening news. It was common for the National Guard to be summoned to ensure that demonstrations remained peaceful and orderly. When they did not, the Guard would use tear gas to break up the crowd. The soup was about to boil.

In May of 1970, the course veered sharply at Kent State University in Ohio, the state where Izy's great, great uncle had first settled and mined for coal: O-Hi-Oh. National Guardsmen confronted and dispersed the student antiwar protesters with a barrage of tear gas. Soon afterward, soldiers opened fire into a group of fleeing students; four young people were killed. Izy was shocked. "Ohio once prided itself on its stand against slavery. Where was their sense of freedom of expression?" The national sky turned foreboding and dark.

"If students are going to defy orders, they are taking their life into their hands. I can't see why you're surprised. I've been telling you this would happen!" Missy exclaimed.

"The students were fleeing. They weren't defying any order," Isabella argued.

"I'm certain that if the National Guard fired, they were provoked!"

"That's why one student was shot in the back, huh, Mom?"

"We weren't there. We don't know what really happened. The Guardsmen themselves are young, confronted with angry young people. They had to be nervous!"

"Young and in the National Guard for one reason and one reason only: to avoid Vietnam. They're doing what they can to escape getting killed. That's why they're nervous. They are looking into the faces of their own generation protesting the thing they themselves are afraid of in the first place."

"Well, at least they are doing a decent thing. Working for their government, not against it!"

"Right. Working for their government shooting students in the back. Did you actually read this article?"

"An article that was written by the liberal press. They are on the side of the communists, if you ask me. If they weren't, they wouldn't print this nonsense. It's demoralizing the entire country."

"Only because this whole war is demoralizing. In fact, it's immoral. We have no business in Vietnam to begin with!"

"I think it's terrible they bring this into our homes every night. Now, this. It's awful."

"It is awful, mom! And like it or not, it is in our homes. You know Matthew's in Vietnam? Don't you get it? It is in our homes!"

Isabella felt a sense of urgency, dedication, and ire. The list of the dead included people she knew and admired. These were boys she had gone to school with, sat next to in class—now they were dead or missing. God only knew where they were or if the missing were being mistreated.

Ronny and Izy often discussed the war. Izy always asked about Matt, so Ronny read his letters to her over the phone or brought them when they met. Izy would hold the letters and smell them, searching for hints of what it might be like, allowing herself to imagine the place from where they had been written, the person who had written them, and the horror that surely surrounded him. One letter had a dirt smudge on the paper. Izy rubbed it until some came off in the swirls of her thumb. For a while she wouldn't wash that thumb, it gave her a feeling of connection to Matt. She read the letter again and again, studying the pen strokes and sensing the unexpressed stress, likely terror, behind them.

Ronny, dear Ronny,

It's not like I thought it would be. When we are at the company base, the flag waves, they play Stars and Stripes and tell us we are heroes, and that we should be proud. But in the jungle, it's hard to remember all that. I try to think about duty and country, but the truth is, sometimes, I'm just thinking about how much I want to live and how I don't want to die in this bug-infested place. I don't mean to complain. You're the only one I tell this to. I am proud to serve my country. What upsets me the most is that in the cities, the people are okay. But out here in the country, they treat us like the enemy. It's hard to believe we're doing the right thing when the people we are here to protect turn on us. I miss you, and Mom and Dad. I hope to be home someday soon.

Love, Matt

Air—a few hundred feet up, sweet, thick like a veil—had to be parted as we sat perfectly still listening to Iron Butterfly: In-A-Gadda-Da-Vida screaming over the speaker between the beats of the Huey's rotor. The smell of jungle and sweat, deafening sounds, the weight of boots, packs, weapons, and ammunition—all helping to pull us out the door. On the ground, we beat it for cover as the last thwaps fade and segue into a moment of pure dread when that sound—the last thread of home, country, father, protection—disappears.

By day we press east and north through tall grasses. We move along a river, then back into the jungle as night falls. We melt into the trees, dark faces, tired bodies, sleepless fears. A night with little rest transforms into gray light: another trek, deeper, farther still.

There is a small band ahead near a clearing: Viet Cong. We drop down and circle in both directions, cutting off any escape they might have. Someone signals and sends a grenade through the thick air, low, into the clearing. Then, rising up, we fire at anything that moves until nothing does. Twelve bodies, all young, men in black pajamas and headbands. Are there more?

We fan out searching, ferreting those who remain. I'm thinking about who

174

had made the kills in the clearing. No one knows. My eyes electric, sensitive to motion, peculiarity, and the slightest indication of danger lurking.

My brain catches a pixel of light, a flicker. I freeze, scanning. There: a body, lithe, flush against the trunk of a tree. Nearly invisible but for a twinkle of light. An eye. Bold, dangerous, hiding in plain sight. I squeeze off a single shot. The apparition might not be alone. Then a sound, thick, guttural, he slumps out of sight in the undergrowth. Dead for sure. A weapon cracks. Close by, a body falls, one of ours. It's a trap! Dropping down, signaling to fall back, someone radios for help: Fumigate the jungle!

The minutes seem like hours. Overhead jet engines come out of the distance, shrieking: whoosh! An explosion. Another, and another. Balls of flame and black smoke bombard us. The ground shakes. The smell of exotic chemicals chokes the air. I can't breathe. A Cobra swoops in to pick up the wounded comrade while the rest of us clear a line through the jungle, sizzling and toxic.

Dark settles under a half moon high in the Southeast Asian sky.

In the jungle, too dank to produce a snap of a twig, is a rustle of greens. I jerk awake, watching—alert and tense. We are in trouble. There. Movement in the shadows. They begin to weave toward the light of open grass, down low in the darkness, creeping, then up to take a look around. A single shot brings a heavy package falling from above me, black, crashing into the foliage and to the wet sticky earth. Another shot. Nothing. Then rustling on my left: a struggle, a scream, a groan, and a thud. Huddled in the grasses, low as snakes, we wait. Before long, the greenery comes alive with bodies moving from the jungle. The radio: "Found out! Compromised! Come get us out!" Weapon fire erupts, cutting down the first wave, then a second, but still they come. "Come get us out!" Several bodies fall with shrieks of pain, metal tearing their flesh. "Come get us out!"

Izy sat upright in bed gasping for air, eyes searching the darkness, believing a bullet was about to pierce her heart. "Matthew!" Izy cried out in the silence of her room. If only for a split second, the dream had transported her to another country where she had tasted terror and traded fear for survival. It was another five minutes before her heart rate slowed, allowing her to take a deep breath— she was grateful it had all been a nightmare.

Isabella spent her spare time at protests, where she was frequently hauled off in mass roundups, fingerprinted, and charged with disorderly conduct or unlawful assembly. Later, she'd be let go or put on probation. Isabella didn't care. She was compelled to flail at something. Isabella wanted to bleed.

As time progressed, Izy's work attitude degenerated. In 1969 a day was set aside as War Moratorium Day. Those who held antiwar sentiments were either to boycott work or go in in protest wearing black armbands. Even though she wasn't scheduled that day, Isabella went into the office dressed in army fatigues she had bought at the army surplus; she distributed armbands she'd made. She was summarily thrown out by security and written up for insubordination and "seditious behavior." It was a means of telling her to get in line with the program.

The Phone Company had strict rules and took security seriously. Izy was to understand that they weren't going to treat such measures lightly. They suspended her for two weeks without pay and put her on probation.

Upon her return to The Phone Company, Isabella began talking to her fellow workers about her antiwar angst. Some were younger and shared similar opinions. Isabella was happy to exploit the situation. She had a plan.

The capture and control of communication is one of the most critical aspects of a successful revolution. The switchboards ran both sides of a long room. Each side held thirty positions and each position consisted of a dozen twin cords. Izy and her coworkers started at the ends of the boards and worked toward the middle. They dialed the main number at Norton Air Force Base, one of three military bases located near The Phone Company. They dialed out through both cords of each set and every set in each position. Then they closed the keys and let them ring into the base indefinitely. Impulses—1,440 of them— fired through the system simultaneously, all destined for one number. Certainly the number had multiple incoming lines, but not that many. Directing a test call to Norton, they got an "overloaded circuit" recording: Their plan had worked. After successfully blowing up Norton's switchboard, they went on to the next military base on the list. Once she had done it, Isabella was flooded with satisfaction—and terror.

"Oh, my God. We did it!"

"What if we get caught?"

"We can't get caught. How could they know?"

"But what if they can, and we do?"

"Listen!" Isabella said. "So what if we do? We did it for a reason. It shouldn't matter if we get caught. We've sent a message in protest of the military establishment!"

Nothing happened for 24 hours; it seemed like they were in the clear. But the second night when Isabella came through the door, she was detoured off into a conference room. They were waiting for her.

"These gentlemen are Special Service Investigators, Stevens and Parker. They have some questions for you, Miss Reinhardt. Sit down, please." Mrs. Langley, the head of operations, said; she gestured to a chair across from the men. Isabella sat down, her hands and feet ice cold. She straightened her back and repeated to herself, "Relax, stay calm."

"We understand that two nights ago a number of phone calls were placed from this location to Norton Air Force Base and other military facilities. Do you know anything about that, Miss Reinhardt?"

"Is there a problem?"

"Do you know anything about the calls?"

"We place calls to Norton from here probably every night."

"These were not ordinary calls, Miss Reinhardt. They were numerous and I think they would not have passed casually without notice. You were on duty that night. Did you make any of these calls?"

"Is it a crime to make phone calls?"

"Actually, it is Miss Reinhardt. If you used the equipment in this building to make unauthorized calls, or if you used the equipment to intentionally damage other equipment or, worst of all, if you used it in an act of sabotage, then it is a very serious crime, indeed—it's a felony. Now, what knowledge do you have of the incident that transpired two nights ago?"

Isabella took in a deep, slow breath to buy time, trying to assess the severity of the situation. She didn't like what she deduced. "Are you arresting me?"

"No, we are questioning you. However, your cooperation will determine whether or not you or your cohorts are arrested in the future. So I think you better explain what happened two nights ago in operations."

"Well, since this is 'very serious,' I don't think I should say anything. You might misinterpret whatever I might say."

"Very well, if you refuse to talk, we can't make you, right now. But we will talk to everyone who was on duty that night. Someone is going to tell us what happened. And if no one does, then we will bring charges against everyone."

Isabella was sent home on suspension without pay until further notice. She held tight and didn't call anyone. After all, she was dealing with The Phone

Company: AT&T. AT&T was the most powerful corporation in the world, as powerful as most nations. Isabella knew what laying a "shoe," or a tap, on someone's phone line wasn't hard to do. Paranoia kept her company as she just waited.

When Isabella was summoned, she was told that the ranks had been broken. To avoid trouble, the others had given up her and Francy as the perpetrators. "That's not fair. I am ready to take the rap, but Francy had no singular role. They're just getting her for spite. Maybe because she's my friend or 'cause they don't like her. Francine had nothing to do with it. I instigated it. It was my idea and I am responsible. None of the others were in on it, although they did participate; they'd be lying if they said otherwise. But they wouldn't have, if not for me," she confessed.

Isabella was fired. Charges were filed for misdemeanor vandalism. Isabella was booked, but mysteriously the charges were later dropped. She was crushed. She was looking forward to being on trial and to have a forum for her opinions and her political dissent! On the other hand, The Phone Company didn't want a forum for anything or a public record of such a stupid stunt being perpetrated by an employee at one of their offices.

Though certainly disappointed, Isabella felt she had at least done something. Later she would come to see it differently. Later, she would be embarrassed that she had done it, let alone endangered peoples' jobs. At the time, however, Isabella felt like she had become part of something noble and worthy.

Out of work, Isabella was trying to figure out what to do next when the phone rang.

"We're at Daniel Freeman and she's pretty bad. You'd better get down here," Uncle Willy said with urgency.

Isabella raced to the hospital, slammed the car into a parking space, and burst through the doors. The desk clerk said she was in X-ray, downstairs. Isabella jumped into the elevator, descended, got off, and followed the signs as fast as she could. A hand from a gurney reached out to stop her as she passed; she pushed it aside, then looked again. There, on the gurney, was a bruised and discolored face, bloody and swollen beyond recognition—except Isabella knew it was Missy.

At first there was only a gasp from Isabella as she stood without breathing. She tried to look away but couldn't rip her eyes from the sight of her mother. Missy couldn't speak. Her mouth was swollen and her split lips were out of shape. Isabella fell to her knees beside her and sobbed—an act of selfishness, but the best she could do. Missy stroked her head with her hand.

Isabella struggled to get beyond her own pain. "Don't worry, Mom. I'll take care of you. I'll take care of everything and we'll get through this." Isabella was composing herself with images of Missy helping Ronny. "How bad is the pain?"

Missy rocked her hand back and forth. Isabella wanted to cup her face in her hands, but there was no part that was not damaged. Isabella held her one good hand. The other was in a splint.

"He beat her, of course. She dragged herself out to the front lawn and collapsed. Neighbors found her and called the ambulance. They called you but you didn't answer. So they called me. By the way, where were you?" Uncle Willy's query stung. The last person Isabella wanted to tell where she'd been was Uncle Willy.

"I had an appointment. My father probably got her twisted up in some convoluted conspiracy. Or maybe one of his imaginary people told him to do it. I was afraid it would come to this."

"You shouldn't have left her alone there with him."

"Excuse me? I shouldn't have left her? I begged her to come with me. You think I should have stayed in that house with her?"

"She's your mother."

Isabella felt a sting of guilt because deep inside, she agreed. Nonetheless, she muscled it out of the way of her anger, a much more comfortable emotion. "She's your sister! Where have you been all these years? What have you ever done to help her? Don't get in my face about what *I'm* supposed to do!" She was being brazen but felt responsible. She hated Uncle Willy for digging at a gaping wound. "Actually, this is maybe a good thing," she thought to herself, pulling back on track.

"Broken ribs, arm, and wrist in two places. Her front teeth are gone. One had been pushed up into her gums," Izy told her cousin, Kathy, who had called when she heard. "It took days before they could even get in there to find that out. He'd slammed her face down on the edge of a table. She's bruised everywhere, but mostly her face, which was blue-green before turning a sickening brown and yellow. She has stitches below her lower lip, under her eye, and down her cheek. She was hospitalized for a week, then I brought her home with me."

"Isabella! That's awful. My dad told me. Sorry I took so long to call," Kathy said on the phone.

"It's no problem. Nothing you could do anyway. How's school?"

"Good. Hard. But I like it. I like being at school. It's nice to get away, on my own," Kathy said. "What are your plans? I mean, she can't go back there."

"She knows that now. And that is the benefit of all this."

Isabella couldn't tell Kathy, who was on scholarship at the University of Illinois, that she had been fired and was a failure. Everyone was so proud of her. Isabella was proud of her, but also a little jealous.

Isabella didn't tell her mother, either. Instead, she said, "I'm taking time off to find a better job." Isabella longed for the sabotage incident to go away but, of course, it didn't.

"I'm a complete failure, Mom. In the hours when you needed me most, I wasn't there to protect you. I feel responsible for this. Maybe if I hadn't left you… ." She continued the thought privately in her mind, "or if I'd killed him when I had the chance."

"Everything happens for a reason, dear. God has a plan and we just have to trust in him for the answers. You didn't fail me. I'm glad you weren't home. Oh, I can't even think about that! And I just can't take much more of this mush!" she said, managing a change of subject and a smile with her broken face.

"I think I'll make you a milkshake. At least it's a treat. Better than blended carrots or broccoli."

"Thank you, honey. I hate imposing on you like this."

"You're not any imposition, Mom." Isabella knew it was time to have a serious talk. "I think we should talk about where we go from here. And I've been thinking, you could stay here for a while, indefinitely, at least until we can figure out, you know, everything."

"I can't stay here. I'd be intruding. I've talked to David. He and Kate have an extra room, and I'm going to stay there for a while. It was Kate's idea. David is insistent, and I think it's best. Besides, they're closer to both work in the city and, of course, church. It's going to be just fine."

"Mom, I want you to stay with me."

"I don't think so, honey. You only have the one bedroom. They have an extra. This will be better. For both of us."

Feelings of failure overwhelmed Izy. She was ashamed her mother didn't want to stay with her. She had failed her mother on top of everything else. On the other hand, she knew that if Missy did stay with her there'd be trouble. There were elements of Izy's life that her mother disapproved of. Francy would become an issue. They would disagree about war, of course, but also about other things Izy had never put into words, things that created the discomfort and uneasiness between them that was just beneath the surface.

But there was also relief, for which she felt even more horrendous guilt. "You can't stay at Uncle David's forever. What will you do long term?"

"I'm not sure. I'll figure out something, but if you have any thoughts... ."

"Is there any money?"

"No. I've been able to pay the bills with what I make, but there's nothing left over. In fact, what you don't know is that the Water and Power has put him on permanent disability. He hasn't gone to work in the last year. They just can't handle him anymore."

"You never told me."

"What good would that have done? Only worried you or upset you. He mostly stays out in his little house. I probably should have left, like you always said, but I thought, he has no one and I am his wife. Thought I should do whatever I could as long as I could. I'm sure Christ would not have abandoned him. I guess I wasn't much help in the end."

"How did it, well, happen anyway?"

"He forbade me to go to church, read the Bible, or pray. He resents my working. He prevented me from leaving for work on occasion and made me late. But I had to work. Some days it was the only thing I had to keep myself sane. I had to have my faith. So I went to church. And I figured I could read my Bible and pray. It's my right to do so. I didn't do these things to defy him. They were necessary, or at least a comfort. I tried to seclude myself when I read and prayed. I wasn't being deceitful. Well, maybe I was, I don't know. Anyway, he interrupted me unexpectedly and went berserk. I'd never seen him like that. I don't want to talk about it. It's over, and I want to put it behind me. I just want you to know that I appreciate your help and understanding, Isabella, and I'm sorry that my life has intruded on yours."

Isabella carefully hugged her mother. If she wanted to go to her brother's, fine. Isabella would try to be okay with that. The trip back to the nightmare house was just to get her personal items, papers, and car keys. Isabella went with her. The house was dark and quiet. She moved quickly, gathering her things. The crazy man never showed his face.

Isabella followed Missy to her brother's house, then drove aimlessly for hours. Aching and hurt, Izy went home and drank vodka until she fell asleep.

The phone woke her up.

"If your mother wasn't already overburdened, I would be telling her what I just learned. What did you think you were doing, young lady?"

"Uncle Willy. You heard."

"Of course I heard. I was utterly embarrassed for you. You are irresponsible and ungrateful. I'd think if only for your mother's sake, you'd try to pretend you have a modicum of the good sense you should have. Your mother, if she knew, would be ashamed!"

That hurt, sure enough. "I did what I thought was right."

"Right? You think treason is right?"

"It's not treason. It's protestation and I have a right... ."

"You have no right to do what you did! You should be charged, tried, and locked up by rights!"

"Hey, wait a minute. I can understand your getting all bent out of shape, having gotten me the job and all. And I am sorry I let you down. But you've got no right to get in my face. You're part of the problem, part of the establishment that just goes along without even thinking about what you're supporting, just because the government says it's right. You're the one who should be ashamed of yourself!"

"You're lucky I don't come over there right now and give you a licking the likes of which you'd never forget. Your problem is your mother never licked you, and your father, well, that's another matter!"

"Shut up about them. Say, where do you get off? You asshole! Where were you when I was growing up, huh? Were you looking out for me then, you jackass? No, you and all your weenie brothers just left us there in that house with that nut. How dare you call now and pretend you have any business... ."

He hung up. Isabella was shaking. She fell back to sleep. She dreamed in red and black of a carnival set out in a forbidding jungle full of mean clowns with weapons and chasing other scary people. She heard ugly noises, shrieks, and grotesque laughter. Wherever she went she couldn't seem to spend her tickets, her huge wad of tickets. She needed to get rid of them, but no one would take them from her.

Isabella awoke to her new reality. She had little money and needed work.

While she searched for a job, voices, loud voices, talked about her inside her head saying things like "Out of control!" "Make a difference!" "Life comes 'round on you." "You could be a supervisor in an office!" "She's not afraid of hard work!" "We're all worried about this girl!" "Do the right thing!" Isabella tried not to listen, but the voices were overwhelming. Then sometimes she'd scream, "What the hell is the right thing, anyway?"

LUNAR ORBIT

Work came in the form of a clerical position at Rockwell International in the Communication Systems division. The manufacturing plant built equipment for military contracts and commercial airlines. Every day Isabella wondered what they would do if they knew what she'd done at her previous job. She had certain misgivings about the fact that they built equipment for bombers and nuclear submarines. At least they didn't manufacture munitions. One thing they did manufacture that captured Isabella's imagination was radio systems for the Apollo missions to the moon.

Man had walked on the moon, complete with eternal footprints. It was a grand thing. To be part of such a grand thing had to have great merit. Even if similar radios were on the planes that were flying over North Vietnam, it balanced out, right? She wanted it to. She really wanted it to, and so she reasoned she was there to further the exploration of space—the last frontier! The concept of the moon missions outweighed any misgivings she had.

The work was repetitive and tedious. Isabella spent entire weeks compiling labor hours spent on each contract, collecting and calculating data, then reporting in detail that which simultaneously protects taxpayers and costs them a fortune. The pay was good, much better than at The Phone Company, and she was enthralled with the work out on the production floor. Somehow it seemed real, tangible, in a way that brought America's strength right down to nuts, bolts, and soldering irons. She spent her spare time with her mom looking for a place where Missy could live on her own. Missy didn't make very much money at her job. Apartments were expensive, especially in the inner city. But fortunately, there was time to search and decide.

At Rockwell Isabella worked with engineers fresh out of respected colleges back east. They were bright, young, and excited to be in California, and they were more sophisticated than anyone she'd ever met. She was awed by them, fascinated by their stories of college life, and accepted without question that these engineers were all men.

Her desk was one in a huge bay. The floor was laid with linoleum tiles edged in black from decade's worth of dirt, haphazardly mopped and waxed into immortality. There were no dividers or any privacy. Desks were lined up, row after row, gray upon gray. The engineers, engineering assistants, secretaries, and clerks sat side by side at their designated locations. There were windows to the outside at the back of the bay. At the front were double doors that swung out to the giant production area resembling the inside of hangars or warehouses.

During another weekend sojourn with Missy investigating apartment options, Izy noticed that her mother found fault with them all. One had poor ventilation, another had no sunlight, yet another had carpet that smelled or neighbors who yelled. With her meager salary her prospects were grim. As they drove away from yet another rejected possibility, Missy spoke, "I'm remembering a small trailer park on my way to work." Her voice turned optimistic. "I think I'd rather have my own little box than one of these tiny boxes inside a big box." Izy's heart lifted looking at Missy and seeing her smile.

"How much will it cost?" Izy asked.

"I inquired at the office quite a while ago. I can buy a small trailer for $5,000. I know I don't have it right now, but I'm saving. David and Kate have been very gracious, but I don't want to impose too long. I've asked God to help me." Isabella drove on knowing that she would be the one to help.

Out in production at Rockwell, there was a sense of excitement over a new radio system that could be plugged into racks on ships and planes. There was a cacophony of voices, tools, and equipment that oozed energy.

Many of the workers were women. Some of them were amazing creatures who defied the laws of gender balance. They had riveted during the war, driven trucks, even flown aircraft. What they lacked in femininity they made up for in moxie. They were not impressed with the little boys from college telling them how to build their radios. The bosses—who sat in offices, wore ties, and earned many times what the grunts did—didn't impress them either.

"Thunderbolt's on a rampage again," an engineer told Bill McNally.

"What about this time?"

"Can't say. She threw me off the line. Said if I didn't get back to my desk, she'd toss me through the doors. I'm not going to tangle with her. You'd better go talk to Gainer."

"Were you doing or saying something when she lost it?"

"I was just explaining that she could be more efficient if she placed her wires, held them, and crimped, all at once. You know, we've been talking about that."

"Oh, gads! Well, I don't know if Thunderbolt's the one you should have tried to sell it to. I'll go talk to her."

It was going to be too good to miss. Isabella grabbed up some papers so she could look as if she had business on the production floor and discreetly tagged along at a distance.

"You know, you can all shove your little techniques right up your tight asses!"

Gainer, was already interceding, "Thunderbolt, we hired these guys to help us cut our labor... ."

"Well, then let's do something that matters. That little Georgia cracker's out here picking at how I crimp wires. If we want to do something, let's get going on modernization and leave my techniques alone! I was crimping wires when you were both suckin' tit!"

Bill McNally stood tall and cleared his throat. Larry Gainer, the production floor supervisor, and Reba Therabolt turned to see that he had arrived. "Well, if it isn't the chief babysitter come to reason with the likes of little ol' me, I'm a-bettin'! Well, stuff it, McNally!"

"Okay, Reba, okay. I heard you out, now let me hear Bill. Can you go back to work, please?"

She cursed and headed back to her workbench, flicking her soldering iron defiantly.

"Bill, don't even start with me. You can't come out here and tell Thunderbolt how to build boards."

"Maybe so, but Rick's assignment is to do whatever it takes to keep the physical time on these boards to a minimum. You know how shaky this contract is, as well as I do. So we got to have a little cooperation."

"Don't expect it from Thunderbolt. And don't expect me to clean up the debris of your department's blunders. Now, if you have a reasonable proposal for overall improvements, fine; otherwise tell them to keep their incremental suggestions to themselves and, in particular, leave Reba alone."

McNally lowered his gaze in defeat and turned tail for the office bay. Isabella couldn't help be impressed that a tie could be sent away with his tail between his legs. Isabella liked Rebecca Therabolt—Reba, or Thunderbolt, as she was most known—more than anyone she'd met in a long while. Isabella watched her work from a safe distance and admired how she handled tools—as if they were extensions of her fingers—and the way the other assemblers asked her for help instead of asking the foreman, Gainer. He paid it no mind; sometimes he himself asked her for help. Thunderbolt knew everything!

Thunderbolt wasn't pretty or even close to pretty. She had an accent that suggested she came from the country, southern country. She was a good-sized woman who wore jeans and denim shirts. She wore a plain wedding band, dinged and marred, on her left hand, and no other jewelry or adornment of any sort. Her hair was bristly, no particular color and with a good deal of gray intermixed. She smoked like a chimney, talked like a man, and cursed more than anyone Izy had ever known.

She ran with a group of older gals, like herself. They were all the same cut: surly and self-sufficient. Isabella secretly called them the Silver Cats. At lunch break, Isabella would move closer to them every day, daring to be obvious and longing to be noticed.

Francine had a new boyfriend. He was a law student at UCLA and drove a red '65 Mustang convertible. He was good-looking, smooth and sophisticated like the college boys at Rockwell. When Isabella went for drinks with the college boys, Francy would come along so Francy and Isabella could catch up.

"How's work? Day shift?"

"I feel like I should wear diapers and shake a rattle. It's ridiculous. But it fits better with Grant's schedule at school. I trade for every weekend I can. I miss you, Izy! I don't have any friends. Rats and suck-ups. Wish you hadn't gotten fired."

"It's all for the best. I like my new job. Say, when are we going to spend some time?"

"Next week. Grant's going to his parents for his father's birthday. I thought I'd spend the weekend with you, like old times."

"You're not going?"

"No. Grant doesn't think the timing's right."

"Timing? What timing?" Izy's hackles went up, her intuition piqued. "Are you his girlfriend or not?"

"Grant knows best, I think. His family is a bit upper crust and he needs to find the right time to introduce me."

"Upper crust?" A second of pause for calculation, "What does that make you, lower crust? What's that supposed to mean? How can you stand by for an insult like that? You're doing it again, Francy. This guy's trouble."

"He's not! It's not an insult. I am lower crust. We all are. He's the smartest and the richest man I've ever known. Like it or not, that makes him special, and he likes me! This is the one, I can feel it! So it's worth waiting for. I don't mind. Why should you? Are we on for next weekend or not?"

And so their plans were hatched. Francy's favorite things besides boys were movies. All that remained was the usual debate over what to see. "Let's see Love Story."

"Again? I don't think so. Wasn't that good the first time. Let's go see M*A*S*H."

"How about Five Easy Pieces—Jack Nicholson—and then the diner for pastramis?"

Later, when they returned to Isabella's apartment, Izy asked, "Wanna smoke some grass?"

"Are you kidding?"

"No."

"Where'd you get that?"

"From a guy at work."

"You ever smoked it before?"

"Yeah, in high school a little. It's no big thing." Isabella lit the joint, took a big drag, and while holding it in, handed the joint to Francy. She shook her head. Isabella exhaled and took another drag.

"Are you out of your mind, Izy?"

"Oh, I hope so! The sooner the better!"

"Damn it! Give me that thing." She took it from Isabella, looking back and forth between the joint and Isabella. Then she took a hit and choked; Isabella laughed.

"It's not like Virginia Slims, Francy! Take a smaller hit, hold it in, and then let it out. You want it to mellow your brain before you exhale. You'll get used to it." She tried again with greater success.

Isabella could feel the gentle whoosh of calm take effect; she tried to remember to watch for signs of Francy's kicking in. They traded the remainder back and forth until it was barely there, clutched in the jaws of an alligator clip that Izy had lifted from the production floor. Isabella turned on the stereo. Francy put albums on the turntable and they fell back listening to Sam Cooke,

Night Beat, Curtis Mayfield's Magic, and the Impressions.

They zoned for a while, then, when the paralysis wore off a bit, "So what do you think?"

"About what?"

"The grass. What else?"

"No effect. Disappointing."

"No effect? Is that why you sat here for three hours without saying a word, stoned on R&B?"

"No way! Three hours?"

"Uh-huh. It's after one in the morning."

"I don't believe it. Wow! Is that what it's like, being stoned, I mean?"

"Pretty good, huh?"

"Yeah, but don't tell Grant."

"Hey, Grant's probably doing it when he's not with you. That's the thing on the campuses these days."

"Not with Grant. I mean, he's a pretty straight arrow."

"Right, well, we'll see. But I won't say anything to him. Hell, I don't even like him."

"Izy! You don't like boys at all."

"Careful now. Someone might get the wrong idea if you go around talking like that."

"Well, you don't. Tell me the truth. You ever done it with a girl?"

"Absolutely not, Francy, don't even talk like that."

"I see you looking at me, sometimes. I wonder." And she sidled over closer to Isabella.

Isabella didn't back away. "You're just stoned."

"Maybe. Maybe I just want to know what it would be like. Wouldn't you? Girls do it with girls. That's how we learn to kiss. Didn't you ever kiss a girlfriend? Just to know what it was like, to learn with someone safe?"

"What would that be like?" Isabella knew what she was talking about, stalling, nervous, wanting to be cool and aloof. "To kiss a woman, touch a woman, you know, do it with a woman." Francy took Isabella's fingers up in her hand, brought them to her mouth, and touched each one with her tongue. Isabella felt a stab of sensation in her gut.

"Do you want to kiss me, Izy?"

Isabella sat there staring at her parted lips, sat still, riveted, wanting Francy to be in charge but not knowing why. Francy kept coming to her, closer by inches, breathing deeper and slower, while Izy felt tingles of stimulation. She waited until Francy's lips touched hers, then Isabella returned the kiss, gently, felt their tongues just touch. It was a thousand times more sensation than Isabella had ever felt before.

Isabella's coolness melted. She felt herself sliding into a rhythm she didn't have to think about. Natural, innocent exploration. Just the two of them, sharing, trusting each other completely in an intimacy that was tenderly given, not taken. The feel and the taste of Francy's body dazzled Isabella. Afterward, she laid back as the sun broke and thought of Francy showering, strolling around naked, putting on her underwear. Then came the conflicts. Nothing is simple.

They went to the beach for breakfast, then walked along the shore. Isabella wanted to talk about what had happened, about how everything had changed for her, but she didn't know how to begin. It had changed nothing for Francy. She seemed just the same as before. For Francine, it had just been an interesting way to pass the night and express a new high. For Isabella, it was shattering.

They spent the rest of the weekend shopping, talking, and eating. But underneath all that, Isabella was trying to organize a long list of confusing thoughts, feelings, and desires. She had made love with her girlfriend. She had liked it. A lot! Am I a lesbian, she wondered, just as Francy had suggested? A queer? God destroyed Sodom and Gomorra for acts of homosexuality. Now I'm a wanton slut and a homosexual? That's got to be bullshit! How could someone like God give a damn who diddles your sexual organs? It just doesn't make any sense at all. Sex: what a nightmare of contradiction!" Isabella spent the remainder of the day trying to understand the true nature of sexual desire.

On Monday, back at work, Isabella put the Francy incident safely away next to the secret of Santa Barbara Island. She was just about to begin stalking the Silver Cats during lunch when she was startled by her personal favorite of the college boys.

"Hey! Whatcha doing?"

Isabella flinched for a second, thinking he might have known what she was really planning to do. "You startled me, Jim! I'm about to eat my lunch, what's it look like? Wanna join me?" Izy flushed for a moment as if she'd been found out, then realized nobody knew anything.

"Sure. Have a good weekend?"

"Yeah. You?"

"Yeah, guess so. Say, we're having a party next week at Ricky's house at the beach. Wanna come?"

"Guess so, can I bring friends?"

"That's the whole idea. Should be a real blow out, frat style, starting in the afternoon on the beach with volleyball, a barbecue, then party, party!"

"Sure, sounds great. I'll be there with bells on, or in this case, a bikini, I guess."

Izy was tired of waiting for the Silver Cats to notice her, maybe invite her into their club. She decided bolder action was needed. The next day at lunch, Izy was waiting. As they settled into their usual section of the cafeteria, Isabella walked right over and said, "Hi, Mrs. Therabolt. My name's Isabella Reinhardt and I've been watching you since I've been working here." She was golden that far, then it began to fall apart as Isabella felt Thunderbolt's gaze upon her. "I was wondering if, I mean, I would like to... ."

"Spit it out, kid. What? Sit down. It's a free table. Sit where you want to. Whadya say your name was, Kid?"

"Isabella, but my friends call me Izy."

"Great, Kid." And that was that. Isabella was "Kid." She never knew whether Thunderbolt ever cared that her name was Isabella or if she just saw her as a kid. Maybe she just liked her for finally being bold. Much later, Thunderbolt told Isabella that she had been watching her prowl around, craving attention.

Thunderbolt introduced the Kid to the other Silver Cats: Maryann, Ginny, Erlene, Donna, and Belva Jean. They politely said, "Hi," then went right on as if Isabella wasn't even there. They jawed about their husbands, some lazy, one laid up, another mean; their kids, mostly grown; housework; and how women got the worst part of the deal: Work all day, then go home and work there, too. They never mentioned the production floor, the bosses, or the snot-nosed engineers. Isabella soon learned this was their time away from all that. Discussions about work were reserved for time on the clock.

From that day on, Isabella ate her lunch with the Silver Cats. She listened and learned. Reba wasn't book smart. She was a natural at everything the boys had studied to learn. She was like great Uncle Micheil, Aunt Mary Beth, Uncle David, and even Izy's father. She was one of those people born with an innate sense of how things work.

Whenever Isabella had some downtime, she'd go out on the floor to visit with Reba. Izy was careful to keep it all businesslike and not cause trouble from her foreman, Mr. Gainer. Thunderbolt began to teach Isabella the fine art of soldering and assembly. More importantly, she taught Isabella the difference between how a thing ought to be and how it more often was. And that's what the snot-nosed engineers had to learn as well. Some would learn willingly, others would take the hard road to understand—sure that no old broad from Arkansas could teach them anything that their fine universities hadn't gotten to in four to six years.

At the party that weekend, some of the Silver Cats showed up with husbands in tow. They were mostly lumpy men with rumpled clothes and country manners.

It started out with about twenty-five or so in attendance enjoying the day, then more showed up for the food. By dark, nearly a hundred people were at the bash. Francy was there with Grant and a couple of his friends.

Izy took Ronny to the party, glad for the time to catch up with her. Late in the night, Izy was sitting at the little breakfast bar in the kitchen area of the beach house sipping vodka when a guy slid in beside her and started a conversation.

"So how do you come to be here?"

"I work with the guy who lives here."

"Oh, so you're one of the Rockwell people."

"I guess you could say that."

"I'm a friend of one of the fraternity brothers of the guy who lives here."

"Ah. That would make you a Pi Kappa Alpha by association."

"No, no, absolutely not. I didn't even go to college. I just know the brothers from parties, you know how it is. Some of them live in my condominium complex."

"What do you do?"

"I invent things. My name's John Martin. What's yours?" He stuck out a hand.

She shook it, "Isabella Reinhardt. But you can call me Izy." And then she noticed the wedding ring on his finger and decided to get some air.

Work was boring. Isabella began to seek ways to get it done faster to gain time to spend on the floor with Thunderbolt. Isabella hung out with the engineers, trying to learn everything she possibly could. It was easy. Everything her father had taught her laid a foundation of understanding upon which to overlay new data about advanced electronics, ciphered communication, and silent intelligence technology and its limitless capacities.

She hung out in test and learned to set up standard routines. Isabella loved to watch the wave-soldering machine and the silver sheen of the molten metal coating the backs of the circuit boards. Soon she learned to load it and set the wave.

The college boys slowly began to modernize the factory. First came the automatic component replacement devices: Operators just had to load the grids and the equipment placed and crimped the leads. The engineers learned quickly and became more knowledgeable, their improvements more intelligent. Soon the operators just had to keep the component trays loaded—the machine would spot, place, and crimp. The most magical equipment was brought into the security-restricted areas where the Apollo systems were built. Isabella set her sights on the Apollo Project, which paid more and would provide a way to help out her mother.

Isabella became a fixture on Thunderbolt's line, sitting with her and watching without raising even a glance from the foreman.

"Kid, you should go to college!"

"What? You're anti-college, how can you say that?"

"Whatever made you think that?"

"Well let's see, you make fun of the college boys, and you can't stand any of the managers. Seems like you're real clear on that."

"Well, then you ain't taken my meaning, Kid. The plain fact is I wish I'd gone to college myself. It's a privilege to learn and one I could only dream of where I grew up."

"But you... ."

"Listen, I don't mind them college boys being smart so much as I mind them being dumb. Books can't teach you everything. Life's a pretty good teacher, too. I guess I just want my due for what I've learned. I get all up and a bit frisky with the boys when they come out here spoutin' what they read in a book without any respect for how sometimes things ain't exactly that way. Besides, those boys all went to school right outta their mommies' arms. Parents paid. They've had the lap of easy. 'Bout time they learned the world's a mite bit more complicated than they're used to." Then she lowered her voice and caught Izy's eye, "Maybe I'm a little envious, too, I guess. Maybe that, too, just a mite." Then back to her work. "But you're young and have no ties, you're a damn fool if you don't put that brain of yours to good use. And working as a flunky ain't the way to do that. You got to get a college degree if you want to get respect. That's just how it is, Kid!"

"Me, an engineer? I guess I could. But why would I want to? Seems so like getting in bed with the establishment. Going to college like the rich kids who could afford to avoid the draft. And besides, I couldn't afford to do it. I have to work and now I want to help my mom. Ah, forget it, Reba, I'll be happy if I can be like you."

"Well, then you are a dang fool, Kid!" She laughed and worked, let it all settle on Isabella, disregarding her reaction for the most part. Thunderbolt was a sagacious old Cat.

Isabella submitted an application for any position that was attached to the Apollo contract. Her application got pulled for a position as production timekeeper, the reciprocal of what she was doing already. Isabella was a logical candidate and excited to be given an interview. The interview went well. Isabella was sure she would get the job, and so was everyone else. She was horrified when her clearance check came back with her father's history of mental illness, his confinements—all of which was held against her for some reason. And if that wasn't enough, her antiwar arrest record and the vandalism booking came up. There was no possibility of working on the moon project in her lifetime. "Sorry, Isabella!"

She was completely and utterly flattened. For weeks Isabella moped around trying to accept the fact that she was ruined. She searched faces desperately trying to figure out if all her coworkers knew that she was a criminal with a nutcase for a father. No one said anything, but Isabella was sure they were all looking at her. She avoided the Silver Cats, not wanting to explain why she didn't get the job. Isabella tried to concentrate on her work and figure out how she was going to recover from this failure.

"Missed you, Kid."

"Yeah, me too. I've been kinda busy."

"Wouldn't be the job you didn't get?"

How did she know? Isabella wondered.

And as if she could read minds, "Not much goes on around here I don't hear, 'specially if I'm interested: clearance. Say, don't feel bad. You got to be lily white to get on that project. Hey, come on! Look, Kid, why do you think I don't work on the best project in the plant, huh? I got a past, too." She touched Isabella's chin with her finger and tried to lift her face, but Isabella couldn't let her see the tears she was holding back. "You can't be ashamed of who you are, Izy. You got to wear it like you earned it, because you did. Whatever it was, and I don't even need to know, because I don't care one way or the other. It is and always will be. See, the thing about being a grown-up is you get to do whatever you want. You just have to be accountable for the choices you make. So own it. Get on with it. Make better choices."

Isabella nodded without looking up. Thunderbolt clapped the Kid on her shoulder and walked away, left Izy by herself. As she left, Isabella looked up to see her swagger off. She wanted to run after her, hug her, thank her, for just that wee bit of something that felt like a life preserver in her sea of awful. At that moment, Isabella set in motion a new plan. She would try a college class at night school.

During her first session with a counselor, Isabella discovered a lot of things she didn't know existed. For example, you could challenge a course. If a student thought she already knew the subject matter, she could request to take a test and get credit for the course if the score were high enough. Isabella also learned that you could get a certain amount of credit just for working. "This might not be as bad as I thought," she mused. "I guess I owe her big time for this one." She set about challenging classes she thought she might be able to pass. By the time she was done, Isabella had amassed forty challenge credits—the maximum. That was a year's worth of school.

From there, now a sophomore, Isabella chose a path that would lead to an engineering degree in electronics; she signed up for her first classes. It would not be easy like high school was. No more faking it and no more just getting by. She'd have to make it on her own; if she didn't, no one would care. They'd just flunk her out and be done with her.

Isabella settled into a relatively disciplined routine of work, school, and homework. When she had time she'd check on her mom. She got off work at 4:30 p.m. and had just enough time to catch some food before heading to class, which let out at 9:00 or 10:00 p.m. Then it was home to study. When she finished her homework, she'd reward herself with a joint and a martini. One night, while she was relaxing after studying, the telephone startled her.

"Izy, you gotta come get me."

"Francy? Why? Where are you? It's nearly midnight!"

"You just gotta come, right now. It's an emergency, I swear!"

"Francy, love, I'm busy, and I got to get to bed, work tomorrow... ."

"Izy, we had a giant fight and he hit me. I'm afraid he might come back here. I don't want to stay here by myself. Pleeeeze, Izy! Come get me."

"Grant. This is you and Grant? Grant hit you? Bastard! Can't you drive yourself?"

"He took my keys and I think he drove off in my car. Besides, I'd be afraid to go outside. What if he's out there watching to see if I leave?"

"Damn it, yes. I'll come."

"Be careful, Izy."

Francy's cheek was bruised, her eye swollen shut; there were marks on her arms in the shape of hands. A few items were broken and Francy was huddled in the dark, terrified. It was then, in the dark and amid the debris, that Izy knew there was cause for concern.

Bolstered by Izy's arrival, Francy ran around packing what she wanted to take. "It'll only be a few minutes. I got to have some things!"

"Well, hurry." Just then the door banged opened. Isabella took in air and breathed out, "Well, if it isn't Mr. Tough with the ladies. I think you better put the key down and get out. Now!"

"I think you should butt out. This is none of your business."

"Now, that's where you're wrong. Some bully beats up my best friend, it's my business."

"I didn't beat up anyone. Ask her, she was the one out of line."

"Out of line is you lifting a hand to her."

"Yeah? Well, now you're out of line!"

He lunged for Isabella, who moved quickly into the bedroom and behind the door, where she and Francy tried with all their strength to close and lock it.

But the two were no match for the force of Grant's weight. Izy looked quickly around for a weapon. Nothing. She let loose the door, fell back, and grabbed a pillow, shaking the feathers all to one end. When Grant came through the door, she came up off the floor and into his chest with a strength she didn't know she possessed. He fell to his knees, the wind knocked out of him.

"Francy, we're going NOW!" And as for you, you touch her again and I'll find you. You gotta sleep sometime. When you do, it'll be payback!" They left.

Francy was hungry so Isabella stopped at a drive-in.

"He was jealous. He just got jealous and crazy."

"I've seen Grant, Francy, what did you do to make him jealous?"

"Well, I was tired of waiting for him to, you know, ask me to go steady or better, to marry him. I just told him that I was interested in, maybe, seeing other guys or something."

"Are you interested in seeing other guys?"

"No! But I wanted him to think that because I think he really likes me, and I thought if he thought he could lose me, he'd say he didn't want me to be with anyone else. Then I'd say, if we were engaged or something, it'd be different."

"You were gaming him. See what it got you?"

"How was I to know he'd go off like that? I thought he loved me."

"Well, he doesn't! No one who loves you beats you."

"It's not just that. He said awful things like I was lucky, you know, lucky someone like him was paying attention to a... ." She trailed off in silent sobs.

"Francy, he had no right to talk to you like that. He's a jerk!" Izy sighed, determined to help her friend, but not certain how to do so, being deterred by her self-destructive patterns. "Oh, Francy! You're an ass at times. You practically beg for guys to abuse you, but you don't deserve what they do to you. Can't you believe that? You believe anything they tell you. Why can't you believe what I'm telling you? I do love you. Don't go out with these bums!"

"But he seemed so right, so everything: good looking, rich, going places. Except he wasn't that great in bed, really." She looked sideways at Isabella and Izy laughed.

"There, see. He's a bum fuck! Waddaya want with a bum fuck, you being a great fuck and all."

"You're not so bad, you know." Now she was smiling and acting coy. Isabella didn't want to get into that and regretted having brought it up. But it seemed to lighten Francy's mood. Isabella felt she should just let it go. "Oh, Izy, maybe I should go lesbo: you and me, together. We'd be great, don't you think?"

"Forget about it and eat your burger," Isabella blew it off with a smile. "I got to get home and get some sleep." Deep and dangerous water, Isabella thought. It was never going to happen again, not ever. Francy had her ways. Sex was just as easy as drinking to her. It meant little. She didn't even consider what they had done as cheating on Grant. It was just a little sex thing between friends. She didn't understand how insulting that felt for Isabella.

She watched Francy chomp her burger, munch her fries, and suck down her shake. Isabella knew that if she were a man, she'd know how to love Francy, treat her special so that the scars could heal so she could believe in herself and, maybe someday, choose to love her back.

The next morning while Francine was still asleep, Isabella got up and went to work, then school. When she returned home around 10:00 p.m., music was blaring and Francy was bouncing off the walls with manic enthusiasm.

"Wow! I'm so glad you're home. I know you're going to be proud of me. I've decided to get my life in order and get a career, just like you, Izy. I'm going to be a Marine!"

"Whoa, whoa, hold it. What are you talking about?"

"I've decided to join the Marines. See here, I can get training in any one of many high-tech fields, money for college when I get out and, who knows, maybe a career as an officer. I could do it, Izy, I know I could."

"Oh, I'm sure you could, Francy. You can do anything you want to. But you don't want to join the Marines. I think it's a good idea to start thinking about your life in terms of a career. But not the Marines."

"Grant wouldn't have bounced a Marine around last night! I also get trained to fight and defend myself. That could come in handy."

"You can take self-defense classes. You don't have to go into the military for that. Once you go into something like the Marines, Francy, you're in. You got to stick it out and, well, I don't think it's the best idea you've ever had. Now, we can go see a counselor at my school and get you into some courses... ."

"You don't understand. I am a Marine! I signed up today. It's done!"

"What are you talking about?"

"I took the bus to the recruiting office and signed on the dotted line. You are talking to a basic trainee, Francine Marie Gavin, property of the USMC!"

Isabella searched her face for a hint of humor or practical joke. Instead, she saw sincere enthusiasm spilling over a grin from ear to ear, Francy standing at attention, her hand in a salute. "Okay, now this has got to be some joke you think is funny, right? Tell me it is, Francy!"

Francy dropped to the sofa, pulling Isabella along, "No joke and it's not funny, it's what I need: discipline, purpose. It's going to be great!" I leave in a week for Parris Island."

"Parris Island? Francy, are you completely nuts? You're not going! There must be someone I can contact and explain that you did this insane thing under extreme emotional distress and it's all a giant mistake!"

"If you did something like that, I'd never forgive you. This is what I want. And I didn't do it under emotional distress. I sat here this morning, calmly, and thought about my life. It's going nowhere. I want this. It's going to give me structure, and I'm going to learn a lot. I can't date until I'm out of basic training. That ought to appeal to you."

"You have to join the Marines to not date? Francy, please don't do this!"

"It's done." She fell over into Izy's arms, which rose automatically to cradle her weight. "And I want you to be happy for me. Come on, please, be just a little bit happy. I need you to be on my side, Izy, please," she purred.

It wasn't her manipulation. At least Isabella didn't think it was. It was bigger than that. As much as Isabella hated the military and everything it represented, and as much as she was disappointed that Francy would do such a thing, it wasn't about Isabella. It was like up in the airplane, she could see a twist in the fabric of life. Francy was headed in a new direction on a path away from Isabella. She had the right to make that choice if that's what she wanted. So Isabella listened to her vision of the Marines as she recited every word from the brochure she'd been given. Isabella watched Francy bounce up and punctuate her chatter with sweeping body language, then fall back on the sofa. Isabella tried her best to smile. She nodded. Over the next couple of hours, a new truth settled in: Francy was leaving.

In the weeks and months following Francine's departure, Izy experienced a mixed bag of events and emotions. She worked and sought overtime whenever she could fit it into her schedule; she was promoted to engineering assistant. She studied and attended classes. To fill the quiet spaces that generally made her feel alone and uncomfortable, she drank and did her share of social drugs.

Missy bought a small mobile home in Gardena and some used furniture. Isabella felt bad that everything was so humble, but Missy was elated. Isabella was reminded of the red kite riding the breeze, flying free. Missy had been freed.

They went to the nightmare house to collect her things accompanied by Uncles David and Willy and Cousin George as part of a contingency plan.

Missy gathered some of her clothes and personal items, photographs, the box of Grandy's things she'd saved for herself, some papers and books, kitchen items and, of course, her Fostoria. It was there, safely hidden in the corner of the closet, wrapped in protective newspaper and boxed as if ready for a quick rescue.

The men were appalled by the house. They did not encounter him, although Isabella sensed her father lurking in the shadows and the rubble of her childhood home. He was in there somewhere, underground, listening and interpreting everything through his lens of paranoia and chaos. Inside Isabella was a small girl who wanted to find him and take him with her, take her Daddy with her. But Isabella knew her Daddy was long gone. Isabella shushed the small girl, telling her to be quiet.

In 1971 an article entitled "A History of the U.S. Decision Making Process in Vietnam" was published in The New York Times: The episodes associated with the escalations of U.S. involvement had been prefabricated to create a justification. The Johnson administration had flagrantly lied to the American public about its intentions, claiming it had no long-range plans for war, while all along committing troops to Vietnam. The article stirred growing antiwar sentiment, even among Richard Nixon's silent majority. Blind acceptance of government rhetoric began to melt; the sentiments of more and more red-blooded Americans were shifting.

Francy made it through boot camp and came home for a brief visit. Her long hair was cut short and neat. Isabella was surprised to see how smart she looked in her uniform, how happy she seemed. She shared tales of grueling training and a rigorous schedule and was proud she'd survived. Izy listened and hoped for the best.

Ronny took a promotion and was transferred even farther away, so Isabella saw even less of her. However, they talked on the phone regularly.

"I've got to read this one to you. It's not that I want you to be upset or do anything, just that it upset me, and I have to share it or I'll lose my mind!"

"Go for it, I'm listening."

"He writes:

'Ronny, I feel I've failed you, and Dad, everyone. But I couldn't help it. I can't explain it, exactly. They sent us out with a bulldozer underneath a Huey to dig out a hole in the jungle: our new home.

'The watch posted, we settled in to get some sleep. Some smoked grass to settle their nerves. It's done. I didn't partake. I wanted to be sharp. I prayed sleep would come. But it did not. I'm not even sure I minded the sleepless nights. Sleeping, even when I was exhausted, was never deep and always troubled with dreams of ghastly shapes and colors, loud noises, and fear. When I awake from such dreams, it is always to mixed feelings: freed from the nightmare of being awake in a nightmare.

'But on this night, suddenly there were shots and chaotic shouting: 'They're coming, oh, God, they're coming!' At the edge of our hole, I could see specters in the darkness all around lobbing explosives. The noise reverberated in the dirt behind me, creating more confusion than damage. They were coming, a dark hoard, like a swarm of mosquitoes, screeching horrible sounds. We were like fish in a barrel. I felt pain in my leg and knew I was hit, but it didn't even faze me, adrenaline surging, and terror rampant. I was shooting at anything that moved above me.

'Then the chaos in the hole began to calm. I grew more terrified. I forced myself to the ground, lying prone, my blood running into the dirt beneath me. It was quiet except for the voices above. I wondered if they were all dead. Was I alone? Prisoner of war?

'I'd heard stories, awful stories.

'Single shots were fired from the rim of the crater at anything that moved, any sound. I was sweating, rivulets running from my hairline down my face, into my ear, along my nose, annoying, tickling. I lay still. I was close to the wall of earth, was I in the shadow? I prayed to God that I was in the shadow, afraid they'd see the sweat. I waited, wishing I could understand the words from up above. A thud, at least two sets of feet touched down in the hole and began to prowl. I heard the sound of items being stripped from bodies, more single shots across the way moving toward me. Faces came into my mind with each shot, yet I could not help thinking, praying to God to let it be anyone but me. Please let me live!

'Ronny, I was so scared. I tried to be brave. I just couldn't. I was begging God, pleading to live, like a coward. I'm so ashamed. I cannot do this anymore. Please don't hate me.'

But he never even signed it. He doesn't tell me about his wound, like it's not important. He's not important. Only his shame matters," Ronny said softly, with more impetus than a shout.

It was a long while before either of them spoke.

For Izy, the loss of Ronny's camaraderie was as painful as the dread of knowing Matt was caught up in ruthless torment. She ached for his tour to be up so he could come home.

By the fall of 1972, Isabella had managed to earn an Associate of Arts degree in general education, which led to another promotion to junior engineer. She was writing test routines for quality checks and final-stage burn-in for completed units. The Silver Cats threw her a party to celebrate. The college engineers were still developing their street smarts and gaining respect. As they grew in stature with the Silver Cats, they began to take Isabella seriously and offered to teach her if she were willing to stay after work or come in early. They came to her celebration party, as well. So did John Martin.

Isabella saw John when she had time to attend events hosted by the college boys. At a Halloween party, he won a prize for best costume. He truly deserved it: He dressed in a horse form that fit around his body, false legs in stirrups dangling on the sides so it looked like he was riding this great, goofy creature.

"How did you come up with that?"

"Mickey Mouse Club, actually. Remember on roundup day when they came out on their horses... ?"

"Oh, yeah! That's amazing! Where'd you learn how to make one?"

He pointed to his temple, "It's all up here. I can do that. I see something and I just know how to make it. Currently, I'm building an airplane using fiberglass. It was pretty simple to translate that into this."

"An airplane! Damn, I'm impressed!" And she was, but he was a married man, so the interaction ended pretty much at that. She did, however, think he had a very cute way of smiling while not bothering to hide his pleasure over her compliments. Isabella made a point of finding out who John's wife was. She was nothing expected: dark, sultry, exotic even, and never with John. She was usually at the opposite side of the room, standing next to someone else. John was tall with dark hair and a strong aquiline nose. His slender, robustly-delicate frame was a puzzling contradiction.

The U.S. involvement in the Vietnam War ended in January 1973, making President Nixon and his secretary of state, Henry Kissinger, heroes for a brief and shining moment. By then, everyone wanted out. Even the most gung-ho warmongers, convinced we were not going to sweep north killing everything in sight, knew we had to find a way to end the agony. Their bitter disappointment was drowned by the tidal wave of relief the whole nation felt. The heinous battle for colonial domination in Southeast Asia had ended. The people who lived there would be free to sort out their future and America's children could come home, those who still could. The rest would end up in a murky category: forever missing in action.

The real sorrow was that those who did return weren't children anymore. They were adults now, robbed of their youth, painted with memories that no one should have to carry and, all too often, snared in a world halfway between madness and impotence.

Some came home, made a life, and rode the crest of the baby boom wave. Isabella met them, studied with them, and worked with them. But she also encountered grown children who battled giant mosquitoes in the dark corners of their world. Grown children who got lost in the middle of conversations, or urinated on patios at parties, forgetting where they were. Others continued the drug habits they'd acquired in the jungle, becoming casualties that didn't make it into the official record.

His unit killed or left for dead in the jungle, Matt refused to go out again, convinced his luck had run out and that God, who knew his selfish desire to survive no matter what, would turn his back the next time. The army accepted his decision with disdain. Although he had been wounded and was awarded a Purple Heart, they sent him to collect dog tags from the dead and bag crispy critters, those burnt in napalm attacks. He spent the last month there burning excrement in the fifty-gallon drums used in outhouses on the bases. He came home shamed by the Army for his fears, ashamed of his life, and convinced he was less of a man than his father had raised him to be. Eventually, he drifted into a life of vagrancy and, finally, into drugs.

An unprecedented number of young people attended college during the Vietnam years. Baby boomers entered their parents' world better educated and with a sense of power no other generation had ever felt before. Yet, no American generation had been so battered by disillusionment or come of age doubting the authority of the United States Government. One way or the other, it was their time and they were going to force change.

RETURN TO EARTH

Her two years with the U.S. Marine Corps finished, Francine came home. She had abruptly married a fellow Marine: her new husband was former Staff Sergeant Redmond Butler. She returned with hope in her heart and a commitment to settling down; she talked of family and children. From the moment she met him, Izy didn't care for Redmond Butler, but she shared Francine's hope. Izy hoped that, regardless of her opinion of the marriage, it would be just what Francy needed.

Everything seemed to be settling. It was time for the nation to regroup and the baby boomers to get on with their lives. The evening news was easier to watch. Songs were about love and liberation instead of war and paranoia. Bell-bottoms ruled and midriffs were bare. The boomers' energies were focused on starting careers. The issues of the past distilled down to women's issues and inequities in the workplace. Women were anxious to roar. Headlines told of flaming brassieres and one other pesky bit of business: the controversy over a curious incident that happened in 1972. It involved the arrest of five men in Washington, D.C., who were caught breaking into the offices of the Democratic National Committee. Uncle Clay was on it immediately, sure there was something significant and sinister behind it. Izy anticipated Clay's calls and, when she could, drove north to Oregon.

School was a challenge. Courses were far from fundamental. Physics, calculus, and solid-state electronics made up the core; chemistry, programming, and computer and mechanical science were thrown in for laughs. Uncle Clay encouraged her to talk about her classes when she was at his home on the Umpqua; he provided a special place for her to study. It was small but looked out toward the river carving time into its banks. He would say to his wife, "Lil, let's take a walk and let Isabella concentrate on her future!" Izy knew Lil didn't appreciate her visits. She made it clear more by what she didn't do or say than what she did. Izy was drawn to Clay, and Lil's subtle snubs were a small price to pay for the support she received from her uncle.

Work was evolving as well. More and more automation was being developed, resulting in less and less dependency on the skill of production workers. Special-purpose computers were also arriving on the scene.

"Soon they won't need us at all. We'll be outta jobs!" Maryann complained during lunch one day.

Izy tried to be encouraging, saying, "That could never happen. You guys are walking encyclopedias of this business."

"We know the old ways, all right. But things are changing. Look who they're hiring now. They have no experience, no training." Erlene chimed in.

"Union's got something to say about that!" Ginny stated.

The Silver Cats were not happy about the handwriting on their wall. But Thunderbolt was silent. She smoked her cigarette and stared into the distance.

The truth was the Cats could see the future and knew that the changes were also the end of an era. The era of Rosy the Riveter, the age of hand-built aircraft and equipment, were coming to a close. Carol, Maryann, Ginny, Erlene, Donna, and Belva Jean watched as their expertise was programmed into machines that didn't talk back and could work in the dark. They all belonged to a union called the International Brotherhood of Electrical Workers. The union was organized to protect against management decisions that ran contrary to the interests and well-being of the workers. The Silver Cats took their concerns to their local. With the end of their contracts looming on the horizon, trouble began to brew.

Labor issues at Rockwell were not the only brews. G. Gordon Liddy and James W. McCord, Jr., members of an enigmatic group referred to as The Plumbers, were convicted of burglary, wire-tapping, and conspiracy in the incident at the Democratic National Committee headquarters. The headquarters were located in the Watergate Hotel, so the press tagged the story "the Watergate incident." And it just wouldn't die. In the spring of '73, a special prosecutor was appointed to conduct an investigation to discover who had commissioned the break-in.

During summer break, Isabella and her mother took a trip to the Midwest. At first glance Aunt Emily, the Foursquare Flame, appeared ordinary, small in stature, thickset, and unpretentious. When she moved or opened her mouth the impression mutated. Isabella laid eyes on Emily with singular interest.

"Margaret Isabel! Little sister, little sister! Come here, let me have a hug," Emily grabbed Missy in bear-like arms, lifted the tiny woman off the ground, and set her down. Missy was taller, not by a lot, and distinctly more slender.

"Emily! Oh, it's good to see you. It's been so long."

"Since we put Mother to her rest. And who exactly is this young woman with you?

Emily turned her broad grin upon Isabella, who smiled, still piercing Emily with scrutiny. "Emily, this is Isabella."

"No. No, it can't be the little tomboy. Grown up and very lovely? Is it possible?"

Isabella was pleased to draw that comment, but of course, Emily knew who she was. "Hello, Aunt Emily."

Emily looked Isabella over good and long and came to rest on Isabella's brown eyes. "She's slender like you, Missy. She doesn't look much like you in the face. She's tall like her father, and her features are her father's. All but those brown eyes. Those belong to Grandma Empee.

"You knew Grandma Empee?"

"No, never laid eyes on her. But when I was young, I heard plenty of stories about her. If you want to really know about that old woman, you'll have to ask your Uncle Clay. What I do know is that everyone who had firsthand knowledge of her said she was a mean one! She didn't have much use for anyone, and most kept clean out of her way."

"She sent her sick brother to work in the mill and to his death," Isabella added.

"How do you know that?"

"Grandy. She told me that Indian Grandma was cursed by the whole town for her inhumanity."

"Dad never had a good thing to say for her. Course, he never had a bad thing to say for her, either. I guess the strongest message was that he said little about her at all, his own mother. Well, what are we standing out here for? Let's go in the house. You coming, Floyd?"

"No. Got to get back to my work. Nice to make your acquaintance, ladies, I'll be seeing you on Sunday, I expect."

"Thanks for picking them up and getting them here safe."

"My pleasure, Sister Emily."

The tea kettle screamed as the women entered the little parsonage. Emily hustled to the kitchen, shut off the flame, and turned, "I figured you'd want tea after the trip."

"Tea would be wonderful!" Missy said. "What a cute, little parsonage. It's wonderful, Emily."

"It's home for me, that's for sure. Has been from the moment I walked in. Mind you, it didn't always look like it does now. It needed a little repair, but nothing a hammer and saw couldn't fix. It's small, but I prefer to think of it as intimate. I remember the first day I walked in here. I just knew I was home!"

"How so?"

"Do you remember when we brought Mary Elizabeth home on the train from St. Louis?" She directed the question to Isabella.

"Sure, I remember when she came home. I don't remember your being there."

"I didn't come to your house. We got off the train and I went to spend the night at Willy's. I caught the train to Des Moines the next morning. That's when I came here. I had postponed my arrival to be with my sister, get her safely back to California. But I had put it off as long as I could. I was offered the opportunity to pastor a church of my own, something I had wanted for years."

"And back then, Isabella, it was a very big deal for your aunt to be given such an opportunity. It was a real credit to you, Emily, that the church council finally agreed." Isabella could tell Missy was proud of her sister.

"Well, as you can see, it's a small community and a relatively small church. But I must admit, I was pleased to make the breakthrough. I had traveled almost constantly from the day I was ordained. I was weary of it and anxious to settle down."

"I know, Aunt Emily. You were out on a mission from God, rampaging across the country, routing crooked churchmen, repairing plumbing, and staving off storms!"

"Woehoe! What's all this?"

"You were sent into situations, like the pastor who was using the offerings to bankroll a dice game?"

Emily threw back her head, boomed a laugh, a gold tooth glinting at the back of her mouth. Her belly shook. Oh, my Lord! I haven't thought of that old rascal for years. Where'd you hear all that?"

"Mother told her, and I guess I've told her, too. But you know, Isabella and Mother were the best of pals when Isabella was growing up. I dare say, Isabella knows more about us than we know ourselves!"

"Did you really command the storm? You remember, at the prayer meeting where they didn't have a tent? And you were in the newspaper."

"Truth is, I've been in the newspaper a few times. Let's see now. Oh, yes. I know what you're referring to, the thunderstorm in Oklahoma, no, Kansas it was. No, Isabella, I did no such thing."

"But Grandy said you raised your hand to the storm and prayed."

"I did that. But it was the Lord God Almighty who held back the storm."

"Do you really believe that?"

"Is it easier to believe that I could do so?"

"No."

"Did she tell you the story of the Sermon on the Mount?"

"Yes, of course."

"After the sermon, Jesus blessed the five loaves and two fishes, and they fed the multitudes."

"Yeah. That was a miracle, right?"

"And then Jesus went into the mountains to pray. Before that, he sent his disciples to get into a ship and cross the Sea of Galilee."

"Right. And that's when he walked on the water."

"Jesus came down from the mountain. A storm had come upon the sea. Jesus walked out across the stormy water of the Sea of Galilee to meet them. Can you imagine?"

"Frankly? No, I can't."

"But that's not the end of it. When Peter saw him, he was afraid, he thought it was a ghost. Jesus said 'Be of good cheer. It is I. Be not afraid.' But Peter had to test. Peter was a curious character, always on the fringe of doubt, struggling for his faith."

"That's not how he is portrayed. I mean, Peter is the rock upon which the church is built."

"How very Catholic of you, Isabella," Emily said with a grin and continued, "Peter was not a rock unless it was the block between his ears. I don't mean to degrade him. It is his very contrary nature that makes him so interesting. This is not about Peter, other than it was his nature to test, and he said to Jesus, 'Lord, if it is you, then bid me come to you on the water.' And Jesus did so. Peter got out of the ship and began to walk on the water, just like Jesus."

"Right, but then he sank into the water."

"Yes. Now that is curious. He has the nerve to ask Christ to bid him come. Imagine that. 'Bid me come, walking on water.' But then, once out there, he saw the winds whip the water and he became afraid."

"Makes sense to me. I think he was crazy to be walking on water to begin with. Please! What kind of a nut would do such a thing?"

"Exactly. Some kind of nut or someone who had unfathomable faith."

"There is no amount of faith that would get me to step onto water and imagine I wouldn't sink into it!"

"Then, Isabella, I don't recommend you try it!" Emily asked if they wanted more tea from the steaming kettle. Missy said yes; Isabella declined.

"That's it? End of story?"

"What do you mean, Isabella?"

"What does that have to do with the storm and prayer meeting in Kansas?"

"You're a smart girl. You tell me."

"I don't know what you're talking about."

Emily looked over at Missy. "She did get Gunter's brains, didn't she?"

"Damn it!"

"Don't use that language in my house, young lady!"

"Well... ," Isabella started to say "hell" but thought better of it. She was considering whether to blow off this aunt along with Uncles Micheil, Willy, and David when Emily continued.

"Isabella, I'm sorry. I shouldn't have spoken to you like that or made reference to your father. I'm a Hume, you know. We're all a little fast with our mouths."

Isabella melted with those words, partly because of the humility in them and partly because she was aware that she had some of that fast-mouth tendency herself.

Emily continued, "I just want you to figure out the connection for yourself, and I know you can."

"You want me to see that you have to have the faith to walk on the water or halt the storm."

"I want you to see that God can work miracles through you if you have unfathomable, unwavering faith. If you step out on the water in defiance of all reason that dictates, you will sink into waves!"

"You know, I am torn between envy and resentment when I encounter people like yourself and my mom who have faith in God. It's all so simple for you. Everything in life can be explained, rationalized, justified, sanctified, but most important of all, distanced because this life is temporal. You are betting your whole life on the speculation of a second, eternal existence. I find that a form of avoidance, in a way, a means of accepting life on terms other than those you would set for yourself if this life were all there was."

"Isabella!" Missy said, partly embarrassed and partly astonished by this declaration—an affirmation of Missy's greatest fears with regard to her daughter's spiritual life.

"Go ahead, Isabella. I want to know what you think," Emily reached out a hand to quiet her sister.

Isabella considered her mother for a moment through her peripheral vision. She wanted to look over at Missy, but knew if she did, she wouldn't speak her mind. "On the one hand, it would be wonderful to rely on the certainty of God. To have faith that there is a plan and that God cares for us as individuals, that there is another chance after life on Earth. Grandy believed all that with great sincerity and openness of heart, and I respected her faith as I do yours, Mom's." Izy could not avoid it any longer. She looked at Missy, then back at Emily. "As it turns out, Aunt Emily, I don't have unwavering faith, and I don't know if I fathom faith at all!"

Missy's eyes dropped to her lap with a sigh that almost went unnoticed.

Emily looked at Isabella. "I might point out that you are betting eternity on your intellectual assessment of spiritual possibilities. And perhaps you don't have faith," Emily continued, "but you're at least honest about it. A lot of people's problem is that they pretend to have faith. Instead, and in reality, they have fear."

"What's that mean?"

"It means they, like you, have their doubts but are afraid it might all be true, so they pretend to have faith just in case. You're not one of them, Isabella. And I believe God respects that authenticity."

Sunday morning Missy and Isabella attended Emily's church service. Isabella heard her Aunt preach for the first time that she could actually remember.

There were flashes when Emily's eyes met Isabella's—Isabella was sure her aunt was speaking specifically to her. "God gives each of us a thorn to bear and we should thank God for that thorn. When we feel its prick, we must thank God for the opportunity to recognize our humanity and to be humbled before He who would love us despite our thorns, our warts, our blemishes, our frailties." Isabella liked that part. She felt she knew what it meant.

"We are put upon this Earth to rise above our weaknesses, our primal natures, and to seek God's higher purpose for our lives. It's one thing to live a good and decent life. That's fine, there's nothing wrong with that, there will be no disregard for such a life. But there is much, much more for the soul who aspires to be Christ-like. What does that mean? Christ did not settle for a good and decent life. He went out of his way to make a difference, to matter, and he changed the world. You can change the world if you have faith and seek to know God's higher purpose for your life." Isabella was moved. She felt that if Emily went on, she'd not be able to stay in her seat. Just when Isabella thought some unknowable force might propel her forward, Sister Emily called to bow heads. She prayed for her congregation to know their potential to serve God and to learn to have compassion for all others through knowing themselves.

During their stay in Iowa, they ate meat, corn, and potatoes, drank hot and cold tea, and spent an inordinate amount of time in church, talking about God, and reading or quoting the Bible. It had been a long time since Isabella had been confronted with that aspect of her life. In recent years she'd put a lot of miles between herself and the faith she once had in a God who might have answered her prayers, but never did. She watched. She listened. She yearned to be cradled in the certainty that her aunt and her mother shared. At one point Izy closed her eyes and consciously forced herself to let go of her disbelief and claim the promise of God and the purity of renewal through Jesus. But it all fell with a thud upon her reasoning and her eyes sprang open. Isabella was respectful of the universe and its omnipotence in contrast with humanity's vulnerability. But she lacked any sense of faith in a sentient, fatherly God.

"I remember you when you were just a little thing," Emily told her. "Any time I'd see you, you'd ask about Kathy. You were precocious and outgoing. And your mother, well, she fussed over you as if you were the center of the universe."

"What about my father?"

"What do you mean?"

"You didn't mention my father. But you knew him."

"Yes. I knew him, only a little. What can I say about that sultry German?"

"Sultry?"

"Sultry. Gunter was a molten mass under the surface. Most of what went on for him was buried in his head. He's a brilliant person, very intelligent. But he used his intelligence viciously."

"That's not a nice thing to say."

"I don't mean to insult your father, but he is a difficult man."

"You don't know the half of it."

"I imagine I don't."

"I want to know more. Don't worry, you won't insult me, I promise."

"He was handsome and stylish, critical of anything that did not fit his idea of things. He had strange ideas contorting his mind early on. Some he asserted, but the rest never saw the light of day. Sometimes, it was what he held in that was the most disconcerting."

"He never held much in around us."

"Well, he changed. When he went into the service he had a great sense of humor and seemed to be a swell guy. He used to draw cartoons when he was billeted in England before he shipped out to Europe. We knew about them because he would send some home to Missy. He signed them 'Rhino' with a funny caricature of himself with a big, upturned horn like a rhinoceros. Clever, he was very clever."

"I don't remember anything like that about him."

"After the war he was very different. I think his dark side was lurking there even earlier, but after he returned home, it seemed to me it loomed larger and consumed him before too long. I've always wondered if Missy would have married him if she had waited just a year. But then, maybe she would have anyway. She was pretty smitten. He was a hero, you know. Won the Distinguished Service Cross. Very complex character, your father."

"I know about all that."

"He was crazy about you."

"No. He never really liked me at all. He thought I was his enemy and stupid."

"Maybe later. But in the beginning, you and he were best friends."

Isabella recalled her mother's words, "Yeah, Mom says the same, but I don't remember it that way."

"Well, that's how it was. In fact, I dare say it bordered on perilous."

"Why perilous?"

"Because it was nearly obsessive. He spent all his time with you. He was convinced you could do anything and treated you more as a pal, like an adult, when you were still in diapers. In a way, I guess it was a good thing. You were quick to learn and he was a willing teacher. But it was… , it felt… ," Emily searched for the right word, only to repeat, "perilous."

Isabella let that sink in, then changed the subject.

"Tell me about when you first came here. That must have been a little strange."

"Oh, yes, I was going to tell you about Floyd coming to get me at the train station."

"You mean Brother Floyd Fenister, the one who brought us here?"

"The very one. I arrived with two suitcases—good-sized ones, banged up, marred, but still holding together and containing everything I had in the world. You don't acquire much on the road. You can't. And maybe that was part of why I was so weary. I'd left so many things behind. Anyway, Sister Fenister told me how Floyd had been all riled up the whole day. First, I should tell you that the founder of The Church, Sister, lived her life and died surrounded by controversy and scandal."

"I know about her."

"Right. So into town I come, a woman pastor." Emily put her head back and her belly shook again with laughter. Isabella smiled to see it. "I'd held services in Des Moines, but other than that, these good people had no way of knowing me, except maybe by reputation.

"Anyway, here I come. And all day Floyd's fussing, 'Who could be comfortable confiding in a woman about sin? What about church business? What if there's some trouble that required a pastor to step up and take charge?' He was sure it wasn't going to work out.

"Nevertheless, dutifully, he left his house to pick up this Reverend Sister Evans. He was polite and tipped his hat, escorted me to this very parsonage, but refused to do more than carry my two bags onto the porch, it not being proper to go into the house alone with a woman. I guess no one had ever schooled him on proper etiquette in the presence of a woman minister. I could see it was not going to be easy."

"How'd that make you feel?"

"Oh, I guess I felt compassion."

"Compassion? I'd think you'd be put off or something."

"If you want to break ground you'd better be prepared for the lumps and bumps! I thought quickly, then commended Floyd for his conviction and assured him I was fully able to get those big old bags inside on my own. He nodded, a bit befuddled, wondering if he shouldn't take them on in, but equally certain that he would not. Finally, he turned and went on his way. I'm pretty sure that, at that point, he didn't know what to think."

"What did you think?"

"Well, I thought he would rather be befuddled than improper. I thought he was polite, and that was something. I thought he was a good man, and I was glad for his thoughtfulness on the matter."

"Today, things would be different."

"I imagine you're right. Things are very different today. And not always in a good way, Isabella."

"Don't you, of all people, agree that women should have equal opportunity in the world?"

"Yes. Yes, I guess I plain have to say yes on that. But I'm not altogether aligned with the style of things today, even so."

"Bra-burning. That's a style you're not aligned with."

"There you go! You got it. I resent it!"

"But why?"

"Because it is improper, vulgar, and inappropriate."

"It's supposed to be. It's a protest. The purpose is to outrage."

"Well, it outrages me, all right."

"If women had burned their undergarments a long time ago maybe you'd have had it easier being a minister."

"And who says that would have been a good thing? First of all, Isabella, why in the world would women want to be equal to men? Women are already superior. They are the ones endowed by God to house life and bring it forward.

What conceivably is more sacred and important than that?"

"I thought we were cursed."

"Yes. The pain and suffering is the curse. But we are also blessed with incredible significance, a power that cannot be equaled but can be subjugated if we allow it—and we seem to allow it just about everywhere. But not completely so. Grandma Empee's people passed on the lineage of the Huron through the women. Here, read this book."

"Huron! So you are curious about her, too."

"Yes, she is part of me, of us. She is why I am short and stout and why you have those brown eyes."

"My father hated my eyes, always; he called me his brown-eyed pig."

"That's an awful thing to say to a child. Don't own it, Isabella. Push that away from you and embrace your mixed heritage. It gives you an opportunity to understand the world better."

After Iowa, mother and daughter traveled to Danville to visit with Micheil and Renée. Isabella and Uncle Micheil ruffled feathers as they tested each other. But the stay passed without incident. They learned that Patrick, the younger son—a missionary in the Congo, renamed Zaire—lived a dangerous life under tyranny, and that Micheil Junior still had not been heard from.

On the last leg of their journey, the women visited Kathy at the University of Illinois. The younger women made the most of their limited time together, catching up and renewing a friendship that did not need constant tending to be strong and true.

Kathy told her cousin that her brother, Patrick, was going to be married.

"Your father never mentioned it."

"That's because he is marrying a local Zairian woman, and Daddy won't hear talk of it at all."

Izy recalled Grandy saying, "...it will always come 'round on you!" For a moment Izy felt a tinge of compassion for Uncle Micheil, as it was apparent he was meant to face some daunting music.

The trip gave Izy time to observe her mother in ways she never had before. It was an illuminating and a surprising treat. Missy was like a tulip at first opening, when you can get just a hint of what might be inside. Her money was tight; she wasted nothing and hunted for bargains. She dressed in her own sense of style with bright colors, something Isabella never realized she liked. Now Missy wore perky pink, sunny gold, emerald green, royal blue, rich red, and often floral patterns. She wore a hair ribbon or flower and always earrings. Izy felt as though she were meeting her mother for the first time.

The damage to Missy's face had faded. She got new front teeth and her smile could light a room. She invited company and served little dinners or lunches. Nothing extravagant: a couple of friends from work or someone from church. She was a gracious hostess. Occasionally she brought out the crystal to dazzle and make even a fruit salad seem special.

There was one lady who Missy chummed with: Emma Hannay. Emma was alone in the world. Her mother, father, and brother were all dead and Emma had never married. Emma lived in the mobile home next to Missy. The two went shopping, weeded their little gardens, and traded recipes. They became best friends, alone together. Missy was building one thing she had never had: a life of her own.

"You know, I'm very proud of you, Isabella."

"How so, Mom?"

"You're working and going to college, it's admirable. I wish we'd been able to help you get an education. I know you don't have much time for anything, and I want you to know that what you are doing is remarkable."

In the fall, the International Brotherhood of Electrical Workers walked out of contract negotiations and set a date for a strike. That was all that anyone was talking about at the plant. Well, that and whether or not Nixon was a crook who should be impeached. The political news that had once roused Izy now stressed her out. When she did contemplate the news or media speculation, she'd wonder, "If a president could be murdered, if he could be an outright liar and a crook, then what was there to believe in, anyway?" The strike was a welcome distraction from the headlines.

The company told its office employees that since they were not members of the union, they would have to come to work or be fired. The union made it known that in the event of a strike, they expected the office staff to refuse to cross the picket line.

The Silver Cats said that if the non-union employees stayed out and supported the strike, the union would protect their jobs. It was standard practice. After lunch one day, Thunderbolt suggested that Izy go with her outside for a smoke. "What are you thinking of doing, Kid?"

"You mean the strike? I don't know. I feel I'm a part of you guys, so I should stay out."

"I think you should cross."

"What?"

"Now don't go getting all riled. Just listen. This is really a lot of saber-rattling by the union. There's no stopping what's inevitable here at the plant. Even if the union succeeds in slowing things down, all that's going to do is delay people losing their jobs."

"But Ginny said... ,"

"Ginny, Maryann, they're clinging to what's familiar, and I don't fault them. But it's the end of us. Maybe not right away, but it is coming. Pretty soon if you don't know about these new machines, you won't know anything at all. And we don't know a thing about them. In no time, what I do will be unnecessary. Already, they're bringing in these components that have whole boards in tiny little boxes. It's just the beginning—and you can be a part of it. But you gotta use your head, not your heart. Now don't you tell the gals what I'm telling you, but you cross—don't make no trouble for yourself."

"I can handle trouble."

"Yeah, I'll bet you can, but this is trouble you should avoid. I'm real proud of you, Kid. But don't mess up and ruin everything."

When the line went up Izy crossed, reluctantly. It was hard to go against the Silver Cats. Izy felt she was betraying her friends, and she was, right in front of them, a traitor. The Cats watched her cross, stunned. They lobbed nasty words: "Scab! You little traitor!" She felt it deeply. Oh, how it hurt.

The strike lasted three weeks. In that time Izy filled in and made a fair tour of the floor, doing a little of everything. If Izy respected them before, now she really had an appreciation for their skill. The Silver Cats' work was much harder than they made it look. It made sense to lower costs by eliminating manual labor and jobs that required years of experience and special skill, talent even. The product could be made faster and priced cheaper. The company could bid lower on contracts and get more work, which would mean more jobs. The taxpayers could get what they wanted for less. Izy was convinced Thunderbolt was dead right and seeing the arc of the future. So why couldn't she be a part of it?

The union workers returned, but the Silver Cats cut Izy out of their circle. All but Thunderbolt, who made time to smoke cigarettes with Izy; she asked about school and winked at her across the floor as she passed. Izy was kind of broken-hearted. Over time she gravitated toward the college boys for companionship. Somehow the Silver Cats had forgiven the boys for crossing, but Izy was different. Her crossing had hurt them in a deeply personal way.

In August of 1974, under the threat of impeachment, Richard "Tricky Dick" Nixon resigned. Deeply troubled by the implications and needing to sort her inventory of tiny boxes, Isabella made her way north. She selected the longest route possible: the coast highway, then inland to the central valley, through the rolling hills and oak trees, across the Oregon border at Klamath, along the Cascades, then down into the Umpqua River Valley. Uncle Clay had much to say on the subject of Nixon and the resignation. Isabella listened respectfully but didn't want to hear about presidential paranoia, so she tuned it out as much as possible, then sought a way to change the subject. From high up in the tree, picking cherries, she said, "Say, when I was in Iowa, Aunt Emily said I should ask you about Grandma Empee."

"That old woman? Leave the bright reds to ripen."

"I will. Yes, Grandy said you were the only one of the children to ever meet her."

"True enough. Be careful up there. You know I'd get up there and pick them myself, but for this old knee. Avoid growing old, Isabella."

She smiled without even thinking about it. She liked being up in the tree. It filled her heart with pleasure to be able to do something for her uncle he could not do himself."

"Grandma Empee?"

"Well, let me see." He took a few steps to the glider swing and sat down, looking up to watch his niece plucking the sweet fruit, one by one. "It was during the good weather, must have been spring, no, summer of '17. Dad took me with him on a trip back to Garden Grove. It was the greatest adventure of my life, mind you. I'd never been anywhere but our farm community. I met his brother, my Uncle Micheil. He was married with a family. He introduced his eldest son with pride, and his other children as well. Anyway, we don't even get settled before Dad comes to me and says, 'Come on son, Micheil and I are going for a walk. You come along.'

"The three of us head out the door walking south out of town. On the way Dad says, 'You might as well know, son, you're Indian, by my mother. Half on me and a quarter on you.' I say, 'Real Indian?' He answers, 'As real as can be. Your grandmother is full-blooded Huron and mean as a skunk. But we think you should meet her anyway. That's where we're off to.'"

"Here, Uncle Clay, trade me baskets." The old man rose and walked over to where he could grasp the basket Isabella had lowered on a jute rope. He loosened the rope from the looped handles, set down the bounty, and retied the empty basket. Isabella whisked it up and begin filling. "Go on with the story. Tell me everything."

"We walked a good distance kicking up dust as we went down the dirt roads. Finally, we came upon a sturdy shack with a lean-to on the side. Under the lean-to was a wood-burning stove with a crooked pipe run up through the slanted roof to carry smoke to the sky. As we approached, a woman came out on the porch and leaned against the post supporting the porch roof. She had piercing, dark eyes set into sallow, chiseled features, and long, gray hair pulled back into a braid that went to her waist. She was short and square-shaped; she did not look well but stood straight, nonetheless. She wore britches made of tanned leather. I had never seen a woman in britches and I have to tell you, Isabella, I wasn't sure what to expect.

"'Good day, mother Empee. I've brought you a grandson to have a look at,' my father says. 'A filthy grandson, I'd say,' she replies. I looked down at my clothes all covered in the dust of the road. My father says, 'We've come by a long walk. I'd say he comes by the dirt honestly.' She looks at me again and says, 'Take your clothes off, boy. I'll wash 'em for you and have a look.' Well, I looked at Dad. He gave no signal. I looked at Uncle Micheil, none from him either. So I untied my high tops, pulled off my socks, then looked again, but no utterance. Both of them watching me, scratching their chins. So I untied my britches and took off my shirt, handed them to the woman. And I'm feeling a bit silly. But that was it."

Isabella was intrigued and stopped her picking to look down as he talked gesturing with his hands, his thoughts deep into his old memory.

"Now I should tell you, Mother'd handmade those clothes for me just for the trip. That old woman, she went to the stove and put wood on the coals. 'Fill this tub with water from the well, boy,' she said, and motioned me to the back. I did as she said, my pale skin naked, in nothing but my long johns and feeling the sun on my back. Now go on with the cherries if you want cobbler tonight!"

"Okay, okay, I'm picking."

Clay smiled, pleased to be sharing his memories with his niece. He continued, "The old Indian put the tub on the stove and heated the water. As it boiled, she poured lye salts in and stirred the water with a stick. She looked at me and tossed my clothes into the brew, stirring and singing a tune. When she was satisfied, she pulled out the shirt and pants with the stick and threw them on a line, steaming and dripping.

"Then she sits on the step and looks at me with my arms wrapped around my naked self. 'You've your grandfather in you, and he died young. Got the sugar disease.' She was referring to diabetes, of course. 'They cut off his feet and he was useless,' she went on. 'Then his heart gave out. Probably the same will come to you. No feet and useless, then dead.' What a wicked old witch to say that to a boy. She went on, 'Let me see your hands.' I showed her, palms up. 'Well, you're a working man anyway. There's a feather. Do you know what they say about me?'

"About now, I can imagine what they might say, but I answer, 'No, I don't.' 'Good,' she says. 'It's all lies anyway.' Then she pulled a pipe from her waistband and put the stem between her teeth. 'Got a light, boy?' I answer, 'No. Never smoked.' She says, 'Don't trust a man don't smoke.'

"She looked at her two sons, then back again. And you should know, when that old woman stared at you, you felt run through! She took a sliver of a tree to the stove and lit the pipe. She drew in and coughed, no doubt with the sickness that was in her, and then her eyes narrowed. 'If you've come looking for something, there's nothing here. Just me, and I don't like you none. I don't suppose you like me either.' By now I was pretty sure I didn't, but I didn't answer. She sat down on the step and said, 'No matter. We're bound by blood, boy, but we ain't kin. I left my kin 'cause they were stupid fools. Do you know that, boy? Listening to the lies of white men. Yeah, boy! White men like your grandfather. Lying comes natural to 'em. Probably a lie or two in you, too, boy, by the color of ya.'

"'First they come with their dirty robes and their pox, killing off my people by the thousands. They come like it's a gift they bring. But it's a curse. They want to herd the people here, then there, always promises, always lies.' She paused, puffed, coughed, and spat. 'They split us up to weaken us: half south, the rest east. No good came of it. 'Course that was the thinking of the devils. Fools don't learn. My family chose to stay, corralled, like animals. I choose different. Turns out my choice brought me freedom but nothing else. I have lived among white fools in a white man's world. In your world, boy, men pass their name and curse their daughters. In the world of my people, women pass the name; they choose

220

the tribal council and keep the medicine. My Clan was Bear. The Bear women were powerful and wise. That small part of you that runs with my blood is Bear. Remember that, boy. Your daughters will be Bear women and you should honor them for who they are.'" Isabella paused again and looked at the sky as her uncle went on.

"I never had any daughters, only my son. So maybe she was talking about you, Isabella. You have her blood. You are Bear, as well." For the first time, Isabella felt a depth of dignity rise up in her. She closed her brown eyes for a moment, letting it all settle in on her.

After a bit she lowered the basket down, descended, and repositioned the ladder, then climbed up again with yet another basket. Uncle Clay watched her without speaking. He waited until his niece was high in the tree again before he continued, "The old Indian pulled out a small pouch, opened it, and poked more fuel into her pipe. She got up with some difficulty, but once up she stood her full height, stretched, and lit her pipe again. The men shifted, but not much. I stood stark still, watching every move, filling up with questions but not enough to make me do any asking. She sat again and spoke, 'I can see that you are blue-eyed like your father and his father. A big part of you is a fool. I can smell em and I can handle em, but I don't have to suffer em.'

"She went on lecturing me about the clan and their ways, their customs, and the fools in her life, in the family, not the least of whom stood behind me. But they spoke not a word. I can't remember everything she told me. She kept on till the sun had gone over the roof. I was standing in the shade half-naked; the wind had picked up, giving me a serious case of chicken skin. She never offered us a seat, a drink of water, or any kindness. When she was good and ready, she rose, went into the old shack without a word and closed the door."

Isabella returned to Earth, certain she'd gotten all that was ripe and ready. She positioned the baskets so they could manage them all in one trip back to the house.

Clay continued, "We all stood there waiting to see if she'd return. Then I felt the two of them looking at me, and I turned to see them waiting for my reaction. It occurred to me that the old woman wasn't coming back out any time soon, so I ran to get my clothes off the line. They were still damp. Worse, the lye water had nearly shredded the shirt mother had sewn and eaten holes in my britches. I looked at them, and they looked at each other and laughed.

"I put on my cold, tattered britches and tied the arms of what was left of my shirt around my waist to cover the holes. My father and uncle clapped me on my bare back and shook their heads, grinning. 'Well now, boy, you've met her. Stay away from her at all cost!'"

"Whatever happened to Grandma Empee?"

"Not too long after that, but long enough, we were already in Los Angeles, a letter came from Micheil Junior, my cousin. He told us his father had died and explained what was going to happen to the family. The older ones were going to work and the younger ones would stay with their mother. It's a curious thing: Both brothers died young and left families to fend for themselves."

"Grandma Empee," she reminded him.

"In the letter, he mentioned the old Indian woman was dead. Lungs gave out, couldn't breathe, probably cancer. Died alone. There in her shack, didn't find her for days. It's not a nice thing when the dead just lie there. Especially off in the woods in an old shack. Afraid she was part of the food chain by the time they came and took her away. Eyes, nose, lips, throat, and fingers— all eaten, pretty much."

"Gross!"

"I guess, but it is the natural order of things. Tribal people came and got her. Don't know what they did with her. Somehow, I have this feeling that was fine with her."

Isabella contemplated the bizarre end of her Indian Grandma and wondered if it was poetry or penalty. "At least you got to meet her," Isabella said as she entered the house.

"Yes. I think I'm grateful for knowing who she was, bitter as that may be. On the walk back to town that day, after initiating me as a genuine member of the Hume Clan, they shared tales of her villainous ways. When we got to town, Dad got out a silver dollar and gave it to me to buy new clothes, saying, 'Guess life owes a dollar.'"

"That's what she meant!"

"Meant? Who meant what?" Clay said as he dumped the cherries into a strainer.

"When Grandy was dying, she was looking into heaven and told you that."

Clay paused, "Yes. She said that. A message from Dad."

President Ford pardoned Nixon of all wrongdoing in the Watergate incident. In a subdued and riveting moment on live television, he said, "By taking this action, I hope that I will have hastened the start of the process of healing." He retained secretary of state Henry Kissinger in his cabinet, which came as a relief to Izy. He didn't do anything really great or important after that, in most minds. Izy thought he tried to be an honest president, especially since his predecessor in the Oval Office was a crook. He appointed George Bush to head the Central Intelligence Agency.

"Keep an eye on this Bush. What he does in the Middle East will mark our future!"

"How so, Uncle Clay?"

"Oil, Isabella, oil."

"What does Bush have to do with the Middle East?"

"There's the crux of it. Oh, yes, Isabella, there's a brew already simmering in that part of the world. And the question is: What will Bush do? Cool it or heat it?"

Francy was having problems in her marriage. Her husband, Redmond Butler, was born and raised in Alabama. He was ruggedly handsome and his body was solid. He had a tattoo of the Marine Corps emblem on his bicep. His thoughts were two-dimensional and his manners crude.

"What can I say? I don't like him. I tried. I really did try, Ronn. But smashing beer cans on one's forehead gets old really fast," Izy explained over the phone. "At first, Francy thought he was just wonderful. 'Virile' I believe was the word she used. But I think she's growing weary of old stories and boorish behavior. She's ready to leave the Marines behind, but Redmond doesn't seem to be so inclined. More and more, Francy comes over alone and hangs out here until she gets a call ordering her home. I think this relationship is going south, and while I feel bad for Francy, I confess, I'm relieved. Besides, Redmond wants to move to Alabama. I don't think Francy's going."

Izy was confident that, painful as it might be, divorce would free Francine to make a new life for herself. Francy was older now and would surely do well without Redmond. Izy thought of her mother: How curious that these two women who were so different might have something in common. Izy watched the dissolution of the Butler marriage with a sense of relief and expectation.

At her work, Izy was taking on more and more complex problems and solving them with confidence. She went to meetings and participated at higher levels in the decision-making process. Sometimes a report she had generated would end up as the basis for a new direction, purchase, or strategy. Izy observed the bosses and formed opinions on their leadership styles and competence as managers. She became more and more convinced that she could do what they do, given a chance.

In 1975 Izy got a phone call from the City of Los Angeles. Gunter had run afoul with the law. After Missy left the nightmare house he had continued his modifications to the structure. He had also boarded up the front door and windows—the property was an eyesore.

The neighborhood at large did not appreciate the modifications; particularly bothered were the people who moved into Shelly's old house next door. The fact that they were black didn't help: It fed Gunter's racial paranoia and, in turn, kindled frustration in other neighbors, especially the man next door on the other side who noticed that the "nut" had lights on under the house and made all manner of banging and crashing sounds late into the night. He filed a complaint.

When city officials showed up to investigate, Gunter didn't answer their knocks at the door. Since the phone had been disconnected, they nailed a notice to the front door for Gunter to appear in court, which he ignored. As a result, the planning department filed charges in court for unauthorized structural modifications and an assortment of other building code violations. Barraged with noise complaints, the police added on disturbing the peace, failure to appear for previous citations, and anything else they could tack on for emphasis.

The real problem was that Missy, still on the deed, would be a party in any legal action. Intervening on behalf of her mother, Izy called the contact listed on the paperwork Missy had received in the mail. She was told, "…and make sure that your father shows up for the hearing!" Izy laughed out loud at that. "If the City of Los Angeles cannot get him out of his lair, how on earth do you expect me to?" She explained she had absolutely no way of contacting or influencing her father, hadn't for years. She assured the person on the other end of the line that Missy had nothing to do with the debacle. She said she would be hiring a lawyer to represent her mother, then said goodbye.

As Izy hung up the phone, a familiar, dark cloud settled around her, thick and damp. She took in a slow, deep breath and ran through memories she thought she had put firmly behind her. She started to experience small, jerking motions—random muscle groups responding to an innate need to flee but held in check by the sound of her own voice: "You cannot run from this!"

In her search for an attorney, Izy was given the name of Milton Feldner, whose office was way out in the San Fernando Valley. She dialed the number and left a message; he promptly returned her call. Isabella briefly explained the situation; he told her she should come in to see him right away. Isabella cut class that night, picked up Missy, and drove out to the Valley to meet Mr. Feldner.

He was a short, balding Jewish man, not all that old, who was intrigued by Isabella's story. He agreed to represent Missy—he was confident he could get her extricated from the case.

"What about your father?"

"What about him?"

"Do you want me to represent him as well?"

"You don't understand. He's nuts! He probably wouldn't even talk to you, and if he did, you probably wouldn't understand what he was saying."

"I do understand that your father is mentally ill. He is in trouble with the authorities and may be incompetent to defend himself. Do you want me to help him, assuming I can?"

"Well, yes, when you put it that way. Of course, he is my father. I would want to help him if it were possible. Sure."

"Can we arrange to see him?"

"That's another matter. There's no way to get hold of him. That's the city's problem. He's in that underground maze somewhere. He won't come out, even though they've posted notices for him to appear. My father just ignores them."

"Phone?"

"Long gone."

"Then we'll have to go there ourselves. What do you think he'll do if it's you two standing at the door?"

"My mother is not going to that house!"

"I'll go if I can help him, Isabella," said Missy.

"No, absolutely not! If anyone goes, it'll be me. I am his flesh and blood. I am his daughter." And as Izy said those words, a whole new frame of reference began to align in her consciousness. It was an uneasy idea at first, but it continued to permeate her being and a new sense of responsibility dawned. Izy was no longer his victim, she was his link to the outside world, if there could be one. She was in a position to help her father—and it was like sunlight after a storm. Everything had changed, but Izy did not comprehend the portent. "When do you want to go?"

"Well, considering he is expected in court in thirty-six hours, the sooner the better. How about tomorrow afternoon?" As she and Missy drove home, Isabella tried to calm herself by talking about anything that might deflect from what she had just agreed to do.

Isabella went to work in the morning, busying herself until it was time to leave. She told her boss she had personal business and headed toward the rendezvous. Mr. Feldner was waiting in his Mercedes-Benz.

Isabella had one advantage over the city: She knew where he'd be. She passed the front house by and, with Mr. Feldner in tow, made her way through the overgrowth of trees, plants, grass, and weeds. Beside the creek, some calla lilies still poked through. Spider webs hung like drapes from tree to tree. Mud, hidden in shadow, made sucking sounds beneath Mr. Feldner's elegant loafers. Once past the garage, she could see the little house where Grandy had lived.

Her heart pounded in her ears as she beat on the door. "Daddy? Daddy, it's me, Isabella. I want you to open the door and let me in. I have to talk to you. You know that I have to talk to you. Daddy?"

She waited. There was the slightest sound inside the house, confirming he was there. "Daddy. You are in big trouble. There finally is a conspiracy, Daddy! We have to talk. I know you hear me. Look out here and see that it's me, Daddy." Isabella saw a flicker of movement between the boards nailed to the window next to the door. A raspy, weary voice from the past spoke to her, "Who is that man with you?"

"Daddy, this is Mr. Milton Feldner. He is an attorney, and we are here to talk to you about what the city is doing. We're here to help you if you'll let us. Now, Daddy, open the door! This is serious. This time you *are* in trouble!"

"Go to the back door of the house." He was going to let them in. Izy knew he meant the back door of the other house.

"Okay, Daddy. We'll meet you there."

They made their way back toward the back door—past the garage and through the overgrowth, sloshing in the mud and shaking off the cobwebs.

Having beaten them there by way of his tunnels, he was waiting, waving them in as if every second the door remained opened was an opportunity for the legions of his persecutors to breach his domain.

The place smelled of excrement and urine. Everything was the color of clay and sand. Isabella barely recognized anything. The only flooring was a catwalk across the expanses of the former rooms turned open chasms around the supports from the cellar to the earth below. The kitchen and bathroom were completely gone.

He took her breath away. Her father was covered in filth, his hair long and unkempt. He wore heavy-duty coveralls and a makeshift truss on the outside of his clothes. Cardboard boxes, cut up and taped around his feet, served as shoes. His delicate, artist's hands were gnarled and deformed from labor and the dank environment in which he lived. His face was old. He was thin. His eyes searched Isabella's and, for a moment, she glimpsed a flicker of her Daddy, or maybe she had imagined it.

She struggled to get the words out, "Daddy," pausing, "this is Mr. Feldner." Isabella turned at last to Mr. Feldner and was glad to see he hadn't fainted. "This is my father, Gunter Reinhardt."

Mr. Feldner treated the aberrant creature with complete dignity and respect. Suddenly and simultaneously, Isabella felt ashamed of something she could not grasp, yet grateful for something she did not understand completely. Mr. Feldner explained the charges and liabilities.

Gunter interrupted with his version of what was happening, which included threats from Martin Luther King whom he claimed had not been killed after all: He'd gone underground to lead a plot to take over the neighborhood. It was the plot, Gunter insisted, that had brought about this conflict.

Mr. Feldner never contradicted Gunter. He persisted in his assurances that, if Gunter failed to appear in court, they would take more drastic measures against him, which could include forceful arrest and, worst case, seizure of Gunter's property. He calmly told Gunter that if he would agree to appear in court in the morning, he would accompany him as his legal representative. Mr. Feldner stressed that if he did so, there was a strong possibility that something drastic—such as his ending up in jail or even a mental ward—might be averted, and that a simple continuance could lead to a settlement out of court. Gunter lapsed in and out of coherent dialogue, but he seemed to like the little lawyer. Isabella felt a wave of relief. Maybe this could work out after all. Mr. Feldner talked with Gunter for over an hour, patiently reiterating the facts of the case and reassuring him that he would be treated with consideration of his rights.

Gunter was definitely warming to Mr. Feldner; he decided to take him on a tour of his work. Mr. Feldner agreed, thanking him for his offer. Isabella had a moment of panic.

Mr. Feldner seemed oblivious to any danger as he climbed down into the bowels of the structure in his very nice suit. Gunter stopped every few yards to point out some aspect of his engineering of the construct that was unique. Isabella was jerked back to her childhood when he explained the rounded ceilings and eggshell design.

Gunter talked about the trains, but the trains weren't there anymore; maybe they were in his mind. Isabella saw an old cardboard box she vaguely recognized. "Perhaps they were in there," she thought. Gunter led them through the tunnels and showed them his time capsule: a huge room at least fifteen feet in diameter, maybe twenty. Inside the time capsule he was storing things of "great significance for the generations to come." Isabella saw some of his canvases there, damaged by the moisture. It was all so much more elaborate than Isabella remembered. "Daddy has been busy," she thought. Bits and pieces of her childhood, hardly recognizable, were scattered around the dungeon. So long as he talked of things technical, he seemed coherent. When he went off in more subjective areas, things drifted into his strangely fantastic world.

All in all, they were in the nightmare house for about three hours. Gunter assured them he would be there in the morning. Mr. Feldner offered to pick him up and drive him downtown, but Gunter said he could get there on his own. Isabella wasn't sure about that, but they took what they could get under the circumstances, and left Gunter inside the house.

It was after five o'clock when Isabella and Mr. Feldner arrived back on planet Earth. Mr. Feldner asked Isabella if they could reconvene at his office. Isabella agreed and they parted. She drove away, trying to picture the man she had just met riding downtown on a public bus. Sometime on that drive back to the valley, Isabella realized that Gunter wouldn't show.

When Isabella arrived at Mr. Feldner's office, his secretary said she could find him two doors down and that he was expecting her there. "Two doors down" was a bar. Mr. Feldner, calm and collected in the presence of her father back at the nightmare house, was sucking down gin martinis. He'd tossed one back before the one in front of him. The empty glass still stood next to the one he was working on.

"Sit down, Isabella, dear. You want something?"

"Sure. Vodka, rocks, lemon," she called to the bartender. It crossed her mind that maybe Daddy caused everyone to drink. Well, except her mother.

"He's not going to show, Mr. Feldner."

"Call me Milton. After what we've just shared, well, I think we're on a first-name basis, don't you?"

"Sure." Izy actually felt more comfortable as she saw his cracked facade lay bare how unnerved he really was. It was a validation of something. She wasn't sure what. "He won't be there in the morning."

"We've done our best. And I'll be there. I think you should be as well."

The bartender dropped off her vodka. She sipped. "Yeah, well, I have this recurring nightmare where he somehow manages to entangle me in his life, and I wind up trapped in that house with him being a wild man. I mean, you haven't had the pleasure of seeing him at his worst. Anyway, I think I'm going to pass. Just please make sure they take my mother completely out of his mess, okay? She gulped the rest of her vodka.

"That will be no problem, I'm confident." He lit a cigarette and his hand trembled. He offered one to Izy. She took it and lit it. Milton put his hand on top of hers, looked at Isabella, and slowly shook his head. Izy pulled as much of the smoke as she could deep into her lungs, hoping for a buzz, wishing it could be like that first drag under the bleachers with Gina. Man, were those days gone!

ILLUSIVE BUTTERFLY LOVE

High above the proceedings light entered from windows near the ceiling. Babbling voices created a quite roar, an atmosphere of orderly chaos. The room was huge. Two-thirds were rows of seating: hard, wooden benches behind a wooden railing. Beyond that large tables were positioned among a smattering of people huddled in small conflabs or filling out papers next to impressive stacks of thick books. Men mostly, inexpensive, crisp suits wielding briefcases and shuffling blue documents, signaling with their hands to come here, wait there, or read this. The judge sat high up at his desk while several people milled around him.

They entered unnoticed and navigated toward the front of the room where they found seats near the rail. The man talked to the women in a quiet, firm voice, then turned and passed through the gate in the rail. He went to another man seated at a table below the judge on the left. Words were exchanged, an arm pointed. The man moved to the other side of the room where a tall man in a dark suit stood with two other attendants. The man handed him a document that was perused and examined, discussed and explained. Hand motions punctuating the conversation and heads nodding in agreement, the four moved to a table below the judge on the right. The tall man spoke with a clerk, who rose up and addressed the judge, who then reached out for the document.

The four men talked together while the judge read and conferred. Then the judge spoke to the four. They replied by nodding in further agreement. The judge spoke again and banged his gavel to the general disinterest of the occupants of the huge room. An individual on one side of the judge motioned to the bailiff, who stepped up and accepted a piece of paper with a nod.

The man returned through the wooden gate to the side of the two women.

"That's it?"

"That's it. You're disappointed?"

"Yes. What kind of court is this? Where's the drama, the focus?"

"This is an arraignment court. It's strictly business, no drama. Hundreds of cases move through the logistics of this courtroom every day, Isabella. Gunter is accused of misdemeanor violations."

"I guess I thought it would be quite different."

"Well not here, not for this. Especially since he's a no-show. If he had been here it would have been a little more formal. I covered the details of your involvement, Mrs. Reinhardt, on the phone yesterday and in a brief, which I just delivered to the prosecutor's assistant. They accept the explanation and agree to extricate you from the charge. You're clear and out of it, no problem there."

"I'm so relieved. But what about... ," Missy hesitated.

"What? I can see it in your face," Isabella interrupted.

"Gunter's not here in time to answer the charges—boom! The judge issued a warrant for Gunter's arrest. It will be delivered to the marshal's office today. That means they have orders to apprehend him, take him by force, if necessary." Missy gasped, covering her mouth with her small hand and shaking her head.

Isabella looked into Milton's face for a moment. "I knew I shouldn't have come."

"They may have to hurt him. They'll take one way or the other now," Milton said. "But you did. Why?"

"I don't want him to be hurt again," Missy said firmly.

"It won't be the first time," Izy said. "Why do you think I came? When will they do it? Oh, how I hate him!"

"Isabella! You mustn't say that," Missy exhorted.

"They will make a peaceful attempt at least once, post another notice on the door like they did before. And you love him."

"He'll ignore it, he can't help it, Milton, and you don't know what's in my heart. I hate him!"

"Isabella!" Missy raised her voice.

"You hate that you love him," he said.

The Ocean of Peace accepted the falling sun gracefully, quenching its light, bidding the stars to come play. Clear night, no haze, Isabella sat huddled in a ball on her small balcony, peering out toward the nightmare house, sipping vodka and smoking a joint. She reached out with her mind in an attempt to touch his.

Out across the ether, searching, scanning, and stretching. Failing to sense any contact, she drifted into a narcotic dream state, paralyzed by images of dungeons with dark, clay walls and giant rats with empty eyes in merciless pursuit of her.

"We're very impressed with your design for this fixture. Excellent work! I'd like to see you take on even more challenging projects this year, Isabella, and so would the project office. We're recommending that you be transferred to the commercial aviation design team next month."

"That's great! That's what I want! Thank you!"

"Well, you've earned it. You've shown very impressive development. You know that the government is pressuring us to hire minorities and women. It's damn difficult to comply, none is trained or capable! The government doesn't care about that. Meet the demands or else. So we're counting on you in more ways than one. Once you've completed your college education, we'd like to give you even more visibility."

"I don't want visibility. I just want to work with electronics and do something that matters."

"It matters that we continue to get these contracts. Your visibility will matter to everyone who has a job here. That's something to think about."

Later at The Station with Jim, her favorite of the college boys, and over a couple of vodkas, Jim told her he could see their point. "Isabella, there wasn't one girl in our engineering class, not one! There were two coming up a year back, but only a couple out of a hundred or so. Once you get that degree you'll be in an elite league and very much in demand."

"I'm not sure what visibility means. I just want to work and do a good job. Visibility sounds like one of those things where you're on the spot." Isabella thought about the movement to recognize women in the workplace, about the National Organization for Women. She felt responsibility, desire, and fear curl up into a little knot in her stomach.

"Yes. But you would also have advantages. It's the way things are going. If Gloria Steinem gets her way, women will run everything."

"Well, Jim, you have to admit, things right now are completely biased against women."

"Maybe, but it is a man's world. Men created everything that exists today, and for women to come along and want equality in it, well, they have to earn their place."

"Does that mean that men assume responsibility for the flaws in the world *they* created?" She held up her hand to stave off his response. "Ok, ok, no one's perfect, I take it back, sort of. Anyway, I guess that's fair, so long as women have a chance to earn their place and make it in the world."

"You've *got* a chance. No one's holding *you* back."

"True. I guess you're right on that point. But maybe they're only doing it because they're being forced to. Do you think ten years ago they would have been as enthusiastic?"

"Ten years ago was there a woman who could perform at the level you are now?"

"Thunderbolt could have."

"No degree."

"Right! That's the point, why not? What a waste of an excellent mind, her not going to college."

"She's good where she is because she's familiar with it, but outside her area of expertise she'd be lost."

"Just the opposite of you."

"What's that supposed to mean?"

"It means that you came here with all the book knowledge and no experience. You couldn't find your way to the floor. But she and the others helped you. If Reba had the education, she'd be a giant! She's smart and something not many of us are: wise."

"That's what upsets me about all this. It's just luck that Reba is in the position she's in. She's not an engineer, that's for sure. You, on the other hand, might be someday."

"Someday? I'm doing work comparable to you right now. Why aren't I an engineer now?"

"Engineer is not a title that can be handed out. It's earned. You need to finish school and walk out with that paper that says "engineer" unequivocally. It's like doctor or lawyer. It's a profession and certain criteria make you one or not. Take a paramedic: You might find one who's a better natural healer than a doctor, but he'll never be a doctor until he completes the educational requirements to be one. Understand?"

"I guess so. Say, where is Reba anyway?

"I heard she was out sick."

"I haven't seen her in days."

"Me either."

"In fact, no one is here tonight. Where is everyone?" Isabella gulped another vodka and went home without admitting to herself that she had hoped to see John Martin.

INTERLOGUE

He heard noise coming from two directions at once. Uncertain of which way to go, he instinctively started moving toward the small house. He found his way through the absence of light, taking comfort in the familiar smell of the clay as he pulled down the ladder. Before he could climb up, he caught a glimpse of two figures above him, shadows who spoke with authority. He turned and disappeared into the darkness. They followed. To him, they appeared to be phantasmal intruders after his soul, after his very marrow. They had invaded his dwelling, intent on having his brain. Evade and resist, he told himself! With no escape route, he was surrounded, ambushed, and snared before he knew what was happening. He found the sledgehammer where he had left it at the mouth of the time capsule. He ducked into the chamber, adrenaline pumping, his inner voice screaming, "Fight, fight!"

He felt the pounding in his chest but also the quickening of his mind as he rose up against them to assault their advantage of surprise. "How many are there?" he thought, "A legion?" He swung at the first glaring light in his face. He made contact, but there were others. Desperate and blinded, he wielded his weapon ahead. From behind came a painful blow to the seventh cervical vertebra. He thrust out the hammer to break his fall as he was jolted forward. The second strike came to the frontal bone above his left eye. Another hit his right kidney, sending a wave of agony through his torso. The next crash, into his diaphragm, took his breath away as he went down on his knees. The final blow, to his cranium, the parietal bone, sent him into a world of emptiness and oblivion.

The officers shackled the maniac's hands and feet. The beast lay limp and bleeding as four burly men lifted its body out of the dungeon and into the wagon that would take him away.

Isabella was at the plant early, anxious to get a few minutes with Reba before the day's work began. "I wanted to tell you myself: We got our notice to post credentials. It's happening, Reba, I'm going to graduate! I'm really going to be a college graduate, an engineer, and I owe it all to you. Can you even know how much I appreciate you in my life, what you've done for me, what you mean to me?"

"Ah, get on now. I didn't do anything. You did it yourself, all of it. Don't be silly!" But she was grinning. They looked at each other for a minute. Then they broke into laughter. When Thunderbolt's laughter turned into a raging cough, Isabella stopped laughing.

"I know that cough. What's the doctor say?"

"Says I'm fine, no problem. Don't you worry, Kid, I'll dance at your graduation party and probably on your grave. Say, that's real fine! I'm proud of you. So are the others, they're just, you know, still miffed. But you mustn't let them or anyone slow you down, not for a minute. You're going to do just fine, you will. And as you do, well, I'm going to be there, cheerin' for you all the way."

"I feel like none of this would have happened if you hadn't, I don't know exactly, hadn't been in my life to put me wise, encourage me or whatever. I just want you to know, I'll never forget what you've done."

"Everyone touches someone. Can't help it, Kid. You gotta go with what you have. I had the war. Now that sounds bad in a way, I know. But as awful as the war was, it gave some of us an opportunity to do things we never would have gotten a chance to without it. Changed my life. An awful thing like that war changed my life for the better. You got a way out ahead of you, who knows where you can go. I just hope you run for it, hard and fast. Don't waste it. Don't look back or let the past drag you down."

"Isabella, sorry to interrupt. You're wanted on the telephone. It's urgent. I think you better come take the call."

He was in a straitjacket, shaved clean of the mane and beard, scrubbed, damages bandaged. He was obviously sedated and visibly damaged. She had tried to prepare herself, but the sight stabbed her just the same.

"Daddy."

His eyes looked at her with heavy, sad lids. She felt small pains in her throat and in the muscles of her face as fluid rose and filled her eyes. She looked away and then back.

"You don't look too good, Mr. Reinhardt. How do you feel?" Milton asked.

"Not that good." Gunter scrutinized the man before him, "I know you."

"Yes. Yes, you do." Milton extended his hand to touch Gunter's arm drawn across his body in lieu of a handshake.

"I've come to help you if you'll allow me."

"Help? What's that mean? Help how?"

"Well for one thing, maybe we can get you out of this rig. For another, I'd like to get you some clothes and talk about your arraignment."

Milton Feldner excused himself and went out of the room. Gunter watched him leave. Isabella stood with her father as he looked around at everything in the room, his eyes, utterly unable to. "I'm sorry they hurt you, Daddy."

"They must have broken in. I'm worried about the house left open."

"I'll go have a look. Don't worry, Daddy."

"Does your mother know?"

"I called her."

"She didn't come?"

"Well, Daddy... ."

"Don't start a sentence with 'well,' it makes you sound like an idiot!"

The words stung, but she was able to stabilize herself and dry her tears. She continued, "I think it's best if Mom stays away right now. The last time you saw her you hurt her. Do you remember that you hurt her?"

"I remember she abandoned me."

"She had to, Daddy, you hurt her."

"She should come home where she belongs. She's my wife! Thugs come into my house, brutalize me and abduct me, and she doesn't even come to see if I'm alive or dead." Despite his medicated state, it was clear that Missy was a throttle for his emotions.

"I think we should concentrate on getting through this. Mom doesn't have anything to do with this situation. This is about you. I'll keep Mom up to speed, but I think it's best she stays away. I told her to. If you want to be angry with someone, be angry with me."

Milton returned. Mr. Reinhardt, they are going to remove the jacket. You will be handcuffed, but at least it will be an improvement. I'll need you to sign some papers. Before you do, I'll go over them with you."

"What's your name again?"

"Feldner, Milton Feldner. We met at your house. You showed me your remarkable engineering."

237

"Feldner. What kind of name is Feldner?" Isabella's stomach turned over twice. "By the look of you, I'd say Jew." "Yes, Mr. Reinhardt, I am Jewish. Is that a problem?"

"Up against the Jewish establishment, it might be good to have a Jew on my side. But that's the catch. How can I know you are on my side? How can I know you're not a conspirator?"

"It's up to you to decide. I am willing to help you if you want my help. If you would prefer someone else… ," He paused and turned to Isabella. "Why don't I wait outside? You can discuss it with your father and let me know." He stepped out of the room.

With pursed lips, Isabella just looked at Gunter, waiting.

"You brought me a Jew?"

"I brought you a lawyer, a good lawyer, highly recommended. What does it matter what he is? You're German. He doesn't seem to hold that against you."

"I like the little Jew. He's bright. I remember he is bright. They are all bright, clever. You are very grown-up Isabella. Not exactly pretty, certainly not beautiful. There is something about you that is attractive. You don't look like your mother." He was studying her closely.

"I don't think my appearance is the issue we should concern ourselves with at this time." Even as she said it, she was desperate to hear what he would say.

"You remind me of someone, someone, yes, you have my father's face, I think. I think you are my father, all but for those eyes. You know, father would not speak with anyone who had brown eyes. He would speak *at* them if absolutely necessary. He was a particular man, penetrating, discerning."

"I am not your father! And he was a cruel man. He was probably a Nazi. Please don't say that I resemble him!" She waited, wanting to turn and leave. She felt a wave of futility and despair threatening to overwhelm her. She reminded herself that he was sick. "He's disconcerted, probably free associating, not to be taken seriously. He isn't really this way." She figured that after all this time, had he been saner, he would probably be curious about her—who she was and what had become of her, his daughter. But part of her did not believe that for a second. Part of her looked back at him and saw his desire to inflict pain and humiliation.

"Tell the Jew to come in."

"No, I will not. You will treat him with respect or we'll just leave and you can get yourself out of this mess." He looked at her with his eyes narrowed, assessing her resolve. Then he nodded his head cautiously in agreement.

When Milton returned, he proceeded with the legal tasks at hand in his same objective manner. Two psychiatric assistants entered. One waited while the other removed the jacket, unbelting it, untwisting it up and over Gunter's head. Then the other assistant manacled his wrist to the bed rail and they both left. With just the gown on, Isabella could see the bruising to his body and knew he must be in great discomfort. She was pretty sure they needn't have hurt him that badly.

Later, on the phone, Missy said, "I should have gone."

"No. You absolutely should not have gone! Milton is handling everything. Frankly, I'm not so sure I should have gone."

"What does Mr. Feldner think is going to happen to Gunter?"

"Worst case, they'll condemn the property and probably sentence Daddy to more time at the state hospital. But Milton says maybe not if Daddy will cooperate. He's going to talk to the city about his voluntarily going into a program of medication and therapy and working with the city to obtain retroactive permits to make appropriate repairs."

"He's not serious."

"He's serious. I just don't know what Daddy will do with the opportunity. The issue is going to be 'appropriate repairs.' Daddy will most likely have to fill in the tunnels and put back the flooring in both houses. Well, I'm not optimistic. But Milton is. Course, Milton thinks Daddy will take the medication. Right there, we start off with a real obstacle."

"I'll pray. Maybe if God will speak to Gunter's heart, he'll cooperate."

"Momma, if God gives a damn about Gunter why doesn't he just heal him of his illness and let us all live normal lives?"

"I don't know why, dear. I just know that God does care about Gunter."

"If you ask me, the only evidence of his care is disdain, even wrath!"

"Isabella! Don't you ever say anything like that ever again!"

"Why? Will God disdain me?"

Isabella got very drunk. She went to the nightmare house as she promised Gunter she would. Sure enough, the boards were broken and the house was unlocked. Clutching a bottle of Smirnoff, she entered, went down into the tunnels, and proceeded out to the time capsule where she sank onto the clay floor and drank, weeping and cursing God. "All my life, all I ever wanted was for you to fix him and give us a normal life. Is that so much to ask? I can understand about the other prayers you've never answered, but why, damn it, why can't you fix him? What did he ever do to you? What did any of us do to you? If you exist, then I think you are nothing but a cruel tyrant who enjoys torturing people with adversity and maladies. Who the hell are you anyway? You son of a bitch! Ratshit bastard! I hate you! She fell hunched over on herself into sobs, then silence.

Finally, there was only her blood pressure to mark the moments. God did not reply. She looked out behind lashes so wet they sent beads of tears flying when she blinked. She wiped gobs of snot from her runny nose with her hands, then wiped her hands on her clothes. The first thing she saw was a seascape: Angry, dark, a moon breaking through the clouds and striking light upon a wave cresting over a large rock where the sea surges and droplets freeze like lighted crystals caught in the depths of space and time—this was his ability to press his emotions through a brush onto canvas. She looked at the damaged oil painting, struggling with the credence that he had the right to ruin them. They were his after all. But what a waste, such a loss. Talk about stupidity!

She wandered out into the chasm under the house and found the familiar box she had seen earlier. She opened it and found the H.O. trains packed away: a miracle! In all this madness, they were safe. She made a decision. She went back to his paintings and stripped the canvases from their frames—those that were salvageable and not lurid—rolled them up and put them under her arm. On her way out she picked up the box of trains and took both with her.

In 1978 small news articles relayed trouble in the Middle East. Once known as Persia, Iran was an exotic and colorful country, often laced with intrigue. Its ruler, Muhammad Reza Shah Pahlevi, was a pal of the United States government. Uncle Clay told Isabella that the Shah had kept his throne only with the help of the treachery of the Central Intelligence Agency. The Shah was terminally ill and desperate to solidify his rule, making it possible for his son to assume the throne. In his persecution of any opposition, he had exiled his archenemy, a religious zealot known as Ayatollah Khomeini. Living in Paris, Khomeini was out of Iran but not out of touch: From abroad he conducted a campaign of terror. Uncle Clay kept up on every detail with fervor.

At home under Jimmy Carter's administration things were relatively calm.

This nice man from Georgia with a gentle style and moral fortitude had begun a healing of the Vietnam wounds by pardoning draft resisters. He was focusing on the environment. He called a meeting at Camp David and invited Israel's Begin and Egypt's Anwar Sadat. The Soviet Union and the United States were talking about a strategic arms agreement and SALT II.

However, not all was optimistic. Carter had failed to come to an agreement with Congress on key domestic legislation, inflation was on the rise, and Americans were asking themselves, "Could a really nice man be an effective President?"

Her crisp, black robe absorbed the sun's rays and heat was building under the mortarboard. Izy just knew her hair was matting in the shape of the cap and would look awful. She felt a bead of sweat roll down her head, pause at the back of her right ear, and then race down her neck. But nothing would dampen her spirits today.

After a seemingly endless wait, she heard the orchestra play the opening notes of Pomp and Circumstance. Within seconds the long line finally began to move forward toward the cool of the auditorium, the sound of the music, and graduation. Speakers Izy had never seen or met had much to say about things she didn't find all that interesting. Her mind drifted, she was imagining what the future might be like now that she was a degreed engineer. Her thoughts wandered through the events of recent months: Milton's ardent negotiations with the City of Los Angeles and Gunter's agreement to a medication regimen— one that would be less debilitating, they promised. Would he adhere? Could he? Without invitation, one thought popped to the forefront: "If Gunter were not insane, if he were healthy, if my father were here today... ." Instant suffering! The thought had to be stopped at all cost! She pulled her mind back to the audience applause as the conferment began. The schools of business and law were first; engineering followed.

Within minutes of exiting the auditorium, Isabella was encircled by her mother, Francine, Ronny, Jim, Rick, her boss—Bill McNally, and John Martin. To her utter surprise, Thunderbolt and the rest of the Silver Cats were there, as well. "You came! I can't believe you came!" She grabbed each in her arms and hugged them. "Does this mean I'm forgiven?"

"Well, let's just say it's forgotten in the wake of bigger things!" Erlene said, amid the hugging and back-patting. When Izy came to Thunderbolt, who mattered most at that moment, the old gal's head was way back, her lips stretched straight across her face as she tried to hold it all back. She couldn't: The tears spilled down her cheeks. No words passed between them, just heat and a handshake, one woman to another—one generation passing life and hope to the next.

Isabella wrapped up her presentation with confidence, certain she had hit all the marks and held the audience's attention. The distinguished staff members of the Secretary of the Navy listened and nodded when she landed on her chosen punch line. She thanked them and turned to take her seat, accepting her boss's appreciative nod from across the room; she listened as the meeting concluded. At the usual reception, refreshments and jovial banter masked the urgency with which Rockwell wanted to land this contract.

"I think you can be proud of yourself, Izy," Bill McNally said, having made a point of approaching her near the cheese platter. "You may have just pushed us up and over."

"You think so? I'm glad."

"Actually, I want to talk to you about your future."

"Yes. Good. I'm wondering when I will be promoted to engineer."

"Well, of course, that is one option at some point, but there are other possibilities you should consider."

"What other possibilities? I mean, all I want to do is engineering. That was the whole reason for going to college, the degree, everything. What other possibilities could there be?"

"You have a good head on your shoulders in more ways than one, and the company would like to put you out in front where you'll get a lot of visibility—something that will benefit you and us at the same time."

"Doing what?"

"Wil wants you to consider going into Contract Negotiations."

"You're kidding?"

"Not in the least. It's a great opportunity for you. You'll be spending your time with really big brass: Navy, Air Force, Army, congressmen, senators maybe."

"Why on Earth would I want to do that? I mean, I can help get work for our plant by making presentations, or something like that. But I don't want to spend time with military people."

"Don't think of it that way. Think of it as an opportunity to meet and work with some of the most influential people in our country. It would mean a promotion, more money, and a front office. I want you to talk to Wil."

"Do it anyway. It's important. Do it for me. Hell, do it for yourself!"

At The Station on Friday night, Isabella talked to just about everyone she thought might have sound advice. Jim said, "I told you! Right time, right place. Go get 'em!"

Reba said, "Is that what you want, Kid? Don't let them railroad you into doing what's in their best interest and not your own."

John Martin said, "You can do anything you want, Isabella. Just make sure this is what you want." Francy was concerned that Izy might have to move to Washington. Isabella said she thought not, but she would have to travel.

Isabella started researching contract negotiators: middle-aged white men with bellies, bad habits, and ironclad ideas. She scheduled a meeting with one, Banister. "What can I do for you, honey?" Right away, Isabella didn't like him.

"I want to learn about what you do, where you do it, and how."

"What for? Are you doing some paper, or just curious?"

"I'm considering a career."

He laughed and lit a cigarette, blowing smoke around her head. "I don't think it's a good idea, a little girl like you locked up for weeks in some hotel with a bunch of men smoking, drinking, using foul language, and telling dirty jokes. That's what it is."

"Why does it have to be that way?"

"'Cause it is, honey gal. That's how it's always been. It's no place for you. You wouldn't like it none."

Isabella left with her dander up. She hated the idea of being ushered out, dismissed out of hand as some "honey gal." She didn't like Banister, but she was sure she didn't want to try to reform him or fight him. That was not what she wanted her life to be about. She felt a little sick.

"Your father wants to know where his paintings are."

"I guess I knew he'd miss them. I have them. They're with me."

"He wants them back," Milton said firmly.

She thought about that, ignored it, and went on, "How's he doing? I mean, is he on the medication?'

"Seems to be. He's reporting for his therapy sessions on time. I'm optimistic."

"What happens if he blows it?"

"Probably back into the hospital. It would be like a parole violation. They can pick him up."

"I'm glad for him. Maybe he'll be okay after all."

"He wants you to bring the paintings back."

"I don't think so."

"Isabella, they are his, his work. You have no right to take them."

"Don't I? He's ruining his work. I want to preserve it. I think I have the right to *something*. If I can't have him, then why can't I have his work?"

"Because it's his. He didn't give you permission."

"He did in a way. He told me to go to the house and make sure everything was okay. I determined that I should take the paintings to protect them. That's what I'm doing. I'm protecting them."

Isabella had put on her best business clothes for the meeting her boss had scheduled. Fortified with arguments and resolve, she went into McNally's office. She didn't beat about the bush: "I think I want to be an engineer. I don't want to negotiate contracts."

"Well, that's a little tricky."

Isabella thought about sentences that began with "well." "Nothing tricky. I just want to be what I am: an engineer."

"We don't have any women engineers and, right now, we don't have slots for any new engineers, period."

"I'll stay where I am, doing what I'm doing. Just give me the title I've earned.

244

And that'll be good enough."

"Wil said you canceled the appointment."

"I don't want to do it. So why waste our time?"

"I think you should consider your future carefully."

"I have. Carefully."

"Consider it again. You are making a mistake."

"I get a funny feeling when you say that."

"Can't run your career on feelings."

"No, wait. It's a scary feeling, like maybe you're threatening me. Are you threatening me, Bill?"

"Of course not. I'm your friend, and I'm trying to help you. But you can't be an emotional female, making decisions because something gives you a feeling."

Isabella left the meeting with something gnawing at her. It was akin to resentment. She could recognize a threat, no matter how subtle or perversely wrapped in good wishes. It was a survival instinct. What really irritated her was that reference to feelings. McNally had made it seem as if she were some emotional ninny. The more she thought about the conversation, the more she hummed inside, warmer and louder as the day progressed. By break time, she was fuming. "I think they intend to make me do this negotiation thing!"

"They can't make you do anything."

"Oh, yes, they can. They can say, 'do this, or else.' I felt that's what Bill was saying."

"Or else what, Isabella? They can't do anything to you."

"Of course they can, Reba! They're in charge. They say what happens. They could say whether I ever get to be what I've worked so hard to be, an engineer. It's up to them! That's what they can do!"

"Well, that's the great thing about this country, Kid. They're free to apply pressure to get you to do what's in their interest. And you're free to choose not to submit to their pressure."

"Free not to submit?"

"Leave. Go somewhere else. You're an engineer now. You can go where you want to. You know, Kid, it may turn out that you have to leave. Here, you're just what they think you are: A cute, young lady who is bright, worked real hard, and got a degree. Ain't that swell. But in their heads you're still that clerk, that assistant. Go somewhere else and be what you are, meet your destiny!"

It had never occurred to Isabella to leave. "Leave Rockwell? Leave you, and everyone? I couldn't. I don't want to."

"Sounds like you're at another one of those crossroads, Kid. If you don't pick the right path for yourself, you'll settle for being buried in other people's expectations of you! And if you do that, you'll grow bitter and start finding excuses for disappointment. The truth is: You will choose. You will choose to do something. Or you will choose the coward's way out and do nothing. It's time, you know, time for you to grow up!"

She sat and watched the Silver Cat walk away from her. She knew it was time for her to walk away, too.

LOGARITHMIC CHICANERIES

The seasonal changes in Southern California are subtle. Deciduous trees turn color late and are outnumbered by evergreens: cypress, pine, spruce, eucalyptus. The weather cools and dries ahead of the rainy season, which comes in winter and turns everything a rich green in a good year. Holiday weather is mild compared to the east, and sometimes warm enough to go to the beach. The festive spirit resides largely in the heart—and no one exuded it more than Izy's mother now that she was on her own. Every year she made a point of telling Izy to bring as many of her friends as possible to her holiday feast! "Mom! The place looks wonderful! Great tree."

"Thanks, honey! Emma helped me."

"Is she coming over?"

"Yes. She hasn't anyone at all. I hope you don't mind."

"Not at all. Francy and Ronny will be here later. Jim's coming too. And John."

"Now, this John, he works at Rockwell?"

"No. He's a friend. A friend of Jim's really, but I like him. He's divorced. His wife was, let's just say, less than reliable in many ways. He was born in Canada, he's a pilot, and… ," she flushed almost imperceptibly, "I really like him."

Missy paused for a tiny instant, noting all the signs—the flush, the aversion of eyes, an inflection—before asking, "Where in Canada?"

"Quebec. His family is French. He speaks French when he wants to, which is almost never. Anyway, I've known him for a long time now, and I like him."

"You said that. Is this someone I should pay special attention to?"

"Not really, well, maybe. I don't know. We're just friends. But I do want you two to get along."

Missy made her own decision to pay special attention.

The doorbell rang and the guests filed in.

"Welcome!" Missy greeted everyone in her green dress, a plaid apron, and a plastic poinsettia in her hair. "Come in! Let me take those." She grabbed coats and ferried them to the back bedroom. "My place is small. I hope we all fit."

"We'll manage, there's plenty of room," Ronny said.

"Seems even smaller tonight," Francy said to the side so Missy didn't hear. Izy frowned at her slight.

"I brought wine and, for you, Missy, sparkling cider. I know you don't drink," Jim handed Missy the bottles.

"Momma, this is John Martin, you remember, from graduation?"

"Yes. Yes, I do." Missy then took a gift, "Thank you, Jim! Ronny, so good to see you."

"Yes, we don't do this often enough. Guess it's the price for growing up and getting busy. The decorations look great, Missy!"

"My friend Emma helped; she made the centerpiece."

"Looks it." Francy whispered to Izy.

"How rude, Francy! Can't you be gracious?"

"What dear?"

"Nothing, Mom, can I help in the kitchen? Rolls in the oven? Serving dishes out? Crystal is magical."

"I know. It makes the table sparkle."

"It sure does, Mom." She took Missy in her arms and held her amid the hubbub for just a moment. Missy felt a rush of tears but pushed them away. "Thank you, Isabella. I love you very much."

"We need to find a few minutes to talk," Isabella pinched up her nose for emphasis. "I wanted to get this done before everyone arrived."

"What dear?"

"Milton wants you to think about divorce."

"Divorce. I don't think so."

"He's missed two sessions. Milton thinks he's off the medication. There's bound to be more trouble. I agree with Milton. You should distance yourself from him."

"I'm his wife."

"I'm his daughter. And believe me, if I could divorce him, I would!"

The tears welled up and over this time. "I'm sorry, Mom. I shouldn't have brought it up. Here, wipe your eyes." She handed Missy a tissue, then they put on their party faces and carried on.

Before dinner, Missy read from the Bible, St. Luke, Chapter 2: "And there were in the same country shepherds abiding in the field, keeping watch over their flock by night. And low, the angel of the Lord came upon them and the glory of the Lord shone round about them; and they were sore afraid."

Isabella could sense Francine's anxiety and began to worry a little.

"And the angel said unto them, Fear not for behold I bring you good tidings of great joy, which shall be to all peoples. For unto you is born this day in the city of David a Savior which is Christ the Lord. Our heavenly Father... ."

As she bowed her head, Izy glanced at Francine who was glaring at Missy. Izy took a deep breath.

"Bless this food and make your gift real to each one of us as we celebrate the birth of Christ and strive to live Christ-like in all things. Amen."

"You know, Missy, you have some pretty, let's just say, traditional ideas," Francine said, still glaring.

"I don't know what you mean by traditional?"

Izy decided it would be best to get in the middle of this and deflect whatever it was that was feeding the pungent tone of Francy's voice. "Traditions are wonderful, I agree. I guess I'm just a traditional girl, myself!" All eyes went to Izy on that one, for no one thought of Francy in that way.

"I mean, you use this old crystal, it's old-fashioned, all the swirls, and what's this on it?"

"You mean the etching. It is hand-etched crystal. And it's not only old-fashioned, they don't even make hand-etched crystal anymore. It's very valuable. Beautiful!" Izy defended.

"I think it's very beautiful," Ronny chimed in, sensing the mounting tension. Jim kept his attention on his plate, and John watched the drama unfold.

"Maybe, but it is old-fashioned, like that old tea kettle, those china cups, and even serving tea. Old-fashioned. Traditional. The way things used to be. Not the way things are now. People don't serve tea. No one serves tea. You're sort of old-fashioned."

"It's good to value things from the past, I think. Don't you think so, Ronn?" Izy was feeling desperate. She knew Francy was reimbursing Missy for her silent disapproval. She could understand. But she didn't want it happening now, here, at this table. She didn't want anyone to attack her mother.

"Yes," Ronny was in step. "I think old things and ways are charming and valuable."

"Your generation is a little out of touch with the modern world. I mean, I don't imagine you listen to much rock 'n roll, or even know what disco is."

Izy's mind was processing, looking for a way to dissuade Francy from taking this course, but it was Missy who calmly began to speak. "You are correct, Francine, I am not a modern person. I am of a different generation. I also know you think it is a form of insult to imply that I am not 'with it.'" Izy felt something she was completely unfamiliar with as Missy spoke. "I do respect the past. I am proud to be part of my generation, mine and that of my mother's before me. We are survivors, and we may not be as clever as you, but *you* have no excuse—a great deal has been given to *you* and your generation." Missy was on a soft roll and everyone was listening. "We invented most of the things you take for granted: airplanes, automobiles, television, photocopiers, telephones, clothes and dishwashers, dryers, permanent press, and hairspray. When I was born, diseases *you* don't even think about today used to kill thousands.

And that doesn't even take into account the two world wars that we fought against incredible odds to make the world free for you to express your opinions and do mostly as *you* please! We were far from perfect. We made mistakes, for sure, and I have made my share. Nonetheless, my generation invented, researched, discovered, created, and died for the world *you* take for granted. So if you think I am a traditional, old-fashioned gal, then I say thank you, Francine, thank you very much!" That said, she turned to Emma who was smiling in admiration, clinked her glass, took a sip of sparkling cider, and resumed eating among her stunned and tongue-tied guests.

Ronny broke the silence, "All right, Missy!" Jim looked at Francy without lifting his head to see her speechless for the moment. John smiled and winked at Izy, who sat dazed, wondering where that had come from. She decided there was nothing left for her to do, certain Francy's attack had been thoroughly foiled.

After her conversation with Reba, Izy purchased a book about how to write a résumé so she could prepare her first. She felt tentative about taking a new job, but curious. On weekends she searched the classifieds for interesting jobs. After submitting a few resumes with no results, Izy enlisted the services of an employment agency, a headhunter, who was intrigued by her credentials and determined to match her up. Sure enough, it was not long before Izy received a phone call, "He said he wants to meet the young lady who got an engineering degree by going to night school."

"What does that mean?" Izy asked.

"It means he's impressed. It is impressive. It also means you should go over there and talk to him. This could be what you're looking for. Go on, show him who you are and what you can do. Give this one your best effort. It could be the shot of a lifetime."

The building was ordinary on the outside, lacking in pretense except for the main entrance where a low stone wall encircled a statue. Around the circle, outside the wall, flagpoles were equidistantly placed and international flags snapped in the ocean breeze.

Inside was different. The walls were lined with rich, old wood that evoked an air of luxury. The floors were marble. In the center of the lobby was inlaid the company logo: a heart, an electrical pulse, and the name "CardioStim."

She walked to the reception counter, the sound of her heels echoing with her every step. "My name is Isabella Reinhardt. I'm here to see Mr. Timothy Vanderfluer."

"It'll be a moment. Make yourself comfortable. I'll let him know you are here."

Isabella could not imagine comfort at this particular moment. She was petrified. To control her frenzied nerves she decided to walk around the huge room and take slow, deep breaths. First, she looked up through a staircase and counted one, two, three floors, each ringed by wood, opening to a skylight. In the lobby glass cases displayed the history of CardioStim, some of their products, performance statistics, and images of the men who had marshaled the corporation to greatness—all flaunted tastefully, setting a tone, and sending a message.

"Ms. Reinhardt?"

"Yes."

"Mr. Vanderfluer will see you now. This way, please." The woman was maybe fifty, dressed in a suit of muted blue and a silk blouse exactly the same color. Her silver hair was perfectly coifed, her nails manicured. She walked ahead with a crisp step through a softly-lit maze of elegant cubicles, live plants, and well-dressed people. Offices lined one wall; through the odd open door, Isabella eyed demure, elegant furniture. They turned into one of the doors.

"Mr. Vanderfluer, Ms. Reinhardt."

"How do you do, Ms. Reinhardt. Please come in and sit down. I must tell you, I am most impressed with your résumé."

"I'm impressed with everything here. It's nothing like Rockwell!"

Smiling, "I imagine not."

Sensing defeat and fearing a bloodbath as a result of a civil war, the Shah, his wife and family, and a small group of aides boarded the Royal Iranian Boeing 707 on January 16, 1979, and fled the country. "The self-exiled Shah hoped to find refuge in America, but the White House today made it clear that the United States would not welcome him. Consequently, the Shah has taken temporary refuge in Egypt. There were rumors that the Shah's longtime political opponent, Ayatollah Khomeini, is already en route back to Iran. Many expect him to assume leadership of the country and quell the revolution."

"Francy, turn off the television and get out! He'll be here any minute, and I don't want you here."

"No problem, just the news. But why do I have to leave? What's the big deal? Where are you going, anyway?"

"The big deal is I'm asking you to leave before he gets here. Is that so much to ask? We're just going to see his airplane. But I don't want you here when he arrives."

"Maybe I'll just hang around and make sure he checks out. Oh, my God! A dress, no less! Say, you look pretty good." Izy's style had mutated over time. She mostly still wore slacks, but she chose richer, warmer colors now. Her hair, worn short, was soft and casual, usually tousled.

"What checks out? Checks out how? Just go! Please! I'm asking you as a friend, go."

"All right, all right. But I think you're in over your head, Izy."

"I'm not. You've always wanted me to date. Or at least that's what you're always nagging me about."

"True, but this guy? I mean, no one builds airplanes."

"Yes, they do. There's a whole association of people who build their own airplanes. He's going to test it soon. The FAA inspector's been out and given the final OK. He's showing it off to me tonight and I can't wait! So, here, take your stuff." Shoving and kissing, "Out, out, out!"

The doorbell rang. Isabella opened the door—a single rose was offered. "Come in, please, thank you. Make yourself comfortable. I'll put it in water right away." In the kitchen, she paused to let her heart slow down and grabbed a vase.

At the small, private airstrip, in a hangar, John showed her his craft. The machine was small, low to the ground, and low winged, with a single engine in the front, a bubble, and a fuselage painted white with red and blue trim. "It's a KRII, made of fiberglass. I beefed up the construction so it will withstand greater stress in aerobatic maneuvers."

"Tell me about that."

"Aerobatics? That's my passion. I love it! Loops, rolls, spins, diving and soaring. It gives you the greatest feeling of being alive, hanging near the edge of disaster, yet surviving, conquering. It's the most incredibly exhilarating sensation. I can't give it justice with words. I want you to experience it."

"Me? Wow, I'm not sure. Sounds pretty crazy to me!"

"Well, it is, in a way. If crazy is letting go of all restraints and rushing to the brink of destruction without falling over the edge into oblivion, then aerobatics is craziness. But it is also freedom. Crazy is freedom. To be sane, to give the appearance of being sane, we live in tight mazes of reason adhering to 'appropriate' social and cultural norms. But it confines, constrains, binds up the spirit longing to express itself without fear. To venture up there, fears must be left behind."

Izy was riveted by his passion. She saw hints of her Aunt Emily in his ardent description of freedom. "But you have to perform, or you die."

"Yes, but first you must allow yourself to exist, to live what you truly are inside, to risk the possibilities. Then your performance will come as a matter of training, practice, and self-trust. There is a particular maneuver called the 'hammerhead.' It starts with a quarter loop into a vertical climb," his hand soared as he spoke, "virtually straight up into space until the plane can no longer climb, gripped by gravity, trapped by physics, the engine all but stalled. The plane pivots around its axis, the nose moves out in an arc, going from pointing up through the horizon, then down to Earth below." His hand mimicked the feat as he described it, his eyes glinting. "Then, the plane is falling, virtually out of control, on the edge of total chaos, picking up speed, compelled by Mother Earth to return. If all goes well, the pilot wrenches back control and goes into a quarter loop to horizontal flight." Now his hands were on the imaginary controls, "It's amazing, terrifying, and thrilling all at the same time!"

"You must be crazy! How high up are you?"

"Aerobatics are performed in geographical boxes prescribed by the FAA. So, it depends. For example, here, in this area, there are several boxes. My favorite is over the ocean, south of here, off the coast of Orange County."

"What box?"

"The aerobatics box is a three-dimensional space where aerobatics are allowed under FAA rules or where approved competitions are held. The pilot has to stay within the lateral and altitudinal limits of the box. During competitions, boundary judges determine when a competitor has left the box. But ordinarily, you're just honor bound to respect the lines."

"Well, how do you know where there is a box in the sky?"

"Every inch of the sky has defined specifications. In the training you learn how to find the box and its dimensions. But to answer your question, I usually perform aerobatics at safe altitudes a couple thousand feet above the ground. Real pros, like the ones at air shows, execute maneuvers at altitudes of only hundreds of feet, sometimes lower, close to the tarmac."

"I still say you're crazy to be up there out of control."

"It seems out of control, but it never really is. The maneuvers are very precise, with specific positions for the components of control during each phase—the aileron, rudders, wings, and engine are within designated parameters at all times."

"So it isn't chaos at all."

"No, more like the edge of chaos. Some of it is intuitive, some counterintuitive—the pressures, G-forces on the body, the plane. It is about control, but also a bit of sheer madness!"

"And you do that in this little plane?" That *you* built?"

"Well, not yet. My test flight is next weekend, and I won't be doing aerobatics maneuvers in the beginning. I've been flying a Citabria—it's designed to do aerobatics. Very different from this one; I rent it. Soon I'll have my own to fly. Jim says your birthday is coming up."

"It is, next week."

"Is it too late to ask you to spend it with me? I'll take you flying. First in the

Citabria and then, after the test flight, in this plane. What do you say?"

Izy looked pensively into John's eyes, gauging this man who was asking her to trust him, up in the sky, out of control, on the edge of chaos. To her utter shock, she felt his mind meet her halfway. She knew his thoughts as clearly as her own. The two were in that moment as one, locked together, exploring each other in ways she had never known. She did not have to speak. John knew that his invitation was the very present Izy was hoping for.

The following evening at Izy's, Francine was sipping a glass of wine, "Well?"

"They made me a job offer today. Project Engineer, starting next month at, get this, three times my salary at Rockwell! Imagine, me working on cardiac pacemakers. Who would have ever thought?"

"I don't care about that. What happened Saturday night? I called you all day yesterday but you weren't home. Come on. Give!"

"We went out. It was good. That's all."

"But what happened? Give me details!"

"I can't give you every detail. I'd think you'd be happy about my job offer. I'd think you'd be proud of me. Something!"

"Well, sure. That's good, but what did you expect? You're intelligent, educated, experienced. Predictable, I'd say. So, did you get it on?"

"Francy, even if we did, I wouldn't tell you. That's very personal and, frankly, none of your business."

"So you didn't. Something went wrong, huh?"

"No. Everything was good, very good."

"Then what, why, and if not, when?"

"None of your business."

"I'd tell you. I do tell you. What's the deal?"

"Let's just say it's perfect the way it is. Telling would make it less so."

"You know, sometimes, when you act like this, I'd say you think you're better than me, if I didn't know better. But I do know better. Right? I do know better."

Isabella said goodbye to Rockwell with mixed feelings. She was excited to be starting work at CardioStim. It was everything she had wanted when she set out to obtain the degree. Even more, medical devices, bio-electronics, was an awesome field. She was humbled by the possibility of saving lives.

But then there was the leaving behind of so much. She had been at Rockwell for over nine years, longer than she had been at any school—even college, since she changed schools and transferred credits to pool her credentials. It was not a small thing to say goodbye to the young engineers and the Silver Cats.

In her cubicle on her first day at CardioStim, surrounded by elegant fabrics, rich wood tones, and her own desk and phone, she was struck by the contrasts to Rockwell. The atmosphere was quiet and soothing, not overcrowded and hectic. She set about the day with enthusiasm, starting with a staff meeting where she would become acquainted with her new coworkers. She was given manuals and other reading material: company policies, technical procedures, product specifications, brochures, employee handbook—reading for a good, long while. She would be working on a project named Remote Fix that was expected to provide noninvasive programmability to existing devices. She had a conceptual idea what that was and gave it her undivided attention, leaving hardly any brain cells for anything like melancholy.

The day sped by and the next thing she knew, it was dark outside and she was all alone in her reading. "Time to knock off and head home, Izy. There'll be plenty opportunity for extra hours soon enough."

"Hi, Mr. Vanderfluer, I'm just trying to get a leg up on so much information. I'm a little overwhelmed, to tell you the truth."

"Of course you are. There's a lot, I know. But I have great confidence in you. With a chuckle, he said, "I just don't want you to burn out the first week, so at least take a break, get some dinner. There's plenty of time. Tomorrow afternoon you'll have your first team meeting. Your teammates have been anxious to have you come on board. You'll need to be fresh for that." He turned as if to leave, then stopped, "It is so unusual to find someone like you. I do hope you are up for this."

"What do you mean, Mr. Vanderfluer?"

"Well, I'm going to be honest with you, Izy. We are under a lot of pressure to fill in our ranks with minorities and women. Frankly, it is difficult. Some people think we should hire them regardless of their qualifications. I'm not one of them. There are blacks, Mexicans, Asians, and women, like you, in colleges. They're bright and capable. I believe we should bend over backward to find them and give them priority in our hiring until it has been clearly demonstrated that color and gender are not the limitations some believe them to be. That's why we waited. We were looking for you, Izy."

"Are you saying I got this job because I am a woman?"

"I'm saying you got it because you earned it, deserve it, you're a perfect fit, and you were worth waiting for. But not everyone is going to think that. Not everyone is going to grant you the credibility you should have. You are going to have to earn their respect, even though you shouldn't have to. Do you understand that?"

"Yes. I do. And I don't mind. I wouldn't want respect for anything other than what I earn, day by day. That's okay with me, Mr. Vanderfluer." She looked into his eyes, finding no deceit or malice, "I won't let you down."

With a nod and a smile, he left her cubicle. She put all the literature in her brand new briefcase, a gift from the Rockwell gang. She stood and looked out over the maze of cubicles, thinking what a strange world it was. Strange to her anyway. Then she exited the building through the employee entrance and walked to her car.

The team was made up of individuals from engineering and science. They had expertise in mechanical engineering, metallurgy and programming technology, and she, electronics. Izy was the only woman in the cool room when the door closed to start the first meeting. She introduced herself without pretense and settled in to learn. She felt some eyes glued to her and noticed others avoiding her. She wished Reba could be there with encouraging words, but the days of her being cradled were in the past. It was time to make it, or not, on her own.

She decided she would speak only when there was something intelligent to utter. Her training with Gunter would serve her well. She knew how to frame articulate questions and, since it was her first meeting, now was the time to ask. She held herself at an objective pitch, not effusive or aggressive. The room warmed a bit as the meeting progressed. When it was adjourned, she was pleased she had successfully negotiated the first hurdle of her new world.

On Wednesday the phone in her cubicle rang: There was something at the front desk. Upon entering the lobby she saw a large vase of gorgeous roses on the desk—the same color as the single rose John had given her. "I'm Isabella

Reinhardt."

"Then these are for you. Lucky you!" said the receptionist, who noticed the stunned look on Isabella's face. "There's a card."

"Yes. Thank you." She took the card and read, "I wanted everyone at CardioStim to know that you are special, loved, and my valentine. JM." She flushed.

She left her roses at work to avoid the possibility of damaging them in transit and so she could enjoy them for more hours each day.

"American interests in the Persian Gulf region are further threatened. In addition to the loss of access to Iranian oil and the cancellation of an uncompleted seven-billion-dollar arms contract, today revolutionary forces in Teheran overran the United States embassy, seizing seventy employees for more than two hours. All personnel in the region are on notice as tensions continue to mount. Meanwhile, the Shah has requested permanent asylum in Morocco, The Bahamas, Panama, or Mexico." The television was becoming a source of stress, mounting daily. Izy switched it off resolutely.

Despite the unspoken barrier between them, Isabella kept in contact with Missy out of love, but also due to a sense of obligation. Isabella felt compelled to look out for her mother, taking up the slack of her father's inability to fulfill his spousal responsibilities.

It was during one of her visits that Isabella presented her gift idea for Missy.

"Okay, it's here. Now, you just sit there, no, okay, stand here. Oh, no. I'll get the door, you wait, anywhere you want."

"There's a truck. What is it you've done, Isabella? Oh, my goodness."

"Don't worry, it's a good thing," she said opening the door. "Yes, this is the right place. It will go just in here. You're going to set it up, right?"

"Set up what, honey? What are they going to set up?"

"Mom, I decided it was time that you had a proper place to keep your Fostoria. Now, just relax and wait. I hope you like it."

Missy watched out the window of her little mobile home as the men took the mahogany cabinet out of the truck and up the steps into the dining room. They removed the protective wrapping and set it against the only wall that would accommodate its size. When they brought in the glass front doors, the workers turned on the inside spotlights to better see as they were assembling. The lights illuminated the rich grain and deep color of the elegant wood and the beveled edges of the glass doors and shelves.

Isabella turned to look at Missy. She stood in the middle of the room, her hands cupped over her nose and mouth, her eyes large. "Well, do you like it, Mom?"

"It's... ." No words would come.

"If you don't like it, I can exchange it. I picked this one, but if you'd like another... ." Missy reached out and grabbed her daughter in her arms and held her close. "It's the most beautiful thing I have ever seen, honey. Thank you."

With work obligations and her desire to spend more time with John, Izy's visits with Francy were growing less frequent. When they did spend time together, there was a heightened air of tension between them. "He doesn't even have a job. What kind of man doesn't hold a job?" Francine inquired with disdain.

"It isn't a matter of holding a job. He hasn't lost jobs. He just doesn't need to work. He invents. He makes money from his inventions by licensing the rights to businesses that want to incorporate his inventions into their products, whatever. It's completely brilliant."

"Well, I don't like it. Doesn't seem proper. Everyone we know has a job. What kind of security is that?"

"You don't have to like it. It's my business and he must be doing all right. He lives well, has a custom engine for his airplane built by Pratt & Whitney, and owns his condo and car. Security is an illusion. Besides, I would think you'd be happy for me."

"I want you to be happy. That's why I'm concerned. I want to make sure you'll be happy."

"I already am, more than I've ever been. Don't worry."

"What about his previous marriage? Something went wrong. Maybe you should think about that."

"It went wrong because his wife was a cheating slut!"

"But why? He must have done something to make her do it."

"Sometimes, people are just not right for each other. You, of all people, should understand that!"

"What's that supposed to mean?"

"Just that. You and Redmond Butler, for example. Redmond was alright, but together you were not a good fit."

"Oh, but he was a good-looking boy. It's just too bad he was such a gun-rack toting, beer-guzzling jackass!"

"His good looks didn't help hold together your marriage. In the end, it came down to whether or not you were right for each other. John and I are a nice fit. He is the one I've been waiting for all my life."

"So the price is right?" Izy turned to look at Francy. "You once told me you were waiting for the price to be right."

"It figures you would remember that line."

"Well? You said it."

"OK. In the broader context of meaning, yes. I give over my complete and unquestioning trust and, in return, I feel completely safe and accepted, sheltered, and loved. The price is right."

"What's that got to do with sex? We were talking about sex when you said that."

"Sex is a byproduct of trust. Nothing is about sex. Sex is an outcome of other things in a relationship. There's something special going on between John and me. I can't explain it, but it's something I've waited for all my life. And yet, I never imagined it could feel this wonderful. It's hard to convey it—it's very special, and the sex part just happens."

"Like between us, Izy? What about between us?"

"Yes. That was about trust in a way. It was also about being high, and I don't want to talk about that."

"Aha! You don't want to talk about it. Have you told your ever-so-beloved John about that?"

"No. And I don't intend to. That was a thing that happened, past, and done."

"Thanks so much!"

"Don't take it like that. You know what I mean. Past and done for both of us."

"How do you know it's past and done for me? How do you think that makes me feel?"

"It was past and done for you when it happened, Francy. Don't go getting your nose out of joint now."

"But it isn't done. I love you, Izy. I've always loved you, and I loved making love with you."

"I don't wanna talk about it."

"Why, because it makes you uncomfortable? Are you sure you should be with a man? Sure you're not a lesbian? Are you absolutely sure you don't want to spend one more night with me?" She crossed the room to where Izy stood with her back turned, went up close and pressed into her and kissed her on the neck.

Izy turned and put a stiff arm between Francy and herself. "Don't do that. I don't understand you. Why would you start this now?"

"Better late than never. I should have seen this coming a long time ago and headed it off then. But I didn't." Francy was melting and moving. "You know what I think? I think you should slow down and reconsider this whole idea." She was steamy and coy, tendrils of her ample sensuality curling out from her being. "You don't want to marry some guy. When have you ever been interested in guys?" Francy was turning her head, playing with a strand of hair at her neck, lips parted, looking at Isabella.

"Stop it! You don't understand any of this, do you? I love John Martin, not because he is a man. I love him because he is a human being, first and foremost—a wonderful human being. And because we have a connection." Izy looked at Francy so desperately trying to manipulate her. She felt sad knowing Francy would not understand even if she tried to explain, but she gave it a try.

"His gender is secondary. Don't you understand? That's the point. He is a human being with whom I have a special feeling. It is not only about sex. Sex comes out of that feeling." She didn't want to hurt Francine, but she wanted to be heard. "What you're doing right now is a cheap seduction." That stung more than she intended, but at least she had Francy's attention.

"What if I tell you that you are very sexy and that I think you could turn on anyone you wanted, including me. What does that prove? Your behavior is despicable." Izy's frustration was interfering with her compassion, but not her reason. "It just hit me! You liked it fine when I didn't date, when I was alone.

You've got some little thing working in your head, don't you? I see it now. How could I have been so blind? I'm your fallback. Oh, my God! All along, I've been your faithful fallback. Now all that is threatened. I love you, Francy, I really do, but right now, doing what you're doing, I think I also hate you."

Francine's face was flushed; her eyes fell and filled with tears. "I'm sorry. I am. I just... , I don't know what I'm doing." She tried to hug Izy as she started to cry.

"Don't cry, Francy. Just forget it. I'm sorry. I shouldn't have said that." Izy knew that it was all painfully true. This path had veered. Izy knew it. She wondered if Francy knew as well.

CardioStim was a solid environment. There was an atmosphere of nobility and purpose that permeated everything and thrilled Izy. It was as if with every breath, Izy grew in confidence. For the first time in her life, she felt as if everything were coming together, instead of falling apart.

It was not explicitly agreed by the men on the team, but no meeting began until Isabella was present. Her approval and input were sought after. When she made suggestions, she was crisp and erudite. She grasped the fundamentals quickly and began to incorporate subtleties that measured both her intuitive understanding and adaptive creativity. In their meeting with management, they presented a project that was on schedule and with incremental features originally thought impossible, as well as ideas to make manufacturing it more cost effective. Isabella did not seek to grab acclaim. She made certain the credit fell equally among the team members. Everyone noticed.

Even her life outside work seemed orderly. She had waited for John. In the back of her mind she was aware she'd been somewhat calculating. Nothing overt, but some sense told her to be patient, and she had been. When she wasn't at work she anticipated spending time with John. This became more and more the order of things, until it seemed reasonable to think about cohabitation.

Izy had no illusions about Missy's or Uncle Clay's opinion on the subject and she dreaded the inevitable. She and John had never discussed marriage. And he had recently been through a contentious divorce. To Izy, the formality of marriage at this point seemed just that—formal.

Alone in her small condominium, which she purchased shortly after starting at CardioStim, her old companion, the television, helped her avoid contemplating the subject. "The White House seems unaccustomed to these new political developments in Iran. Up until now, Cold War politics have dictated that every confrontation be defined by U.S. and Soviet polarities. The adjustment to a fundamentalist, religious revolution that denounces the United States and the Soviet Union equally seems to befuddle President Carter and his advisors. There is also growing tension over the health of the Shah, critically ill and seeking admission to the U.S. for medical treatment. President Carter has made it clear that he will not provide a haven for the Shah, but advisors are concerned about the impression that the U.S. is abandoning one of its oldest and most loyal friends."

Isabella turned it off. Her worry for the President took her far afield of her own issues. There was nothing crafty about Carter. Izy was convinced he was honest, genuine, and forthright. But she was also sure that a degree of craft and cunning might be required in the Oval Office.

"These improvements are remarkable."

"And they're all Izy," Vanderfluer acknowledged.

"Isabella, you are a very sharp, young woman! What really gets me is how you work through these guys around you like heat through butter. I'm telling you, you are really something!"

"I'm glad you think so. I like what I'm doing."

"What I have in mind is broadening your experience some."

"What do you mean?"

"I want you to go ahead and finish up on this project, really go for it, incorporate all you can. When it's complete, I'm going to bump you up a level in technical complexity, market value, the works. I think you have the savvy for much more and we should take full advantage of it to our mutual benefit. I'd like to set you up with a mentor and a development plan as well."

"Thank you, sir." She turned her head to Vanderfluer, "I appreciate the confidence."

"I'll set up an appointment with Human Resources. I don't want to push too hard, Isabella, but I do want to move you along. I want to fast track you but not derail you. I want a full battery evaluation and psychological workup."

"A psychological workup?"

"It's standard procedure for high-potential candidates. It's routine, nothing out of the ordinary: standard indexes, quotients. Nothing to worry about."

But she did worry. Her feelings on this subject were thick with apprehension. Izy didn't trust anyone from the psychiatric trade. After all, they had made a mess of her father's situation. And harking back to her childhood days in a cold, dismal hospital, there was that painful, haunting question: Could she be crazy as well? Did some strain of insanity lurk in her genes, hiding, waiting to sabotage her life at some point?

The nose of the plane rose up maybe twenty-five degrees above the horizon, rolled to port and steadied, then about thirty degrees below the horizon. Izy gripped the safety harness with all her might. John mentioned rudder and elevator positions, deflected, neutral something in the direction of the roll. She tried to listen, if for no other reason than to avoid thinking of what they were doing in the invisible box in the sky. "That's the easiest maneuver, usually the first one a pilot learns. It's not even a competitive form. Now, this is a snap roll."

The plane jerked. Izy closed her eyes, her stomach contents rolling with the plane. "That's really a horizontal spin with one wing stalled. How do you like it?"

"I gotta tell you, I'm petrified, but it is thrilling," she managed into the intercom headset.

"Do you want me to stop?"

Part of Izy wanted nothing else but to get down on the ground, or at least to a straight and level flight pattern. Another part knew she had to come to terms with it. She said, "No. I want to do this. What's next?"

"Easy, the Barrel Roll, not a competition maneuver, but one of my favorites! You'll see. It's fun!" The plane lifted up as if to loop but then rolled over in a big circle, corkscrewing through space, with the wheels of the plane on the outside of the roll. "That felt different."

"Positive Gs, that's why. Probably one, maybe two. Okay, now try to relax, I'm going into a spin."

As the plane nosed over into a stall, it began to orbit its own nose into Earth, going around in dizzying circles. "John, tell me you can stop this!"

"Don't worry, one or two more."

"Enough. Up, make it go up, John!"

"Okay, up we go, no problem. Now, that's where the living becomes vivid. Agreed?"

"Vivid, very vivid. So does the dying. Dying becomes vivid too, John."

"Can't have one without the other. Can't live without risking death."

"People do."

"No, they don't."

Izy entered the suite of offices that were so high in the skyscraper, they seemed to exist in the realm of the angels. She could see the entire basin laid out before her all the way to the ocean. This was her second visit. The first she had spent in a small, isolated room with no windows where she took test after test: language, numeric, pattern analysis, psychological profile, and personality index.

"I have your results and I will go over them with you before we provide them to your employer. You're a very bright, young woman, Ms. Reinhardt, but then, you already know that."

"I suppose I owe a lot to my father."

"Tell me about him."

"What do you want to know?" She felt caught in her own words. "He was very intelligent. He took great pains to educate me early, to take advantage of my mind when it was most agile."

"He's passed away?"

"No."

"You used the past tense, 'He *was* very intelligent.'"

The man's words hit as some form of indictment. "I don't see him very much. We no longer have a relationship. I guess that's why I used past tense."

"Tell me about that."

Was this where all her dreams crumbled? She had been denied clearance at Rockwell partly because Gunter was a nut; now was she about to step on a landmine? Why had she bothered to say anything about him in the first place? Maybe this little man would have asked anyway. She determined not to lie.

"Parents and offspring often grow apart, especially in the rebellious, teenage years." She smiled to assuage any concerns that it might be more.

"What caused you to grow apart from your father?"

"Completely different priorities about almost everything."

"What are your priorities?"

"Ah! A way out," she thought to herself and replied, "I want to be useful and to make a difference. I want my life to count for something. I think most people want that. The trick is to find a way to be useful in a world so devoid of strategic, cohesive thinking."

"Tell me about that, the world devoid of strategic, cohesive thinking."

She pondered a second on the nature of the little man's job. He seemed to repeat whatever she said back to her in the form of an open-ended question. It was useful that she realized this. "Sometimes I think about humans as a silly species. We have many similarities, the most significant being our fears, hopes, vulnerability—the questions we all have and the answers we all seek. Yet we act out of our own ego states as if the answers are some prize that can be possessed like a winner in a competition. Somehow, that is sad to me."

"What about competitive nature as a means of surviving and the survival of the fittest?"

"Absolutely! That is how we got where we are. Today the world is much different than when humans emerged as the dominant species. We're not battling the other species to see who will get the food, water, make it through the night, or the winter. We have banished every other species to the brink of disaster or, at least, submission. We have definitely survived. Now, will we survive ourselves? I suppose you're sorry you asked."

"Why do you think that?"

"You just don't quit!" The little man smiled slightly, acknowledging her comment without being beguiled. "Does everyone who comes in here dump their personal philosophies on you?"

"Do you believe everyone has a personal philosophy?"

"Yes. Even if they can't articulate it, their life is the outcome of their fundamental principles, beliefs, and precepts, whether or not they are conscious of its manifestation. What do *you* think of all that?"

"This time is set aside for you, not for me. Let's focus on what you think and how you function. How is your thinking different from your father's?"

"Ouch," she thought and tried not to react too much. The little man was cleverer than he seemed. She decided against further evasiveness. "My father is mentally ill and, frankly, it is difficult for us to have any relationship at all, let alone understand how we differ in our thinking."

"Mentally ill. Has he been diagnosed?"

"He has been hospitalized, and I'm sure the psychiatrists who have encountered him have labels for him. I'm not sure I'm completely versed in their diagnosis or, with all due respect, whether they understand him at all. I can tell you they have used the term 'paranoid schizophrenic.'"

"You are a very fortunate young woman, Isabella."

"How so?"

"Statistics are that twenty-five percent of the offspring of severely mentally ill parents are themselves afflicted with mental illness. Those offspring not afflicted are often suicidal, severely depressed, and rarely as high functioning as you are."

"As I am?"

"Why don't you ask the question that's bothering you?"

Isabella spent a few seconds trying to deceive herself into ignorance, then said, "You're very clever. And you're right, of course. I've always wondered if I would go insane, as well."

"Of course you want to know, and the answer is probably 'no'!"

"How can you be so sure?"

"There's a timetable. You are old enough, past several thresholds—it is not going to happen. And you are fortunate, even remarkable! I'd say the odds of your sitting here with me being considered a fast-track leader in a Fortune 500 corporation is one in a hundred thousand."

"Is that why I'm here?"

"Yes. And now that we've gotten acquainted, let's look at these results. Each score is put into context with three comparators. The first is a relative score for managers in the United States, in all fields, shown in black; the second is a relative score of executives in the Fortune 500, shown in green; and the third is a relative score for managers at CardioStim, shown in blue. Your mark is in red against each of these." He laid out each test and explained one by one. Izy saw that her red marks surpassed high marks everywhere. He made projections of her ascending to the highest echelons of corporate management. This did not impress Izy—but his words about her sanity, those were a relief.

The gloved hands moved with measured care, decisively manipulating the scalpel. The initial cut was in the axilla about five centimeters along the line of the pectoral muscle, exposing pectoral tissue. Then, skillfully, the surgeon continued the incision below the muscle in order to form a pocket. The subclavian vein was then punctured with a long needle and a sheath was inserted, providing a smooth entry into the vein and preventing a possible hemorrhage.

All his preparations in place, Dr. Ibsen turned to the nurse and requested the lead, which the nurse picked up with both hands, removing the sterile packaging and dumping its contents onto the stainless steel work surface. Dr. Ibsen placed a guide wire into the valve of the sheath, picked up the lead, fed it through the valve, over the wire, and into the vein toward the heart's ventricular chamber. Izy saw the look of intense concentration on the surgeon's face. He watched the real-time X-ray images displayed on overhead monitors as the claw of the lead zeroed in on the target tissue. Once in position, the lead bit into the tissue; the worst was over. The pulse genitor was attached to the proximal end of the lead and placed in the submuscular pocket. The wound was closed with absorbable sutures and the procedure concluded.

"No. It actually isn't typical. I use this procedure on young women and girls. It is a more cosmetically-friendly placement. But other than that, the basics are typical."

"I never thought about scars."

"No one did in the beginning. The idea of saving the life so far outweighed any thought of cosmetics, it wasn't considered. But then when the young ladies grew up and had to live with keloid scar tissue, we wondered if we could do better. Any physician, even surgeons," he said, grinning at his self-deprecation, "have to be concerned with their patients' overall well-being. I admit, there are those who are so focused on the physiological science that they don't take time to consider, let alone assess, the psychological. But that's not how it should be."

Izy liked this big man; at work in his cath lab, he seemed even bigger. Big was his craft, as well: medicine, cardiology. These were wizards who could probe a damaged human heart and restore it back to whole and functioning. It was awe inspiring. Her mission was to break through the awe and sustain an objective, curious mind so she could assimilate Dr. Ibsen's knowledge and experience into her work. And that was the truly stunning thing: It was *her* work! She created tools for these wizards. From time to time, thoughts about the import of her job— the scope, the responsibility—overwhelmed her.

"I want to be of service to you. I came to understand how I could do that. I realize I am taking your precious time, but I promise I will use this gift with diligence."

"I don't mind giving you my time. It can be frustrating to host individuals from corporations like yours who see the visit as an obligatory ritual, thinking I will be impressed that they've shown up. I'm only impressed when someone listens intently and brings back what I need to serve my patients."

Isabella easily built relationships with the physicians and surgeons she met. Her lack of medical knowledge was not an impediment—it allowed her to be a student. Her curiosity and craving to understand was compelling. She was not there to impress them with anything other than her genuine appetite for knowledge; it was in the fabric of her being, the disciple. Isabella observed each physician's unique style and manner. Though spiced with dashes of arrogance, she decided it might be a necessary ingredient for summoning the nerve to do what they did. She formed strong bonds with these wizards and enjoyed collaborating on the magic.

Milton spoke with a tone of disappointment and concern, "Well, he's still in the house but he's canceled meetings with the city engineers. He doesn't go to therapy sessions and there is no record of his picking up medication this month, though he may still have some in his possession. It doesn't look good. I drove out there, but he wouldn't come to the door. I left a letter explaining the prospects. Nothing."

Izy asked, "How does he even get food or anything else? What does he do all closed in like that?"

"He told me once in a lucid moment that he ordered canned goods via mail order. He had been going to the store, but the children threw things at him and hit him. I mean, he can be pretty frightening when he's lost in his madness. Course, he's not as scary as he was when we saw him before the marshals took him. His hair is grown out, but not so much. He seems to be shaving, at least once in a while. He's cleaner."

"Go figure, he'll threaten me and beat my mom, take on the city and its marshals, but won't defend himself against children?"

"It's so frustrating to see him lose it. I feel helpless to do anything for him. When he's clear and we talk, he demonstrates an impressive mind."

"He's very smart. He wanted me to be as smart as he is. But I wasn't. I'm not. I tried to be. Everyone expected me to be. I think you have to be crazy to be as smart as he is. Or maybe if you're that smart, it makes you crazy. Sometimes I think of what... ," she paused. "I think too much sometimes. It's a waste. A complete and pitiful waste."

"We'll do the best we can for him. I have to be honest with you, Isabella. I'm not sure it's in anyone's best interest for him to be on his own."

"Then why don't you help society put him somewhere he can be safe?"

"It's not that easy. Society hasn't a clue what to do with Gunter. If society, with all its applied expertise and knowledge, doesn't know, how can you, or I for that matter, know what to do?"

"Is it a matter of all the applied expertise and knowledge being leveraged to do something meaningful, or is it leveraged to avoid social involvement?"

"Society will tend to avoid anything for which it hasn't a ready solution. That's why sometimes it's necessary to force society to face issues in a way that demands solutions to be found." Isabella knew very well the meaning of those words. She just wasn't sure how it applied to her at that moment. "In the meantime, we really can only wait for either Gunter or the city to make a move."

Those words were no comfort to Izy.

Izy had avoided it, thought it over, and finally decided John had to know. She found the right moment and told him about Gunter.

"I guess I should have told you about this. I wanted to. But I was afraid."

"What were you afraid of?" John asked.

"People have a strange reaction to the subject of mental illness. They are okay if it's a joke about some abstract crazy person, or if they can pigeonhole the victim into some cliché. But when it is a real, live human being, out of control and crazy right in front of them, they mostly want to give them a pill to stop the behavior, or club them to the ground and cart them off. And I don't even find fault, really. I can understand that. I've had some pretty awful thoughts about my father at times. It's just that when I tell someone my father's insane... . Well, okay, I've never told anyone that. I just couldn't. You probably can't understand any of this."

John looked at Isabella, sensing what was beneath the surface. "I think I can understand, enough to know this is a huge burden to carry all alone. You're not alone. You know that, don't you?" Isabella hung in his arms feeling suspended in a bubble of protection from the specters of her life. Was this someone, at last, who could know and not run away? Could someone face this with her? The intense closeness drew her and captivated her. It also cleared the final hurdle between them.

Finding no safe solution, President Carter, persuaded of the urgency and the humanitarian merits, contacted the Teheran government to gain assurance there would be no retaliation if the Shah were permitted to receive cancer treatment in the U.S. The Shah arrived on October 22nd and survived surgery on October 26th.

Isabella's heart was heavy when she heard the news; her intuitive mind sensed trouble. She understood passion. It was difficult to imagine others did not. It was a mistake. It might be a humane, even courageous, decision; nonetheless, it was a strategic mistake.

Gandhi might have known what to do. It occurred to her that his death had been an incalculable loss to the world. He was on to something, something so profound, so course-altering, it could not be fully fathomed while he was alive. Izy's mind drifted to an altogether different direction and she thought of someone she hadn't thought of in a long time. "Maybe presidents have to turn and swim toward the sharks before the sharks come in for a bump!"

On Saturday, October 27th, Izy and John were working on their costumes for a blowout party the coming weekend. "What on Earth are they?"

"Hi, Mom! They're aliens. But wait till you see. John, can we fire them up?"

"Sure, help me out here."

The fiberglass head sat on a base that strapped onto John's shoulders. Since he was already over six feet tall, the head rose almost to eight feet. "Look in there, he can actually see out through that cleverly-disguised opening. Now, let me get the rest of it." Isabella draped his body with a cape made of shiny silver material. "You can get the effect. But wait. This is the best!" She turned off the lights. "Okay, honey!" With John at the controls, the huge eyes lit up. "Now say something!" The voice came out distorted and metallic in sound.

"How'd you do that?"

"Simple. It's just electronic distortion of John's voice."

"And who is this lovely lady?" John's metallic voice echoed in the garage, making Missy laugh.

"We're almost set."

"You two! I brought you something for lunch. I made extra in case you're hungry."

"Starved! We've been working all day, Missy. What is it?"

"Nothing fancy, just a casserole. I'll heat it up." Missy left them in the garage and went to the kitchen. Isabella finished cleaning up and followed.

"I want to talk to you, Isabella."

"What's up?"

"I talked to Mr. Feldner on the phone again yesterday. He is convinced that your father is going to wind up back in Camarillo."

"Yes, probably."

"I don't want them to hurt him. Is there anything we can do to prevent them beating him up so badly?" She trailed off, fighting her pain at hearing herself utter the words.

"Do you have something in mind?"

"Maybe if we went to talk to him."

"I don't want you anywhere near him, Mom."

"But if I could persuade him. If we could just get him to surrender this time."

"I don't know, I'll think about it."

Telling John about Gunter had created a place where Izy could go to work out difficult moments; no more struggling alone. "You've got to understand the conflict I feel about this. On the one hand, I think if I can find some way to coax him out of that fortress of his and let the cops suddenly appear, then cuff him and take him away calmly, it can work. On the other hand, part of me thinks that

272

would be some kind of betrayal. I don't know, John. What do you think?"

"I think it's an awfully big conundrum. Now, my dad's dead and has been for a long time."

"Really? You never speak much of your family."

"We are somewhat estranged. But that doesn't mean I don't love them. If I had to choose between sweating out my dad's getting brutalized by law enforcement or planting the kiss of Judas to protect him from the beating… , whoa! That's a rough one. Let's look at it logically first. Is he likely to hurt anyone else?"

"Oh, he's capable of inflicting injury to preserve his fixation of the moment, his sense of persecution. In the past, he's always gotten the worst of it. You know, they're afraid of him. They show up with a full SWAT team, weapons, they don't take any chances with him. His file says he's dangerous; they respond accordingly. I don't know. It could happen. He could hurt someone. I suppose there is that to consider in favor of doing whatever it takes to get him into custody."

"Okay, let's go to the other side of the equation. Talk to me about the betrayal."

"Well, it's something about respecting him enough to let him carve his own destiny. Like it might be easier for me, for Mom, to have him go peacefully. It is less upsetting than the violence and the feelings associated with his getting hurt. But if he wanted it to be easy, he could surrender. He somehow wants this intrigue; the persecution serves his mania. He's the one who creates the violence by his refusal to cooperate, and as his daughter I feel I should respect his design. I know that sounds goofy."

"No, keep going. That has something, go with it."

"I can't know what is in his mind, what his world is like for him. I cannot know him like other people know their fathers. The only thing I have is a thin tether to him built on… . There's a word, but it's not coming to me."

"Acceptance?"

"Yes. The only relationship I can have with my father is to accept what he carves out for himself, regardless of the anguish it may rise up in me. It's about respecting his life the way he is creating it, without judgment or reservation."

"Can you do that?" John paused, waiting for Isabella to process. She did not answer.

Work was a splendid means of escape. Isabella continued to gain respect, and her accomplishments were mounting with the progress of her team. Being at work was a perfect elixir for stress and pain. Sometimes she would park in the front of the building and enter through the lobby to look at the company history on display, smell the wood, and walk past the great heart logo on the marble floor. She would be filled with a sense of dignity that pushed out all other possible thoughts.

Once at work, she had only the patients to consider, people who would live, and live a better life, because of what she and her colleagues did each day. She snatched every opportunity to meet with cardiologists to watch, listen, and absorb. She took pains to incorporate what she learned, which helped her form strong bonds with the physicians, not only in cardiology, but also with internists, neurologists, oncologists, and other medical specialists.

Her mind expanded and hatched new uses for implantable, bio-electronics. Isabella realized that pacemakers were only the beginning of what could be solved with the technology. Once the little computer was in place, its electrical impulses could be deployed for all kinds of things. What about precise drug delivery and data collection? Or the supervision of other, smaller implants. She imagined unbounded possibilities!

She met each new challenge with enthusiasm and worked hard on finding appropriate solutions for moving forward and achieving optimal results. She saw contributors as warehouses of knowledge and was eager to grasp their same sense of purpose and fulfillment. Once in a while she encountered difficulties, but nothing that gave her cause for concern. She loved her work. She loved this new company, its mission in health care, and the growing diversity of its workforce at all levels. Most of all, she loved the way it consumed her pain.

"I'm hungry. Let's get started!" Isabella announced as she laid the pizza on the table. She observed that Francy was sullen and not making eye contact with anyone. "I've got the perfect wine to go with the pizza."

John was chatty, on edge all through dinner. Francy left as soon as the dishes were washed, dried, and put away.

"All right, what's going on?"

"Nothing. Nothing's going on."

Isabella looked at him. "You think you can lie to me? I can read your mind, honey. I know something's wrong. I bet I even know what it is. So let's have it."

"Francy and I had a little difference of opinion while you were at the grocery store."

"I see. Francy coming on to my honey again?"

He didn't answer. Isabella sighed. "She can't help it. It's just her way. She's insecure, and I think you and I really trigger some strong feelings in her."

"Well, I don't like it and, frankly, Izy, I tolerate her because she's your friend, but I don't always like her, I don't trust her. And furthermore, I don't think you should have any respect for someone who pretends to be your friend and then tries to make it with your boyfriend behind your back!"

"I want you to like her. And she is my friend. But I'm glad you didn't take her up on it. I know how seductive she can be."

"Francy is a very sexy woman. She, all by herself, is intoxicating at times. I mean, that's why I get so bent. And tonight, well, I had to let her know I wanted her to cut it out!"

"You didn't hurt her."

"No. But she wouldn't quit, so I did shove her away, and I think she got the message!"

Isabella felt tormented. It did hurt that Francy would do such a thing. But it was also nothing she did maliciously. It was part of her survival, a constant search for self-esteem in all the wrong places.

Around the world, thousands of miles away, Iranian students were holding rallies. With their voices and banners they demanded that the United States return the Shah for trial and that the fortune he stole from the people of Iran be returned to them. In the capital, Teheran, the temperature was white hot in the early morning; it built energy as the minutes turned into hours and the sun rose higher in the sky. The students—charged, inspired, and urged by the incendiary, powerful Imams who taught them—mobbed the city streets, churning their way toward the United States Embassy.

The news of American hostages taken at the embassy shook the nation, none more than Izy. Upon hearing yet another broadcast of their plight, she was overwhelmed by feelings of empathy. She shut off the television and virtually collapsed.

"What's the matter, Izy?" John asked her as she lay curled up on the bed, sobbing. John was troubled by it. "Izy, please talk to me." But she did not; she lay in a tight ball and wept. He grabbed her up and settled for comforting her without knowing the reason for her distress.

Once quieted, she lay still in his arms, then slept. Later, she volunteered an apology. "Sorry. I'm sorry. I didn't mean to lose it."

"Don't apologize. I just wish I knew what upset you."

"It's not anything specific. It's more like an overwhelming dread of something so terrible I can't even imagine what it might be. I've had these feelings before. Usually I can reason that they are feelings, nothing more, and push them away. For some reason, today I lost control. Maybe it's the hostage thing. Those poor people. It's horrible. Yet, sometimes I think I can understand how angry the Iranians must be. I don't know, John, I don't know. It just upsets me. I wish Gandhi were alive. He seemed to have such clarity. And things are not at all clear. Why is every damn thing in the whole damn world so complicated?"

"Don't know, Isabella. I can see that it is upsetting. It is awful. I wouldn't want to be in Carter's shoes. It's a bad situation all around." He pondered for a moment. "Sometimes, when I have inner conflicts that are unresolved, I let them ricochet around and manifest in completely disjointed ways instead of expressing what it is I really feel." He paused and looked at her, extending himself, touching her heart with his, and getting a direct hit. "Izy, what have you decided to do about your father?"

"I'm not sure. I'm... . I'm so conflicted. And I guess I'm running out of time. I'm going to have to do something. Maybe that's it. I feel mounting pressure to do something and soon!"

"I can't decide for you, Izy. But whatever you do, we'll do together."

But that was only partially true. There were some things Izy would have to do on her own, and the events leading up to action included a final visit to Milton's office with Missy. One last time, she would attempt to get her to agree to sever connections with Gunter.

"I've made up my mind. I am not going to divorce him under any circumstance. I cannot and will not abandon him!"

"But it is just a legal tactic to shield you from anything he might do that has legal or financial consequences. Besides, I don't see how it has anything to do with abandonment, at this point."

"It is the abandonment of a sacred trust, a promise to stand by him, look out for him in sickness until death parts us. When I made that vow, I didn't exclude horrible sickness. I didn't say except for the unspeakable horrors of schizophrenia. This is exactly the reason why a promise like that is made. These moments of abject horror are why it is crucial to have someone who will stand by. It is all about these moments, Isabella. When no one else will stand by. Oh, Isabella. You just don't understand!" Missy broke into the sobbing she had been holding back, bending over her lap. Isabella put her hands on her mother's back and rubbed softly, silently.

But Isabella did understand. While her mother wept, she began to question her motives. Was there any other way to protect Missy from Gunter? Did Missy really have to break her vow in this way? "Momma, this is just a piece of paper. It dissolves a marriage; it does not break a bond of love or your vow. We can still stand by him together. If you want, I'll make a vow with you here and now, we will stand by him no matter what. But I think it's best if you sign this legal document. It doesn't have to mean anything we don't want it to mean."

"Then why would I sign it to begin with?"

The finality of the words cemented Izy's decision and compelled her to action. She would have to travel back to the nightmare house one more time, this time alone.

"Daddy? Daddy, it's Isabella. I know you're in there. Listen to me. I want you to open the door and let me in!" There was no response at all. She beat on the door with all her might, "Daddy! Listen to me! I have to talk to you! I know you can hear me. I have your paintings. I have them here with me. I am going to the other door. I want you to open it and let me in. Go to the other door, open it and let me in!"

She turned crisply and walked through the jungle, past the garage to the back door of the front house, just as she had with Milton. When she arrived, she beat on the door. "Okay, Daddy! Let me in! I'm here! Open the door!" She waited, trying to see inside, but couldn't. "I'm going to get something and come in, one way or the other. Maybe I'll pick up this old two-by-four and bust in the door. I don't remember it's being all that sturdy. I'm coming in, Daddy. Open the door!" When there was no response, she grabbed up the three-foot length of wood and began heaving it over her head against the door. The bashing was weakening the wood. She decided to pause for effect. "Daddy, open the door!" She heard the lock turn; the door moved slightly, then nothing. She placed her hand on the edge of the battered door, pushed it open, and peered into the darkness of the nightmare house.

After her eyes had adjusted, she entered. He had stepped back into the shadows but watched her as he closed the door behind her. His eyes showed white around the irises. He held his sledgehammer raised slightly as if to guard himself. "Where are my paintings?"

"I have them. They're safe."

"You have them here?"

"I have them. I have come to give them to you. But I want something in return."

"The devil Jew sends a minion to negotiate?"

She ignored that, "I'm worried about you. How are you doing? Food, are you getting enough food?"

"Food? Why do you worry about food? There are fruit trees, nuts, and roots outside. I can eat if I want to. Why do you worry about food?"

"How do you… how do you get food? Do you go outside?"

"Why do you ask if I go outside?"

"I, I just want to know that you are okay, that you have food. You're my father. I have a right to care. I have a right to something. I have a right to care."

"Do you?"

She paused, looking at him, searching her heart. She decided it was not wise to lie to him. "Sometimes. Sometimes I care so much it's more than I can endure. Other times, well, I wish you would, I wish you were… ." She paused, then surrendered, "I can't stand the thought of you at all, and I wish you were dead."

He seemed to accept that. He nodded his head slightly. "Food is not a problem."

"That's good. That's a good thing. You are eating. I want to talk to you about medication. You're not taking the medication."

"You take the medication."

"The medication is for you, not me."

"You take it, then tell me I should."

"Why? What is it like? The medication, it's bad?"

He sucked his tongue to the roof of his mouth, "If I don't mind my mouth stuck together, dry as dust, muscles cramping till I could scream from the pain, and blurred vision so I can't work, or my extremities jerking when I least expect it. I do mind. I mind very much! And all of this I should endure? Not because it has any hope of making my disease go away, but because it will allow you and your society to ignore me!"

"I'm sorry. I'm so sorry. I wish it could be better. Maybe they can give you something else to help with all that."

"You want me to be something I'm not, a product of drugs on top of other drugs, turned into some vegetable without a mind or soul just so you can be comfortable, so you can feel safe? I don't think you have the right to feel comfortable or safe at my expense. I know who you are, what you do." Those words pierced Izy, making her feel conspicuous. "You live in your world conforming to all the rules, fulfilling expectations, seeking to please. It won't get you anything in the end because you will give over all that you are to be what you think you are *supposed* to be. They will abandon you, deceive you, and betray you. And you, you will have nothing inside because you gave it over to them."

She was quiet, riveted by his clarity and put off balance by his message that convicted her of a truth she could not name. He was uncharacteristically lucid. "There must be residual effects of the medication," she thought, or else this was just an extraordinary moment. She couldn't tell which, nor did she care. "I'm afraid if you stay in this house, you'll get hurt. I don't want that."

"Danger, you speak of danger. A threat, you're threatening me?"

"No. You threaten yourself with your own actions. You made a commitment to the city and you have broken that promise. Eventually they will work through their bureaucratic requirements, and then it will be more than a threat, as you well know. And I don't want you to be hurt. Is that so hard to understand, to believe?"

"It is only through the blood of the Lamb that the truth can be made known to the Jew master."

Her heavy sigh was unavoidable. She felt the weight all around her, but kept focused on her mission. She tried to keep him engaged, but felt him slipping away. "What truth? Tell me about the truth."

"The truth will set you free. The truth hurts. I am the way, the truth, and the light."

"You are a light, Daddy. You are my light. You shine on me every day, whether you know it or not."

"Then you see the truth."

"I want to see the truth. I want to see the way out of darkness, this darkness. I want you to show me the way out of this darkness." Then something flickered in her mind, a memory threaded into her head. She started to hum and sing, "Friendship, friendship, just the perfect blendship. When other friendships have been forgot, ours will still be hot!"

He penetrated the fog between them for an instant as if to see something more clearly. "You know that song?"

"Yes, Daddy. You used to play it for me and dance for me." She felt pain in her throat and her eyes but held tight, her mind with his.

"Isabella?"

"Yes, Daddy."

"Why are you here?"

"I want you to come out with me, outside."

"Oh no, I couldn't do that." She was losing him again. "It's not safe out there. Can't go out there."

"Tell me why, Daddy." She had to come up with another strategy and quick, she was stalling.

"What do you want, Isabella?" His voice told her that the hopeful moment had passed.

"Daddy, if you don't come out and go with me, the men will come in here again and take you out, whether or not you want to go. You know I'm telling you the truth. That's what's true. If you come out now, with me, it will be on your terms and no one will hurt you, I promise."

"My terms?"

"Yes. What terms do you want?"

"I want the paintings."

"You got them, no problem."

"And I want your mother."

Isabella's heart seized. "You want Mom. What does that mean, exactly?"

"I want her to come home, here, and then I will go with you."

That was never going to happen. As certain as the sun will rise, she knew if

Missy came in here, down here, it would spell disaster. Her mind raced for something to say. "What if Mother meets you outside when you come out with me?"

"I'm not going out. Why have you come here? You are intruding, come to betray me." He looked menacing and raised his hammer. Her adrenaline surged and fear rose with each heartbeat. She needed to engage his intellect.

"The medication, do you know how it works?"

"What?"

"The medication they give you, do you know how it works?"

"It's nothing remarkable. It doesn't cure anything or change anything. It's just a powerful sedative. They give it to people they don't want to deal with, don't know how to deal with. They give it to make us shut up and behave. It does nothing. It only makes people in your world more comfortable and enables them to ignore me, to pretend I don't exist."

"I can see why you resent it. I would resent it, I do resent it." She was conflicted and confused. She had to keep focused.

"What do you think we should do?"

"Do? There is nothing to be done. All that is necessary has already been done. Everything is in place and unfolding accordingly."

She felt him slipping away. She had to think. "What do you think could be done to make the drugs more effective? What could be done besides the drugs? You know more about it than the doctors. Tell me what you think." She watched his face shift. His brow furrowed, questioningly, then lifted in pursuit of his answer.

"They don't comprehend what is happening. They see things in increments. They see the effect and think it is the cause."

"Cause? You know the cause?" It occurred to her that his powerful mind knew more about the disease plaguing it than all the experts in the world.

"The brain is an electrochemical machine. The chemicals are manufactured and released by the body in conjunction with tiny, micro-electrical circuits. The body is just a computer. But they don't care about that. They just want me to take tranquilizers, massive amounts. Tranquilizers don't do anything. It's a complex problem, electrochemical in nature. Tranquilizing does nothing except subdue me. That's what they want. They could not possess me, enslave me, so they want to destroy me. Put me to sleep. Keep me incarcerated inside my own head. They are deceptive. They want you to think they are helping me."

Isabella recognized her brief inclusion in his world. Her conscience was in conflict. Here in this precious moment, he was present, needy, and vulnerable. This was her father, her Daddy, whom she loved and cared for. There, at that moment, she was with him, not against him. But her mission was to use that bond to manipulate him for what had once seemed a greater good. But was it? And this feeling of inclusion, of being with him—was it just self-satisfaction? What should she do? Her heart wanted to align with him against them. But there really was no 'them.' How could she have it both ways? Or could she?

What an absurd paradox that this brilliant man was excluded from helping to solve his own problem. It was a tragic conundrum. Unless… . Isabella saw a road, a path emanating from her solar plexus, stretching out in front of her, forking toward the future, one tine veering sharply, unalterably.

Isabella began laying out for Gunter the plan that was forming in her brain. It was utter nonsense, ridiculous. She darted between telling herself it was a ploy, then unreasonable, then imaginable, then no, maybe, never—then yes! It was a risk in so many ways. It was full of impossibilities, the odds were overwhelming that it would never work out. But it was all she had and it was a voice in her heart screaming to be heard. She'd have to trust herself to figure out exactly how it could be done.

Across America, Iranian students demonstrated and Americans fought an internal battle of bigotry versus tolerance. The American hostages were seen blindfolded and beaten; ultimately, they were accused of crimes against Iran. Emotions were molten on both sides. At home some scorned anyone who appeared to be of Persian descent. Carter's non-violent response—sanctions— triggered an oil crisis. The ricochet effect was felt in any industry dependent on oil or its richest byproduct: plastics.

CardioStim's business was completely dependent upon plastics—in more ways than management had ever stopped to think about. Work became a crisis center. It would take wisdom and ingenuity to get them through. Izy's creativity and ability to get out in front of a problem were invaluable assets.

As the days came and passed, Izy came to believe that the hostages were actually a perfect fulcrum, something Carter did not seem to understand. His well-meant intentions were cementing their fate. Izy thought about what Gandhi would have done if he were a hostage; it did not require much imagination. What she couldn't fathom was what he would do if he were in Carter's place. But her thoughts were foiled: Gandhi would never be in such a position.

Whenever she felt herself spinning out of control, trying to make sense of an insane world, Izy would grab her imaginary boxes and cram them with the disturbing thoughts and feelings. Then she could dive into her work with greater focus and intensity. This freed her to discover new options and new solutions where there seemed to be none. She was instrumental in helping CardioStim to negotiate the hazards of the oil crisis with minimal damage. Management recognized her contributions, and Isabella Reinhardt was propelled to prominence among the highest ranks of the corporation.

UNFOLDING PARADIGM

Uncle Willy died in his bed of heart failure. Aunt Abigail blamed her husband for not abiding by his diet. Willy thought he could overcome his transgressions with insulin, but eventually, his toxic blood destroyed his heart. "If the death certificates of people who died of diabetes-related malfunction of the heart, kidneys, whatever, cited diabetes instead of an organ failure, diabetes would be the number one killer in this country. They always say it's heart disease, but half of that is due to diabetes!" Uncle Clay told Abigail, his arm around her as they left the grave.

"Willy was stubborn."

"Willful and stubborn. Had to have things his way. Mom should have given him a few good lickings when he was a kid. So you see, in the end it was his charm that killed him, for he always weaseled his way into this and out of that. Now look what's happened. Guess he couldn't get his way."

"Now, Clay dear, that's no way to talk today. Even if it is true, let Willy go to his rest with love and without judgment," Missy gently held Abigail's hand as they walked. Inside, she was glad that her brother was his acrimonious self to the end.

"Oh, all right!" Clay shut his mouth, convinced that Willy's selfish behavior meant that he left his wife alone for no good reason at all! He didn't calculate how much of his frustration was about his late wife's similar failure.

Emily stood at the grave as the others left. From a distance, Isabella watched as Emily looked down upon the casket that held her younger brother. She, too, had recently been diagnosed with diabetes.

Emily's face lifted toward the sky. Isabella wondered if she was experiencing vulnerability or was invoking some miracle. Perhaps she was surrendering to an inevitability descending upon her. Even the Foursquare Flame was mortal. Then Isabella heard her speak but could just barely make out the words. "Not yet," she thought she heard, "I have unfinished business!"

A contingent of cousins attended the funeral. They were strangers to Isabella, and she knew that Katherine Margaret, dear Grandy, would find that sad. It occurred to her to mount a reunion; she put it in her mental to-do file. She made small efforts to talk with each cousin, but found little in common. She realized that they were only characters in family stories; she didn't know them at all.

Most of the day, Izy stayed close to Kathy who in turn, stayed close to her father. Attending his young brother's funeral had hit him hard. Today he was neither impertinent nor arrogant. Today he was contemplative, and Izy saw him through different eyes. He had seemed fragile and uncertain as Uncle David, once again, spoke parting words over a Hume.

Micheil and Renée went home the next morning. Kathy and her husband stayed on for a visit with Izy, who was tickled to have them. Her husband's name was Stanley Dietz, Dr. Stanley Dietz, a neurologist. Kathy met him at university and they kept in contact after graduation; their friendship blossomed into romance. Appreciating that the two women might want some time alone, Stanley left them to do some reading. For that, he got extra credit respect.

"I understand exactly what you're saying, Izy. But it doesn't add up. The number of people with psychosis is insufficient to warrant such an extended and expensive program of research. The payback just isn't there in the end. It's better when all mental illness is included, but you want to focus on schizophrenia. There's absolutely no payback in that and no way to predict if you will develop data in your research that can cross over to other disorders. I reiterate, all together, it doesn't justify the extensive program you've laid out in your proposal."

"What if we expanded it to all brain disorders, including neurological disorders like multiple sclerosis, Parkinson's, and such? Or what about just neurosis?"

"I am afraid that would be too broad. What precipitates one may be entirely different for another. We just don't know. You have not convinced me that there is any program that could be inclusive that would also provide the focus to get meaningful data or create anything of value for a specific disorder of the brain. We would be starting from zero, maybe less than zero because all diagnosis today is very subjective."

"You're right. It's just that this matters to me more than anything."

"I'm sorry, Izy. I can see this means a great deal to you. But it's not going to happen, so forget it."

"I suppose I will, for now, but there has to be a way." Izy left the office of CardioStim's CEO. She didn't work directly for him, but they were well acquainted, and she appreciated the time he allotted upon her request. Izy was a highly-valued employee, a blossoming executive, someone whose personal concerns were taken seriously. Izy valued his opinions. If she ever did come up with a means to execute her plan, she'd need support and critique along the way.

On her own time, she had developed a proposal to expand the use of corporate technology on a research methodology; she hoped this would eventually provide some answers. From her initial study of the market size, she knew it would be difficult. Mental illness, although devastating, did not affect the masses, not like heart diseases. Isabella hoped to strike a chord of urgency based on the horror and hopelessness of the disorders. By this time she well understood the intricacies of corporate finance—she knew that research dollars needed to pay back in direct proportion to the risks involved. In the medical device industry, the risks are high and the criteria strict. The hazards of the development process and regulatory hurdles can easily delay paybacks. If the returns are not projected to be significant, investors would be reluctant.

She drove home that evening preoccupied with other frustrations. She put away her disappointment and shook off feelings of failure. She started mulling options and rethinking her ideas. Stopping by the mailbox, she extracted advertisements, bills, and a letter from Iowa. She couldn't wait to open the envelope. She ripped it open, cutting her finger in the process.

Dearest Isabella,

I am writing to tell you it was grand to see you again. You are such a wonder to me. I remember you as a baby, a little girl, and now you are a woman. Like Kathy, you are out in the world, educated and doing things I never even dream about when I was your age.

Willy's death has given me pause for thought. I realize that it is for me to do the things I have in my heart before I am too old or too ill to do so. I want you to help me with one of these. I'm not sure how or when, but I want you to go with me to Europe, to France.

My Robert is buried there in a grave honoring the brave soldiers killed on the beaches of Normandy. I have never seen his grave. I have the information. It was sent to me, but I never went over there to find him. I know it may sound silly, but I feel I have to go before I die. I hope you can understand that.

At any rate, one reason I've never gone is my fear. I've never been outside the United States and, I confess, I'm scared to go alone. Would you go with me? I'll be happy to pay for your trip. Don't worry about the cost, I've been putting away for this for years.

Love in Christ,

Your Aunt Emily

The idea of Emily afraid of anything was a new concept entirely, but also endearing and compelling. She understood completely about Emily and her Robert. She would gladly go. And, of course, Aunt Emily needn't spend her little savings on Izy's expenses.

She wrote back, rather than telephoning. It seemed to Izy that the import of the mission itself had taken on a measure of formality and even ceremony. It had to be a letter. They began to correspond regularly and then talk on the phone from time to time. At first, the notion was almost one of whimsy, but as Izy engaged in the preparations it began to take shape.

It so happened that CardioStim had given Izy an objective to travel to Europe to scout out suitable sites for offshore manufacturing. Lots of candidate countries had been mentioned including Great Britain, France, Germany, Netherlands, Belgium, and Switzerland. Izy decided it was the perfect opportunity to slay multiple and proverbial birds. Once she had planned her time slot and laid in her itinerary, it seemed ideal for her to meet with physicians on behalf of the company as well. Soon, a month abroad was scheduled, complete with a side trip to The Invasion Memorial in France. Emily would be fulfilling the mission to visit her Robert in the spring while Izy fulfilled her objectives for CardioStim.

From Chicago, Kathy was sending literature to Izy on the latest research on healthy brains versus those diseased with psychoses, especially schizophrenia. One fact was now evident to everyone involved. A genuine baseline of information about the functions of "normal" brains was virtually non-existent. Most information was purely speculative, based on observation of outwardly manifested behaviors rather than physiological algorithms or biomechanics. Izy and Kathy spoke on the phone regularly. Often Stan would get on the line with some pertinent comments, and sometimes they arranged conference calls with informed and/or interested individuals.

It was on just such a call that Izy's phone indicated she had a call waiting. She found Ronny on the other line, in tears, got off her conference call as soon as possible and called Ronny back.

"When did it happen?"

"Just this afternoon, at his work. He just died. His heart, they think."

"How can I help you, Ronny? What can I do?"

"There's really nothing, except I had to talk to someone, someone who knows, who could understand. I feel so strange. I'm so devastated. But, well, it is so hard to explain."

"Maybe you have other feelings too," Izy said, knowing a lot about mixed feelings.

"Yes. I do. He was my father. With everything, I cannot say I'm sorry he was my father. I don't want you to hate me for saying that."

"Years ago I probably would have misunderstood that, but I know exactly what it is to love so deeply the very person for whom you might also have other feelings just as strong."

"Yes. That's it exactly. Because in spite of how much I loved him, how much he mattered to me, I am also relieved. I feel unspeakably sad, and at the same time, it is as if I have exhaled after a lifetime of holding my breath."

Izy understood what Ronny expressed and was grateful to be someone with whom Ronny could share such a thing. She also had a moment of realization. It was a different thing from knowing something in your mind. It was knowing it in your soul, your depth of being that no one, absolutely no one, gets out of here alive!

Izy flew to Des Moines to pick up Emily and they flew to New York Kennedy Airport together. Emily had never been to New York. Izy had allowed plenty of time for a taxi into Manhattan before the evening transatlantic flight to Paris since Emily mentioned she had a stop she wanted to make. Actually, Izy had invited her mother to join them, but Missy had no interest in Europe and didn't seem to want to see The Big Apple, either. So it was Izy and the Foursquare Flame on the town together. Emily was dead set against seeing any Broadway shows. Izy opted for the afternoon ferry past the Statue of Liberty, Ellis Island. Everything seemed to make Emily's eyes wide and she expressed her astonishment with intermittent sucking sounds through her pursed lips.

"Think about Grandy, born just out there, at sea, coming into this very harbor so long ago. Now, here we are, Aunt Emily, on our way back to Europe. Life is sure full circles and patterns."

"Yes, it is. I know that Grandy told you a lot of stories, but she could not possibly have conveyed to you how determined, courageous, and genuine she was all her life. Sometimes I marvel that someone who was so mistreated and unloved as a child could be full of love, acceptance, and compassion for others.

She was quite somebody. Not the way a person is famous, recognized, or rewarded. But in the way she lived, walked, talked, and had faith. It is amazing to be here and to think of her as a newborn baby on that old sailing ship."

"The *Limerick*."

"Yes." She chuckled. "The *Limerick*. Here in New York Harbor over one hundred years ago and just about this time of year, too." The wind was blowing, the water was parting for the fat width of the ferry, and birds were calling from the sky near the island where the lady stood. "Isabella we're going to take a fast visit to this address before we head back to the airport."

"But I was thinking... since we're here, The Empire State Building..."

"Our church sends money to this young man. He lives here in New York and has a wonderful ministry. I want to see him while I'm here. I'll probably never have this chance again. Let's go."

When the ferry landed, they took a taxi to the address Emily had shown her. It was not a nice place. The street was littered with debris and there was a smell of filth in the air. Izy didn't really want to get out of the cab and was terrified they'd never get another one out here. Emily was hell-bent on her mission.

The address led them down steps into a large basement. Once inside, Emily began asking about her young man while Izy had a look around. Inside, it smelled clean and looked orderly. There were three sections. One was a kitchen, closed off toward the back, but, over the smell of cleaning materials, you could detect that a meal was underway. Then there were a few offices up front where people were busy with small tasks, looking up only to smile and look back at their work. In the middle was a huge, open room with cots in neat rows and long tables, end to end.

"Morris! Morris Bosley!" Emily's voice boomed, joyously."

"Sister Emily! I'm so glad you could come!"

"This is my niece, Isabella, Isabella? Come here. I want you to meet Morris, who runs this place. My niece, Isabella Reinhardt."

"Welcome to The Open Hand Ms. Reinhardt."

"What is this place? A homeless shelter?"

"Yes. We specialize in taking in the homeless who are not accepted elsewhere."

"Why is that? I'd think shelters wouldn't discriminate."

"The truth is, there hasn't been so many homeless on the streets since the Great Depression. The financial woes of the Carter administration have made parts of this city disaster zones in terms of jobless, desperate vagrants: whole families, mothers, and children. It is very bad. But that is a mask for another problem that isn't on your evening news.

The laws regarding mental patients are very interesting. When patients get out of line, and the severely ill often do, they often become disenfranchised from whatever anchor to a life they might have had. They may be sent away to a mental facility for some period, usually ninety days. Then, they are just ousted into the streets. The hospitals are no help to them. While there, they tranquilize them so they don't cause trouble. But once out, they are just as incapable of fitting into society as they were before hospitalization, only now, they don't have that anchor, whatever it used to be: an apartment, maybe they once had a job, or they were clinging to some form of disability. Suddenly they have absolutely nothing, including the reason to reestablish themselves. If they were getting checks from some source, sometimes families, they have no address to receive them. They are just out there, alone in more ways than you or I can imagine.

Other shelters can't take them because they only help families and children, and some of these individuals are pretty wild. So, we take as many as we can. It makes us pretty unpopular. We have to come to a place like this just to exist. But someone has to have a care for these pitiful creatures. It's not their fault. They deserve better. Can you imagine turning cancer patients out onto the street naked to fend for themselves until they are eaten alive by their disease? It's a tragedy. Your aunt and her good people listened to our cry for help and send a little money each month to help out, and it is much appreciated. We get a little from the government as well. But as you can see, we are only a small bucket in the sea of need."

Izy looked around again and saw Gunter staring back at her from every corner. For every face, there was another tragic story, a stolen life, a fractured family. She saw tired, vacant eyes, dead eyes, individuals no one wanted. And yet they weren't like Gunter at all. Because his eyes, his blue, eyes even though they might be tired, had a look about them. They were angry. She began to realize that the rage inside her father was what kept him from crumbling under the weight of the disease. "Aunt Emily, why did you decide to help this man?"

"It was one small thing I could do. In a tragedy, where I felt ignorant and impotent, it was one small thing I could do."

"Why did you bring me here?"

"I was compelled to do so as if you needed to see this. You will have to tell me why I brought you here beyond that." Morris gave them explicit directions to the subway and they managed to get all the way to Kennedy, clutching their suitcases and handbags, Emily assuring Izy they were surrounded by angels, protecting them as they went. All the time Izy wondered if God threw out the angels that were crazy to suffer here on Earth. Gunter's tragedy had never loomed as large in her mind as now. What if circumstances had been just a little different? What if Gunter was left to the streets of New York? Even in the City of Angels? He would be set free in just 18 months. Where would he go? She had made him a promise, now she had to keep it, somehow. Time was running out. She had done far too much talking and had accomplished nothing!

She was vexed all the way to the airport. They checked into the first class lounge just minutes before the first boarding call was given. They had a private jetway from the lounge to the first class section of the airplane and went swiftly to their seats and buckled in. A tall, elegant stewardess offered them a beverage. Emily took tea and Izy asked for vodka on the rocks. She waited for Emily to rebuke her, but it was not forthcoming. She took it down gladly, washing away the agony of the lost souls at that shelter. "Tell me about Robert."

"He was a good man. I was lucky to know him."

"Grandy said he was handsome."

"He was. He was all that and more. He had a rich soul. That's what got him killed I'm sure. He was brave, loyal, caring, and honest; all the qualities that forbid a person from shirking their duty. He hit that beach proud to give his life and was dedicated to his men and his mission."

"How do you know?"

Emily turned her head to look straight at Izy. She searched Izy's face for something. Izy wasn't sure exactly, but Emily's eyes were piercing into her. Then it seemed she had found what she was looking for. Her gaze softened and she began to speak.

"After Robert's death, I found it difficult to preach or even to pray. It was not just Robert, it was that Sister had been found dead that same year and it was unclear what the cause had been. You know Sister?"

"Sister Aimee Semple MacPherson."

"Yes. The newspapers said it was an overdose of drugs. There was a strong suggestion that it might have been a suicide, although her son, Ralph, adamantly refuted it. Regardless, I could not help feeling betrayed. Suddenly all the scandals about Sister swirled in my head. Sister was a woman ordained by God to do a mighty work. But she was also just a human being. She made mistakes. And with notoriety, there is a price. All your mistakes are very public."

"So you know the dirt on the kidnapping?"

"Well not exactly, but I developed my opinions. I think Sister got herself into some sticky situation. I never believed the kidnapping story. It just didn't tie up. And I struggle with the idea that Sister might have lied. Not a courageous thing to do. Then, when Robert died, and she died with all the suspicions, I found myself caught up in doubt about everything, not just Sister. What was the meaning of all this? How could God give me someone who was my perfect soul mate, my beloved, my match in every way and then not bring him home to me? Did Sister kill herself? Had she really been just some snake oil shyster, everything a hoax? And if not, how could it be that God would allow such things to happen. How could I serve this God? Who was this God I had dedicated my life to? My heart was broken, and I was consumed with myself. I went into seclusion. I didn't want to see anyone, talk to anyone. I couldn't read the Bible or pray. I couldn't imagine my life going on. I didn't have the fire, the passion to breathe, let alone to preach or to be a servant of God. My flame was out, and I was surrounded by bitterness and pain.

"At first, I thought of suicide. A sin, of course, but what did it matter in light of everything in my heart and mind? God had forsaken me. As the days passed, I became more comfortable with the pain until the pain itself became a reason to live."

Isabella could not believe how her perspective of Emily had broadened in the past few months. She listened to her Aunt, noticing little expressions, a turn of the head that reminded her of Grandy.

Emily continued, "I found myself walking in a meadow. I felt the uneven ground beneath my thinly shod foot, and, by the delicate colors spilled across the ground, I realized it was spring. The day was hot, baking in the radiant sunlight and smelling of grass. I turned to a gentle touch on my shoulder and found a man wearing a hat in silhouette against the bright sun behind him. As my eyes focused I saw that the man was Robert himself standing there. He opened his arms and I ran into his embrace. It was really him, strong and alive. But what could this mean? I turned my face up into his and the question didn't need to be asked…

"'I had to see you. You've made quite a mess of things and it's time you cleaned it up, Emily.'

"But I got a telegram,' I replied, 'you were killed at Normandy…

"'And so I was, Emily. But that was only my body that died. And just as I told you in my letter, a great miracle was wrought that day. I got to be part of it. I am glad and proud that I was. You must believe me when I say that everyone dies, but not everyone dies fighting for what they believe in. I was privileged to do so. When it is all done, everyone is dead just the same, but I died knowing my life had mattered. I found a purpose to my life that day on that beach. Every man who fell on that beach made way for others to survive and fight. Can you understand this?'

"'Yes.' I replied, 'I think I can. Was it as awful as I imagine? Tell me if you suffered.'

"He answered, 'It was far worse than anyone could possibly imagine or that I could convey. But it is in the past; any pain or suffering does not exist in my memory now. As you can see, I am safe and well.'

"I said back, 'I'm glad, but somehow that does not make me less lonely, nor can it take away my pain.'

"He said, 'No, and you will ache and be lonely. That is your thorn.'

"'What do you mean, thorn?' I questioned.

"He said, 'I mean, you are very proud and powerful. It is difficult for you to comprehend those who are not, like yourself, endowed with an inner strength. It is easy for you to make yourself believe that they should all face life just as you do. But you can see how the events of one's life can tear at the foundations of character. You endured your childhood, and it never fazed you. You lost your father and, unlike your sister, you carried on. You have always gone where angels fear to tread, but in a single loss, you have come to your knees. Don't you see what you have done? You have run away and hidden, afraid that others will see you are weak and impotent. Even you have been humbled.'

"'It is not just a single loss,' I said.

"'Ah, yes. There is Sister,' as if he could read my very thoughts.

"'You know about Sister? Do you know the truth about her death, her life?' I said aching to know.

"'I can tell you this, Emily: If your ministry was based on Sister, then it is good that you have come to lose her and the illusion that blinded you,' he spoke. 'Did you do all that you did for the glory of Sister, or the glory of God?' And then I was awake in my bed. The visitation ended."

293

"Was it a dream? What?" Isabella inserted.

"I cannot say because I do not know. The dream, the presence of my true love, or maybe God in the form of Robert's likeness had passed, but the question was still ringing in my head. Had I done all that I had for the approval of my mentor or because I believed in the Lord God Almighty, in Jesus the Savior, and in the heaven that Robert had ascended to, joyous in the noble sacrifice?

"I was freezing cold, my hands and feet like ice as if all the blood had been drained from me. I sprang from bed, stripped off my nightgown and stepped into the bath, waiting impatiently for the running water to warm up. And as the warmth began to surround me, I rededicated my life to God, vowing to live and die for the purpose God had ordained me and that no person would come between God and me again. At once, I realized I was not to raise a family after all. Robert's purpose in my life had been fulfilled. My children would be the lost and lonely, and my mission would be to guide the lost and lonely to God's love. From that day forward, I knew in my heart that Robert was watching me, and I lived life to measure up to his example. But never again would I allow any earthly influence to step between my soul and God.

"I made my way out to California, to Angelus Temple. There I waited for the altar call, and like a sinner, I lay prostrate in penance for my loss of faith. When I felt God's hand return to my shoulder, I mounted the platform and told a stunned audience that I had been visited by a heavenly being, which I thought was the best way to explain it, and after having been reminded of my frailties, I decided to renew my vow to God which I had done, and to my ministry, which I would do immediately. I confessed my weakness and my humanity openly before the entire congregation and told them that they should not be consumed by gossip. Nor should they concern themselves with Sister's life or death. The only thing that mattered was their own heart and whether or not it was right with God. Then I visited Mother and assured her that I was going to be just fine before leaving to resume my work."

Izy appreciated what Emily had shared with her. It explained a lot to Izy about Emily's version of God's work versus that of her uncles. She asked herself, "What do I believe about the dream or the visitor?" The time when she and John had connected with the other's mind and heart, could not be explained, yet it was real. But what about God or heaven or Uncle Robert or Grandy's vision. Was it all a metaphysical mystery that foolish humans tried to rationalize when there really was no explanation to be had?

Emily Evans found her husband's grave, marked by a pure white cross and indistinguishable from that of thousands of others who died beside him that day. It was clear to Isabella that Emily was shaken by the stark nature of the place. Despite all the words spoken or written, short of being on that beach that day, the only way to grasp the magnitude of what happened and the sacrifices made was to stand silently and be humbled by the presence of all those crosses.

"Reunion? But there's so many of us now!"

"All the more reason to do it. I don't think Grandy would like the fact that we are all so far apart, and we don't really know each other anymore."

"Yes, she was all about family. She would like that, I guess, and if it were possible, she'd come herself."

Izy expected, at any moment, Emily would try to convert her to Christianity, but her Aunt only encouraged her to believe and to seek God for herself, on her own terms. "If your heart is open to the possibility of God, God will find you and touch you, Isabella."

"I don't know what to think. I know all the rules and the rituals are a stretch for me. I know there are many things that are beyond our mortal understanding, and I get really irritated by people who tell me they understand, or worse, try to explain the unexplainable."

"I feel assured when you speak, Isabella. I know that what you speak is true for you and that is essential to faith in God."

"What does that mean, Aunt Emily?"

"It means that the first step on the path to faith is to open your heart to the unknowable and be true to what God places there for you. It is of no importance what anyone else believes or says they believe. All that matters is what flows between you and God. Be true to that always."

He found her huddled, weeping inconsolably. John gathered Izy in his arms and surrounded her with himself, trying to make her feel safe. After a while, she quieted, limp from the catharsis.

When she could, she said, "I'm sorry. I don't mean to be so weak. It's just that I am such a failure, John." He said nothing but listened. "I told my father if he would give himself up to the authorities, I would provide him an opportunity to fight back. I'd find a way to put his brain to work on his behalf. I had this idea to save him. But it's all come to nothing now. How can I face him again? What will become of him when he is released? I've screwed everything up. I've betrayed him."

"I know you want to find the cause and then a solution. You've told me. I believe in your dream. Why do you say it has come to nothing?"

"I made a proposal to CardioStim. They are interested in long-range research to broaden the use of electronic stimulation in other parts of the anatomy for other physiological issues. I thought this might be a good fit or, at the very least, I wanted it to be. But it isn't. After all, they run a business and make decisions based on market viability. Mental illness just isn't up there in the top tier of profit. There are decades of research ahead and a fortune to be spent with no idea of when it might provide a return. I've racked my brain and can't think of what to do next."

"What do you need? If you could do anything, what would you do?"

"I guess I need to get some collective energy working, focus on the questions. Stunning little is known, really known, about the disease."

"How would you go about it?"

"I know some of the right people already. Kathy is a psychiatrist and Stan is a neurologist. I could find other intellectual components and talents through my contacts. I need specific medical experts and someone who is a wizard with computers, math, and data analysis. I guess I'd get them all together in a room and lay out the challenge, assemble a team, point them in the direction and see what we could come up with. People working together, collaborating, can do almost anything."

"Then why don't you do that?"

"I don't know. Money I guess. I'd be asking them all to show up out of the kindness of their heart, the least I should do, is foot the bills"

"Would twenty thousand dollars cover such a meeting?"

"Sure. Easy. I guess I could use my next bonus. But Gunter will be out before I get that and what will I do with him? He has nothing now."

"There's something I should tell you. You're not the only one who keeps things to yourself. It hasn't really been important until now." He paused, lifting her face. "I know where you might be able to get the money."

"Money?"

"Yes, money. Lots of money, but you will have to get it on your own. I can point you toward it but I cannot get it for you."

"I don't understand."

"My family is rich."

"Your family, rich?"

"Very rich. But we're not close anymore, to put it mildly. In fact, I am the outcast, the black sheep, or maybe prodigal is more accurate. After all, I left them. They did not abandon me."

"Your family. You've never talked about them." She thought for a moment, her head cocked to one side. "I guess I never asked. I figured there was some dark secret. It seems to me, most families have dark secrets. I didn't want to pry. I never dreamed money was your secret."

"Oh, we have a few darker tales, for sure. But the truth is, I love them, just don't like most of them. I have a theory about generations that have their wealth handed to them. I am the fourth generation, and it is pretty corrupt at this point. No sense of ourselves or the world around us. Money that has no foundation in struggle or risk is crippling, an easy comfortable twisting of the perspective. But that's another story. I ran away from them, not because they are bad, because they are not. They were born into their world just as your father was born into his. But I wanted to escape it, to untangle myself from it in the best way I could."

"So are you rich, John?"

"Not really. Like I said, I ran from them and when I did that, I also left behind the money, most of it. I have a small bundle; it's enough. They do have money, and they do grant funds to research projects. I could get you time to make your case, but I doubt anything I could do or say to them would be of any help to you. They think of me as, well, foolish and irresponsible."

"That must hurt."

He looked at her for a long time, deciding whether or not to go to the place where he had kept his darker side, his choices, and their consequences. She saw his eyes turn just slightly glassy, then he blinked them clear again. "Life hurts. Everyone carries their hewn tree on their shoulder. I can't complain about mine."

"Your parents?"

"My father died quite a while ago. Worked himself to death in his ivory towers. That convinced me that I had to flee the life he wanted for me. I mean, he built upon what was given to him and, in the process, traded away most of his time here on Earth, only to hand it to his children who face a similar fate or worse. My siblings have no sense of struggle or sacrifice."

"Siblings?"

"A brother and sister. They bask in their situation. They have money without being able to imagine what it might be like to have nothing, a life without prospects."

"Tell me about them."

"I think deep inside my sister feels it too. She tries to apply herself in all the right ways—ways of which our Mother approves. She sits on charitable boards and works for hospital programs. But I don't think she allows herself to ask why she feels she needs to. My brother's older than me, very stable, very connected to the right clubs, the right charities, and the right sports: the right lifestyle."

"Right sports?" Never knew there were any right sports."

"Oh, yes, Izy. Example: a one-on-one game of hoops is inappropriate. If you want to sweat, tennis is an acceptable way, and at a proper club, with the proper attire. Golf is appropriate, even racquetball. Anything you do at a private club is appropriate.

"And that gets close to the heart of my objections. My great-grandfather made his money in lumber as an ax-swinging jack in the northwest who built himself an empire. My grandfather took that empire and added industries that he learned from the ground up: paper milling, hardware, construction. I'm not saying they were saints, but they knew what it meant to risk everything for what you believe in and face the consequences of ruin if you are wrong.

My generation is removed from all that. I can't explain it, but I know that there has been a departure from what it was that made the money have meaning. Now it is just wealth: safe, secure, and insular."

"Why would they be interested in mental illness?"

"I don't know, Izy. Maybe they wouldn't. For all I know, there's no reason why they would."

THE PARTICLE OWNER

Veronica grew distant: a signal to Isabella that her friend was hurting. Busy or not, Izy would track Ronny down and probe until she found the source of her friend's pain. And there were ample roots. Despite the fact that Ronny had inherited her mother's self-deprecating sense of humor and preferred to be in public with a smile and a joke, puns being her weapon of choice, there was little joy in her life.

But then there was Izy who epitomized marvels, energy, and ever-abundant optimism. Ronny was thrilled to hear that Izy was organizing a reunion luncheon for the three: Ronny, Izy, and Francine. It had been a long time since they all had been together. Although they talked on the phone, it had been a year since Izy and Ronnie had seen one another. On the day of the luncheon, Ronny selected a dress to wear, tailored and in a muted color. Her blonde hair was trimmed just below her ears. She was heavier now and purchased clothing that hid her generous buttocks behind graceful lines. She never wore jeans anymore.

Izy was a busy executive with a crowded schedule. She had an executive assistant who handled her arrangements and kept her work life somewhat sane. After talking with Ronny, Izy had instructed Mrs. Walters to block out a long lunch, to make the arrangements with the other two women, then safeguard the slot with her life! So when Izy arrived at the office that morning, she was given a printout of her day displaying in big red letters LUNCH WITH RONNY AND FRANCY! in the noon to two slot. She smiled and enjoyed a flush of excitement then put it aside to get on with her work.

One of the things Izy had done at CardioStim was to leap on the opportunities that she saw in a new device introduced to her by her secretary, one day. Mrs. Walters, who now worked with smooth elegance and efficiency, came to Izy asking permission to attend a seminar on something called word processing. She was determined, so Izy agreed.

When Mrs. Walters returned, she had literature on a product manufactured by Wang Laboratories. It featured a keyboard similar to that of a typewriter, but instead of pressing an embossed character at the end of a mechanical arm into an inked ribbon and onto a piece of paper, it displayed electronic images of characters on an electronic screen. Corrections were easier, copies were unlimited, and files could be stored on 8-inch squares called floppy disks. The very idea made large file cabinets seem absurd. Izy instantly thought about the floor space currently consumed by storage cabinets at all CardioStim facilities. After agreeing to allow Mrs. Walters to purchase a Wang Word

Processor, Izy recognized its potential, which brought Reba Theabolt to mind. It was as if in a single crack of thunder, a bolt of lightning, she understood the true nature of Reba's vision.

She began her own investigation and soon had Mrs. Walters place an order for something called a Personal Computer made by Apple Corporation. It didn't take up a whole room or require a special environment such as raised flooring and humidity controls. It was simple to use and anyone could make it do rather amazing things. She gave it to one of her engineers and encouraged its use. Before a quarter had passed, its potential, like an infection, had spread throughout her department. The box was in constant demand, and so Izy bought more.

In no time at all, CardioStim had gone PC. Within a year, the big room with the mainframe was ripped out, and a new, systemic network of desktop computers was revolutionizing the work. Terms like database, disk storage, hard drives, and software were filling their vocabularies, changing minds about the concept of data processing and storage. CardioStim was on the crest of a new age, largely because of Izy! Izy knew it was all due to two women in her life having vision, and Izy, the wisdom to listen.

She often thought of Thunderbolt and from time to time had gone to visit her. After Thunderbolt retired from Rockwell, she was diagnosed with an all too familiar disease: lung cancer. But she never complained or talked about death. She relished hearing the latest developments in Izy's world, smiling and nodding in affirmation as if she could see the future as clear as day. The end, for Reba, was a blessing. Having witnessed the harrowing process, Izy made a decision: the cigarettes Izy enjoyed so much, had to go. It wouldn't be easy, but then, nothing ever is.

Izy's morning was so typically congested that she barely made it out the door, Mrs. Walters chasing to catch her on her way. She found Ronny in the parking lot of the restaurant went inside, swooping in on Francy, seated at the bar, with a whirlwind of greetings that seemed to annoy Francy.

"Hi, honey! How are you?"

"Good to see you."

"It's been too long."

"I'm so glad Izy called to set this up."

"She didn't call. Some broad called," Francy snapped. There was an uncomfortable second as the jab of Francy's words hit the otherwise happy occasion. Izy decided to brush it off.

"You're referring to Mrs. Walters. She's far from 'some broad', and she was able to get us all together again!" The mood picked back up, Francy ordered another whiskey to go as they were lead to their table.

"Well, don't you look grand, Izy, all spiffed out in your suit. And you all dolled up. Don't you both look lovely," Francy said, acerbically.

Izy ignored the tone, assuming correctly that Francy had arrived early and had had a few. But she was disappointed. She had wanted this to be a fun time. "You look good too, Francy," she lied. Francy did not look good. She was bloated with weight, her skin looked older than her years, and darkness surrounded her eyes. Her features, once beautiful, now seemed permanently set in a sardonic knot.

"Did Mrs. Walters pick out our food as well, or do we get to choose from the menu?"

"Please, Francy, I just wanted us to be together and catch up with each other. Can't this be a celebration?"

"Certainly. Let's celebrate. Let's celebrate our young executive here. What do you make now? Six figures, I bet. You are proof that one person can have it all, aren't you, Miss Yuppie? Or are you? Do you have it all?"

"I'm not going to do this with you, Francy. If you want to hate me, there's nothing I can do about it. But will you at least tell me why you hate me?"

"I don't hate you, Izy, I love you. Surely you remember. I'm the one who loved you and cared about you, I thought I was someone who mattered to you. Guess not, cause you've gone off and left me and don't even care about me, and you have Mrs. Walters call when it should be you that calls, but you're too busy, too God-damned busy to call a friend. This friend, anyway. I take it you called Miss Veronica, here!"

Izy felt embarrassed. It was true. She never had time to spend with her friends, and if she took time, she was more inclined to call Ronny than Francy. She looked at Francy and reached out her hand. "I'm so sorry, Francy. You're right. Will you forgive me?"

"In a pig's eye, I will!" Francy raised her voice. "You can't make years of bullshit disappear with one sentence. And don't go touching me! Who the hell do you think you are, anyway?"

Everyone in the restaurant was looking at them. "Francy, please. Can't we just have this time together, let me make up for the past?" Izy's eyes were pleading. Francy, knowing she had the upper hand, stood up, turned to meet the stares from other tables and leaned in hard with that sardonic smile, "Whassamatta? You assholes never seen lovers quarrel? Uptight bitch!" She said to a stunned woman at the next table. "Whadya think you're lookin' at?" Francy said to a stunned woman at the next table. Then she turned and walked out.

"She's jealous, Izy. Don't take what she says to heart."

"How can I not? First of all, Francy has never known love. I think we are the only ones who love her."

"There you go, Izy. You're the one who loves her. The rest of us tolerate her."

"See? That's exactly what I mean. She has such a low opinion of herself that she behaves badly. Then people just leap on it and affirm her low opinion. I confess I don't keep up with her like I used to. I don't know why. She's hard work. Maybe sometimes I'm too tired to put forth the effort." Izy shook her head. "What an awful confession. Francy needs constant support and yet she is too wounded to accept it easily. I know she creates much of the unhappiness in her life, but I can't shake the fact that she's struggling against overwhelming odds."

"But that's the grim truth, Izy. Unfortunate or not, her life is her responsibility. We all have our hurdles. Are Francy's greater than mine or yours?"

"Maybe. I don't know. It's not a contest. And it's much more complex, Ronny. I don't think Francy has any sense of herself and, furthermore, she's right about something else. I care more for my career and my dreams than for either of you. It is the truth."

"And why not? What's wrong with caring about what you do? What's wrong with having dreams and passion for them? "So much has changed since we were born. if things are perceived as having changed rapidly over the last generation, they're changing at warp speed now."

Isabella sat down and her eyes landed on the business card holder that sat at the far edge of her desk. She read the title above the embossed CardioStim logo, "Outstanding Leader of 1986" on her business cards with a level of satisfaction; then went quickly on to her stack of incoming mail. It was opened and placed in priority order so she could move through it efficiently. Thank goodness for Mrs. Walters!

The invitation was printed on thick, luxurious paper in an elegant font. At the bottom, a tastefully designed crest was stamped in gold foil. "How distinct and peculiar," she thought. The satisfaction she had just felt was now lost to the grip in the tightness of her chest. The message was succinct:

Dear Ms. Reinhardt:

We have received your petition for endowment consideration. You are cordially invited to Maison Eveque for an audience with the Board of Governors of Saint Martin Guerisseur May 4th of this year."

Isabella was struck with a strange sensation that smacked of insecurity and uncertainty. "What have I gotten myself into this time?" she wondered and breathed deeply. She told herself this is wonderful but found it difficult to keep her breathing deep rather than rapid and shallow.

"My God, John. What are you, related to a saint?"

"No. I am not. Not that I know of anyway. I think it is an identity that my family embraced several generations ago when my great-grandfather grew wealthy and influential. As I told you, they are all very pleased with themselves and steeped in their own importance." John cautioned her to resist being overly impressed. He told her that she would be meeting with his Mother, Frederique, and also his sister and brother. In addition, there would likely be four others who are not family. They're the brains. Mother is the brawn," he explained.

Shortly after the formal invitation, a packet arrived with information on Saint Martin Guérisseur, its purpose, and designs. Saint Martin was the patron saint of France, Martin the Merciful, The Glory of Gall, and was actually born in the Roman Empire, in what, today, is called Hungary.

After a career in the military, he converted to Christianity and devoted his life to religious pursuits. He spent most of his religious career in Gaul or France where he sought an opportunity to humble himself, embracing poverty and fasting regularly. During his ministry, he was renowned for many miracles, medicinal solutions, and his visions which bordered on the bizarre. Isabella thought of Emily and her vision while simultaneously pondering the possibility that Saint Martin might have been psychotic. The most profound and prevailing assertion by all accounts was his affinity with the wretched. "Ah, the wretched. There's a hook. What is more wretched? There may be a method here. How fitting that this organization should bear the name of such a man. If ever anyone was in need of miracles, a healer, here we the wretched stand!" It also occurred to Izy that Saint Martin's epiphany occurred during his military career. Somehow she was sure that there was a connection between her father and this legend. Coincidence or destiny, her hopes began to mount, and she was determined to make the most of it.

Izy bought French Language tapes, books on French Canadian culture and history, as well as anything she could find on Saint Martin. She had two months to prepare and she used every minute.

But her confidence deflated when she arrived at Maison Eveque outside of Montreal. The limousine that picked her up at the airport floated through the imposing gates as they opened onto the property, parting an elaborate M and E.

The sleek, black Mercedes continued through a natural landscape of soft, rolling lawns, sculptured hedges, and graceful gardens. They passed small cottages, then buildings that might house equipment or vehicles. Further ahead, behind more ornate wrought iron stood the main house built of stone and with huge beveled glass windows which caught the light and sparkled, giving the impression one was traveling toward an enormous granite mountain laced with quartz.

For a moment, Isabella could not recall what outrageous cause had brought her to such a humbling circumstance. She wished she were in a taxi so she could order the driver back to the airport without further delay.

Once they had arrived at the granite palace, Isabella, feeling completely subjugated by the chauffeur, was seamlessly passed off to the butler who escorted her to a secretary. The secretary led Isabella over parquet floors through a maze of richly colored furnishings and brocade fabrics, up a staircase beneath a carved ceiling to double doors that opened to the library. On the walls hung oil paintings of ancestors with familiar features, the only evidence connecting John's simple tastes and temperament to this splendor. Seated at a large table in the center of the room were the seven Governors of Saint Martin, enveloped in plush wing chairs and engrossed in each other's mumblings. The secretary initiated introductions with a respectful "Ahem," and then, "Allow me to present Miss Isabella Reinhardt with petition 1784 before you. Madam Frederique Vanse Martin, matron of the Martin Family and Chairman of the board of Governors of Saint Martin Guérisseur."

Madam Martin raised her gaze and paused to examine the young woman before her. Isabella nodded and smiled. Madam Martin smiled as well, but it was not a warm smile. It was polite and appropriate. "Miss Reinhardt, the board of Governors welcomes you in the presentation of your petition. This is my daughter, Angelique Martin-DuBois," Frederique continued with a tiny nod to her left, "and my son, Charles Martin." She turned to her right ever so slightly and added: "Doctor Louis Lateur, Chief of Medicine, Montreal Memorial; Peter Eclatè, Chief of Research Saint Catherine Center for Neurology; our legal counsel Simon Racheĺ; and last but certainly not least, our business advisor, Raymond Allison. Please proceed, Miss Reinhardt."

Isabella had no time to discern if there was an ally in the group. She recognized the need to proceed calmly and with reserved authority. "Look at each person, relax, smile at least some of the time, and for God's sake, don't make any mistakes!" She told herself. "Remember the objective is to get the money!" There was a least a technical ally in Peter Eclatè from Neuro-Research and she had someone to defer to in case she faced an onslaught of tough questions. I might even be strategic to defer to his expertise in the field. She had decided to direct her remarks broadly, but to make key points with tactical precision, whether it was medical, technical, or financial in nature. As she spoke, she wondered if she was being evaluated for anything besides her presentation of facts. In the tiny seconds when Isabella's eyes were captured by the unflinching gaze of Madam Martin, poised and restrained, she wondered if the woman was curious about her as a person.

Isabella was accomplished in her presentations. She had researched her content and planned skillfully. She had prepared immediate, intermediate, and long-range models with comprehensive requirements, contingent actions, and probable outcomes of each. She could feel the board's rigidity slacken as the physicians became more interactive and animated. The brother's arm found the table, and he leaned in. The daughter's head turned as she followed the conversation. The lawyer sat quietly, nodding occasionally. But when Raymond Allison began to contribute to the discussion in a supportive manner, Izy felt successful.

When all was said, she was excused. The Secretary escorted her to a parlor downstairs where she was told to wait. The butler entered and asked if she would like tea. Gratefully, she accepted his offer which brought a bit of comfort, a sense of home in the foreign setting. When it came, she wondered at the need for two servants to present a single cup of tea. The butler opened the door and the tall and graceful Madam Martin entered the room. Isabella stood and, by some miracle, did not spill her tea. "Miss Reinhardt, I thought I should speak with you. Do you mind if I join you for tea?" She spoke perfect English with only the slightest inflection of the "j". But when she turned to the Butler, she spoke in French.

"Enchanté, s'il vous plaît," Isabella replied, hoping her pronunciation was nearly proper. as she settled gracefully into the chair opposite Isabella.

"I understand you are a friend of my son, Jean."

"Yes, Madam."

"You must understand that your friendship with Jean can have no bearing whatsoever on the outcome of this petition. Our work is not about endorsing the whims of my children, but rather strict adherence to the charter and mission set forth by my husband's grandfather many years ago."

"I do understand. And it is precisely the charter that inspires my belief in our mutual interest. 'Bring the lamp of hope where darkness imprisons the wretched and nourishes despair.' There is nothing more despairing than a human mind incapable of trusting its own sensory information."

"It is true that Saint Martin Guérisseur pays particular attention to the sick, and yes, has even more interest in the wretched. Nonetheless, each year, we set out our agenda and we must comply with this agenda. If we allow ourselves to be swayed by each sincere and well-intended petition, we would become entangled in the myriad of the world's needs. It is my responsibility to ensure this does not happen."

"I appreciate such a responsibility as well as the focus. I ask no other indulgence than for you to imagine you yourself in a place where nothing makes sense. To the extent to which you are able to perceive the world, everything seems menacing and calculated against you. Imagine if the entire world seemed to harbor only disdain and malicious intent with regard to your safety and your purpose in life. Imagine there is no escape from this horror, and each morning is just another day in a maze of paranoia and distorted thought. Imagine you are intelligent and capable, with dreams and aspirations but are doomed instead to this torture. Further, when you do have a rational moment, you are able to realize what you have become and the futility that surrounds you. Finally, imagine that society has only one solution: drug you into a stupor and ignore you."

"Your plea is impassioned even if somewhat impertinent, Miss Reinhardt." Isabella was pretty certain there was an insult packaged ever so delicately, even politely in those words. "I believe your passion is for good reason. However, I must tell you this is not within our scope of consideration at this time. I do not want you to build false hope only to be disappointed. Furthermore, I do not want you to assume that we can give this any consideration other than strict objectivity."

Not easily set back on her heels, Isabella replied, "I ask only that you consider it as if there is no other lamp in the night save the one you hold. In fact, Madam Martin, it is the case as truly as I sit here and state it!"

The older woman sat still, holding the young woman's gaze. Then, calmly as ever, she said, "Excuse me, I must leave you now," rose and left the parlor. The butler returned with Isabella's things, signaling an end to the visit. Isabella grabbed up a biscuit for her empty stomach's sake and departed the granite palace believing she had failed to penetrate the heart of the woman who clearly held sway over the considerations of Saint Martin Guérisseur.

In the car back to the airport, she recalled Grandy's admonition about life and adversity. Muscling her sense of failure, disappointment, even frustration out of her way, she also remembered that sometimes a person has to set their mind to a thing, come what may. Perhaps Saint Martin was too easy a solution to her problems. Perhaps she should have known that. Isabella began to develop a plan "C".

John exhaled down toward his shoes. "I was afraid of just this."

"Just what exactly."

"My relationship with you would do more harm than good. You see, my mother sees me as the Martin family's charcoal gray sheep." He used the French pronunciation of his family name. "I'm sure she uses the term 'objective consideration' loosely. My fear is that her consideration will be only too subjective and not in your favor, as a result of my unfortunate influence."

"Well, I don't see it that way. I see that I failed to capitalize on a great opportunity, which I would never have been offered to begin with if it weren't for you. Besides," she gave him a mischievous, grin, "it was worth it just to see what you've run away from. I can understand how it could be overwhelming, and yet I can't imagine what it took to walk away. You are more of an enigma to me now."

"There! That's it!" John was not feeling any humor at all. "I don't want to be an enigma! I just want to live, be me, fly my plane. That's why I left all of it behind me!"

"Why?" How could you just walk away from the possibilities a life like that offers?"

"It's not as you think. There are far fewer possibilities than you envision.

You'd be surprised how ensnaring money, old money, can be. The truth is not that I walked away. I had to get away, I ran to escape it, all of it. All that you witnessed and a whole lot more, that is not me! As long as I affiliate myself with it I am judged by it, held up to the scrutiny of those who have long since forgotten what life is really about. My mother cannot comprehend earning a living, paying bills, embracing a challenge. And she cannot understand that I love the very elements of life she cannot even grasp. Away from it, her, them, I am free to fly, dream my own life and exist as just John, the person I am inside. Can you understand me, Izy, can you?"

Izy looked into the scrunched up expression on John's face and reached out to the man she loved. She reassured him that she didn't need to understand, only to trust. How different, she thought, his life had been from her own. How very different their mothers were. Still, they were both refugees from their earlier lives.

John and Izy together put up the money to initiate work on her plan. She would need to meet with the clinical talents from science, especially bio-electronics, neuro-dynamics, and psychology. The legal aspects and government regulations alone were staggering.

Isabella reluctantly researched government grants, obtained the appropriate forms and completed an application. It would mean relinquishing ownership of intellectual properties. The government exacted a high toll as compensation. In a way, this was reassuring, but not enough to offset her apprehension. On the other hand, it was a means to the end she was now dedicated to achieving. The greater the adversity, the more her resolve was solidified. She looked over the forms one last time, sealed them inside the envelope, and sent them away with postage and hope.

As a backup to plan "C", Isabella also began writing letters to any charitable foundations whose charter seemed to align with her own.

Some accepted her query. Others declined. Isabella acknowledged the acceptances with gratitude and contacted the declinations directly seeking to understand their objections. Mrs. Walters helped out tremendously with phone calls, appointments, and coordination of what had become an even busier schedule.

The months passed quickly. The meeting was coming together but the money was not. Her initial inquiry to the government returned a mountain of paperwork. The National Institute of Health wanted a detailed plan with schedules, budgets, risk assessments, and endorsements. All of it was possible but chokingly time-consuming. Izy turned her face up as if to ensure a last breath of air before submerging into the waters of bureaucracy.

She received invitations to make presentations to three charities expressing an interest in her preliminary proposal. She prepared for each one individually, molding her thoughts and offerings to specific formats and guidelines. The days so dense, time did not exist except in the transition between appointments and tasks. Her world had compressed into a quest for means, method, and mechanism. Urgency her constant companion, she clung to a faith she didn't even know she had. And then one day, Mrs. Walters stepped into Isabella's office as said, "Ms. Reinhardt, you have a phone call from Mr. Peter Eclatè. I told him you were busy, but he insisted.

Peter Eclatè had mixed news. The good news was that Saint Martin Guérisseur had found Izy's presentation so compelling, that they were going to make a small fund available to her cause. The less heartening news was that the funds were offered with the expectation that the results, though desperately needed, would likely be disappointing and doubtlessly dissuade further investment based on futility. The assumption was aggravating, but Izy was also grateful for this tiny chance and welcomed the offer without reservation. A small fund of five million dollars was a lot to Isabella. If she was clever and careful it could go a long way.

Then came the condition that made her heart sink: the funds would only be available if a representative designated by SMG sat on the board of governors of the organization overseeing the research. The SMG-designated representative was to be Jean Martin himself! And there was the trap, laid and sprung. Isabella had become the bait. Her brain swam in circles as she wondered what to do. She could not allow herself to become the means by which John was forced back into the grasp of his family and his cunning and virulent mother.

That night at dinner, John announced to Isabella that he had received a letter from Saint Martin Guérisseur, in fact, from his mother, explaining the details of the proposal.

Fredique Martin was thorough.

"I'll do it."

"You must be joking!"

"And we will make no argument about it nor protest in any way."

Isabella had ceased eating entirely and stared at John. "I don't understand. You have said repeatedly that you wanted to be free of your family, the foundation. How can this be your response? It contradicts everything you have said."

"Simple. I want you to have the money. She wants me to resume involvement with the foundation. It's what she has always wanted. But she wants something else as well. She wants to force me against my will to return to the fold and do something she believes I do not want to do. There is a subtlety in that I will not afford her! So, I will do it willingly, quietly, without ado. I will not give her that one small satisfaction."

"But then she wins."

"First of all, the big winner is the research. Second, I assure you, it will be only a partial victory if I do it without some big battle."

"But she's made me the bait in this trap, and I'm afraid you'll end up resenting me. I feel there's a wickedness involved."

"Oh, my Izy, you are intuitively wise. My mother is a bit of a viper. The truth is, I made a choice to involve you with her. If anything, you may resent me for putting you in this vise. You are beginning to feel the second edge of the sword. However, it is entirely possible that Madam Martin underestimates one critical factor with which she is relatively unfamiliar."

"And what's that, John?"

"Isabella Reinhardt!"

The first meeting of the Reinhardt Foundation was held at the Del Coronado Hotel in San Diego. The board arrived over the afternoon and evening of a Friday and met for cocktails and introductions.

"Congratulations on your marriage, Izy. It's just like you to get married like you cross off an item on your "to do" list. I can't say I'm not disappointed."

"Thanks, Kathy. You're not the only one. Mom was fairly furious, as furious as she has ever gotten I think. And John's mother, well, she is, I think it is safe to say, outraged!" But really, the whole concept of the marriage, well, it seems superfluous somehow. It changes nothing for me personally. And a wedding, well, it's a fine thing, but more stress than I wanted. There was no payback for me. No one seems to understand that at all. No one! Except for John. Anyway, thanks for coming, I know this is an imposition."

"I am anxious to learn what it is you are putting together for us."

"Katherine, Stanley Dietz, this is Doctor Ivan Myers, Neuro-Surgeon at Yale

University."

"Of course, we know of your reputation, Doctor Myers."

"Likewise, pleased to make your acquaintance."

"Doctor Myers, this is my husband John Martin, and Milton Feldner. And this, everyone, is Mrs. Walters, the most brilliant administrator in the world." They chatted politely, then went up early to their rooms anticipating the early morning business.

Mrs. Walters had reserved a conference room and they entered to fresh fruit, pastries, juice, and hot coffee. Izy waited for everyone to arrive then dove directly into the agenda.

"As I have made clear from the beginning, I have a very personal and passionate obsession at work as we begin what I hope will be a meaningful relationship that may change mental health care in the world for future generations. You've all received the basic proposal, and I want to started today by answering any questions you might have."

"What are the legal implications of using Mr. Reinhardt as a human guinea pig?" Doctor Myers asked.

"He is an enthusiastic participant. You must remember the ultimate concept of data collection is his, to begin with."

"I feel it is extreme and I have reservations!" Dr. Myers asserted.

"As do we all, doctor. There is much we can do without taking that drastic step. And we will, but it is an interesting proposal."

"It is that, indeed. A unique utilization of a high-risk procedure. I hope we do not find ourselves without other options."

"Agreed. However, if we are faced with the prospects of such a risk we must remember the proposal is his entirely. We would merely supply the expertise and technology. I think our only problem will be to constrain him within protocols for the experiments."

"Yes, but what if something goes wrong? What if there are problems, complications? There could be complications. What we are talking about is very risky and full of opportunities for surprises and unexpected developments. I want assurances that we are not liable in some way."

"We are liable. We are exposed, and accountable for how we proceed. How could it be otherwise? But that does not mean that it is faulty or inadvisable."

Milton interjected, "Mr. Reinhardt has been under medication for 22 months. He is rational and articulate. He has availed himself of legal counsel and has elected to participate of his own free will. I will act as his counsel, looking out for his interests, Isabella has secured separate legal counsel for the foundation so that I cannot be biased or compromised."

"But this man is legally insane."

"But not legally incompetent. He is in full charge of his faculties, able to determine for himself what he wants to do. And I believe he wants to do this more than anything in the world."

"I assure you this will have to pass muster with the University's Legal department."

"We should arrange a meeting as soon as possible to begin surmounting those hurdles."

Izy rejoined, "Are there any other questions?"

"Yes, where will Mr. Reinhardt go when he is released in two months?"

"The foundation has arranged for Mr. Reinhardt to move to the Bennett Institute, a private facility in La Jolla. That is why I have brought you all here so that we can tour the facility together this weekend."

"Tomorrow afternoon, Ms. Reinhardt, I mean Mrs. Martin, Sorry."

Izy smiled, "No problem Mrs. Walters. The Bennett Institute has agreed to set aside a suite of offices and rooms for our project. The Institute is dedicated to understanding the nature of mental illness. They have agreed to allow our project to be facilitated at the Institute so long as they are granted recognition for the body of our work along with the foundation and of course that they are reimbursed for expenses. They will also participate in any financial recoup beyond our obligations to our benefactors.

"My father is a curious and intelligent man. The greatest tragedy, beyond the agony and humiliation of the disease, is that a great mind has been lost to the world and to the man himself. His choices are: (A) to remain a wild maniac and careen through social boundaries until he is confined to a state mental hospital where he will be tranquilized into a state of numb existence accompanied by unpleasant side effects; (B) be consigned to the streets and whatever fate awaits him there; or (C) fight back in the only way he can: with his intellect. In this choice, he recognizes the opportunity to battle his enemy, to find a solution or die knowing his efforts will pave the way for a solution to be found. He chooses the latter.

"If there are no further questions, let us move on to the financial business. Our benefactor Saint Martin Guérisseur has placed at our disposal a modest fund of 5 million dollars with stipulations laid out in the documents before you. The stipulation of greatest interest is that the money be used to better the world of the mentally ill on this planet by aggressively striving toward scientific, humane, and therapeutic options. This is completely aligned with our own charter and goals.

"We must make measurable progress within a short period as the money is already allotted according to the financial schedules included in your packets. This will be more difficult than it may sound, considering the insufficiencies of the foundations on which we begin. As remote as it may seem, we must challenge ourselves to make significant inroads against the hopelessness of schizophrenia within the next twenty years."

"Can we even hope to be successful within that time frame?"

"We must push against the boundaries of reason. We carry the hopes and anguish of thousands and thousands of families as we tarry in our labor. We are starting from zero, in uncharted territory, but five years from now we will at least know what we don't know today. In a decade, we may even know something that will, like a seed, grow and prosper into a possibility. Today we take the first step by showing up, willing to believe." Izy looked around at the silent affirmations and felt she had done her best to answer the question any of them could have asked. So she continued.

"The money has been placed in a safe annuity fund where it will multiply and protect our research during these first five years. Incremental limits have been placed on expenditures to ensure we stay within the structure prescribed in your packets. Each of you is now a member of the board of governors for this foundation and have a duty to spend this money wisely, with a focused vision toward a miraculous future that will be ushered in by dedication, effort, and courage."

"And a dream, Isabella, don't forget the dream!" Isabella smiled at Mrs. Walters, who nodded convincingly in reply.

Doctor Stan Dietz chimed in, "My wife and I are interested in the comparison of Mr. Reinhardt's electrochemical profile to that of individuals who do not demonstrate the characteristics of mental illness. The problem is in coming up with an appropriate "norm". This is our challenge."

Katherine Dietz added, "One thing we have to work with is an enormous amount of data collected from epileptic patients during inter-ictal cycles while

313

being monitored in a more limited but similar approach. However, this does not give us the chemical end of the equation, only the electrical brain wave data. Nonetheless, we are hoping for some jewels once the data is examined with our particular focus."

"I can see the challenge," Doctor Myers interjected. "Have you considered including the chemical aspect of certain epileptic patients over a shorter period of time but enough to give you the data you require?"

"Yes we have but we run into difficulty with the FDA-approved procedures already in existence. We could initiate a separate protocol for a clinical trial. It may be our only alternative, but we will pursue every other possibility prior to committing those resources in that direction.

"I am working on the protocol for Uncle Gunter's activities and regimens over the course of the research. I think you'll find it interesting and, of course, I'd value your input. I've brought copies of what we have for everyone to review." Kathy laid out inch thick spiral-bound notebooks on the table. "Light reading to put you to sleep tonight."

Izy watched the board members pick up the notebooks and begin perusing the contents with curiosity. Within minutes, questions were being asked and answered, discussions ensued. Her eyes shifted to John who met her gaze. It was really happening.

Izy drove up to Camarillo State Hospital with Missy to greet Gunter on the day of his release. They had brought clothes for him to wear: slacks, a knit shirt, and a jacket a pair of shoes. He looked pale, thin, but handsome when he met them, and Missy was so proud of him. Izy chauffeured as her parents sat in the back seat together, patting each other's hands. As she caught glimpses in the rearview mirror she felt a tightening in her throat and had to use significant restraint to keep her emotions in check.

They stopped for lunch and drove to the cliffs at Torrey Pine cliffs to look at the ocean. These simple things that they did, they had never done as a family. Just being together, peacefully, was a miracle.

When they arrived at the Institute, Gunter was greeted with deference. He was no longer a maniac chained to the wall, filthy and reviled by his keepers. He had a foundation named after him and a place where he could ply his mind against his monster. He was the subject of a research program. He was a man with a disease and the wit and courage to fight back.

Gunter was escorted to his suite which included a bedroom, bathroom, sitting room, and a study where he could read, work, or watch television. On the walls were his paintings, preserved and re-framed. On the shelves, the HO trains, clean and shining, sat on golden tracks set inside Plexiglas to keep them immaculate. A row of windows looked out to the Pacific Ocean and pines which had been blown into abstract shapes by the constant onshore breeze, each one, a work of art.

He walked through the suite, pausing for a long look out the windows. He took in every detail, then turned to look into the brown eyes of his daughter. Izy looked deep into her father's eyes and accepted what he offered without diminishing it with words. Izy was a dreamer but she did not imagine for a single moment that Gunter Reinhardt would ever offer her anything more valuable than what she gleaned in that moment of silence.

Isabella Martin was busy indeed. She was given the responsibility of building and starting up the new European facility, which she had recommended CardioStim commit to The Netherlands and allow them to take advantage of generous government incentives that would dramatically reduce the cost of construction and operating costs over the first ten years. She had twice the responsibilities and began a shuttle lifestyle between California and Europe, where she took up residence in a village near the construction site.

She lived in a restored estate which had once belonged to a wealthy landowner. It had modern plumbing and basic conveniences such as telephone service but, other than that, was rather primitive. There was a fireplace in each room for heat. The beds were covered with big, down-filled comforters, but were relatively uncomfortable. There were no showers in the bathrooms, only hand-held nozzles in claw foot tubs. Everything made of wood or metal had been worn smooth by the many hands and feet of earlier times.

When she was there, Isabella worked. When John joined her, they would travel.

In Bremen, she found the ship manifest that included the Reinhardt family. They had left on a vessel that landed them in Galveston, Texas. She had no idea how they had come to be in California from there. She did learn that the name Reinhardt was relatively common. The manifest included the city in which the family had originally lived before beginning their journey. So Izy visited a small village called au Rheine. Her research there turned up a family whose history was quite erratic. They were described as being strong and prosperous, pillars of the community one generation, then there was little mentioned about them the next. One man, Boris Reinhardt, recognized in Berlin, was acclaimed as *erfinder extraordinair* which meant he was a great inventor. Isabella believed she had found the roots of her family.

Over an extended weekend, she traveled, alone, to Edinburgh where she made her way to an ancient Presbyterian church made of stone. Beside the church was a small cemetery, and there, on an old stone cross she found the weathered chiseling: Sean Prebble, died 1873. She knelt down on the grass and touched the chiseling. She whispered, "Great grandfather, I wonder if you had it to do over, would you have stayed with your wife and daughter? On the other hand, had you stayed, you might have perished in the mines. When I was a child, I thought you were a villain. You and all the other men who seemed to trite, brutal or inadequate. She paused. Now I see that we are all teachers for each other. I think Katherine was destined to be tested so she would become strong and courageous. You would have been proud of her. Isabella saw pictures in her mind of characters in her own life; some she had not thought of in years. "Everything happening perfectly, unfolding like a rose. Time is the storyteller and in the end, Great Grandfather, it was you who got shortchanged by your own folly and cowardice. When Katherine saw into heaven, she did not see you. Was that because she didn't know what you look like? Was it because the only real hell is running away from your life." Isabella stood up and said, "I want you to know that I hold no ill feelings in my heart. Rest in peace and know that your life did have meaning and I thank you."

In La Jolla, the research progressed with mixed results, and Gunter Reinhardt's original proposal, risk-ridden or not, was looming on the horizon demanding serious consideration.

"I don't care about your fears! All of this is a waste. We are pissing away valuable time and money and getting nowhere!"

"It is unheard of!"

"No one would do this!"

"Not indefinitely!"

"It is outrageous!"

"It is! You are correct! I don't dispute that. But this is also an outrageous opportunity. There has never been a Gunter before. He is unique, and I believe we must move forward in support of his ideas. You know it is not for the sake of the research alone. It is for his sake as well. Do you not see the passion in this man? How can we offer him nothing when he is willing to risk everything?"

"If we consider this action, we must proceed with great care."

"Agreed."

"Absolutely."

"Lay it out again. We must go over and over this to be certain, very certain."

Izy proceeded with the overview, again. "First, Gunter will undergo a detailed, thorough physical examination to quantify and qualify every aspect of his physiology so that we have a baseline for the study and can monitor any deviations as we proceed.

"Once we have that physiological baseline, and Gunter is ready, we have arranged for him to undergo some state of the art diagnostic procedures. This technology is very new. A magnetic field will be applied to his body, specifically his head, which causes a specific alignment of atoms in the bone and tissue. Then radio waves are directed at the alignment in such a way as to create a resonance of energy. When this effect is stopped, the absorbed energy is emitted in the form of a weak radio wave, varying in molecular density and structure. A computer then creates an image based on the detailed radio transmission. The result is a very precise cross-sectional image. This will be used during the procedure to ensure proper placement, particularly of the depth sensors. This same procedure will be conducted periodically during functional analysis later on.

"When the baseline data is complete, we will fly my father to Weil, Germany to undergo surgery. He will be in the hospital there for at least two months while we monitor his healing, review the status of the implants, and conduct functional testing.

"Assuming the outcome of the surgery is satisfactory, we will return him to the Institute where the experimentation can begin with calibration tests and early data assessment.

"When we are confident of the data, we will begin the formal collection process. Doctor's Katherine and Stanley Dietz are working on the details of that phase. I will turn it over to them to carry on the agenda."

When all had been debated, digested, and decided, Isabella adjusted her schedule accordingly. Upon returning from Europe yet again, she grabbed a nap and headed to the Institute, bracing herself for what lay ahead. She escorted Gunter to the San Diego Airport and accompanied him back to the land of his fathers. She was exhausted and seriously double jetlagged by the time they reached the hotel near the hospital. She got Gunter settled and fell into a deep, if brief, sleep, black and dreamless.

The next morning, Gunter was checked into the hospital at 5:30am and prepared for surgery. Doctor Myers greeted him.

"Mr. Reinhardt, we are about to begin a great project together."

"Yes, we are," he said, "but it's my brain. Don't forget. You must be careful!"

"I shall be. And may I say, this is the most courageous thing I have ever heard of in all my life."

"It is not courage. It is frustration, rage maybe. I hate doctors. Doctors have made my life miserable."

"I can understand that. I will do my best to change your opinion. Everything looks good. We will begin."

A technician shaved his head, exposing old scars. Next, the anesthesiologist pushed a solution into the IV tube. "You are going to get drowsy now, Mr. Reinhardt. I will see you in the O.R."

Izy held Gunter's hand until his eyelids drooped, then closed. The technicians moved him onto a gurney, and they paraded down the hall toward the double doors of the surgical suite. At the doors, Izy veered toward the surgical administration station. She took scrubs and entered the locker room. She removed her clothes, put on the scrubs, put covers on her shoes and a bonnet on her head then turned and exited into the hallway where Gunter slept quietly. She paused to look at her father as he lay helplessly, his life completely in their hands, then passed into the washroom to scrub in.

Inside the OR, the clock read 8:30am as the technicians lifted Gunter's limp body onto the table, face down into a fixture that cradled his face and chin, exposing his shaved cranium.

Professor Klingman entered with an air of authority, approached the table, turned and studied the radio emission images already hanging on the light boards along the wall. He made a mark on Gunter's head three centimeters above the left ear, up and over the longitudinal fissure of the brain to the opposite side the same distance above the right ear. A nurse used a scalpel to trace the mark, just breaking the surface of the skin. A tiny line of blood appeared. Then a complicated system of devices was brought in. The first was designed to hold the head absolutely still by literally inserting screws into the temples and securing the skull in a large halo-shaped frame. Once satisfied with the positioning, the nurses moved in to attach a pressure cuff and drape the body leaving only the tiny cut line exposed.

Next, a device was affixed to the halo to allow three-dimensional navigation within the brain. By the time this was all in place, Izy could not tell who or even what was on the table. She could no longer see Gunter's head at all. The large overhead room lights dimmed as the task lighting increased over the table. The operative field became the brightest area in the room. The surgeon and nurses mounted a small platform that raised them to a comfortable level at which to work. Izy turned her attention to the monitors to track further progress. This entire preparation took just over an hour.

Professor Klingman began the process of cutting through skin and subcutaneous layers that make up the scalp. The scalp was retracted to expose the skull. Izy was amazed at the size of the opening produced by a single line. Eventually, a large area of raw wet bone was visible and then the drilling began which unnerved Izy with its whirring sound, the smell, and a fine mist of fluid mixed with bone dust. "You worried?"

Izy smiled beneath her mask and tried not to appear aghast.

"You should not. This is perfectly safe. I will tell you when to worry." Professor Klingman resumed his work.

It was Izy's fervent desire not to draw attention to herself. She was an observer with inherent concerns. She made a greater effort to contain her horror and be unobtrusive.

Once the appropriate number of burr holes and incisions had been made, a neat chunk of bone was removed with great care, and reserved until it would later be replaced. On the monitor above her, Izy could see the first of the meninges: the dull gray dura mater. This portion of the procedure took another two hours.

The flights and stress weighing down on her, Izy struggled to maintain her composed demeanor, desperately wanting to lay down or to sit down at least. There wasn't anything to sit on. At least she only had to watch. And she absolutely had to, if she had to glue her eyes open. She would endure. She knew a lot about endurance.

Doctor Myers entered. The two surgeons spoke, nodding, pointing, using terms familiar to them, mystical to Izy. Then Doctor Myers came over to Izy. "We will now open the dural layer, Isabella."

"Now you can worry!" Professor Klingman said. "Now is when we begin the danger with infection, from here on and for the duration of your experiment." Izy nodded her understanding and put her faith in The Plan.

The two surgeons carefully peeled back the dura in large neat pieces and staked each one back out of the way. Once out of the way, the next membrane was exposed: the arachnoid, so named because it crawls like a spider, hugging the contours of the cerebral cortex. "This is where we will place the arrays, but first we must insert the depth sensors. They are the difficulty, the tricky ones, dangerous. Let us get them out of the way."

At this point, some discussion ensued between the surgeons regarding position, direction, and angle. They consulted the computer navigation, the imagines on the wall. Once they came to an agreement, the surgery proceeded. "We want to minimize the discussion once the brain tissue is exposed, Isabella. We must make our determinations as close as is possible now." More sterile draping was placed, minimizing the risk of infection. The Arachnoid was cut, opened, and lifted back. Next, the pia mater membrane was opened. When complete, another two hours had passed.

There in the center of the lights, lay the tissue that formed the brilliant, but malfunctioning brain of Gunter Reinhardt. Izy stared transfixed, imagining there was a way to heal that brain with her own will. She decided it was an appropriate moment to have a word with God, should he be listening. So in her own mind, she said "Well God, there it is, if you ever had the perfect opportunity to do something, this is it! Course, I don't imagine if you were going to heal him, you wouldn't need all the cutting. Tell you what, I'll settle for one single prayer in all my life being answered. Let this crazy idea work and not kill my father in the process, okay?"

Why was that brain matter flawed? Was it flawed? Was Gunter's anomalous brain functions just part of the spectrum of humanity's brains? Was he as perfect as anyone else, all of us making up what it is to be human? But it was so wrong. So wrong for him to believe that the world was a master conspiracy against him, tormented. That cannot be right. It certainly wasn't fair. Was anything ever fair? Isabella's mind was swimming in thoughts that were partly diversion, part exhaustion and yet, questions she had known existed inside her for a very long time.

Another two hours passed during the placement of the depth sensors. Izy was nervous remembering the surgeon's concern to minimize the exposure of

320

the brain tissue. This compounded the headache that was splitting her own head wide open. She watched them intently. They were riveted on their work, paying her no attention whatsoever, but they didn't seem upset. She tried to relax and moved her head in all directions to relieve stress.

Almost ten hours of surgery had elapsed before the inner meninges were closed again with only a tiny sterile conduit exiting the wound with wires. There was the lingering danger. She looked at the tiny tail, which led into the brain tissue, deep into the folds of the brain in the frontal lobe. It had been a very long time since Isabella had made prayers. She was certain today was a record. She wasn't even sure whom exactly she was speaking to, and she didn't care. She was simply imploring any higher power that could receive her message, "Make a miracle happen here, for us, right now and forever as long as that little conduit remains." And then she thought, "The risk would be minimal if the wires didn't have to exit the brain. We need to do this without wires." But that was not possible.

The Doctor placed the arrays of electrodes: eight across the frontal lobes where abstract thought, creativity, conscience, and personality exist; four to the occipital lobe where vision is interpreted; and two each to the temporal lobes on either side to cover hearing, smell, and taste.

Then came the process of closing the dural layer and replacing the skull piece. Once the final sutures were in place, a temporary sterile bandage was applied.

The surgical field was adjusted, the navigational apparatus was removed, screws were extracted, and his wounds bandaged. The halo device was moved. Gunter was gently repositioned with the left hemisphere, neck, and shoulder carefully exposed. There was more re-draping, and temporary bandages were taken away. All the wires in a sterile conduit were run under the scalp, behind the left ear, down the muscle of the neck, and into the left pectoral region. Once in place, the scalp was sutured and completely bandaged. On top of the bandage, Gunter's head was wound round and round with thick sterile gauze so that he appeared as a Hindu with a very large head. All in all, the procedure took fourteen hours and the device itself had not yet been placed. That would be done another day.

Izy in sterile dress stayed by Gunter's side in recovery. Unable to keep open her eyes open, her head dropped on the bed next to her father and they both slept.

"If I didn't know better, I'd think you were praying."

"I was. I am."

"You believe in all that nonsense?"

"I don't know what you mean by nonsense."

"God: some benevolent or malevolent being that pays attention to the supplicants of inferior sub-creatures on one of his or her planet creations. That nonsense."

Izy smiled at the absurd characterization. "You're right Doctor Myers. I recognize it is completely possible that God is not in the least interested or involved with our day to day tribulations. But it can't hurt and maybe God does listen."

"I can't even give you that, Isabella. You are an engineer, a scientist, a pragmatist. Surely you do not believe in God."

"I am surprised at you, to be perfectly honest. You are Jewish. Don't you believe in Yahweh?"

"I am a Jew. That does not preordain that I am religious. My education seriously interfered with my faith. It is difficult to see the universe through the scrutiny of science and believe in supreme beings."

"Actually, it is because I am a scientist that I do believe in God."

"How so?"

"The universe was formed 15 billion years ago from the explosion of a single sub-atomic particle that contained the entire mass of all we know to exist. It existed in such a state of stress and pressure that the atomic structures we know could not even exist. There was only chaotic soup, virtually substance without structure, a cauldron of immense density and pressure."

"Yes. The big bang theory."

"In one convulsive moment, unable to contain itself, that particle burst forth, spreading, spinning, and hurling everything out into cold empty space where it cooled and condensed and formed structure, structures that eventually became the energy and matter we know today."

"Yes. All astrophysics, mathematical extrapolations from the echo of that cataclysmic event are still evident today. What does that have to do with God? It seems to me that it explains away the creation of the universe by a single entity or even a group of entities. It turns creation into an equation of inevitability, a fluke event."

"Ah, but that is exactly where you are wrong. Think about what you just said."

"I said 'An equation, an event. In other words, a completely explainable phenomenon.'" Doctor Myers paused and looked at Isabella who still smiled. "What?"

"Whose particle was it?"

BARTER FOR HOPE

The Reagan years passed prosperously and rapidly, congested with advances in every aspect of life imaginable. There was change: deregulation, patriotism (although Uncle Clay said it was nationalism), attempted assassination, militarism, the first trillion-dollar budget, the first woman on the Supreme Court, invasion, and the slogan, "JUST SAY NO!" The fall of communist Europe into desolation and ruin as well as the demise of the Berlin Wall sent Germany into a state of change not known since the end of World War I. Floods of immigrants—poor, needy, and desperate—threatened economic stability. The immigrants were not all East Germans. They were from everywhere east of the wall, often they were what the Germans called "zigeuner," or gypsies.

Isabella's operation in the Netherlands was fraught with controversy over the right-wing sentiment whipping up in neighboring Germany, in particular in Dusseldorf where Izy shopped. A smoldering undercurrent of fascism alarmed Izy as well.

In the United States, the era heralded a focus on democracy, capitalism, free trade, entrepreneurism, and the stock market as never before. Business was hip, no longer the enemy. M.B.A.s flooded the job market, a dime a dozen.

Izy was relieved that the country had a president who seemed to bring a sense of strength and stature to the office. In Europe, she tried to explain to her colleagues why Americans had elected a thespian to the highest office. She reminded them that though he'd been a second-rate actor, he'd done a pretty good job as governor of California. Maybe acting was just his way of bumbling along until he found his true calling as a decisive leader.

But nothing deterred Uncle Clay from his relentless derision of politicians; he resented Reagan all the more *just because* he was an actor. On a return flight, Izy popped into Portland and drove a rental car to the Umpqua Valley. She didn't have much time but had to check in on the old man, see that he was alright. Uncle Clay celebrated her surprise visit by making his special chicken pot pie and cherry cobbler. Placing the pie in the oven, he said, "It is absolutely insane to elect a man whose profession is affecting, feigning whatever is necessary in order to entertain and delude. He's in the White House even as we speak, pretending to be the President of the United States. It's sheer lunacy! What is this country coming to? I tell you, we deserve what we get. I worry about the future. Actors for president—the very idea!"

Isabella considered what Uncle Clay had to say. But he no longer seemed the oracle to her that he once had. He hated all politicians, pouring out his personal bitterness on anyone who dared to lead, angry because he couldn't, didn't. She felt sorry for him, but loved him. She decided that anyone elected to the office of the President of the United States was ultimately only doing the best act they could, because nothing could really prepare a person for something like that. In the end, anyone willing to take the risk, to assume the exposure and burden, would likely be overwhelmed by the actualization of the success, no matter who. Maybe an actor's training, the ability to set oneself aside and assume a role, was an advantage. Maybe Izy just needed to have confidence in a president. Uncle Clay sent Izy away with two jars of his cherry preserves and a jar of homemade apple butter.

At CardioStim another struggle was being waged at the highest level. Its outcome would dictate the future of the corporation. A competition among the top pacemaker manufacturers was heating up. The big ones—Saint Jude, Medtronic, Cardiac Pacing, and CardioStim—had set the tone for the past quarter century. Abruptly a scramble was on to be the first to build a new biotechnology empire. The smartest of leaders were eager to make it happen. Now that implanted computers were understood and commonplace in the form of the pacemaker, it was not a huge leap toward the potential of placing even smaller computers in other parts of the body.

Some of the old guard at CardioStim thought it was a passing phenomenon and were unwilling to pay any attention. Others wanted CardioStim to expand into the broader field of cardiothoracic medicine while staying focused on core markets.

When the dust settled, two things had happened: Gordon Fitzer was elected President, CEO, and Chairman of the Board, bringing a very conservative agenda to the table; as well, the board strongly recommended that Isabella Martin be named Chief Operating Officer. Her mandate would be to optimize facilities to better position for meeting the goals set forth in the strategic plan.

The new role would be challenging. To focus on core markets and broaden participation in cardio-thoracic medicine, the company needed a much broader product line. They needed to play a rapid game of catch-up and were considering several acquisitions. It would fall to Ms. Martin to fold them into existing operations with a minimum of disruption. Wall Street would be watching.

When Gordon Fitzer approached Martin, he was determined to gain her support and cooperation. He knew she was aligned with his philosophy and ambition and was key to securing the board's approval for his agenda.

Consequently, he was stunned by her initial reluctance and cool interest.

"Let's get down to it, shall we, Isabella? I know you are not interested in the breadth of my recommendations for expansion. In fact, I am aware that you opposed my perspective. But that should not preclude your stepping into this role now that it is clear the board agrees with me. You will have my full support and I will value hearing opposing thoughts as we proceed. We could be a powerful team for the future of the corporation. And, of course, there is the considerable financial incentive being offered to get you on board."

"You're right. I do disagree with your agenda, and I'm not interested in incentive. Frankly, I think we should let others slash and burn each other with low-cost, low-margin commodity products. We should go deeper rather than broader. The corporation has only scratched the surface for utilization of high-tech applications in our base implantable technology. But as you say, the board has made their decision and we are all accountable to the stockholders. So, I accept their decision."

"We are both stockholders; the compensation package includes significantly more shares. I would think that alone would be incentive enough."

"You can keep all the shares in this package. I want only one thing. If you can arrange it, I will agree to assume these duties and fully devote myself to executing your plans."

"Anything. What do you want?"

"I want the license to the CardioStim patent portfolio relating to biostimulation in the brain, spinal cord, and all aspects of neurological application, and I want it indefinitely."

"For the life of the patents themselves, they are limited."

"Not the way we continue to reiterate them. They will go on in perpetuity, and I want exclusive and unrestricted use."

"What on earth for?"

"I have my reasons. Can you get the board to agree?"

"I don't know. I will have to think about this. Now, let me get this straight. You will decline any additional shares offered in this package in exchange for license to the CardioStim patent portfolio as stipulated."

"I would be happy to provide a more specific and legal definition of what I want, but yes, in general, that's it."

"Give me some time. I'm sure it can be arranged."

Isabella smiled, stood, shook Gordon Fitzer's outstretched hand, turned, and headed to her office.

"Francine Gavin phoned three times. She was rather rude and very insistent on speaking with you."

"Thank you, Mrs. Walters."

"You have other messages."

"I'll take them later." Izy went to her desk, picked up the phone, and dialed.

"Well, it's about time!"

"Where are you, Francy?"

"I'm at your favorite restaurant and I'm running a tab, so you better get down here and cover it 'cause I don't have any money."

"What do you mean you have no money?"

"I got fired. They got this thing where you gotta pee in a cup, they just spring it on you. I don't think it's legal. But they fired me. What am I going to do, Izy?"

Izy put her day on hold and went to collect Francine and take her home. "You know, you really got to do something about this place. It doesn't befit a big shot like you. It's a dump."

"It's coffee for you, love. And it's not a dump, it's just fine."

"With all your money you could live in a palace. This is a dump."

"Truth is, Francy, I'm never here, so why waste a lot of money on some big house. I have everything I need. Now, drink this."

"I don't want coffee. I need another whiskey. You got any good whiskey?"

"You've had enough whiskey. How are we going to figure out what to do with you in a stupor? Come, dear heart, drink at least some of this."

"You know what? You should give me some of your money. You want to fix things? That would fix up everything perfectly. You got lots of money. You don't even have time to enjoy it. I could enjoy it for you. Give me a couple hundred grand and I'll show you what money's for. I could teach you a thing or two. You used to know how to have a good time. Now, you just exist in your corporate world, work all the time, no time for friends. You, with all your superiority, all your looking down your nose at me all these years. You know something? You're a snob! And you have no reason to be a snob. You're not special. You've got everything, everything in the world. It all came easy to you, didn't it? So smart, so sure of yourself with all your ideas. From the very beginning, you held yourself above everyone, too good to fuck, too special, always aloof, too good to elbow with real people. I've always known you were a hot shot, a know-it-all. I hate you, always have, in a way."

"I don't believe you. I won't believe you. I think you're angry and it's covering up great, big chasms of hurt. And you want to hurt me. I'm not sure why. Do you expect to drive me away by creating more hurt and abandonment? I won't let you do that. I love you. And someday you'll believe that. Even more important, someday you will love yourself." Francy gave Izy the bird and didn't finish the coffee. Instead, she wandered to the sofa where she passed out. Izy covered her and wondered what to do. She knew Francy had no savings, few assets, nothing of value, nothing but debt. If she didn't get work soon, she'd lose her place to live. Izy could put her up for a while. But that wasn't the biggest problem. It was that Francine was way over the top and out of control with her drinking. Izy was pretty sure Francy was an alcoholic, maybe worse. And getting fired wasn't going to help. The problem would be getting Francy to straighten up and get a grip on her life, let alone keep it together long enough to get another job.

The weeks passed. To Izy's dismay, Francine was in full self-destruct mode. She was asleep when Izy went to work, watched television all day long, and began her alcohol consumption before noon. She was gone when Izy got home. She stumbled in at three, four, and five in the morning— angry, drunk, and abusive. Finally, John came clean. "It's not that I don't want to be supportive. But there is a thing called enabling. You are enabling Francy to destroy herself. I think it's time for some tough love. You have got to bounce her!"

"And you think that will stop her self-destruction? Where will she go?"

"That's for her to figure out. That's the point. She has to face the situation. You are shielding her, don't you get it, honey? You know this. You know it's the truth."

Izy delayed thinking about Francy, using her work as a distraction, until things started to disappear from the house. Even then she was in denial, but John wasn't. He decided it was time to take an extended vacation and told Izy she was on her own until she resolved the Francy problem. "She is your friend.

I cannot stop you from enabling her right over a cliff. But I can stop supporting you to do it. You have to face this and figure it out. You can do this. Let me know if I can help once you decide what you need to do."

John left in his plane for the first destination that made sense to him: Watsonville, California, and the Antique Air Show. Then it was off to the Reno Air Races and on to Oshkosh, Wisconsin.

Izy took vacation time as well and spent it finding Francy a job. Francy decided her new job was demeaning and that all the people there were "assholes!" After two weeks, she quit and resumed her old habits.

"What's that you have there?"

"It's a present. For you. I thought you might like to make use of these." Isabella laid the wooden box on the table in Gunter's suite. He opened it. Inside were tubes of oil paints, brushes, and a palette. He looked up at her. For a long while, he held her eyes in a way she could not interpret. She was transfixed at that moment. She thought he would speak, but he didn't. Gunter had come through the implantation in excellent shape. He was still on psychotropic medication and, now because of the surgery and the opening in the meninges, he was on antibiotics. He lived in a world that was as sterile as it could be and still be functional. He vented his thinly-veiled disdain for the program collaborators, but was clearly enjoying being the focus of tests, examinations, and challenges.

Every week in the office mail, Isabella received an envelope containing a cartoon strip chronicling the adventures and antics of a character called "Zipper Head" and other actors in his world. Zipper Head performed tasks and functioned in a "Bowl Fish Gold" world as scientists and doctors feverishly attempted to decipher the radio signals emanating from the transmitter inside his left shoulder and attached to the probes inside his head. The illustrations were sardonic but clever; they conveyed much more than the acerbic situations they depicted.

Europe was well established and run by a Vice President of Operations who was thorough and meticulous. Izy visited every quarter and spent a week reviewing critical issues, leaving day-to-day decisions to management. She had more than enough to keep her hopping in the United States.

Gordon was on an aggressive acquisition campaign: a cardiac-surgery supply distributor, a start-up angioplasty company, a heart-valve manufacturer, and a plastics-processing plant. Izy decided the only way to successfully expand at this rate was to develop a comprehensive business system. She wanted it to allow for creativity to cover diverse business needs, but also to require that each entity conform to a standard of quality and compliance that would minimize any threat to the corporation's integrity. She hired a brilliant, young biochemist who also had a degree in international regulatory ethics. Together they began carving out the concepts.

Between quarterly trips to Europe, she bounced around the U.S. visiting acquisition candidates. She personally welcomed each acquired company into the fold and encouraged them to see themselves as a part of a greater mission to make a difference in healthcare worldwide.

In order to elevate productivity and personal commitment, Isabella knew it was essential to ennoble each individual. They were not making refrigerators or cash registers. Any mistakes could cost someone his life or well-being. Generally, she was pleased, but looking out on sea of faces looking back at her, she knew it would not be easy to instill a cohesive and solid sense of dedication over the broad matrix of facilities. She had made a bargain to get what she wanted from CardioStim. She would fulfill her obligations, but began to see a gap between her personal goals and her professional role. She kept a mental calculator of the weeks, months, and years left on her contract.

Isabella's travel schedule left Francy pretty much on her own at the house and, against her better judgment, Izy allowed her to stay. That worked until Mrs. Walters contacted Izy at a new facility in Indiana with urgent news that put Izy on the first available flight home. Francine had been arrested for selling cocaine. Since she resided at Izy's house, Izy was in a lot of trouble.

Izy could not engage Milton Feldner as he represented her father, but he recommended a good criminal attorney who managed to convince the authorities that Francine had taken advantage of Isabella's generosity and that the house itself was not a drug den.

Twenty thousand dollars in legal fees later, Isabella was extricated from Francine's legal problems, now formidable.

Under the Reagan administration, the war on drugs was hot and punishment was swift and brutal. Francine had been caught with cocaine with a street value of fifteen thousand dollars. She was going away. There was nothing Isabella could do but cover her legal expenses for a good lawyer who could minimize her incarceration, or at least, where she would spend it.

John was relieved that Izy was released from Francine's clutch. He vowed he would do whatever he could to prevent it from happening again. It was obvious how Francine had acquired the money to finance her ill-fated deal: While Isabella was away she stripped their house of anything she could sell. Unfortunately, Francine lacked the good sense to know she was in over her head. Izy was devastated, drained of all understanding. She spent a day in bed hunting for a box big enough to hold her guilt, sense of responsibility, and confusion.

Back at work, Izy was opening her mail when she noticed the weekly envelope from La Jolla. Zipper Head was up to something new. The doctors were changing his medication regimen to begin assessing the effects of specific chemicals or lack thereof in his brain. Zipper Head was concerned. The comic wasn't as funny this time. And Isabella found it interesting that the one-reviled medication that had helped him find peace would now be ripped away from him.

Isabella went to the Institute to meet with her father. "Are you sure you want to go through with this? You don't have to."

"I want the answers more than I want to remain in this safe, little bubble of time. We will proceed as planned. Never mind Zipper Head. He's just ink. He means nothing."

"You mean something. You must be absolutely sure."

"I am absolutely sure, and you must promise that when it gets difficult, you will be strong and not deter from the course, no matter what. Swear it to me, Isabella!"

"I swear, Daddy."

And so the next phase of the experiment began. It took a while for the medication to be displaced and for the disease to begin to re-emerge. The monster that stalked Gunter's life was alive and well, but now, like a thief caught on camera, it was being monitored by a determined enemy.

At the Institute things were getting rocky. The paranoia returned and Gunter's mind was not able to hold on to the plan. Instead, it became a conspiracy against him and management took on new challenges. The Bowl Fish Gold, an obvious contrivance, fed his paranoia. They had prepared for this. The windows were made of thick Plexiglas so when things were hurled at them, they bounced off. From time to time, Gunter was restrained and the staff was trained to respect him, but not trust him under these circumstances. Other times, he was withdrawn, virtually hiding out, burrowing into himself, fearful. Izy began to understand her father's reference to "no matter what."

The brief truce ended. Gunter now saw his daughter as the archetype of his incarceration; the very sight of her could send him into a tirade. His knowledge of her involvement became fuel for his conviction that she was head of a plot to persecute him. Isabella found his behavior hurtful; it was difficult to cling to objectivity. The child inside her wanted to avoid the Institute. But the woman who knew the price of discovery felt obliged to be there whenever her schedule permitted. Reams of data were accumulated. From the sensors inside Gunter's brain, a graphically-enhanced display of behavioral patterns in response to a carefully-planned medications regimen was ready for complete and detailed analysis. Changes were observed in both brain chemistry and electrical patterns under various stresses activated during a range of activities and tasks. Once the meds were stopped, electrical activity increased dramatically in some areas of the brain and ceased in others. Isabella was eager to make some breakthrough, a brilliant discovery, and hungry for correlations and solutions. She was frustrated by the amount of data and the struggle to make sense of it. She was anxious to put Gunter back on the medications to which he had come to respond so well and that had put an end to his torture, to her own torture.

They continued to administer significant doses of antibiotics to stave off any possibility of infection. With bacteria and virus the ever-present enemies, anyone who visited him—staff, team members, Missy or Izy—were required to wear prophylactic garments. No one with even a hint of illness, an open sore, or a cut was allowed near him. The entrance to Gunter's suite became an airlock.

Francine did 18 months in prison. After considerable legal maneuvering, eventually she was released on parole to a halfway house for six months. After that Izy wanted to grab her up into her arms and take her home. She wanted to protect her from the inevitable. But John stood like a giant thorn in the side of that plan, providing Izy with literature, personal testimony, and transcripts of ALANON sessions to try to convince her she had to stop enabling Francine. When Francine called, Isabella told her she loved her, wished her well, wired her five thousand dollars to help her start a new life, and left Francine Gavin.

At first Francine left messages detailing her latest obstacle or debacle, decrying Izy for abandoning her. More imaginary boxes were filled, tied with rope, then chains, and shoved to the very farthest corner of her mind. Pretty soon, John made sure the messages were erased before Izy got home; he answered the phone whenever she was in the house. John became aware of the downward spiral: It started with hard times, degenerated to prostitution, arrest, then parole violations. Back to prison. And finally, silence.

In La Jolla, they were regulating the dispensation of favorable chemicals in a precise protocol to isolate their effects.

Meanwhile, the Dietzes were analyzing brain-chemistry data derived from autopsy records. A comprehensive database that seemed to be the beginnings of a documented standard of normalcy was emerging. However agonizingly slow, piece by piece, the team continued to make progress.

Izy was impressed with Kathy's disciplined style and dedication to her work. Her childhood memories of her cousin in a bonnet and ankle stockings gave Isabella a sense of belonging, of family. She felt the whisper of the inescapable storyteller: time.

Izy sat outside the suite looking in the windows of Zipper Head's "Bowl Fish Gold." Kathy found her cousin in deep contemplation. "How are you holding up, Cuz?"

"Fine. I wish this phase were over. I know this is what he wants, and I want it too, but only if it can deliver a solution that will help him. I want him to have more time, quality time. If you'd seen them, Missy and him together when we drove down from Camarillo… . I never saw that, never saw him love her in any way. It wasn't so much what he did on that ride. It was what he didn't do. He was quiet. He sat close to her. He really looked at her."

"Isabella, you have to accept the fact that we may not find a solution for Gunter. Gunter may provide a solution for another generation, but not for himself. Will you be able to deal with that?"

Isabella looked into her cousin's eyes, her brow furrowed. "I guess I'll have to be if that's the way it works out. But it's not over yet. I see him fight so hard, and I'm so proud of him." She paused, struggling to find words for something she had to get out. "I have this friend. I love her very much. She is very fragile and self-destructive. She doesn't have a disease really, well, maybe alcoholism. Is that a disease?"

"Yes. But it is a disease that compels the victim to inflict the sickness upon themselves. It tends to make the victims seem less sympathetic. Probably why some people struggle to find empathy for the alcoholic. Do you empathize with your friend?"

"Maybe. I guess so. Actually, I was an enabler for a long time. I had to stop."

"Good, Isabella. It may seem cruel, but you have to let go. It doesn't help to keep an addict from hitting rock bottom. In fact, the bottom is usually the only place that brings an alcoholic to make the tough choices he or she must."

"I see him in there, fighting against a monster he did not inflict upon himself. And Francy's out there somewhere careening off the edges of life with her monster. I don't know, Kathy, life is really strange. Where is God in all this?"

"I'm not sure. That's bigger than I can tackle. Where is your friend?"

"Haven't heard from her in a long time. Could be dead. It drives me nuts if I think about it. I try not to think about it too often."

"If she's lucky she'll crash and burn somewhere and get into a really good twelve-step program. She'll find a connection to God and maybe, her way back to you."

"Really?"

"Really. It's part of recovery. She'll come back to make things right. And then maybe you can have your friend—wiser, stronger, and in control of her life, one day at a time."

In 1989 the team had sufficient data to make a proposal with their findings to a pharmaceutical company. It was not their intention to market drugs, so they turned over their data to the company the team determined could best develop a new medication. It would take ten years to get into practical use in the United States, but it was a start. The new medication, once developed, would target a chemical imbalance without the use of sedatives. The royalties from the drug would be go back into the research. Izy found this a relief since the money was running thin. In her heart, she was deeply disappointed that the best they could come up with was just another drug. She told herself, "Step by step."

The initial revenue would be security for the data, but royalties were a long way off. They needed to be frugal. Research always holds surprises and most costs money. Izy secretly hoped they would be able to reimburse SMG for their faith in the project and donation, while pushing as far away from Madam Martin as possible.

Since her son had seen fit to marry in such a pedestrian fashion, there had been near-lethal conversations between John and his mother. When it was necessary for Isabella to interact with her mother-in-law, there was excessive civility, but little acceptance on either side.

Meanwhile, research continued at the Institute. The team was developing a concept that included both local drug delivery and electro-stimulation of brain tissue by sending tiny charges through fluids. It was a difficult balancing act—

too much energy and the fluid would cook the tissue. Too little, and there would be no effect at all. The access to the CardioStim patents would pay off if they were successful. The data was providing insight and trends that began to shape their thinking.

The team's confidence was bolstered by some progress. Izy tried to share their enthusiasm while balancing her own drive to make a breakthrough. Gunter was in a phase of the experiment where he was coherent and articulate, able to understand that he had made a difference. Missy was visiting again and Izy was less tense.

In January of 1991, President Bush announced that he had signed Resolution 77 authorizing the use of military force against Iraq. In doing so, he had taken a step toward a violent confrontation with the Iraqi dictator, the maniac who had risen to power largely due to the support of the United States during Bush's tenure as Director of the Central Intelligence Agency. Corrupted by his own power, Saddam Hussein had invaded land he claimed belonged to Iraq: the sovereign nation of Kuwait. This, in conjunction with U.N. Security Council Resolution 678, paved the way for a shift in the desert sands of the Middle East. Bush made clear that this was a message to Saddam that he must withdraw from Kuwait without condition or delay.

At CardioStim the halls buzzed with opinions and gossip. "There is no way Iraq would be pushing the crisis if they didn't have some secret weapon. We'll be lucky if we can get out of this with our skin still attached!"

"That's ridiculous. If they had a secret weapon, do you think Bush would be going to war?"

"They could unleash biological weapons on us here in America if we attack them."

"Bush isn't going to war. It's the United Nations."

"I think we should just go in there and teach those towel heads a lesson!"

"We are the U.N., you dope!"

"What towel heads? You mean Hindus? They're in India, not Iraq."

"We are not! Even other Arab countries are afraid of that maniac! The Arabs are not puppets of the U.S."

"I don't care, they should be taught a lesson!"

"Arabs or not, the U.N. is a euphemism for the world according to American politics!"

"You don't know anything! The Saudis and Kuwaitis are paying for the war. That makes it a world thing."

"That makes it a hired hit on the 'Don' of an Arab family who are out of line! And we're the shooter!"

Uncle Clay was sure it was somehow poetic justice for Bush, but Isabella could not listen to any of it at all. It served to heap anguish upon her and offended her inner sense of balance. She was certain that war would only assure greater, deeper resentments and more violence.

Early on January 16, 1991, the sky over Baghdad was streaked with fire. It was Desert Storm, the code name for the coalition under a mandate from the United Nations Security Council to liberate Kuwait from the unlawful invasion and possession by Iraqi forces. A relatively new and struggling news agency had journalists stationed in the beleaguered capital city and was broadcasting live coverage via satellite as bombs exploded and sirens wailed in the background. For the first time in history, people around the world sat in their offices and living rooms watching war unfold minute by minute. This was not footage taped earlier—a summary of the day's events. This was action happening in real time, uncensored. It ushered in a new global reality and the emergence of the Cable News Network.

"You looked pleased."

"Isabella. Pleased? Maybe. Remembering, thinking." Gunter pressed the mute button, silencing the live telecast of the bombing in Baghdad. Isabella turned her back to the disturbing images.

"What were you remembering, Daddy?"

"First, I am fascinated. How the light of a bursting bomb traveling through the black night is picked up by CNN's sensors, sent up into the ether, and grabbed by a satellite that beams it to receptors at CNN studios."

"It is remarkable. There is so much we take for granted."

"I was remembering when I was young, how I would ditch school to stay home and indulge my curiosity and imagination."

"You ditched school?"

"I didn't think much of school. Neither did you when you were very young."

"I didn't think much of it ever, I guess. Until I was older and wanted a degree. Then it mattered. And then it was interesting."

"I think you are like me in a lot of ways, Isabella."

For the first time, she embraced that thought with pride. "I hope so."

"You do not have the disease. They say you are lucky. I'm glad."

"I've been told that. I'm very lucky. I don't have diabetes, either."

"Is that why you don't have children?"

Isabella looked at Gunter, thinking. She had never wanted children. Maybe it was because she always felt a little like a child herself. Maybe because she had too long been the parent to her parents. Maybe Gunter was right. Maybe she had opted not to pass on the risks to the future until she could also pass on the cure. And there was not enough time, the cure itself would be her offspring. "There are enough humans on the planet, Father."

"Yes. True. Too many humans on the planet." He got up, went to his small desk, and extracted torn pages of a magazine, folded over to keep them together. "I want you to read this article, Isabella. Read it with your mind wide open and think of the whole concept, broadly. I know you will see the meaning!"

She opened the pages to read the title, "Differentiation of Stem Cells." She glanced at the abstract:

The enormous promise of stem cells, both pluripotent and mulitipotent, as they relate to the development of new therapies for the most devastating diseases and the production of many tissues of the human body is an important scientific breakthrough. It is not unrealistic to say that this research has the potential to revolutionize the practice of medicine and improve the quality and length of life.

Isabella looked into her father's face to see him looking back. She nodded her understanding, then put the pages in her briefcase. That she could have a conversation with this man, that he could calmly offer something to read, without demands, without ridicule, was remarkable. The article could wait, for now. But the poignancy of the moment transfixed her. And behind that was something else. The words rushed through her brain like water through gravel toward the future.

They were Hume and Prebble children, evidenced by how they walked, spoke, even argued. Isabella arrived early, eager to see each member of her extended family, over a hundred in all, though only half were able to attend the reunion. They arrived in automobiles, RVs, a taxi. Patrick traveled for four days straight from his home in the Bandundu province on narrow, clay roads overgrown with jungle to Kinshasa, the capital city of Zaire. He wore thick wristbands of copper and malachite. His wife, Matidi, was black-skinned and wore a traditional head wrap of the Bantu women. She was with their children: Pango, Tata, and Kihua.

Isabella spotted the tall stranger as he stood watching the festivities from a distance. She thought it might be some curious local, passing time in the shade of the old tree at the park's edge. She noted his posture—the way his arms were folded as if to keep something from penetrating his heart. Izy knew then that he was no casual onlooker.

John, who arrived with Missy and Uncle Clay, caught up to Izy at the resort and took her in his arms saying, "So this is Aurora, Nebraska. The center of the country. So damn flat you can almost see your way here straight from the airport."

Izy watched Clay greet his son, George, with polite gestures. How was it that this man, in whom Izy found a great friendship, could be so unbending with his own child?

After dinner, in the recreation room, video cameras rolling, formal introductions were made, including mention of those who had passed. The adults told who they were, where they lived, what they did. With each gesture, smile, and phrase, Izy gleaned the common threads woven into the fabric of her kinship.

When it was Patrick's turn, he regaled them with tales of exotic dishes made of peanut flour and deadly, but delicious, viperous ingredients. The children were enraptured by his stories of jungle adventures, introducing yet another facet of their heritage: the courage to venture and explore.

When it was Izy's turn, she was brief, then described her relationship with Grandy. "She gave me something precious, its value inestimable. Something that belongs to each and every one of you." She held up the small, bound book containing accounts of family history going as far back as the 12th century and the green hills and glens of East Lothian, Scotland.

The next day, Uncle Micheil sat with his wife, Renée, on a swing in the shade of a grand, old tree watching the dark-skinned children playing on the lawn, pondering the threat to his world. He didn't notice the two men approach until he saw the stunned expression on his wife's face, tears filling her eyes.

"It's me, Micheil. It's been a long time. You probably don't even recognize me."

Standing next to Patrick was the prodigal son himself. Renée fairly threw herself into his arms, sobbing.

"It's alright, Mom. It's alright." He comforted her as he faced the astonishment on his father's face.

The old man rose and touched his son's arm as if to reassure himself that the man standing before him was real. "Micheil, you're here. How? Where have you been all these years, son? I thought you were a drug addict, lost on the streets of some big city."

"Instead, I am a normal Joe who manages a Walmart and lives in Arkansas."

"But you ran away, so troubled, I thought... ."

"I was troubled, and I was running. But I'm not running anymore."

During the remainder of the reunion in Nebraska, every evening after dinner, Izy read from Grandy's book. Everyone received a copy to take home.

On the last night of their stay, with John fast asleep, Izy stood in the shadows of the room looking at her image in the mirror. She had beckoned Grandy's children to this place for a taste of bittersweet antiquity and something else she had needed to feel just a bit more complete.

She marveled at the many generations before her who passed on what they could to the next. She wondered if her existence was worthy of being the total sum of her parents—the end of the line. She was pretty certain she was not.

Izy reached up to touch the skin of her cheek. It felt both warm and cold at the same time, as being alive and knowing that it was temporary. Someday she would be nonexistent, except in someone's memory, someone's heart. Unable to endure her thoughts any longer, she returned to bed and tried to sleep.

Gunter contracted a urinary tract infection caused by a virus. There was little time to determine its origin, although it was thought to be related to an enlarging prostate that prevented normal urination. The physicians jumped on it with a new regimen of antibiotics. But because Gunter was saturated with antibodies, the effect was minimal. The infection quickly spread to the kidneys,

339

creating cause for concern. Isabella took an emergency leave from CardioStim and stayed in La Jolla with Missy, who calmly prayed for God's will.

Gunter stayed focused on the research, insisting that nothing interrupt their data collection.

After two weeks, the infection became systemic and engaged Gunter's heart valves, turning the prognosis from one of consternation to grim. Terms like cardiac insufficiency, cardiomyopathy, and heart failure peppered the discussion.

Izy kept focused on a solution and encouraged the team to try different options. She ordered the physicians to give Gunter whatever information he wanted, and not to lie to him or mislead him in any way. By the third week, Gunter was extremely fatigued. He was experiencing chest pain and difficulty breathing; his hands and feet began to swell. The doctors placed him on diuretics and put his name on the emergency heart-transplant list. The next day, his heart twice ceased to function; he was resuscitated. He refused to be attached to a ventilator. He lay quietly, Missy holding one hand, Izy the other. Eyes barely open, he struggled to remain the subject of the greatest experiment of his life. And then he was gone.

Missy stroked his head, his brow, "Thank you, Lord, thank you, Lord. Now take good care of him till I get there. Thank you, Lord."

Isabella could not let go of his hand. If she did, she would have to begin processing what had happened, and she simply refused. Gunter could not be dead.

All the other individuals, places, events, influences, experiences, accomplishments, everything—her entire life—had merely been a counterbalance to Gunter. She felt her life start to spin and spin, swirling around as if someone had taken a giant bucket of water and poured it down a toilet bowl in her brain. Centrifugal forces pulled her toward a gravitational void where all consciousness—everything—would be displaced if she dared let go of his hand.

The team was stunned by the swiftness of his departure. The core of their research was gone, abruptly leaving a giant void. Missy had the presence of mind to place a call to John.

"Is she all right?"

"In time she will be, but not right now. She won't leave him, let go of him. I think if you were here, she could, maybe."

John had never felt completely needed by Isabella before. One of the things he loved about Izy was her strength. Even the money, he knew in his heart she would have found a way without him. But maybe this time, Izy really needed him.

By the time John arrived at the Institute, the team was anxious. Izy had refused to let anyone near the body. "It's not at all like her. She's just sitting in there with him, alone."

"I'm worried for her."

"Do you think you can get her out of there?"

On his way down the coast, John had been asking himself the same question. Now, looking through the "Bowl Fish Gold," he realized exactly what to do. He opened the airlock, went through to the room, and waited.

After a few minutes, Izy turned her head to see who was there. John smiled just a bit. "Do you need anything?" "No." She paused, unable to look at him directly as if something might break apart. "I suppose they all want me to let go, come out, whatever."

"What do you want, Izy?"

"I want more time."

"You can have all the time you want."

"You see this hand? It's a remarkable hand. See the long fingers, the strong square palm? I've always loved his hands. He once painted praying hands, and I knew he had used his own hands as the model. Though I'm pretty sure he never prayed."

"Those hands created a few miracles and a few disasters."

Izy managed a small laugh. Then a tear spilled over onto her cheek. "This is so twisted. I would have him back even if I had to go all the way back to the beginning. Once I thought he was going to kill me with a hammer. He did like hammers. I really thought he might. I would go through it all again if I could have him back for just a little longer. It would be different, but I would understand. I would have compassion. I wouldn't be afraid or hateful, so hateful. I would love him, try to help him. If I could do it all over again, with my whole life, I'd find a

341

way to help him."

Izy lifted her eyes to meet John's, her head slowly moving back and forth, her last attempt to reject the finality between her two hands. John simply looked back, steadily and with kindness. She turned her head back for one last look, then kissed the hand, placing it on the chest of her father's body as her shoulders collapsed inward and heaving sobs broke free.

They had previously agreed to retain Gunter's brain for analysis and the team went to work. They did not find what Izy had hoped to discover. But they did have invaluable data.

Isabella was incoherent with sorrow for two days. She opened every single box, long stored in the dark crevices of her mind, emptying the contents in one, undiluted inventory of her life. All the old, musty pains and tribulations pooled around her for a time as she stroked toward some shore she could not see or even know existed.

"This is the beginning of a new story for me. My whole life has been about my father. He has been the single most overwhelming aspect of my life: A great light, warming me, blinding me, burning me, but always shining ahead to show me the way. I have loved him, feared him, hated him, cursed him, and even wished him dead. I have fought him and run from him, but never, for even one minute, have I ever been without him.

"I have to be honest. Gunter Reinhardt was a difficult man. I think he would have been so under any circumstances. He was many things noble and ignoble: artist, racist, engineer, deviant, cruel, but also gentle and loving. Contradictions? Yes. He was the most complex human I have ever encountered. In his lifetime he was loved, admired, disdained, abandoned, beaten, and chained. I suppose there are those who would say he deserved it. And maybe he did. He was no small life force exerted upon this world.

"The truth is, he was punished for the crime of being ill and having the arrogance to be angry about it. I will spend the rest of my days grappling with that. I wish I could have been a brighter, braver, more compassionate daughter. I could not. In that, I failed. I think he may have forgiven me, and I must try to do the same.

"I have played the 'What if' game over the years. What if he had been able to realize the full potential of his intellect, talent, and curiosity? What if he could have participated in the lives around him, giving and exchanging love? What if he could have witnessed my mistakes and accomplishments? It has always made me a little crazy to play that game.

"Gunter Reinhardt represents a very large group of hopeless, helpless people, many of whom are scorned and abandoned to city streets as nameless shades of humanity. Mental illness is a silent tribulation, an unpopular subject, and, an unspeakable shame. Most people turn their backs to the afflicted, afraid to look mental illness in the eye and see what might be looking back: the haunted emptiness of an unavenged disease.

"Approximately 9.8 million Americans suffer from severe mental illness. A quarter of the homeless adults in shelters live with serious mental illness. Among the 20.2 million adults in the U.S. with a substance-abuse disorder, half experience a co-occurring mental illness. But the greatest tragedy is that the medical industry has made more progress curing snoring than finding ways to help these defenseless individuals suffering from the ravages of their plight.

"Gunter never bowed his head to his monster. He used its power to rally against his nemeses. He once told me he would not allow himself to be sedated and inventoried for the sake of society's comfort and convenience. He wanted to thrash on the gates of society until it took notice, until he was noticed. I am compelled to see his conviction as a triumph, an ascendancy of will over ignorance, fear and, most disdainful of all, indifference.

"Gunter Reinhardt is dead, but his mission to be noticed and to solve the mystery of his illness lives on. We will not rest until schizophrenia is understood, until there is a cure—a healing of the afflicted and those who love them.

"All that said, today is also about losing my father. When I was very young, he was my hero, and then, because I was so terrified of the monster inside him, he became my enemy. I had to learn to separate the two: my father and the monster. I am grateful that in the nick of time, I was able to do that."

The physicians and scientists who had worked with him, battled with him, and admired him, carried Gunter to his grave.

John Martin stood with Izy and Missy as did Emma Hannay, Veronica, and Milton Feldner.

"Do you see those men over there?" Milton pointed out a group to Izy.

"Yes. Who are they?"

"They are the civil engineers who worked with Gunter when he was

343

cooperating with the city years ago. They had been so amazed by his tunnels. One told me that, even though it was illegal, it was still a marvel and should be turned into a shrine like the Watts Towers. Anyway, they have come to pay their respects. I thought you should know."

"Thank you, Milton. You were a good friend to my father. I'm sorry he didn't always treat you well."

"It was sometimes difficult to separate the illness from what he might have actually been thinking. He was very angry. I never begrudged him that. I believe that when he was behaving in a manner that appeared cruel, it was just a means of venting his rage. Or maybe not. I think each of us must decide for ourself. Your father always spoke the truth. I never had any illusions about him and he never disappointed me, although he did surprise me."

"Surprise? How so?"

"I think, in the end, he liked me. And it was not just a respect. Mutual respect was something we had early on. I think he decided he liked me and gave me something that, for Gunter, was considered a prize, indeed. He gave me his trust."

Uncle Clay, very old but never missing a step, walked with Missy, who remained calm and strong. She did not feel she had lost Gunter, but rather that for a short time, she was able to have back her prince again—enabling her daughter to finally meet the father whom she had forgotten.

Veronica stayed close to Izy all day and Izy was grateful. It rained lightly all day, and Isabella let the sky do her crying. At one point she reached out to touch the metal box holding Gunter's remains, looking up at what might be heaven, and whispered, "The monster died, Daddy, you are free." She heard the notes of an old song playing in her head and silently repeated the refrain, *"Friendship, friendship, just the perfect blendship. When other friendships have been forgot, ours will still be hot! Da dadada da da da!"* And then she smiled.

CPSIA information can be obtained
at www.ICGtesting.com
Printed in the USA
FSHW020516070519
57913FS